The Public Prosecutor

Jef Geeraerts was born in 1930 in Antwerp. He was educated in Jesuit schools and spent time as a colonial administrator and army officer in the Congo. He gained international acclaim with his *Gangrene Cycle*, four novels based on his experience in Africa. Geeraerts, Belgium's best-known author after Georges Simenon, has more recently focused on crime and noir novels, of which *The Public Prosecutor* is the first to be published in English.

THE PUBLIC PROSECUTOR

Jef Geeraerts

Translated from the Dutch
by Brian Doyle

BITTER LEMON PRESS
LONDON

BITTER LEMON PRESS
First published in the United Kingdom in 2009 by
Bitter Lemon Press, 37 Arundel Gardens, London W11 2LW

www.bitterlemonpress.com
First published in Dutch as *De PG* by
Prometheus, Amsterdam, 1998

The translation of this book was funded by the
Flemish Literature Fund
(Vlaams Fonds voor de Letteren - www.vfl.be)

Bitter Lemon Press gratefully acknowledges the financial
assistance of the Arts Council of England

A CIP record for this book is available from the British Library
ISBN 978–1–904738–38–1
Typeset by Alma Books Limited
Printed by CPI Cox & Wyman, Reading, Berkshire

The sex life of the camel
is not what one might think.
In a single moment of weakness
he tried to make love to the Sphinx.
But the Sphinx's rounded rear
is filled with the sand of the Nile,
which explains why camels have humps
and the Sphinx an inscrutable smile.

EGYPTIAN PARABLE

The primary concern of the judiciary is not to see what does not have to be seen.

NAPOLEON BONAPARTE

Grab one pig by the ear and all the others squeal.

POLISH FARMING PROVERB

1

While the Public Prosecutor was absorbed in his daily morning ritual in front of the bathroom mirror, his sense of satisfaction at the agreeable prospect of spending the entire week at home alone was increased considerably by the realization that he didn't look bad at all for a man of sixty-four. Five foot six, 198 pounds naked, slightly overweight according to American norms, but this was due to his "muscles of iron and steel that had been marbled irreversibly with fat over the years". A few sporadic streaks of grey dusted the temples of his thick, pitch-black hair. His lower jaw was angular, no sign of a double chin, his complexion bronzed, his nose classic Greek, his eyebrows Saracen, and he preferred to reveal his innate contempt for humanity as a whole with a crooked smile and an appraising look.

But there was barely a trace of contempt to be seen this Tuesday morning, 15 May 1999, a radiant spring day with expected noon temperatures around seventy-five degrees. He felt cool, like the cowboy in the Marlboro ad.

"Basically, it's all a question of genes," his school friend George Weyler (Jokke) used to say. The man was now a renowned internist earning ten times the Public Prosecutor's salary, but having to work for it like an animal. "You need more exercise, Alberto," Jokke would consistently complain at the fortnightly meetings of the Rotary Club, playfully poking Albert Savelkoul in the belly with his forefinger. With the exception of horse-riding and hunting, he wasn't much of a sportsman, and he enjoyed eating in the best restaurants, where he had acquired a reputation for being a good judge of wines.

He concentrated on the purple veins that had recently appeared in the bags under his eyes. He pinched the skin between his thumb and forefinger and pulled it carefully, as if it were a piece of elastic. Guy Staas, another school friend and plastic surgeon to many a wealthy lady, had offered to give him a nip and tuck for next to nothing, but Albert thought real men would consider such a thing thoroughly shameful. He wasn't sure why, exactly – perhaps because of his macho conviction that men on the whole are presentable enough and don't need such surgical interventions.

For the second time that morning, he felt that damned pressure in his bladder. Was it what he feared? He suppressed a shiver of horror and forced himself to pay no attention to it, following his personal adage that problems disappear if you ignore them. He moved closer to the mirror, stretched his lips and inspected his teeth. His gums had been shrinking, so to speak, for some time, exposing the root tissue. He considered perfect teeth to be a must for a man of his standing. He was also of the opinion that the vast majority of his countrymen had more tartar in their mouths than ivory. He had no need to worry about that for the time being. He had a sturdy set of teeth, inherited from his mother, who had her first filling when she was seventy-six.

He cast a satisfied glance over at his dark hirsute torso, still comparable, more or less, with that of a forty-year-old athlete. The electronic scales were next, but he decided with a sigh to leave them out of his routine. He stretched and massaged his neck, which cracked, as it did every morning, when he twisted it left and right. But this morning had at least one positive feature. His wife, Baroness Marie-Amandine de Vreux d'Alembourg, had left the day before for a week visiting English gardens with her aristocratic friends. This meant he could enjoy breakfast unperturbed, an important aspect of what he called his "elementary male *Lebensraum*". He was free to take his place at the table in the kitchen, barefoot, unshaven and in a kimono, something that pleased their Polish maid Maria Landowska no end. Amandine always dressed to the nines, even for breakfast, as if she'd been invited to afternoon tea at the palace. She would finish her porcelain pot of yogurt with affectation, her pinkie raised, and gaze absently past the Public Prosecutor and Maria, to whom she spoke only rarely, and then only to give her orders in broken Flemish, a language she barely understood. "One never says *merci* to the staff," was one of the more haughty expressions she and her family had cherished for more than seven generations. Since the birth of their youngest son (September 1965) she had communicated with her husband by impersonal memo. On official occasions or at dinners where communication was unavoidable, they addressed one another with "*ma chère*" and "*mon ami*", as if they were characters in a nineteenth-century French novel.

"Bah!" Albert grunted. He slipped quickly into the grey kimono with Samurai markings on the back ("The life of the warrior is short, powerful and merciless"). It had been a gift from his girlfriend Louise – his treasure, his greatest passion – when she had followed him the previous year to Kyoto, where he was attending a specialist conference on Anglo-Saxon law. Albert had represented Belgium, thanks in part to the intervention of his father-in-law, Baron Pierre Philippe de Vreux d'Alembourg, Emeritus Professor of Constitutional Law at the Université Catholique de Louvain, former Supreme Court judge and author of legal handbooks, and in part because he was one of the few Belgian magistrates who had acquired a DJS (Doctor of Juridical Sciences) at the University of Harvard.

"Bah!" said the Public Prosecutor for a second time when he thought of his father-in-law: ninety-four, still alive and kicking, but completely gaga. He lived alone with a maid and a butler in an elegant town house on Marie-Josélaan in Berchem. He was a descendant of the prominent de Vreux family, elevated to the aristocracy by Leopold I for their part in the establishment of the Belgian Constitution. Fortunately, he knew nothing of the less than ideal relationship between his only daughter Amandine and his former student Albert Savelkoul, which was a result of Albert's young mistress. According to accepted custom, Amandine had cunningly concealed the affair with such skill that even their sons, Didier and Geoffroy, were unaware of it. The oldest, Didier, was a lawyer in Leuven and still single. Geoffroy had a pretty wife, two children and was counsellor to the embassy in Washington.

As he descended the stairs to the first floor, passing his collection of authentic, hand-coloured aquatints by Henry Alken, picturing straight-backed, fox-hunting gentlemen in top hats and tails on ridiculous horses, the god-awful odour of crushed silk haute couture outfits invaded his nose. True to tradition, Amandine had decided to air them a week ago, partly out of respect for the generations of old women who had once worn them, and partly because she couldn't bring herself to throw anything out. He hated the smell with a vengeance, because it reminded him of death: ugliness and decay at its last gasp.

He looked at his watch. Eight thirty. She would still be asleep, his scrumptious little creature, his voluptuous little serpent, with whom he was still insanely in love after seventeen years. He would call her in an hour and tell her he was free. He would use his mobile, since he suspected his wife had been eavesdropping on his land-line calls. His office phone was out of the question. His predecessor had had a tap installed at the switchboard. Only his mobile was safe. He took pleasure in the paranoia he had been forced to create. It was the only way to preserve the privacy he cherished so much.

He stopped on the landing in front of a statuette of Our Lady of Fatima on a simple white marble console with three immaculate lilies in a vase at its side. He snorted disdainfully. "Sanctimonious hypocrite!" She insisted that Maria Landowska renew the lilies every day. It had been one of her dreams to have a Polish maid in residence, a dream that had been fulfilled with the help of one of the canons of Antwerp Cathedral. Maria, a young lady with a *réputation immaculée*, earned bed and board and the princely sum of sixteen thousand francs a month for a twelve-hour working day. She was a thirty-four-year-old country girl from the Kielce region of Poland, strong as an ox and Catholic without being bigoted. Albert had a soft spot for her. When Amandine was away, they would chat together in a mixture of German and Flemish. She would teach him Polish words and he would teach her popular Flemish sayings, and their conversations were burlesque on occasion. Her mother was the village fortune teller, who took her cow – *Czowieka* (Daisy) – for a walk every day.

"*Salve Regina*," he said with solemnity, his eyes shut and his lips pursed, imitating Amandine's habit of greeting the virgin every time she passed the statue. The pressure in his bladder returned. He took a deep breath and opened the door to the toilet. The flow was steady and frothy, and he was relieved. It wasn't what he had feared after all. Jokke had told him that the first symptoms were "anal contractions and lazy urine". Before flushing the WC, he bent his knees slightly to allow gravity to take its course and watched the last drop disappear into the pot, something he had seen in a film about American soldiers at the front during World War One.

He suddenly remembered something he had to look up urgently. "Oh, what a beautiful morning… Oh, what a beautiful day…" he crooned, marched into his office with what he called his "cavalryman's gait", switched on the light and immediately found what he was looking for on the bookshelf: a small black volume bound in artificial leather with the words *The Teaching of Buddha* embossed in gold on the spine. The bookmark was still at page 440. He started to read:

> THE LIFE OF YOUNG WOMEN.
> There are four types of women. Of the first type there are those who become angry for slight causes, who have changeable minds, who are greedy and jealous of others' happiness and who have no sympathy for their needs.

He slammed the book shut. "Marie-Amandine de Vreux d'Alembourg to a tee," he barked and slipped it between the South African and the Spanish versions of the New Testament. The majority of his wife's lady friends belonged to this category. Louise belonged to category three, the good companion type. Category two wasn't much better than category one. Category four covered the beatified cunt type, the kind that bored a man to the point of weariness. Albert wasn't even remotely interested in philosophy and related disciplines and was likewise mildly immune to art. He considered the books in question to be little more than curiosa, all three stolen from hotel rooms where a Bible can usually be found in the bedside cabinet. *The Teaching of Buddha* was from Singapore, where he had attended a congress for jurists. The parallel English-Chinese text had made swiping it worth the effort.

He looked around the only room in the house that belonged to him and him alone with gratification. It was devoid of heirlooms and souvenirs from bygone days, the sight of which could depress a man in seconds. One wall was covered with solid wood bookshelves with his favourite authors: Ernest Hemingway, Vladimir Nabokov, Robert Ruark, Norman Mailer, V.S. Naipaul, Anaïs Nin, Henry Miller, Georges Simenon,

Bruce Chatwin, Frederick Forsyth, Gabriel García Márquez, alongside an extended collection of biographies, which he referred to as his "lives of the saints". His desk was an art deco dining table in beautifully grained hardwood. A shabby Afghan rug covered the floor. The only decoration was on the desk: the decapitated sandstone head of an authentic Khmer statue from Cambodia, mounted on a cast-iron base. A glass display cabinet exhibiting three double-barrelled shotguns and two hunting rifles, magnificent examples, well-oiled and gleaming, took up half of another wall. Four sets of stag antlers together with two impressive wild boar tusks graced the wall above.

He glanced fleetingly at his cherished weapons, was reminded of the Scottish Highlands where he regularly joined friends for a spot of hunting, crossed to the window and pulled open the curtains. The room became clear and radiant and appeared to increase in size. He switched off the light and made his way downstairs, looking forward to his first cup of coffee. Maria Landowska was busy in the kitchen, setting the table for breakfast. She was large and sturdy, and there was something stealthy about the way she moved, as if danger was lurking nearby. She was wearing jeans and a green sweater, clothes that were strictly forbidden when "Madame" was at home. When she caught sight of Albert, she smiled and revealed a couple of stainless-steel teeth, a remnant of life under Communism. Her smooth skin, lacking the slightest trace of the ravages of bourgeois society, was pale and freckled and she had prominent Slavic cheekbones. Her red ponytail looked like a bunch of dried flowers.

"*Guten Morgen*, Mr Albert," she said with her boyish guttural voice, her bright-blue eyes looking him full in the face.

"Good morning, Maria."

"What's on the menu this morning?"

"*Drie Eier*."

"*OK*," Albert said in clumsy Polish. "Fried or beaten?"

"Beaten like raindrops on the window."

A cunning smile appeared on her lips. She opened the thermos and set it on the table with a thud.

"Beaten like a farmer beats his wife?" she enquired.

They laughed conspiratorially. He sat down and poured himself a large mug of coffee, while Maria cracked three eggs into a bowl with unparalleled skill, flavoured them with pepper and salt, and started to beat them as if she were mixing two different sorts of animal feed in a bucket. Albert took his mug and drank his coffee as he preferred: first blowing then slurping. Louise always used to say "my wolfie" when he did that.

2

As the years had passed, Albert had grown more and more inclined to leave the course of the day to fate, which he attempted to steer with all sorts of superstitious behaviour. What would be his first deed on this sunny spring day? Something industrious or something that suited his mood? As Public Prosecutor to Antwerp's Court of Appeal, he was fortunate enough to be able to spoil himself with the latter. He decided to let a game of patience settle the matter, three at the most. He had read somewhere that Charles de Gaulle and the Norwegian winner of the Nobel Prize for Literature, Knut Hamsun, were similarly addicted, and had convinced himself that this innocent custom could improve the quality of a person's life. Interesting pieces of information of this sort filled him with respect for important figures.

"Queen of Spades, come to my aid," he mumbled as he made his way upstairs to the second floor to shave, still barefoot and dressed in his kimono. He had enjoyed an appetizing breakfast with all the trimmings and chatted about this and that with Maria Landowska, who had taught him his daily dose of five Polish words. He liked the language because it sounded pleasant to his ear. He was proud of the few Polish sentences he could pronounce without any trace of an accent.

As he walked into the bathroom, he realized he was out of breath and his heart was throbbing in his skull. Two cups of Maria's strong coffee were to blame. This kind of reasoning allowed him to file the problem away for the time being in a remote corner of his mind. He did the same with other matters of an entirely different nature, namely the treatment of delicate cases from the offices of the district prosecutors under his jurisdiction, with which he "involved himself" when he considered it necessary (especially if there was a hint of politics involved). He was aware that he was flirting with the law in such instances, but he was also aware that it was fairly common practice in Belgium. He called it "compartmental thinking", a technique characteristic of primitive peoples that had saved him considerable amounts of time. He considered it a highly appropriate social grace.

He switched on his state-of-the-art Braun electric shaver, a gift from Louise, the Rolls Royce of its kind, which seemed to vacuum away the last tiny hair without a sound. After shaving, he splashed his cheeks with Davidoff and inspected his teeth for a second time. He brushed them to get rid of the taste of coffee, rinsed his mouth with water, carefully examined it to see if his gums had been bleeding and scrambled down the stairs two at a time, something that still came naturally to him. He sat at his desk in his elegant leather-and-chrome chair, a gift from the Brussels firm that had furnished his chambers at the Prosecutor's Office, where an identical specimen had likewise been delivered. He filed this similarly Belgian form of corruption under "shrewd favours that need not be reciprocated per se". He had preserved the firm's publicity brochure, which claimed that the leather was fault-free because it came from Scottish cattle unharmed by barbed-wire fences.

He opened a drawer and took out a round Japanese black lacquered box adorned with a slender bird. It contained a worn-out pack of Johnnie Walker cards. He shuffled the pack and the third card he chose was the Queen of Spades. "Ha ha!" he said. "She heard my appeal." He childishly identified two of the four queens with Louise and Amandine, the latter with the

Queen of Diamonds, which he considered the least interesting. If the next card was the King of Hearts (Albert Savelkoul), his day would be made. He nervously selected three cards from the pack and flipped them over, but there was no sign of a king. At the last moment, when he had more or less given up hope, he flipped over the King of Diamonds. And the *King of Hearts*! "Ha ha!" he exclaimed for a second time. By the time he had placed the Queen of Spades on top of the King of Hearts he had lost interest in the game. His decision had been made: on Tuesday 25 May 1999, under the treacherous sign of Castor and Pollux, he was going to enjoy every moment without the slightest inkling of false modesty. He would show his face at the Prosecutor's Office, peer over a few shoulders and make sure everyone had seen him.

His official car would arrive at the front door as it did every day at nine o'clock sharp. He glanced at his watch. Twenty past eight. He rolled back his chair and reached for his mobile, which was concealed behind a table leg. He quickly keyed in her number. He let it ring twelve times but no one answered. Unusual, he thought, and hung up. She must be in the stables. He produced a scrap of paper from his kimono and read aloud: "Horse: *koń*, judge: *sędzia*, egg: *jajko*, coffee: *kawa*, milk: *mleko*."

He picked up his mobile a second time, but instead of calling her number he stared absently into space. If she didn't pick up this time, that would be a bad sign, in spite of the Queen of Spades. He decided to wait a while. Tempting fate so early in the morning could ruin the rest of the day. He tried to reassure himself. She could only be with the horses at this hour. Was there something wrong with Yamma or Soliman? According to Albert, who had received a pony from his father fifty-seven years ago and was an experienced horseman, Louise was the only woman who knew how to treat horses properly. When they rode together through the Sint-Job-in-'t-Goor woods where she lived, he always admired her natural balance in the saddle and her perfectly coordinated instinctual reactions. He fantasized that they had once galloped across the Asian steppe together on sturdy Mongolian tarpans, centuries ago in the time of Genghis Khan, she screaming wildly, her hair unfettered, he with a bow over his shoulder. He had once told her about it while she was riding Yamma and she could barely stay in the saddle for laughing. He could be a romantic at times, and as he mused on their first encounter he became more and more convinced of it. Their relationship was the result of what he referred to as a chapter in a picaresque novel, the kind of thing that never happens to ordinary men and women. Seventeen years earlier, on Friday 5 March 1982 to be precise – he was still the public prosecutor's first substitute in those days – he had intervened in a delicate case of adultery among Antwerp's upper-crust, which a team of gormless criminal investigators had more or less botched up. While personal interventions in such matters were exceptional, he found himself in a privileged position at the time on account of the simple fact that the then public prosecutor was a political creation of his father-in-law, Justice de Vreux. He was free, for example, to enter the public prosecutor's chambers unannounced, and the man even called him by his first name, something not done in those days.

The official report of the case in question revealed a glaring procedural error: the team of inspectors had burst into the house of the defendant on 7 January 1982 "to ascertain the offence of adultery", fifteen minutes before the prescribed time of five in the morning. The lady involved had fled stark naked into the garden, where the temperature was five below zero. This savoury detail is not mentioned in the report, nor the fact that she was left out in the freezing cold for more than half an hour. She wasted little time in submitting a complaint against the inspectors, with three witnesses to confirm her side of the story. He had summoned the woman to the Prosecutor's Office in an effort to settle the matter out of court. His boss, the former public prosecutor, was on the point of being promoted to adjunct Barrister-General to the Council of State, and preferred to avoid such cases. The lady turned out to be a particularly attractive forty-year-old woman, accompanied at the time by her then sixteen-year-old daughter, the breathtakingly beautiful Louise. He was at the height of his midlife crisis in those days, which his circle of less-than-innocent friends called "the midday demon". He also realized that his life up to that point had been a sexual flop of grandiose proportions. A little drama could do no harm.

In the same period, prompted by Amandine's evident lack of interest in what she called "marital duties" (they had slept in separate rooms since the birth of their son Geoffroy in 1965), he made occasional use of the services of a prostitute in the district surrounding the central train station. But on one of his evening excursions, a plain clothes CID vice squad investigator had spotted him leaving an establishment on Van Wesenbekestraat, the curtains of which were still drawn. Although he had disguised himself with a baseball cap and a pair of sunglasses, the investigator, alias "the Krul", had clearly recognized him. He could be one hundred per cent certain that details of the incident would remain inscribed in the police database for ever and a day. He stopped visiting the area after that evening, aware that the investigator in question would probably have tipped off the CID commissioner general's office, where details of his misdemeanour would be recorded, a fact that could prove embarrassing in certain circumstances. The Krul's own sordid reputation made little if any difference. What the fuck was he to do to defend himself at the Prosecutor's Office, where he was first substitute, *nota bene*, with a file running around full of testimony provided by "nightclub hostesses", forced by the Krul to provide their services for free during his monthly visit to check their papers? Even the man's reputation as a psychopath wasn't likely to tip the balance in his favour. The Public Prosecutor could count his blessings nevertheless. The affair had not affected his career, the Krul had passed away, and Van Wesenbekestraat had been taken over by the gay community in 1990.

His romance with Louise had started at that very moment. It was love at first sight on both sides and he could still remember every last detail. The only risk involved was her age, two years under the legal limit, but he was so madly in love with her he simply ignored it. She was still attending the Dames Chrétiennes Institute on Lange Nieuwstraat, Antwerp's most exclusive school for girls, run by the female Jesuits. The first time he saw her with her mother, she was wearing the school uniform, which excited him intensely. Their first love nest was a friend's flat. He had borrowed the keys and insisted she wear her school uniform to every rendezvous until she graduated in 1984.

Their lovemaking was passionate but conservative. During their first seemingly endless kiss, he had slipped his hand slowly under her pleated skirt. He thought she would be satisfied with kissing and caressing at first, but the illusion he had been cherishing that Catholic schoolgirls in Antwerp knew nothing about love was quickly dismissed. Without mincing words she told him what she wanted. She had been taking the pill for two years and knew all about orgasms and the like. While he searched for her "honey pot", she would unzip his fly and pull out his stiff cock. After she had reached her climax, he would slip her panties out of the way, slither inside, still standing upright, grab her muscular buttocks with both hands as she clung to him like an ailing bird, and when she shouted "*Mate! Mate!*" he would come, howling like a wolf. They would collapse together on the bed and the kissing, touching and other foreplay would start again. The verb "to mate" had immediate success with her every time. Their lovemaking lasted the entire afternoon in the early days, but after a while the single act of penetration evolved into an episode of touching and fondling that raised them to an *état de grâce* so to speak, in which she would come with ease and he would pretend half the time. He called this "the white-lie method".

Although she still had the sinuous snake-like body of her youth, the silky-smooth skin with the musky odour of faintly perfumed chamois leather, and luxuriant East-Indies hair in which he would bury his nose like a hound in search of prey, it didn't make the slightest difference now in 1999; not even the discovery of brand-new variations on the verb "to mate" was of any help. To put it plainly, his virility had been on the decline for several years. It usually took at least a quarter of an hour before he succeeded in producing what he called a "sparrow's orgasm", and during their last encounter he had even had difficulty getting an erection. He tried to make up for it with expensive gifts.

"Oh well," he mumbled, audibly inhaling and looking at his watch. Eight thirty-five. He grabbed his mobile, but something stopped him from calling her. He groaned and gazed at a silver-framed sepia photo on his desk of a young boy on a pony, looking into the lens as if he was about to burst into tears. The pony was a Shetlander with a bushy mane and distrustful expression, waiting patiently for the opportunity to kick someone, if his stance was anything to go by. His name was Pieter. When the pony was found dead in his stable on a summer morning in 1944, Albert experienced grief for the first time.

Whenever he looked at the picture, pessimistic thoughts about the irreversible swiftness of time, growing old and the carefree days of his youth that were gone for ever, would flood his mind. This time was no exception. He envied Louise, only thirty-two and a couple of years younger than his eldest son, no less. In the glory years, he had derived enormous pleasure from reading *Lolita*, and that thrill, nowadays taboo, had played a considerable part in the gratification of his needs, but even sexual fetishes like *Lolita* were now beyond him.

"Oh well," he muttered a second time. He stared into space, his face washed out, listening to a mysterious electric motor start up somewhere deep in the foundations of the goddamned building, looked at his watch, resolutely straightened his back, concentrated on the Queen of Spades and punched in her number. She answered after a single ring.

"Hello..."

Her husky voice.

Albert forgot the world around him. He took a deep breath and asked: "How's that Black Lotus of mine?" They always spoke to one another in the dialect of Antwerp.

"Mmm..."

"And what's my Black Lotus wearin'?"

"Guess."

He leaned back in his chair, enjoying the moment. "Champagne-coloured... satin... undies... thigh length... where a man can take his time, slipping his hand..."

"Well, well..."

"And why would a man do that?" he said, anticipating her response.

"You know why..."

He felt a warmth in his eyes. "Love of my life..." he whispered, his lips close to the phone. He had called her that from the beginning.

"Will I see you today?" she asked impersonally.

"First a quick visit to the office, then I'm all yours. Should I bring anything special?"

"Up to you. Shall I saddle the horses?"

"Of course. By the way, were you in the stable half an hour ago?"

"Nope, why?"

"I phoned."

"I was in the house. Maybe the radio was too loud."

"Maybe..."

"Cheerio. See you later..."

He gave her a kiss through the phone.

He hung up and calmly climbed the stairs to his bedroom, without deigning to look at the Virgin of Fatima. "Judge *sędzia* milk *mleko* coffee *kawa* horse *koń* egg *jajko*," he crooned to the tune of Mozart's 'Que dirai-je maman?', a melody he always had to play for his mother on the piano in the olden days.

Maria Landowska had carefully arranged his shirt, ties and suit on a valet stand in the bedroom. He inspected the flawless, made-to-measure, dark-blue alpaca suit, the striped silk shirt and selection of ties. Without hesitation, he selected a flamboyant Versace number, flagrantly defying instructions "concerning the attire of magistrates and comparable functions", which had circulated among the personnel on his advice six months earlier.

An emblem of the Grand Cross in the Order of Leopold II decorated his left lapel. He examined it carefully to ensure it was correctly positioned in the buttonhole.

3

Albert had once thoroughly enjoyed reading the book *Official and Confidential* on the secret life of the legendary FBI director J. Edgar Hoover. The book contained sufficient and incontrovertible evidence that the man was a scoundrel of the first order, who hated the same vices in others that he himself possessed to a considerable degree. This did not diminish his admiration for Hoover in the slightest. He did not know why, but every time his chauffeur, provided full-time by the Prosecutor's Office via the CID, opened the passenger door for him and said: "Good morning, Public Prosecutor, sir," he couldn't help thinking of Hoover. He had taken perverse pleasure in reading about the way the man had treated his chauffeur. He had apparently been fanatically demanding when it came to spatters on his blacked-out Cadillac, the precise size of the folded travelling blankets on the rear seat and even the shape of the ice cubes for the Jack Daniels he regularly enjoyed with his bosom friend Clyde Tolson, in spite of the FBI's strict prohibitions against homosexuality and drinking alcohol on duty.

"Good morning, Public Prosecutor," said the chauffeur as he held open the rear passenger door of the brand-new, black Opel Omega. The Peugeot had been passed on to a district prosecutor two months earlier. Amandine preferred the Peugeot, and he knew why: Peugeot was the model preferred by Antwerp's French-speaking elite, or what passed for French, a custom dating back to the War, when Dufour's – the best yachts money could buy – still attended to its clients in the language.

"Good morning," he answered in a neutral tone, briefly looking him up and down. J. Edgar Hoover only spoke to his chauffeur to tell him off or accuse him of things of which he was entirely innocent.

"The Kaai," said Albert when the chauffeur had taken his place behind the wheel.

The distance from his house, a desirable residence on Amerikalei, given to his wife by her father Justice de Vreux on the tenth anniversary of their wedding, to the Court of Appeal on the Waalse Kaai was a little less than a mile. Albert considered it the height of luxury, which probably explains why he enjoyed it so much. "Completely absurd," said Jokke Weyler one morning, having gone along for the ride. "Luxury is always absurd, Jokke," he had replied. "But the classes are God's creation, are they not?" One of their more affected expressions.

Antwerp's Court of Appeal on the Waalse Kaai was located next to a tarmac surface littered with garbage bags, which was supposed to pass for a car park. The building itself had seven stories and was a prime example of the ugliness that characterized third-rate Seventies postmodernism. The first floor had hexagonal windows that looked like the wide-open gullets of North Sea cod. Faulty drainage had left the frames discoloured and stained. The building was about twenty-five years old, but wear and tear was visible wherever you looked. Inferior building material and poor maintenance were to blame, an excellent example of what had become known as "Belgian laxity". Albert avoided the Court's public entrance at all times. At the rear of the building, near the Cockerill Kaai, there was an inconspicuous rusty metal door, which was always locked. Only he and the janitor had a key. The door opened into a gloomy corridor with coarse concrete walls leading to a elevator, which stopped only at his offices on the seventh floor. He considered himself a public figure and was not shy of the media, but starting the day in mystery was an exclusive privilege he reserved for himself. He deemed the hard-working diligence of the office staff on his arrival to be evidence that the Antwerp Public Prosecutor's Office was running like clockwork. But he was unaware of the fact that the moment he pushed the button in the elevator, a red light flickered on the seventh floor, announcing to an attentive clerk that "Cardinal Richelieu" was on his way. The remainder of the staff were thus forewarned. He had acquired the nickname on account of the Roman elegance with which he wore his red toga and genuine ermine cape. At the Court of First Instance, they used to call him "line of least resistance", which he put down with a fake smile to his talent for "appropriate delegation". He preferred to limit the latter, aware that his subordinates might imagine they had achieved something while they were only entertaining themselves.

He opened the elevator door, looked left and right into the empty corridor, frowned at the absence of activity and made his way pensively past a row of portraits, former public prosecutors, posing self-importantly like Renaissance prelates with white lace ruffles and ermine collars, draped with medals of honour. This illustrious gallery would include his own portrait in three years time, he thought. His soundproof, studded-leather office door was open. He headed directly towards his impressive Italian desk, with matching designer cabinets in solid rosewood. The interior had devoured a significant portion of the 1996 budget entry for "fixtures and fittings". He sat down in his chair, the leather of which had an unfamiliar odour, vaguely reminiscent of some exotic aromatic plant. He cast a contemptuous glance at the bundle of exposed cables running at floor level along the wall. The computers acquired by the Court of Appeal in 1995 were yet to communicate with one another. Links to the other prosecutors' offices and courts of the land were still impossible, in spite of police reforms. The keyboards were little more than glorified typewriters.

"Hmm..."

He looked up. His secretary was standing in the doorway with a file under her arm. She was close to fifty, a resigned expression on her face, small, pale and chubby, with short grey hair. She was wearing a dark-blue skirt, a beige blouse with a turnover collar and a string of artificial pearls. She was unmarried, took care of her mother, and was completely dedicated to her job as secretary. Albert, to whom she exhibited the devotion of a nineteenth-century maid, saw her as part of a dying race.

"Good morning, sir."

"Good morning, Miss Verdonck." He used his subdued baritone voice. He never addressed subordinates by their first name and even used official titles for his colleagues, a habit inherited from his father-in-law, who abhorred the barbaric manners introduced by the Americans.

"Anything out of the ordinary?" he enquired in his best "Queen's Dutch", the tone slightly elevated.

"Nothing in particular, Public Prosecutor, sir."

"Good," he replied, his chin tucked into his chest.

She deposited the file on his desk and waited.

"That will be all, Miss Verdonck," he said without looking up. She disappeared.

Albert opened the file and rubbed his eyes with extreme caution. Although he was long-sighted by heredity, he only wore glasses when he was reading a book, an activity he confined for the most part to his home life. According to psychiatrists, the obstinate refusal to wear glasses was a sign of narcissism, but after reading a fascinating article on the matter he had become convinced that narcissism was a characteristic of highly gifted individuals and was something to be sought after. In his opinion, there was only one vulgar variant, which he referred to as "secondary narcissism". He was particularly proud of the expression, which was not to be found in the manuals because he had invented it himself, during the Glyndebourne Festival, no less. He hated classical music and only attended concerts when there was no alternative. People determined to identify themselves with one or another famous conductor, soloist or opera singer particularly irritated him. Amandine, on the other hand, was wild about the sophistication of such musical events. Every year she insisted he join her for an entire week at the Glyndebourne Festival, which had an international reputation for being among the most exclusive, and where she had friends among the English aristocracy (Lord and Lady Egremont, Edith and Noël Beiresford-Peirse and the Earl of Carnarvon) with whom she could gossip to her heart's content in her poor English. One evening, after an opera during which he had fallen asleep, the public had applauded, shouted and stamped their feet for little short of fifteen uninterrupted minutes. The episode had angered him so much that he was unable to say a single word at the post-opera dinner. For the first time in his life, he noted something "non-juridical" on a piece of paper in his hotel room that night: *secondary narcissism: hysterical projection of personal deficiency; read inanity.*

He fished his Mont Blanc Meisterstück 149, nicknamed "the cigar", from his inside pocket, removed the cap and started to sign the letters in purple ink without reading them. He finished off his carefully placed signature with three elliptic full stops, designed to lead his addressee astray in one way or another: Catholics wondered which lodge he belonged to, and although the so-called "free-thinkers" knew better, they still had their doubts. The truth, however, was simple. Public Prosecutor Savelkoul did not belong to the Christian People's Party nor was he attached to the Lodge, something quite unique in the politicized Belgian legal establishment.

Having dealt with the day's correspondence, he returned his fountain pen to its place, groaned and inspected the series of photographs hanging side by side on the wall. He felt a little melancholic, as he always did when he looked at the photographs on the wall. He was much younger in most of them: with King Boudewijn, Queen Beatrix, UN Secretary-General Waldheim, twenty years of Belgian Prime Ministers, President Mitterrand, and, topping them all, President Bush, who shook his hand by sheer accident during a flying visit to the University of Harvard, where Albert had "audited classes" in 1989.

4

Albert left the Court of Appeal at ten thirty via the back door. He strode across the car park towards the Vlaamse Kaai, his expression introverted, as if he were deep in thought. He was aware that a selection of people were watching him from the windows above, following his every move with laser precision, and this prompted him to walk with dignity, much slower than his usual brisk pace – evidence, he believed, of his excellent physical condition. He turned into Pourbusstraat, a cheerless place lined with derelict buildings and warehouses, reminiscent of New York's Lower East Side. He walked through an open door and found himself in an ugly brick-paved courtyard with lock-up garages right and left. He produced a bunch of keys, unlocked a grimy plastic roll-down shutter numbered 14, pulled it up, opened the boot of a large black BMW, removed his jacket, folded it inside out, placed it in the boot and slipped into a brown leather sports coat lying beside it. He loosened his tie and tossed it on top of the jacket, closed the boot, got into the car, started the engine and reversed out of the lock-up.

At that same moment, twelve hundred miles away in Rome, a short, thickset, sixty-year-old woman was leaving the Academia Belgica on Via Omero, a grubby bunker-like edifice from the Mussolini era. A silk Hermès scarf was knotted around the strap of her black, crocodile-leather handbag. She had a peroxide blond, razor-cut hairdo with a lock hanging over her forehead in imitation of Queen Paola. There was a hint of disdain in her expression, a feature common among upper-class ladies. She made her way with measured steps to the awaiting taxi, stopped at the rear passenger door and tapped the window, but the chauffeur did not budge. She stepped awkwardly into the taxi, closed the door, fished a visiting card from her handbag, put on her glasses, which were hanging around her neck on a chain, and said in Italian with a French accent: "Viale Bruno Buozzi *settantatrè*."

The thin unshaven chauffeur with Arab looks and a black anorak started the engine and accelerated abruptly. The woman glanced at the meter, which correctly read three thousand lire, and glowered involuntarily. Instead of following the shortest route via Villa Giulia, the chauffeur drove at reckless speed through the "gay park" towards Piazza del Popolo. The woman looked at her watch, opened her handbag, produced two ten-thousand lire notes and held them at the ready. The chauffeur positioned himself at the front of the left lane at the crossroads with the Via Flaminia, and the second the lights changed to green, he cut in front of the line of cars waiting to drive straight ahead and turned right into the steeply climbing Viale Bruno Buozzi.

A little less than a mile further, on the brow of the hill, where the luxury apartment buildings made way for walled villas surrounded by palm trees, the taxi stopped in front of a cheerless, grey-stone, four-storey building with bars on the windows and its inside shutters locked tight. The woman paid, left no tip, got out of the taxi and ignored the driver's derisive gesture. There was no nameplate beside the doorbell, which gave the impression that the building was unoccupied. She rang the bell. It took a while before someone opened. A thin, slightly effeminate young man stood in the doorway, Mediterranean, dressed in a splendid black suit, pink shirt and mauve tie. He smiled as if he recognized her and said: "*Buenos dias, señora.*"

"*Bonjour,*" she replied, appearing not to be even slightly surprised at being welcomed in Spanish.

He let her in and lead the way along a wide marble corridor where an immense chandelier with burning beeswax candles was suspended from the lofty ceiling, as in a church. At the end of the corridor there was a silver-framed portrait with a crystal vase of white lilies on an antique bronze stand. The portrait was of a man in his early sixties, dressed in a black soutane, his eyes narrowed, peering beyond the world in front of him through tortoiseshell designer glasses. His pursed lips and hanging jowls gave his dramatically furrowed rustic countenance a troubled look. A gnarled right hand covered half the left hand, the thumb of which appeared to grasp at something invisible, like the claw of a lobster. The young man paused in front of the portrait, closed his eyes, bowed his head and murmured something. The woman stood beside him, looked briefly at the portrait and closed her eyes. They remained in front of the portrait for a few seconds and then turned into a second corridor where the young man opened a tall hardwood door. "*Un momentito por favor,*" he said with a smile.

The room was spacious and bare and had the chilly atmosphere of a cellar, the only furniture a marble table on gilded legs with lion's head motif and two chairs with embroidered armrests. A small wooden cross without corpus was the only decoration on the white walls. The air was odourless and a deathly silence filled the room. A patio with carefully trimmed boxwoods in terracotta pots was visible through the net curtains decking a large window. The woman took a chair and sat at the table. She sighed and looked at her watch. 9.55.

Albert scurried out of the delicatessen on Vestingstraat, where he had just bought smoked Irish salmon, two boiled crayfish and a 250-gram tin of Iranian Sevruga caviar. The man who served him pretended not to recognize him, but Albert preferred this to the forwardness so typical of Antwerp's population, one of the few things on which he agreed with his wife. He headed back to his BMW, which was unlawfully parked in front of someone's garage, stepped inside and drove off.

The door opened and a small, pallid, bony man in his early fifties with black crew-cut hair cautiously entered the room. He wore a soutane with an exceptionally high clerical collar and a gold watch chain dangling from one of the buttons. He was carrying a black leather file under his arm, decorated on the front with a simple gold-leaf cross. The woman got to her feet. He greeted her with a nod, took his place at the table and said in perfect French: "I am procurator of the Italian prelature. You had an appointment with the prelate general Monsignor Echevarria, but he is unavailable." No apologies were offered for his absence.

The man spoke so quietly, the woman had trouble understanding him. She raised her eyebrows for an instant. He signalled that she should take a seat. The round lenses and black frames of his glasses were reminiscent of one of El Greco's cardinals. He knotted his hands together and held them a couple of inches above the folder. The sleeves of his soutane revealed immaculate cuffs with rectangular gold cufflinks. He looked at her penetratingly and said nothing.

"*Pax*," the woman mumbled, her eyes turned to the wall.

The priest pretended not to have heard this characteristic Opus Dei expression, opened the folder, tapped his glasses and started to read the first page of what appeared to be a personal file.

After a few minutes, in which the silence was virtually audible, he looked up, straightened his back and said impassively: "Your son Didier is on the verge of fulfilling his agreement and becoming a numerary with the Leuven residence of Opus Dei in Belgium. You are aware of this." His concluding words were not a question, but an observation of incontrovertible fact.

"Yes, Father."

The priest nodded and reflected.

"Do you know what this implies, *ma fille*?" he asked, in line with the strictly upheld Opus Dei policy of treating women like girls.

"A great honour for us..."

"For us, did you say? What do you mean by 'us'?"

The woman scowled and a wrinkle appeared between her eyes.

"Let me help you. The honour also extends to your *husband*?"

His question irritated her. The priest stared at her unwaveringly. "Would you be kind enough to answer my question, *s'il te plait*?"

"The sole purpose of my visit to Rome is to talk about the problem to which you refer. On the advice of Hervé van Reyn at the prelature in Brussels on the Avenue de la Floride, by the way —"

"No need for names and addresses, they are already known to us!" The priest's expression turned vacant and cold.

"My apologies..."

An embarrassed silence filled the room.

"My husband... thinks... I'm in England," the woman continued, clearly ill at ease with the idea.

The priest shrugged his shoulders, removed his glasses and stared at the woman with dark-brown, short-sighted, slightly bulging eyes.

"Perhaps we should come to the point —"

"I beg your pardon..." the woman interrupted, but, with a trivial gesture of the hand – thumb and forefinger pressed together as if he was handing out Communion – he repeated his words with a shrill yet insubstantial voice: "I said: perhaps we should come *to the point*!"

"What do you mean?"

"What I mean is the following: that his *entire* inheritance must be made over to Opus Dei *as a minimum*."

"Yes, I'm aware of that."

"*Eh bien*, so what are we waiting for?" he said with a giggle, his arms spread open.

"The matter is more complicated than you think, Father."

"In what respect?" he enquired abruptly.

"Do I have to explain?"

"Do I have to remind you of our primary obligations, in addition to our unconditional obedience to His Holiness the Pope?"

The woman's cheek twitched nervously.

"Mortification, mortification and more mortification, *total* childlike submission, *unremitting* piety and *single-minded* apostolate!" he snapped.

The woman blanched.

The priest's mouth had contorted into a contemptuous grin, exposing his teeth. He wheezed and continued in the same tone as before: "And meditation on the sayings of our founder, El Padre, in *The Way*. When did you last read it?"

The woman heaved a sigh and turned to one side.

"And you call yourself a supernumerary, a married member of Opus Dei?"

"I beg forgiveness, Father..." she whispered.

"Finally! You would do better to go to confession in the chapel after our conversation."

"I was planning to do so, Father."

"A propos, how is your relationship with your husband?"

"I go to confession once a week, to an Opus priest in Antwerp."

"You're avoiding my question. I asked about your relationship with your *husband*."

The woman bit her lower lip.

"Do I have to be blunt?" he snarled. His voice cracked at the word "blunt". He slapped the table with the palm of his hand and glared at her with barely contained rage. Without waiting for her reaction, he snapped: "Do you still sleep in the same room? In the same bed? Do you still give in to the *sins of the flesh* in the matrimonial bed now that your fertile years are behind you? Have you forgotten that your body is a *sack of dung*? That we must *chastise* the body because it is our greatest enemy?"

His cheeks were flushed and his mouth was half open. He moistened his lips. The breath was audible in his nostrils. All at once he blessed himself, slowly and with solemnity, closed his eyes and nervously prayed: "*O Dio, che concedesti al Beato Josemaría, sacerdote, innumerevoli grazie, scegliendolo como strumento fedelissimo per fondare l'Opus Dei, cammino di santificazione nel lavoro professionale…* O God, you granted your priest Blessed Josemaría countless graces, choosing him as a most faithful instrument to found Opus Dei, a way of sanctification in daily work…"

The woman gazed at him motionless. She felt as if she had aged ten years in just a few minutes.

He wasn't sure why, but every time he took the exit for Sint-Job-in-'t-Goor on the E17 on his way to Louise, Albert was always reminded of the same thing: the way he had acquired the farmhouse with its four acres of grazing, their "love nest" in recent years.

In 1991, after roughly six months in office as public prosecutor, the Court of First Instance was presented with a delicate case, which carried such political baggage that he decided it was appropriate to get involved, much to the relief of the then district prosecutor. He went on "retreat" for a couple of days to an apartment on the Zeedijk in Knokke, which his wife had acquired by deed of gift, free of inheritance tax. He studied the paperwork to the last detail. It was a sordid business about the reallocation of fifty-seven acres of wood and heath for building purposes in a protected Green Belt Zone in Brecht near Sint-Job-in-'t-Goor by a well-known Antwerp property broker. In partnership with a notary public and two local mayors, one of whom was the father-in-law of the Flemish Minister for Environmental Planning, the firm in question had set up a system whereby the "fraud" was buried to such an extent under what appeared to be watertight legal arguments and the texts of a series of Royal Decrees which no one remembered, that only a legal expert such as Albert had the brains to detect it.

For a variety of reasons, he decided to approach the case with discretion. In the first instance, the Minister for Environmental Planning was a good friend of the professor who had succeeded his father-in-law at the Catholic University of Leuven, and in the second, Albert was familiar with the broker in question from the fortnightly meetings of the Antwerp Central Rotary Club. He was not sure which of the circumstances was the weightiest. Instead of the customary initial meeting in the chambers of the Court of Appeal, an "exploratory discussion" was organized in a restaurant near Brussels known for the privacy and tranquillity of its *salons*. The meeting started with champagne and a sumptuous lunch offered by the property broker, Walter de Ceuleneer from Roeselare in West Flanders, who arrived in a Rolls Royce Silver Shadow. The other guests were the notary and the two mayors. It was deemed inopportune to involve the minister at this stage in the proceedings.

Although Walter de Ceuleneer – well-upholstered, cheerful, with man-of-the-world appeal – only enjoyed a superficial acquaintance with Albert as his Rotary brother, he succeeded in winning him over in less than an hour. It turned out that both men shared an obsession with hunting and riding. The broker had his own stable and castle in Scotland's grouse country at his disposal the year round. He travelled in his own Lear Jet and rode a genuine Connemara horse after the hunt. To cap it all, he was the type of person who could talk about wine and haute cuisine, who enjoyed a joke, and, as he said himself with an ostentatious wink, was not averse to the occasional bit of skirt. Albert immensely enjoyed the encounter, mainly because his judgement of character in everyday life left a great deal to be desired.

The problem at hand was more delicate than Albert had first imagined, but still relatively easy to solve, with the necessary courage of course. It had been exposed four years earlier by an environmental association of "guys in clogs and mohair socks" who had halted proceedings after the sudden death of their chief negotiator. The affair had been left to simmer at the Court of First Instance during that time, held up by so-called procedural errors discovered at the last minute by one of the big guns at a renowned Brussels legal firm. Another seven months and the case was due to lapse (de Ceuleneer's reasoning was inaccurate. In every instance of forgery, the case in question did not lapse after the usual five years). That was the essence of the matter and the rest was bullshit, de Ceuleneer concluded with a meaningful glance in Albert's direction. He had evidently been informed that Albert did not have a blank record when it came to sweeping "delicate cases" under the carpet. He dropped a few hints to this end with characteristic shrewdness. In 1983 (Albert was still first substitute to the public prosecutor at the time), the Antwerp CID announced an important drugs haul. The street value of thirty-five kilos of pure heroin was little short of spectacular in the early Eighties, more than one-hundred million Belgian francs. The press had had a field day and Albert had even appeared on television in front of a table with thirty-five sacks of white powder. But when the matter finally came to court, all hell broke loose: the heroin appeared to have changed all of a sudden into talcum powder. A month earlier, the "secure space" in the cellars of the Court of Justice, where the heroin was stored awaiting destruction after the publication of the court verdict, had been broken into. According to the public prosecutor's spokesman, only a couple of files had disappeared from the cellar. The man was telling the truth, of course, and since the heroin appeared to have been left untouched, little fuss was made of the apparent document theft. New locks were placed on the doors and that was that. But sparks began to fly when the court was in session and demanded a supplementary expert's report. It then became clear that the heroin had been stolen and the sacks had been filled with talc. Albert had been given charge of the inquiry, together with an examining magistrate who now worked as a legal advisor to a multinational. He could smell the smoke hanging over his head and he reacted accordingly by removing the dangerous statements provided by the accused, two Albanians from Antwerp's criminal underworld, who had confessed that the plastic bags actually contained heroin. Records of the tests done by the forensic police, which supported the confession, also appeared to have vanished. Since the lack of concrete evidence had now robbed the case of much of its vigour, Albert had been particularly clement in his closing speech. The chairman of the Third Correctional Court, a thick-headed old man whose only interests were his stamp collection and his pension, followed First Substitute Savelkoul's remarkable closing speech without question. The two Albanians were acquitted. Where was the heroin? It remained a mystery. An internal inquiry tried to solve the talcum powder issue but to no avail. The Public Prosecutor's

Office intervened and the affair was transferred to the Court of Appeal, where it died an inconspicuous death.

The Albanians' renowned defence lawyer, who had pleaded their case with remarkable reserve and just the right amount of indignation, was naturally aware of the ins and outs of the affair. He didn't breath a word about the break-in at the court house, but he told his clients what had happened to the paperwork. They were good listeners. A little more than a week later, Albert received a telephone call at home during which a man with a German accent invited him to call a certain number in Geneva, identify himself with the code name Beaver and submit an account number. Albert took note. The next day he decided out of curiosity to do what the voice had asked. The people in Geneva informed him that the account was in credit to the sum of one million Swiss francs, the entire amount at Beaver's disposal. *Twenty-five million Belgian francs!* His relationship with Louise was rich with passionate infatuation. In those days he earned eighty-eight thousand francs after deductions, most of which Amandine pocketed for "household expenses". He had to manage as best he could with the rest and with the income from a small parental inheritance, which produced the princely sum of eighteen thousand francs per month. He had just bought a bracelet worth ninety thousand francs for Louise, money he borrowed from a bank. After the telephone call from Switzerland, he did what anyone else in his position would do. He pretended nothing was out of the ordinary and withdrew occasional sums from the account. He had in fact invested fifteen million in stocks and shares, which earned him an average of twelve per cent a year. The sense of independence from Amandine, who had discovered by this time he had a mistress, was incredible. A few days after the money was deposited in the Swiss account, one of the Albanians telephoned him, thanked him in cryptic terms and a deep husky voice for the inestimable service he had provided, and informed him in exotic Flemish that he could count on the Albanian community "for eternity". He heard nothing more after that.

Walter de Ceuleneer happened to have an acquaintance in the Albanian underworld, the owner of an antiques and curios shop in the old part of the city, where he would drop in from time to time.

The Albanian's name was Ramiz Shehu. The man had invested a couple of million, via the property firm WDC, in land with planning permission on Antwerp's Left Bank, which he had purchased at an excellent price and which had quadrupled in value after a few years due to the construction of a supermarket. He had also paid part of the purchase price in cash under the table, a method de Ceuleneer employed to perfection. Since then, Shehu had sold him carpets, antiques, caviar and a second-hand Ferrari Testarossa at such favourable prices they had to have been stolen property. As with Albert, de Ceuleneer had managed to win over the Albanian without much effort and to such a degree that they now embraced each other when they met. One fine day, the man had made it clear to his "Belgian brother" that he was prepared to bring in *specialists* to take care of certain "chores", but de Ceuleneer had wisely ignored the offer. His relationship with Albert was much more intimate. After the miraculous settlement of a case related to greenbelt land in the eastern part of the province of Antwerp (the minister for Environmental Planning intervened and granted building permission), he had invited him to the castle in Scotland, in his Lear Jet no less. The grouse were plentiful and the shooting was exceptionally good. They even stalked deer on another occasion. Louise had accompanied him, but she didn't like killing animals. She spent much of her time with de Ceuleneer's daughter Patricia, enjoying long horse rides in the unsullied countryside.

After the holiday the two became "the Scottish Sisters". He later offered Albert the farmhouse in Sint-Job, which he first had renovated, adding stables and a corral. The notary, who was in on the scheme, drew up the deed of sale in Louise's name. Not a single word was said about settling accounts. And they had continued to be friends, calling one another for a chat on a regular basis, going to dinner with their respective girlfriends and, in the winter, hunting for wild boar in the Ardennes, where de Ceuleneer had a "bit" of land. After the favourable outcome of the case, de Ceuleneer no longer called on Albert's services. He pretended nothing had happened and Albert found their gentleman's agreement just fine.

He drove through the centre of Sint-Job towards the dirt track that had been referred to as the Oude Baan since Napoleonic times. With the exception of Louise's farmhouse, there were no other houses in sight and this suited them down to the ground. The paddock for the horses was surrounded by pine trees, which gave him a positive sense of security mixed with a nostalgic longing for years gone by. He was certain that no one in the village knew who he was. The farmhouse had a whitewashed façade, small windows with blinds and a chimney with a weathercock on a rustic tiled roof.

He stopped at the garage adjacent to the house, which used to be a barn, and tooted the horn. The door was half open. A brown Labrador galloped outside and raced in the direction of his BMW. When Albert opened the passenger door, the dog barked and turned in circles. He grabbed him by the head and shook him back and forth.

"Igor! Good boy! Where's the boss?"

The dog raced into the garage and returned in seconds accompanied by a tall, slender woman in khaki riding breeches, a silk blouse and boots with brown greaves. She had long black hair, small breasts, slanting grey eyes and tanned skin.

When Albert caught sight of her he closed his eyes and held his breath. Dear God, make this last, he murmured to himself. He had recently fallen prey to escalating moments of anxiety, but when she nestled up to him, warm and muscular, and her youthful fragrance reached him from what seemed so far away, he would open his eyes in amazement and inhale the scent of the pine trees. It's spring, he thought, and this beautiful young woman is all mine. What could be better? A different sensation coursed through his veins, which reminded him of being young and carefree.

"You smell like ground rusks," he whispered in her ear.

"Nut case!"

They pursed their lips and kissed, the tip of his tongue caressing her teeth. He had learned the technique years before from a whore. The suggestion of tobacco in her mouth gave him goose bumps and he put his arm around her waist. He sensed a shiver run from her lower back to her shoulders. He thought about the Third Woman according to Buddha.

"I brought some goodies," he said, burying his nose in her hair.

"Mmm..."

"Caviar... crayfish... smoked salmon."

"Weren't we planning to go for a ride first?

"Sure. Is Yamma OK?"

"The vet says it's not colic after all. She must have eaten too much spring grass. Thoroughbreds can't handle it, he says."

"Did you pay him?"

"Yes, fifteen hundred."

"So she's fine?"

"Sure, she's *fine*."

He had to laugh at her Boston accent, which she had picked up from him.

They made their way to the car, Igor turning in circles around them.

"It's high time we bought some sheep," she said with a grin.

"And why should we buy sheep?"

"Igor isn't a Labrador."

"No? Then what is he?"

"A shepherd. Look at the way he's protecting us."

"The Good Shepherd," he proclaimed, "lays down his life for his sheep. It's in the Bible."

"Shit!"

He opened the rear passenger door of his BMW and removed a plastic bag from the back seat.

"We should put this in the fridge."

"Whatever you say, Dad."

He held back, remembering the time he had stingingly reacted to her remark as if it were yesterday.

They went into the front hall, where her "horse collection" was displayed on an out-of-place empire chest of drawers. The showpiece was a polychrome Chinese wooden horse with saddle but without rider, which he had bought her for her birthday from an antique dealer on Brussels's Zavel market.

The living room with its rustic open hearth was soberly furnished, if one did not count the enormous white leather sofa and the twenty or so cuddly toys stacked side by side and on top of one another in the middle. A couple of Henry Alken hunting scenes decorated the walls, not unlike his house on Amerikalei. A .22 FN Trombone rifle graced one of the corners.

She relaxed in an armchair, lit a cigarette and absently flicked through a copy of *Vogue*. He made his way to the kitchen, placed the bag in the fridge and moved on to the bedroom. When he returned five minutes later in riding breeches and boots, tweed jacket and riding hat, she looked at her watch.

"Let's go," he said.

"OK." She stubbed out her cigarette determinedly.

* * *

The gaunt, pale-faced priest stared unwaveringly at the blue-suited woman lying flat on her belly on the floor of the crypt, her arms outstretched, in front of a solid silver railing, the massive marble tomb behind it covered with lilies and engulfed by a vague smell of vanilla. The crypt had an extraordinary oval shape surrounded by a wooden gallery on the ground floor and what appeared to be a second level. The gallery was filled with pews where women either leaned forward with their hands over their eyes as if deep in prayer, stared into the distance or took notes in a writing pad. It was deathly quiet. Every now and then a woman would leave the gallery, noiselessly passing the woman on the floor without disturbing her. The women were dressed for the most part in the same black or grey knee-length skirts, white long-sleeved blouses, flat shoes and pallid nylon stockings. They wore their hair short and there was no evidence of make-up. They walked to the railing, to which a round silver medallion depicting the head of a man in relief had been fastened, touched it with their right hands and raised it to their lips. They remained standing with their heads bowed for a few seconds and then left the crypt.

The priest watched motionlessly as the woman on the floor struggled to her feet. The woman looked at him. He returned a brief nod. Both touched the medal, raised their hands to their lips, and made their way silently to the exit. They found themselves in a corridor with bare marble walls, ascended a flight of stairs and entered a chapel with a simple altar and a red sanctuary lamp. They both kneeled and crossed themselves, walked through the room and ascended another flight of stairs, steep and narrow as a mine shaft. The priest took the lead, climbing two stairs at a time. The woman was unable to keep up the pace and stopped halfway, out of breath. The priest continued. At the top of the stairs he looked down at the woman with what appeared to be a derisive sneer on his face. He glanced at his watch and waited. The woman slowly climbed the remaining stairs.

"Forgive me, Father," she gasped. "I'm not as fit as I used to be."

The priest pretended not to have heard her.

After a maze of corridors and stairs, some leading upwards, some downwards, they arrived back in the corridor with the portrait, where they stood for a moment. The priest walked to the parlour door, opened it with brusque impatience and invited her to lead the way.

They sat in the same chairs as they had an hour before.

He ill-temperedly opened the file, which was still lying on the table, removed a sheet of paper with a typed text, tapped his glasses and started to read.

The woman fished a handkerchief from her handbag and blew her nose. He looked up for an instant, put down the sheet of paper and turned his gaze to the ceiling. "Your father," he commenced, "appears to have bequeathed you – *inter vivos* – a portion of the family property, consisting of a penthouse apartment in Knokke-het Zoute, a villa with garden, pool and concierge in Wijnegem, and fourteen acres of woodland in the Belgian Ardennes. Am I correct?"

"Indeed, yes —" Her voice was toneless.

"And was there an agreement to share assets?"

"Of course not —"

"So you have full title to the assets?"

"Yes —"

"Shares and bonds? Money? Other resources?"

"No, Father," she answered almost inaudibly.

"Are you telling me the truth?" he asked with a penetrating look.

She sat upright and said: "What do you think?"

"Personally, I have no thoughts on the matter, but Saying 367 of our holy founder, *Il Beato* Josemaría's *The Way* states: 'Even the most exquisite dish turns into pork if it is eaten by a pig. Let us not be *animals* like so many.'"

"What are you implying, Father?"

"What am I implying?"

"Yes."

"That liars are worse than *animals*! That's what I'm implying."

"There are shares to the value of roughly ten million Belgian francs..."

He whacked the table with the flat of his hand, snorted and started to laugh scornfully. "Is that everything?"

She nodded and hung her head.

"Look," the priest continued, "before we go any further, allow me to ask you a pertinent question: do you still wish us to negotiate with the Belgian Royal Family on the question of an aristocratic title for your husband, a hereditary title that would pass to your two sons?"

The woman sat upright and a self-satisfied smile appeared on her lips. "My dearest wish, Father. Public Prosecutor General Savelkoul is a commoner and unfortunately my sons bear his name..."

"We are aware of this."

She said nothing and stared at him anxiously. He waited, evidently searching for the correct words. He then spoke with hesitation, as if his sentences were divided into segments.

"We are prepared... to intervene... with the Private Secretary to His Majesty King of the Belgians... The man is one of our cooperators. He is well disposed towards us, although not a member."

"Precisely..."

"He has so much influence... A recommendation from him... always meets with a positive response... from His Majesty...

We speak from experience… His coat of arms does not bear the emblem *Dieu est Mon Epée* for nothing…"

He closed the file and looked beyond her to the figureless cross on the wall.

"We have a notary in Belgium, a supernumerary member of Opus Dei, prepared to do whatever is necessary…"

"Whatever is necessary?"

"He will fill you in on the details," he responded arrogantly.

"Surely not the entire family patrimony?…"

"Rest assured, you will have enough left to live according to your station in life."

The woman nodded.

The priest leaned forward and grinned victoriously. "Now to a completely different matter…"

She looked at him.

"I suppose you are aware of the… er… the Public Prosecutor's extramarital *behaviour*?"

The woman closed her eyes, her frown coinciding with a painful twitching.

"Is my question clear enough?"

She nodded in the affirmative.

"*Alors*…"

"I have known about it for a long time, Father."

"How long exactly?"

"Almost fifteen years."

"Do you know the woman?"

"I have never seen her. I don't even know her name."

"Do you know where they meet?"

"No. I have never tried to find out."

The priest pursed his lips and thought for a moment. "I'm sure you are aware that the committee of inquiry into the suitability of a candidate for a title is particularly strict on ethical matters."

"I come from a noble family myself, Father."

The priest's eyes narrowed. "*Il Beato* Josemaría was Marquis of Perálta, young lady."

"That's not what I meant."

"*Basta!* When do you return to Belgium?"

"My airline ticket is open-ended."

"*Muy bien.* There is a retreat for young ladies being conducted here in the house at present. Would you like to participate?"

She nodded.

"*Muy bien.* Let me sum things up: the moment you are back in Belgium, you will contact the notary we spoke about and make the necessary arrangements."

"And my husband?"

"What do you mean? You did not agree to share your assets when you married. There should be no problem."

"No, the other matter —"

"*Distinguo!*" he snapped, using a typically Jesuit term for discerning the difference between truth and illusion adopted by Opus Dei. "Don't worry about it."

"Can I still count on Opus Dei mediation with His Majesty's private secretary? I happen to know Pierre…"

The priest turned white as chalk.

"*Ma fille*, what do you want? Do *we* arrange things or would you prefer to do it yourself?"

"I will keep a low profile, Father," she whispered. The matter clearly troubled her.

Once again, the priest pressed his thumb and forefinger together as if he was handing out Communion and said: "Women have no need to be intelligent, only dedicated and careful. And do not forget: the sanctity demanded of us by the Lord is founded on three pillars: sacred daring, sacred compulsion and sacred brazenness! We are merely *instruments* in His hands."

He stood up abruptly and thrust his chair noisily under the table. "Let me bring you to the retreat house."

She got to her feet and followed him, head bowed, along the marble corridor towards the elevator. The priest pressed the call button, stood stock-still on the tips of his toes, closed his eyes and waited like a statue, his fingers stiffly intertwined against his midriff, his knuckles white, the leather file clasped firmly as if he feared he might lose it.

After accompanying the Belgian woman to the retreat house, situated in the west wing of the building, which had served as the residence of the Hungarian ambassador to the Holy See until 1945, the priest made his way to his office on the fourth floor. The room was spacious, high-ceilinged and furnished with simple but expensive furniture, the centrepiece a modern desk with a telephone and switchboard, a black Artemide halogen reading lamp, a small wooden crucifix within hand's reach, and nothing else. Two life-size framed photographs adorned the wall opposite, one of John Paul II, whose cunning old man's scowl made him appear angry, and one of El Padre, Monsignor Josemaría Escrivá de Balaguer y Albás, founder of Opus Dei. It was a copy of the altarpiece from the Ardeatino, Rome's Opus Dei Church, and presented him *in pluviale*, dressed in a gold-embroidered cope that accentuated the narrowness of his shoulders, blessing the faithful with a deeply furrowed brow, a discreet halo around his head.

An IBM Aptiva computer, a laser printer/fax, a large photocopier and an enormous widescreen TV graced a long table against another wall.

The priest, Joaquín Pla y Daniel, procurator of the Opus Dei (responsible for relationships with the Holy See), was the great nephew of Cardinal Pla y Daniel – known in his day for his ultra-conservative stance – Archbishop of Toledo and Primate of Spain until his death in 1967.

He rolled back his chair, sat down, placed the leather file in front of him on the desk, the file he had reviewed with the "young lady". He stared vacantly into space for a time, reached out to the crucifix for a second, took off his glasses, carefully polished the lenses with a white handkerchief, returned them to their place, and pushed a button on the switchboard, which connected him automatically to a specific number. He left the receiver in the cradle and waited, his back rigid and tense.

The number answered after the first ring: "*Oui?*" a woman's lucid voice enquired.

"*Prélature belge?*" he asked curtly.

"*A qui ai-je l'honneur?*"

"Joaquín Pla —"

"*Pax, mon père.*"

"My sweetheart. May I speak with the Counsellor?" he asked in an exceptionally cordial tone.

"*Tout de suite, mon père.*"

He waited a few seconds.

"Van Reyn," a high pitched voice broke the silence.

"Hervé? Joaquín. *¿Que tal, querido amigo?*"

"*¡Muy bien! ¿Y tú?*"

"*Yo tambien.*"

They continued in Spanish, a language the Belgian Regional Vicar of Opus Dei, Baron Hervé van Reyn, spoke with some fluency. He had studied philosophy for three years at the Opus-Dei-run University of Navarra in Pamplona and had degrees in politics, economics and environmental planning.

"Good news?" van Reyn enquired.

"Is this a safe line?"

"What a question…"

"I presume you have heard about the problems surrounding the father of one of our candidate numeraries, Didier Savelkoul?"

"To the last detail."

"Can you suggest an adequate solution?"

"I think so."

"I'm listening."

"We first have to ease the father away from that er… whore, then we can get down to business."

"Exactly. And the footnotes?"

"Destabilize the whore and then blackmail. The man is vulnerable enough…"

"Is he corrupt?"

"Corrupt is a somewhat er… elastic term in Belgium, but yes, he is corrupt and in more than one domain, although we have no hard evidence as yet."

"But that is precisely what we need."

"And we'll have it in due course."

"I'm listening."

"We'll employ a private detective to learn more about the whore and her background."

"Good idea. And?"

"There are claims that he has a bank account in Switzerland."

"And?"

"As you know, my family is well informed on banking matters. We have a supernumerary in Zurich who can find anything. All we have to do is ask. Am I making myself clear? By the way, did you see *la madre*?"

"She was sitting in front of me not a quarter of an hour ago. As supernumerary, she relinquished a considerable portion of her family patrimony. Didier's inheritance for one, and a… er… sizeable supplement for arranging an aristocratic title with your Royal Family."

"Aha, excellent news."

"Are you acquainted with King Albert's personal secretary?"

"Saint Pierre? The man is inclined to favour the Charismatic Renewal, but he has never refused a favour."

"Does he have that much influence with the King?"

"His Majesty always listens to his advice. He's even close to the crown prince, a sort of spiritual director. They attend weekly prayer services in the palace together. The Belgian lefties claim he's running the country, and in a sense they might even be right, ha ha."

"So you'll organize the detective and the Swiss connection."

"You can depend on it, but I'll need the documents for the notary."

"Should I send them by special mail?"

"The fax should be fine."

"Is that safe?"

"My private fax, remember. Then we can be sure they don't fall into the wrong hands."

"Business as usual otherwise?"

"What do you mean?"

"Fishing… new members…"

"Twenty per cent of our approaches to potential members have been positive so far this year. We've just purchased three properties to house the new candidates."

"Where?"

"Ghent, Antwerp and Liege. What about Rome?"

"*Calma.* The Prelate is on his way to Peru and Colombia."

"Colombia? I'm intrigued…"

"Problems with the Medellin clan."

"Well, well…"

"They claimed their 'prices' had come under such pressure from competition and terrorism in the interior that they could no longer afford to finance the construction of our new hotel school in Bogotá."

"Ha ha ha, cocaine has never been so expensive. So… don't their children attend our schools?"

"Their Achilles' heel, precisely. By the way, before I forget… is Didier's father a member of the Lodge?"

"No. He appears to be fairly neutral on matters of ideology. I only hope that our plan doesn't create more problems than it solves. He is a senior magistrate after all."

"*Querido amigo*, don't forget Saying 702: 'Never forget that the importance of events or of people is very relative'."

"Never!"

"I'll fax the documents…" Pla y Daniel concluded.

"*Muy bien. Adios.*"

"*Adios.*"

Joaquín Pla y Daniel folded his hands with a satisfied grin, opened a drawer in his desk, produced a packet of Marlboros, fished a lighter from his pocket and lit a cigarette. He inhaled deeply and stared vacantly into space. The drawer remained open. He smoked until the ash of his cigarette was too long and flicked it into an ashtray in the drawer.

Then he jolted, all at once, as if overcome by a violent shock. He stared at the surface of the desk, ran his forefinger over it and looked around the room in desperation. He pressed a button on the switchboard.

"Padre?"

"Come to my office now!" he snapped.

A minute or so later there was a knock at the door.

"Enter!"

The door opened and a woman with the features of an Andalusian farmer, and dressed in the same outfit as the women in the crypt, hurried inside and knelt down at his chair. He touched her head fleetingly as if it was a time bomb, and pointed to the surface of the desk without a word.

She scurried out of the room and returned moments later, red-faced and gasping for breath, spray polish and a duster in hand. She set about polishing the desk with uneasy strokes. He remained seated, his eyes shut, his hands folded around the wooden crucifix, waiting motionlessly until she finished.

Whenever he had to control himself in such a way he always suffered an allergy attack. He rummaged in his desk for a Rhinocort nasal spray, which he squirted awkwardly a couple of times into each nostril and snorted loudly.

After the woman had left the room, he removed the documents from the black leather file and walked over to the fax.

5

Without waiting for the fax from Rome, Baron Hervé van Reyn, Opus Dei's Regional Vicar in Belgium, consulted his telephone list kept in a small beige leather book in which he had noted "important" numbers in minute yet extraordinarily clear handwriting.

He was forty-eight and had the looks that one would expect of someone with old aristocratic blood: arrestingly youthful and fit, the consequence of a moderate lifestyle. His manner conformed perfectly to well-defined criteria: evident class without pretence, and the complete avoidance of anything people of his standing referred to with disdain as "*nouveau riche*". His facial features, reminiscent of the eighteenth-century portraits hanging in his ancestral castle in 's-Gravenwezel, even reflected his manner. He looked as if he had just returned from the barber, and was flawlessly shaven without the slightest hint of cologne. A permanent smile hovered over his lips, as if he was arrogantly suppressing some or other private joke. His glasses were expensive but conventional and he took care to maintain an open, candid and interested expression, conscientious, without the slightest trace of affectation, focused on the world outside, worthy of his family device "*Droit et en avant*". His stylish yet traditional blue blazer was tailored to perfection, his grey trousers had old-fashioned turn-ups, and his shiny black Keith Highlander shoes glistened like the boots of a British Royal Guardsman. His military tie, with the insignia of the 1st Cavalry Regiment, in which he was once a reserve lieutenant, matched his blue-and-white-striped shirt, made to measure by a shirt maker with a shop on New York's Fifth Avenue, diagonally opposite Saint Patrick's Cathedral.

Although he was a priest, ordained in Saint Peter's Basilica in Rome by Cardinal Palazzini, he rarely wore a soutane or clergyman's outfit. He didn't even wear a cross on his lapel. He was a close friend of Joaquín Navarro Valls, head of the Vatican press office, senior Opus numerary, and doctor and bullfighter in a former life. When they greeted one another, they would do so by swapping portions of El Padre's Saying 836: "To serve as a loudspeaker for the enemy is the height of idiocy; and if the enemy is God's enemy, it is a great sin." They had developed the habit of referring to Opus Dei as "the Company", in line with the CIA, convinced that their code word testified to their capacity for healthy irony and bore witness to their intelligence. When van Reyn was in Rome, which was frequently the case, they would dine together every evening at Da Fortunato, a restaurant near the Pantheon, frequented by parliament members, artists, journalists and prelates, an establishment known for its discretion, delicious food and the slightly nonchalant service of the waiters, most of them on the wrong side of sixty.

Van Reyn and Navarro Valls both considered themselves acutely superior to ordinary numeraries, so much so that they insisted on the right to live a distinct lifestyle, without exaggerated penance, a clandestine gentlemen's agreement, which they enjoyed like a pair of naughty boys and gently mocked at one and the same time. Wearing the cilice, a penitential chain with jagged barbs worn around the thigh, and self-mortification with the lash was for other people, not them. They no longer slept on the floor, didn't spray their bed with holy water, took warm showers and limited their "daily obligations" to the recitation of 150 Ave Marias, the celebration of Mass (for van Reyn only) and a half-hour meditation on one of the Sayings. They were relieved de facto of the obligation to do public penance (van Reyn as priest, Navarro Valls as senior numerary), their letters were left unopened, and the only obligation they were unable to avoid was weekly confession. "Confessional tourism" was not permitted, however, and both men were required to confess to a "Company" priest.

Baron Hervé van Reyn had advanced through the Opus Dei ranks at lightning speed, and by pure accident. His family happened to be related to Monsignor Papejaens, Professor of Canon Law at the Catholic University of Leuven in the 1970s, and appointed secretary by Pope Paul VI of a council of ninety-eight consultants from every part of the globe, charged with the task of adapting the Code of Canon Law to modern times. The professor, who enjoyed good food and wine, was fêted by the prelature of Opus Dei in the best restaurants in the country. Papejaens was a human being, of course, and the prelature's strategy enjoyed considerable success. The Codex Juris Canonici, drafted in 1978 and promulgated in 1984, clearly bore the signature of Opus Dei. "Dinner table diplomacy", much praised by El Padre, had proven its worth yet again.

A broad toothy grin took hold of his face as the fax machine buzzed into action. He closed the small leather notebook, stuffed it into his inside pocket, and called a number on his mobile. He never made such calls via the central switchboard. He trusted the secretary one-hundred per cent, but he considered a degree of suspicion justifiable, under the circumstances. He thought for a moment of using the public phone on the corner of Avenue de Floride and Avenue Montjoie, but someone from Belgacom had once assured him (incorrectly) that a mobile could not be tapped.

"Marlowe et Compagnie," said a gravelly male voice.

"*Bonjour,*" van Reyn replied in true managerial style, "may I have a word with the director?"

"Who can I say is calling?"

"I prefer not to mention my name."

The call was transferred without further comment.

"Hello..." The voice seemed at first to come from a distance, but after a click it became clear. A sign that the conversation was being recorded, he thought, but took it as a mark of efficiency and nothing more.

"Am I speaking to the director?"

"Yes. With whom do I have the honour?"

"A client who used your services in the past, much to his satisfaction I might add."

"Thank you. How can I be of service?"

"I would like to pass on the assignment by phone as I did before."

"Quite acceptable, *monsieur*."

"I still have your bank account number, if I'm not mistaken."

"I understand, sir. How can I be of assistance?"

"We would like to have someone tailed."

"No problem, sir. Do you have the coordinates?"

"It's Public Prosecutor General Savelkoul in Antwerp."

"Mm. Do you have an address?"

"Amerikalei 124A... in Antwerp, naturally."

"Is it a house or an apartment building?"

"A house."

"What would you like us to do?"

"Tail him. He's said to be having a relationship with another woman."

"Would you like photographs?'

"If possible, yes."

"I think it would be best to begin by stationing a decoy car with one-way glass in front of this house. But that costs 5,000 francs per hour."

"Did you have problems with payment on the last occasion? If I'm not mistaken, we even agreed to an advance of two hundred thousand. We can do the same this time."

"With whom exactly do I have the honour?"

"It doesn't matter. The advance will be transferred into your account in half an hour."

"You seem to have little faith in our discretion, I must say…"

Hervé van Reyn chortled. "I have every respect for your candidness," he retorted.

"So, the target lives at the address provided and is to be screened for adultery."

"You could put it that way, yes."

"When do we begin?"

Van Reyn thought for a moment. "Let's say early tomorrow morning."

"We'll have to find an appropriate place to keep an eye on the house and a parking space for the liaison vehicle, which will take care of surveillance."

"I imagine you will need to get into position under cover of darkness?"

"Precisely, *monsieur*."

"Agreed. How much should we transfer?"

"The amount you spoke of earlier."

"It'll be taken care of."

"How can I reach you?"

"I'll call you three times each day and you can tell me then if you have any news."

"That's a deal."

"Fair and square, Mr Marlowe."

"I'm not Mr Marlowe, but we're proud of the company name."

"The money should be in your account within the hour."

"OK. Would you be good enough to use a code name when you call?"

Hervé van Reyn thought for a moment. "Perálta, with the accent on the first a," he said, thinking of Josemaría Escrivá, the self-styled "Marquis of Perálta".

"Understood, thank you. I'll hear from you tomorrow, Perálta. By the way, do you have a photo of the target?"

"No, but a chauffeur collects him every morning from home."

"Thank you."

Van Reyn ended the call, walked over to the fax machine, removed the bundle of pages from the tray, put them in a mica-coated folder, placed it on his desk and sat down. His eyes narrowed and his amenable expression faded. How was he going to trace Public Prosecutor Savelkoul's Swiss bank account? Family connections in the Belgian and Luxembourg bank world had allowed him to establish contact with a Swiss national living in Zurich, a member of the council of commissioners of Credit Suisse and an Opus Dei supernumerary. The man could easily penetrate the closed world of the Swiss banking system with the assistance of a number of Opus Dei cooperators. He had helped van Reyn before with what had seemed at first to be a hopeless case. He had discovered that details of incoming and outgoing telephone connections were stored in the computer of every Swiss bank for twelve months. If they could trace the telephone number in the system, additional connections would allow them to establish the code and bank account numbers of certain customers, allowing automatic access to their portfolio, account activity and balance. But that was only one of the methods. Every case deserved its own approach.

From an ethical perspective, such procedures were unacceptable, of course, and were even punishable by Swiss law, but Opus Dei had little concern for the law if its own interests were at stake. The members refer to themselves with good reason as humanity's "general staff" and to non-members as "the rank and file". As a consequence, albeit unspoken, everything outside Opus Dei is shut out, excluded, godless, impure, faithless, damned, outlawed.

When it came to serving the interests of Opus Dei, Hervé van Reyn had no scruples whatsoever. He called this his Sacred Brazenness. He made frequent use of the global network of numeraries and cooperators in the bank world, multinationals, politics, the judiciary, the diplomatic service, the military, the government, journalism, the cultural and academic world, the media, the police, local government. The Opus Dei code word *Pax* opened every door.

He consulted his notebook for a second time and used his mobile to call a number in Zurich.

"*Grüezi.* May I speak to Mr Jacobi, please?" His otherwise perfect German had developed a Swiss accent.

An innocent expression transformed his face as he waited. He smiled engagingly, like an excited camper, and the skin of his face appeared to swell slightly, taking on a doughy texture, without a single wrinkle.

Albert always became a different person when he was riding. It aroused something within him halfway between a *condottiere* from the Italian Renaissance and a prairie Indian on a mustang. His powers of observation were also transformed. He had carried the conviction from early childhood that he was a man of the wild, his senses alert, with what he called a *reptilian memory* – something he also admired in horses – the ability to recall the exact place and circumstances of events even if they had taken place years before.

Around noon that day, the temperature was seventy-five degrees and there was a light easterly breeze. Yamma and Soliman behaved as one might expect of a couple of thoroughbreds in such pleasant spring weather: alert and unpredictable in a manner typical of *correct* blood, as equestrians call it. As usual, Albert rode Soliman, a five-year-old dark-brown gelding with a star on his forehead and three white hoofs, the offspring of Yamma and the renowned stallion Od' Aventure. He had broken him in a year earlier using the Monty Roberts method, named after an American who could talk to horses in their own language. No one else had ever ridden Soliman, not even Louise. This explained why Albert regularly boasted that he and Soliman could understand one another at a nod. He claimed to know instinctively how Soliman would react to something and explained this affinity between horse and rider as a shared *equus* awareness, a secret he tested whenever possible, without anyone noticing except himself and Soliman.

They cantered side by side along a dirt track. At the other side of the woods there was an open pasture with wild pine trees and a single oak, a leftover of Napoleon's obsessive desire to have deciduous trees planted along every road. Soliman had the habit of flattening his right ear and changing his gallop when he caught sight of the oak. Albert knew why. While he was still something of a novice, Soliman had been badly scared by a pheasant, which had fluttered loudly into the air in front of him close to the same oak. He had reacted like an "immature colt", bucked and leaped into the air, his back tense, all four hoofs off the ground. Albert had been thrown from his saddle and had fallen to the ground with a hard thud. It left him with three days of back pain and a sprained wrist, but he had not been upset with Soliman. The horse had reacted "correctly", and what's more, no other horseman would have been able to stay in the saddle in the same circumstances. Louise had enjoyed a good laugh at "grandpa", who always insisted on riding young horses, and had given Yamma's son a telling off for his "quirky behaviour". Albert had bought Yamma for her three years earlier, a thoroughbred mare with an impressive family tree.

Her foal Soliman was too young to ride in those days, but when they read in his pedigree that his father had been Od' Aventure, he had purchased him immediately. In fact, Soliman was the first horse he ever had ridden that was his and his alone.

When Soliman caught sight of the oak, his right ear flattened as expected and his gallop changed to allow him to veer swiftly to the left if the need presented itself. Albert started to talk to his horse, and although he had done something wrong, he refused to tell him off. He tried to give him the impression that he was in full control and did his best to be a little bit ahead of him every time, forcing him to stay in gallop at the moment his ear flattened. That was horse-riding at its best, he thought, befitting a horseman of the old school. He had always spent his holidays on the farm when he was young (when real farms and real farmers still existed) and he didn't consider himself a city person. He knew every last corner of the Kempen and constantly scanned the horizon for changes in the landscape. He could immediately identify every bird call and every bird. Louise thought it was all bullshit: she couldn't even tell the difference between a pigeon and a seagull. When they walked together in the countryside she would mock him a little if he followed animal trails or pointed to rabbit tracks at the edge of a field. He once made a trap from copper wire and got up before dawn to see if he had caught a rabbit. Poaching – an infringement of article four of the 1882 Hunting Code – was a risky business, especially in his position. He marinated his catch in red wine and served it up with potatoes and apple sauce just like in the good old days. She enjoyed it but thought it was a lot of work for something you could buy frozen from the supermarket. Such reactions convinced Albert that he belonged to a generation that had "continued to live the nineteenth century in the twentieth". He had no regrets whatsoever.

As with so many things in his life, his desire to pass on "knowledge" to the younger generation was the result of a sort of superstition that fascinated him to the core – astrology. A few years earlier he had invited a renowned Dutch astrologer of Indian origin to prepare his horoscope. The man had discovered that Chiron exercised an enormous influence on Aries, his star sign. Albert was particularly proud of this fact, since Chiron, the centaur from Greek mythology, was a creature with a great deal of intuitive knowledge it desired to pass on to future generations. Louise, a Gemini, was a poor student and that saddened him. He saw her as a typical example of the post-War soft generation, who had never had to make an effort, took everything for granted and struggled to appreciate most things. His friend Lev Hirschhorn, a diamond merchant from Antwerp who had been raised on a kibbutz, put it like this: "They're children without real experience, not like we used to be back then. We were forced to sleep with a sten gun under our pillows."

Louise could spend hours on end in an armchair, smoking and browsing through fashion magazines, with pop music playing so loud it was impossible to hold a conversation. Fetching a frozen dinner from the deep freeze and tossing it in the microwave was her only domestic chore, that and taking care of the horses. Albert always had a good laugh at the way she groomed them. He knew the right way to go about it, and had even taken the trouble to learn how to hot-shoe horses at the blacksmith's. Cold-shoeing, which was now the fashion, was beyond him, but he thought the purchase of a forge for two horses was taking things a little too far.

Once the oak was behind them, Soliman was completely under his control. They approached a straight path roughly half a mile long where they usually picked up the pace. He knew that Soliman was faster than Yamma, who had once suffered an ankle injury as a racehorse. He always let Louise win. He had once tried to convince her that full gallop with thoroughbreds was nothing very exciting, and that it gave the horse too much power over the rider, but she refused to listen. Everything changed, of course, after her horse bolted one day, something he had only witnessed twice in his life.

The horses knew exactly where they were going to be spurred into action and started to trot in advance, a fault he was willing to overlook. He tried to calm Soliman, but Louise smacked Yamma with her crop and yelled "Yahoo!" She disappeared like an arrow from a bow.

In spite of his seventy-six years, Ernst Jacobi still maintained a leading position in the Swiss banking establishment. He was the son of the renowned Paul Jacobi, president of the Credit Suisse from 1938 to 1971, a man who bore considerable responsibility for the secret laundering of Nazi gold. The "leftist" Swiss press, to the extent that such a thing existed in Switzerland, referred to him as a Gnome, a member of the extremely conservative, anti-Semitic, profoundly religious cast of German-speaking Swiss nationals, who had once been described by Dürrenmatt as "girls working in a bordello while trying to keep their virginity". Jacobi senior had also used the epithet "*cheibe Usländer*", or bloody foreigners, to refer to anyone who could not be categorized as Swiss. He had once confided to a number of intimate friends that a Swiss banker had to be like the owner of a quality hotel: a civilized host who provided excellent service, and counted his takings to the last penny as his guests settled down to an evening cognac. Ernst Jacobi followed in his father's footsteps and respected family tradition. Like his father, he was almost six and a half feet tall, had a large round head that was bald as a billiard ball, thin lips and the jowls of a toad, greedy eyes of cracked grey porcelain behind thick glasses, and was always dressed in a worn-out anthracite suit and a black tie. He looked to all the world like an undertaker's master of ceremonies.

He walked like a crane, slow and lurching from arthritis of the hip, which he refused to have operated upon, afraid of the consequences a full anaesthetic might have for someone of his age. He had been a widower for ten years, was father of nine children, warden of the Augustiner church, devoted knight of the Order of Malta, holder of several Vatican distinctions granted by His Holiness, friend of the Archbishop of Chur – who profited from his generous gifts – with whom he spent his summer vacations in the Graubünden mountains. He was an Opus Dei supernumerary, which he denied when necessary in line with the rule of personal humility, obedient to the prohibition against flaunting membership that had been relaxed to some degree in the 1982 statutes. In addition to two wedding rings, however, he also wore the gold ring with the inset black stone of Opus Dei, but no one had any idea what it meant. He lived alone with an aged Alsatian in a genuine eighteenth-century chalet with a weathered wooden roof hidden among the trees on the flanks of the Uetliberg, with breathtaking views of the Lake Zurich, although he paid them little attention. His primary secret was his executive position on the board of the "*Stiftung Limmat*", a bank network that administered billions of Opus Dei dollars. His greatest strength was being a citizen of a peaceful country in the centre of old Europe, in which historical axes intersected and where creativity was considered a superfluous quality best left to artists and writers, brats that needed constant supervision because they tended to think as they acted and vice versa, patent proof of unreliability.

On Tuesday 25 May 1999 at eleven forty-five a.m. – he started work at eight every day except Sunday – Jacobi was sitting at his desk in a gloomy office on the fourth floor of the imposing Credit Suisse building, Paradeplatz 8. The edifice's nuclear bomb-proof cellars, five concrete shafts thirty metres deep, preserved the secret fortunes of the likes of Mobutu, Ceauşescu, Hailie Selassie, Hassan II, Idi Amin, Bokassa, Stroessner, Saddam Hussein, Abu Nidal, Duvalier, Noriega, Suharto, Marcos, Karadžić, Pinochet and others.

When American journalists demonstrated in 1996, on the basis of irrefutable documentation, that billions of dollars of Holocaust money were locked up in the safes of a number of Swiss banks, Ernst Jacobi responded in an interview in the *Neue Zürcher Zeitung*: "A waste of breath… peanuts!"

The telephone rang. Jacobi, who was examining a file on tax evasion and fraud, blindly lifted the receiver with his giant liver-spotted claw of a hand. A fatherly smile lit up his face. "*Grüezi*, dear Hervé," he said, and listened carefully.

As usual, his responses were limited to a monotonous drone and guarded nods of the head, his eyes fixed on a Gobelin tapestry from Brussels hanging on the wall opposite, portraying a pogrom against medieval Jews who had desecrated the body of Christ by cutting Communion wafers into pieces to add lustre to the sacrifice of goy children.

The conversation only lasted a few minutes.

All he did was note down a telephone number and address in Antwerp in cursive convent school handwriting and conclude the conversation with a formal "*Pax*", something without meaning for either party, given their status, to be ascribed to his obsession for decorum and nothing more.

A rigid grin appeared on his face as he hung up the receiver. He placed the index finger of his right hand on his left wrist and took his pulse in silence without referring to his watch. He waited until his heartbeat had reached what he considered an appropriate number of beats per minute and called a number in Brussels.

"Belgacom?"

"*Oui.*"

"I would like to speak to the director general for International Communications." While his French was correct, he had a marked guttural accent, once described in the Paris gossip rag *Le Canard Enchaîné* as a sickness caused by too much cold air passing through an open stable door.

"With whom do I have the pleasure?"

"A friend..."

"I'll put you through."

"Hello," a neutral male voice introduced itself.

"Ernst Jacobi from Zürich speaking."

"Aha! How is life in Switzerland, my dear Mr Jacobi?" The man's tone of voice changed pitch.

"*Pax*."

"*In aeternum*. How can I be of assistance?"

"We have a technical problem..."

"Continue."

"I have a Belgian telephone number here. We would like to have access to the international call statements for, let's say, the last year."

"Is there an ongoing judicial inquiry into this number?"

"Not that I'm aware of."

"Then what you ask is illegal."

"I'm asking on behalf of Hervé van Reyn."

"Hmm... I see... Can I fax the information?"

"Thank you, my dear director general." Ernst Jacobi hung up without saying goodbye and returned immediately to the file on the desk in front of him as if nothing had happened.

Albert uncorked a bottle of champagne with a loud bang, something Amandine considered evidence of a lack of style, much to his enjoyment. An open tin of caviar with two mother-of-pearl spoons awaited them on a plate. He considered eating caviar from the tin as the height of decadence. They sat on the floor in riding breeches at a squat coffee table, their boots left by the door, both stinking of horse sweat. Igor lay stretched out on a blanket, sound asleep.

As he was about to pour the champagne, Louise lit a cigarette and said casually: "I'm not really in the mood for caviar and champagne."

"What do you fancy then?" he asked light-heartedly, hiding his disappointment.

"Gin and tonic and cheese crackers."

"OK, then I'll have a whisky."

She nodded, puffed at her cigarette and inspected the varnish on her toenails, slowly wriggling her toes in the process.

He closed the tin of caviar with an expressionless face, popped a bottle stop in the champagne and brought both to the kitchen.

"Large or small?" he shouted after cursing under his breath.

"Whatever."

He returned to the living room with a smile a few minutes later, carrying two glasses and a bowl of cheese crackers on a tray.

"*Madame est servie.*"

"Ha, not a bad race, eh?" she said, stretching her back, the contour of her breasts filling her silk blouse.

"Until you lost control of Yamma."

She shrugged her shoulders.

"Chin."

"Chin."

"Louise..."

"Mmm?"

"Do you still love me?"

"Of course, idiot," she said with a chuckle, gazing at him with her shallow, lance-shaped eyes. He felt relieved. Her tone was like the old days, the best days, but when he looked in her eyes she turned away.

"There's something different about you," he said. He took a gulp of whisky and held it in his mouth. He suddenly felt like an old man. The ride had tired him. His legs felt like lead.

She pinched his hand and threw him a kiss.

He swallowed his whisky. "Come, let's talk about something else," he said resignedly.

"Good idea."

"Buy anything new lately?" He knew from experience this was the best preamble to reconciliation. The whisky gave him heartburn.

"No, but I have my eye on something?"

"What?"

"An Armani ensemble, in Brussels."

"How much?"

"No idea. Sixty or seventy, thereabouts. Armani isn't cheap and it's my birthday soon."

"And is it pretty?" The question was out before he realized how redundant it was.

"Did I ever buy anything that wasn't pretty?"

"No, of course not. What colour?"

"Black. Necklace and earrings to match."

"Plus shoes and a handbag..." he said flatly.

"You like me to be pretty, don't you?" She stubbed out her half-finished cigarette.

"Aren't you hungry?" he enquired.

"Yes, but not for crayfish."

"What then?"

"An omelette and a glass of red wine."

He finished his glass and held it at his lips to take in the medicinal smell. Whisky always had an unpredictable effect on him. It either made him aggressive or made him yearn for tranquillity and harmony, like looking at snow-covered mountains at an altitude of three thousand metres with your back against a warm rock.

But this time there was no tranquillity, only melancholy and self-pity, because he had unexpectedly stumbled into a situation that was none of his doing. He headed to the kitchen and poured a second whisky.

When he returned to the living room, she said: "To be honest, I fancy going to Brussels more than anything else."

"And the omelette?"

"Why don't we just have lunch at L'Ecailler?"

He closed his eyes, took a large gulp of whisky and held it in his mouth as before. This was too much, he thought, clenching his fist.

"Cat got your tongue?" she said as she petted Igor's head indifferently.

He swallowed.

"Did you already reserve a table?"

"Reservations aren't necessary for lunch. Besides, I know the head waiter."

"OK."

"Would you rather stay here?" she asked in a soft toneless voice, staring at him intently.

"No, Brussels is fine by me." He emptied his glass, got to his feet, and made his way to the bedroom, his legs stiff.

"Did you bring a suit?"

He turned. "Yes, it's in the BMW."

"Don't forget to get rid of that stupid pin from your lapel."

"I won't."

"I fancy a shower."

He entered the bedroom and stared vacantly at his trousers lying on the bed. His self-pity was so bad it made him furious with himself. I've been mistaken all those years, he thought. She's right up there in Buddha's category one, and I'm too old for a demanding young woman like her. Hemingway called them "rich bitches". He was absolutely fucking right!

As he lifted his right leg to take off his riding breeches, he felt the same dreaded dart of pain shooting from his lower belly to his anus, where it grabbed hold like pair of forceps.

While Albert and Louise were savouring Colchester oysters and sipping Trimbach Pinot Blanc in L'Ecailler du Palais Royal, a renowned restaurant in Brussels' exclusive Sablon district, Opus Dei cooperator and director general of international communications Anneessens was faxing a four-page printout to Zurich. He was no more than a mile and a half away, on Jacqmainlaan. It was two fifteen.

Ernst Jacobi pressed a button under his desk. An elegantly dressed young man appeared in the doorway, but remained motionless, like a statue, a yellow folder in his hand. Jacobi gave a sign that resembled the start signal of the Tour de France. The young man approached the desk, handed over the folder, bowed his head like a Prussian aristocrat and said "*Bitte, Herr Doktor.*"

Jacobi nodded and said: "*Gut.*"

The young man turned and left the office. Jacobi immediately opened the folder, brought the printout to within six inches of his face and started to read with interest, his cumbrous index finger running down the series of numbers. When he discovered the number of a Credit Suisse branch in Geneva, on the first page for Christ's sake, he roared with laughter.

"*Nicht möglich...* unbelievable," he rejoiced, hastily circling the number. He flexed the fingers of both hands several times, as if trying to restore the circulation, and called a number in Geneva.

Baron Hervé van Reyn received a telephone call at three fifteen from a triumphant Ernst Jacobi, who launched into his report without the customary "*Pax*". Albert Savelkoul's code name was Beaver. He immediately provided the address and telephone number of the branch in Geneva, together with the denomination and balance of the account and the market value of the shares portfolio. The latter was superfluous, but sheer villainy forced him to mention it. He carefully dictated each piece of information and waited patiently until van Reyn had noted everything necessary. They agreed to visit one another at the first possible opportunity.

Van Reyn decided after hanging up to keep the information to himself for a while, to take his time and mull over his next move. He had developed a unique procedure to this end: first reduce his thoughts to what he called a "gaseous mass", then "ionize" them until he could attune himself with precision to their "focal point". In other words, a few minutes meditation on one of the sayings of El Padre. He knew all 999 by heart. He opted for his favourite, number 349: "Never compromise, since such is an indisputable sign that you do not possess the truth."

6

The telephone rang at four o'clock in the office of the university student residence Arenberg, which was located on the eighth and ninth floors of a modern apartment building on Tervuursevest 123 in Leuven. Paul Hersch, the forty-seven-year-old Opus Dei numerary who was responsible for the twenty-four students who lived in the building, answered the phone.

"Hello..."

"Résidence Arenbère?" a woman's voice enquired.

"Yes... Who's speaking?"

"The mother of Didier Savelkoul-de Vreux. I'm calling from Rome. May I speak to my son?' She spoke Flemish with a French accent, a drawl the majority of Gallicized Flemish still considered evidence of their superiority.

"Didier is not here at the moment. Would you like to call back in, let's say, an hour?" Hersch's tone was cool and collected, professional, with only a hint of the contempt he harboured for all women, with the exception of his own mother.

"*Bon,*" the woman agreed abruptly. "*Merci.*"

He hung up and snorted. He was pretty sure why Baroness de Vreux, alias Madame Savelkoul, wished to speak to her son. He knew her sort down to a tee, but he wanted to let her suffer a little for the hesitation she had shown when asked to regularize the financial situation of her son, the new candidate numerary. The first thing that came to his mind was to call Hervé van Reyn, but he preferred to wait until after mother and son had spoken to one another on the phone. He intended to be present during the call, of course, listening in with the earphones.

Paul Hersch was a psychiatrist by profession. As Opus Dei numerary, he was "student mentor" in the Arenberg residence where he also lived and where tradition demanded a strict, almost monastic lifestyle. Though a numerary, he did not practise his profession full-time, except when he wanted to break into the soul of some young man or other, something he called "boring holes". He was born into a doctor's family in nearby Mechelen and had been a member of Opus Dei for all of twenty-three years, much to his parents' chagrin. He hadn't the least difficulty in describing their opposition in current Opus Dei jargon: *they had failed in their obligation to raise a Christian family*. He performed his duties with the utmost care, supervising the daily round of prayer and spiritual training that took place under permanent compulsion, *a support to perseverance* they called it. Rise at six thirty. Holy Mass, prayer and Communion in the chapel. Breakfast. Departure to the various faculties. At nine thirty, a team of female numeraries would arrive from the Steenberg Residence in Leopoldstraat to tidy the rooms, make the beds, collect the garbage, bring food for the evening meal, which was prepared collectively, and, last but not least, adorn the statues of the Virgin Mother and the Founder, Josemaría Escrivá de Balaguer, with fresh flowers. The sober evening meal was followed by prayer in the dark, meditation and reading. A period of recreation was concluded at eleven o'clock with a decade of the rosary in front of the portrait of the Founder and bed. Students who wanted to stay out later than eleven were required to ask for special permission, the Nihil Obstat.

Hersch suddenly remembered that his assistant Didier Savelkoul was to give a lecture that evening entitled 'No Christianity without the Cross' and lead the discussion that was to follow. He was actually planning to talk about bodily mortification and self-castigation. Hersch picked out one of the folders from the pile on his desk. It contained the printed text Savelkoul had submitted for inspection. He changed his glasses and started to read.

Only those who are unfamiliar with the Church's history are likely to be surprised about bodily mortifications such as fasting, sleeping on the floor, the use of the penitential girdle or the "cilice" and self-flagellation. Priests and members of religious communities had been using such means for centuries. The Curé d'Ars, for example, as well as Paul VI. In the monasteries and convents, where the members of Opus Dei purchase the cilice, bodily mortification is a daily routine.

The use of the same means by Opus Dei members, be they lawyers, journalists or professors, is a source of considerable misunderstanding. But even this is nothing new: Thomas More also used a penitential girdle. Are such methods outmoded? Every form of penitence will become a thing of the past on the day the cross of Christ becomes outmoded.

It is important to realize that bodily mortification enjoys only a secondary place in Opus Dei. The less significant mortifications are more important, in our daily tasks, in our interaction with others, and in the sobriety of our lifestyle, which often stands in shrill contrast to the norms of our consumption-based society. The irritation some express concerning such bodily mortification often conceals an ambition to live a Christian life without the cross. To use an image employed by His Holiness Pope John Paul II: there are many who want to rise with Christ, but few who are prepared to die with Him. There can be no Easter Sunday without Good Friday.

Just like the Church, Opus Dei is counter-cultural, sailing against the tide of a hyper-sensual society that often produces the bitterest of fruit, as a glance at the headlines or the evening news in our country will confirm.

Mortification and self-castigation must play their part in encouraging us to fulfil our primary task: to do our daily work with the greatest perfection. This is what the Founder, Blessed Josemaría Escrivá, called the supernatural motivation, the lamp that illuminates the way. It is thus that we prepare for our final goal in life: God, to whom we dedicate all our daily endeavours.

Working in the presence of God is the same as praying constantly, the pinnacle of Christian existence. As faithful apostles of the Lord, it allows us to engage in continual struggle against ignorance, God's greatest enemy. Apostolate is and remains the essential element of the Christian vocation. It has to be permanent and intense, geared towards the obligations of our state in life and our daily work.

Hersch pursed his lips until they quivered, carefully returned the typed page to its folder, removed his glasses, glanced at the statue of Our Lady adorned with white roses on his desk, and folded his hands in a moment of prayer, something he did with regularity during the month of May, the month of Mary.

As was his custom when he sat at his desk (at least ten hours per day), Paul Hersch was wearing a black tracksuit and training shoes, which looked brand new because he never wore them outside. This was all part of his image and, as a psychiatrist, there was nothing accidental about the strategies he employed to deceive those around him. The Germans, with their renowned talent for clarity, referred to the phenomenon as *Sitzriese* or sitting giant. The voluminously lengthy torso rising behind the desk gave the impression he was a formidable figure of a man. But in reality, Hersch had abnormally short legs, although he was still impressive when standing upright, in spite of being five foot six. This was probably due to the intriguing smile that seemed painted, as it were, over his broad, pallid peasant face. His bald head was covered with freckles and he wore bulky-framed glasses that did not suit him. His light grey eyes were round and full and radiated what seemed to be dependable loyalty, leaving the people he met with the conviction that he was a sort of new Jesus. Many had fallen into this trap. A student resident once had an argument with him and had cursed him to his face as "the Devil with a smile". The student was asked to leave the residence for good.

Hersch was also an adherent of the method promoted by the American professor Harding, who trivialized every psychological problem he came across and laughed it off. In Hersch's case, however, this could take curious forms. He would roar with laughter when zapping away from an inappropriate TV programme with the same gusto as he did when someone came to him with a genuine problem. Together with Harding, he was also a strong proponent of the "blunt approach". A student came to him one day grieving the loss of his sister. The young man was on the edge of depression. Hersch had asked him with his usual smile if he had had an incestuous relationship with his sister. The student ran off in hysterics. He would exhibit an additional facet of his disturbed personality during the *Praxis*, the application of the rules governing the Sacred Obligations. He had taken over a refined form of spiritual sadism from the Jesuits. His uncle, who had been novice master in the Jesuit noviciate in Drongen in the 1950s, had required aspirants, referred to as *fratres*, to perform a variety of tasks "intended to encourage the virtue of humility": cleaning the corridors on one's hands and knees with a worn-out dishcloth and a tiny basin of water, after which he would soil the place anew with mud-covered boots. On occasion, he would hide a pin in the sheets of one of the novices and then ask him if he had made his bed properly. He would check the bed, produce the pin, and hold it in front of the novice's face. His uncle also thought very highly in those days of the *frater tortor*, a select novice who spent hours in a room with a bench vice, fashioning wire straps which the novices would fasten around the thigh when they walked in prayer through the monastery garden until the pain almost crippled them. The same novice also made disciplines, or miniature lashes, with which he and his fellow novices would flagellate themselves, kneeling at the side of their bed, when faced with temptations against blessed purity. Opus Dei had based itself on such practices, and those of the Founder, Blessed Josemaría Escrivá, himself a Basque, who was given to Spanish theatricality and regularly flagellated himself until the blood spattered the walls. Even the hotel rooms on his many journeys were not spared.

The tracksuit was also just for show. Hersch had never exercised in his life, but he insisted that the residents go for a seven-mile run in the nearby Heverlee woods every week, following the group in first gear behind the wheel of his car, and humiliating the stragglers.

He suffered from a phenomenon that was common among psychiatrists: the projection of his own problems onto his immediate environment, accompanied by the abuse of authority. But Paul Hersch's main problem was his sexuality. Everything that had anything to do with sex (sins against the apostolate of celibacy as he called it) made him angry and paranoid. Every night before going to sleep, he took six drops of Frenactil in a glass of water, a powerful neuroleptic prescribed in psychiatric prisons for erotomania, exhibitionism, paedophilia and excessive masturbation. He warned the students at every opportunity about the dangers of temptation against the sixth and ninth commandments. He terrorized them with threats that every single sin, which "transformed the body into a rubbish bin", had to be confessed the following morning before Holy Mass and Communion, otherwise one would commit a sacrilegious Communion, one of the worst sins imaginable. Every morning, after the students had left, he checked the sheets on every bed, just before the female numeraries, whom he treated as ordinary maids, arrived from Steenberg Residence. Even a wet dream was considered unforgivable. The student in question was obliged to sleep on the floor for a week, after he had sprinkled it with holy water. The showers were always cold in Arenberg and were to be taken in the dark, while praying aloud.

Prayer, prayer and more prayer. Penance, penance and more penance. This is what blessed Josemaría Escrivá had written after all in *The Way*. And recreation was to be filled with song and laughter and more song and laughter, as a sign of sacred joviality and childlike trust in the will of God.

Hersch grimaced, his lips disappearing in the process, tensed his back and held his breath as long as he could. He was convinced this sharpened the awareness that the body was an enemy that needed to be kept under permanent control.

He wondered if he could throw Didier Savelkoul off balance by asking him about his use of the word "ignorance". Savelkoul was a complex case. During his studies at the faculty of law fifteen years earlier, he had spent four years in Arenberg, where he had emerged as an exemplary candidate supernumerary, capable of more prayer, penance and subjection to humiliation than Hersch had ever witnessed. This was doubtless due to his secondary-school studies with the Jesuits, who had almost managed to have him join the order. He worked a two-year internship at a large legal firm in Brussels after obtaining his master's in law, but he didn't seem to be cut out for a law career. While his knowledge of the law was second to none, he was obsessively scrupulous and this made him so insecure that he would even lose the most minor of cases by making elementary errors of logic in his long-winded pleas, something that drove presiding magistrates to despair. For the sake of appearances, however, he was still registered at the bar in Leuven.

He was his mother's favourite – they were like two peas in a pod – but the reputation of his father and grandfather on his mother's side was such a burden it only exaggerated his insecurity. The only way out after the spiritual support of the Jesuits was an "appointment" with Opus Dei, with a view to becoming a member after five years. On the advice of his mother and Regional Vicar van Reyn, who was distantly related to the de Vreux family, he had finally chosen to register for journalism and communication studies. Numeraries were preferably expected to have two university diplomas. He obtained his degree in three years and moved into Arenberg as candidate numerary and assistant to the mentor. Shortly thereafter, Baroness Amandine de Vreux became a supernumerary.

Hersch grabbed the telephone and did what had become his custom before dialling a number: he looked at his hands, which (and he knew this) put the fear of God into some of the students. His hands were striking to say the least, exceptionally broad, plump, unwieldy and above all ugly, with the knobbly fingers of someone with arthritis. He called them "lumberjack hands", although he had never wielded an axe in his life. He could fold back his thumb so far that it no longer appeared to be part of his hand. According to the laws of palmistry, this was a sign of intransigence, lust for power and duplicity, character traits he admired, for example, in a number of Roman emperors.

He quickly punched in the three numbers of an inside line, and pinched his eyes to narrow slits, imperfectly resembling a cat, animals he hated because of their indifference to intimidation.

"Didier, can you come to my office for a moment?" he said in the dialect of Mechelen, the city of his birth. He knew that Savelkoul hated such dialects, and used it as a customary part of his efforts to "destabilize" everyone he met.

There was a knock at the door.

"Yes!" Hersch roared. He immediately donned his reading glasses and fished Savelkoul's lecture from the file in the blink of an eye.

The door opened and a squat, thin, forty-something man entered Hersch's office. He was wearing a dark-grey formal suit, which made him look older than his years, a white shirt and a dark-blue tightly knotted tie. Clasping a brown leather briefcase, he looked nervously around the room as if some sort of danger were lying in wait, and remained standing by the door. The pale skin of his forehead was wrinkled at the temples, like the blisters left by a badly healed burn. A permanent twist of pain stretched his lips and exposed his teeth. He finally moved closer, placed a small narrow hand on the edge of the desk and waited. His fingernails were chewed to the quick.

"Aha, Didier. Stomach pain any better?" Hersch enquired jovially. Savelkoul had eaten virtually nothing at lunch.

"Still a bother. Sorry..." he spoke a measured, educated Dutch, but his soft voice was barely audible beyond a few yards, something that had irritated the court magistrates to no end.

"Forgive me, my boy. Take a chair, relax."

Savelkoul edged a chair from under the desk and cautiously sat down, making sure not to touch the back of the seat.

"The reason I asked you here," Hersch commenced, nonchalantly removing his glasses. "This evening's lecture... So, what do we make of it?"

"Is it not good?" Savelkoul moistened his lips and gulped.

"Take a look. Read it through for yourself. You'll soon see what's wrong with it."

Savelkoul bit his bottom lip and grimaced, a facial trait he had inherited from his mother. He now looked like a fifty-year-old.

"You shouldn't give the idea that we fast all year round," Hersch continued, as he slipped the folder across the desk. "And you need *impact*." He clenched his right fist and punched the air, like a striking worker spelling out his demands.

"Blessed Josemaría only fasted one day a week. I do the same."

Savelkoul pinched his lips and held his tongue.

"Let me come to the point: your use of the word 'ignorance' bothers me."

Savelkoul held his breath and what appeared to be panic took hold of his face. He had copied the text word for word from one of the many speeches of Monsignor Escrivá, but if he dared admit to it, Hersch would be sure to let him have it. He knew the man well enough.

"By the way, your mother called. She's in Rome."

"In *Rome*?"

"That's what she said. She wanted to have a word with you."

"Did she leave a number?"

"No..."

Savelkoul blinked nervously and removed the typewritten lecture from the folder.

"Read it through in your own time," said Hersch indulgently.

"But it has to be ready for *this evening*."

"And is that a problem?"

"But I'll have to start from scratch."

Hersch sneered, waved his hand dismissively and shrugged his shoulders. He looked at his watch, a gold Rolex. "Shall we say... my office in an hour?"

"Did my mother say anything about calling back?"

"No," Hersch lied. "It probably wasn't very important."

"Then I'd better get started. I'll be back in an hour."

Didier Savelkoul looked furtively at his watch, pinched his lips once again and left Hersch's office, chewing on the stumps of his fingers, his shoulders hunched like an old man.

Once he was alone, Paul Hersch's broad face took on a curious, almost frosty appearance. He decided it was time to practise his "serpent's stare", something he did on a daily basis. It inspired such loyalty among his student informants – his "key boys" – that they were simply incapable of withholding information after a couple of "practice sessions". He fixed his eyes on the plain cross on the opposite wall and altered the field and angle of his vision by focusing on an unspecified point in the distance. When one of his informants was in his office, the laws of optics prevented the boy from detecting this procedure, because the focal point of Hersch's gaze was somewhere behind him. It was also important to look over the key boy's head using the periscope principle, which eliminates any possibility of eye contact because the other is literally overlooked. The eyes appear to be directed at a far-distant object, or perhaps some thought in the depths of the boy's mind, which he is diligently trying to keep to himself because it signals the suppression of some sordid passion. Dialogue is pointless in such a situation, and the key boy, driven by an overwhelming sense of superfluity, is left with only one option: get out of the office on the double. But departure is impossible without the permission of numerary Paul Hersch, who at a certain moment will look the key boy straight in the eye, as a snake does when it closes in on a rabbit. And how does the rabbit react? It stands still and starts to tremble from fear. Then comes the miserable moment at which Paul Hersch puts his fundamental principle into practice: if you stick your nose in far enough, you're sure to smell something rotten.

7

At around nine o'clock in the evening, a dark-blue Mercedes delivery van belonging to Bineco Sanitary Installations Ltd, with its offices in Vilvoorde near Brussels, pulled up diagonally opposite house number 124A on the eastbound carriageway of Antwerp's Amerikalei, not far from the European University. The distance between the delivery van and the house was roughly seventy yards. Not the best position, but there was no alternative. Traffic sped in both directions along the four-lane, sycamore-lined carriageway. It was mild and calm and the pavements were deserted. The delivery van, a so-called decoy vehicle, was fitted with advanced observation hardware: a digital infrared camera, an Electronic Number Interceptor 421 telephone and mobile number interceptor (prohibited by Belgian law), an American-made gadget not even the police or the CID could lay their hands on. To round things off, there was a container with the equipment necessary for planting miniature bugging devices, including a hyper-sensitive high-grade steel nail that, when fired into a brick or concrete wall, could pick up everything going on inside.

The Marlowe & Co. team commenced their observations ten minutes after they arrived, having transmitted their position to their Brussels headquarters, where the video screen of a Central Travel Pilot was placed on stand-by. The team consisted of two men, both young, competent, ambitious and well paid. They were wearing dark-green Gore Tex overalls and trainers. They had disabled the Mercedes's suspension to allow them to move about without rocking the vehicle. They adjusted the back, neck and foot supports of two chairs, readying them for hours of comfort. Their first job was to enter the target's telephone and mobile numbers into the ENI 421, to ensure that any incoming or outgoing calls would be registered on the screen. Four one-way glass windows allowed for 180-degree observation without betraying the contents of the van.

The first observer, Joost Voorhout (thirty-two years old) was from the Netherlands, although he had studied electronics in Belgium. His theoretical skills were surpassed by his ability to exploit every imaginable practical application of modern photography and electronics and solve associated problems. He was tall and blond with an athletic build. He came across as a little slow, but his reflexes were sharp as a cat's. His team mate, Jean Materne, was an Antwerp-born twenty-eight-year-old who lived in Brussels and had served for ten years as a first battalion para. He was short and thin with a crew-cut, a large moustache and sideburns, which made him look like a Hell's Angel. He was a bodybuilder, skilled in burglary with counterfeit keys, and an expert in aggressive driving and karate. He had applied for a job with the police Intervention Squad, but psychological tests had correctly revealed his personality to be imbalanced. He considered life to be a permanent challenge, facing and conquering dangers of every sort, and he took pride in the fact that he was genuinely afraid of nothing.

That evening, he had infringed one of his firm's strict regulations: he had brought along his pit bull Rambo, white with brown flecks and pared ears, which lay motionless beside his chair, its bulky head resting on its front paws, its eyes narrow slits. Materne called him "my unlicensed revolver".

At 21.45, they observed a tall, well-dressed elderly gentleman emerge from a side street opposite and make his way towards house 124A. Voorhout fixed on him with the camera's Albada viewfinder and zoomed in.

"We're onto a winner here, Jean," he whispered.

Materne grabbed his infrared binoculars and focused in on the man, who appeared indeed to have stopped at 124A, produced a key and gone inside. Everything had been captured on camera.

"I fancy a cigarette," said Materne resolutely.

Voorhout switched on the van's ventilation system and they lit their cigarettes without losing sight of the house. After a few minutes they observed a second-floor light go on. The camera hummed.

"He's hitting the sack."

"Let's do the same."

"No. Best wait. What if he makes a phone call?"

Voorhout had barely finished his sentence when the ENI 421 started to beep.

"He's using his mobile," said Materne, "but it's not connecting."

"Why would anyone use their mobile when it's cheaper and easier to use the ordinary phone?"

"Yeah... right... Why?"

They laughed. They had a habit of asking each other questions with obvious answers.

"Call information," said Voorhout, without letting the house "out of his sights" for a second.

Materne dialled information and, given the late hour, was connected to an operator almost immediately. "I'm looking for the name and address linked with number 03-6364044 please." He waited with the cigarette between his lips and the smoke billowing from his nostrils.

He noted the information. "Thank you."

Voorhout looked at him.

"A certain Louise Dubois. Oude Baan 2, Sint-Job-in-'t Goor."

The ENI 242 started to beep a second time. The same number. No connection.

"Something's winding him up," said Voorhout and grinned. "Louise. Nice name, eh?"

"Is this the one?"

"Who knows?"

"What do we do?"

"We wait an hour, then we take a peek in Sint-Job-in-'t Goor."

"Shouldn't we input the number? You never know."

"Good idea."

"Better check if Louise called anyone else earlier."

Voorhout punched in the number and pressed a couple of buttons. A number appeared with the same initial figures 636. "She called someone with a similar number at 21.12. The call lasted 190 seconds."

"Someone she knew."

"Possible."

"Try information."

One minute later, Materne noted the name and address: "Johan D'Hoog, Veterinary Surgeon. Address blah blah blah in Brecht."

"Not far from here."

"Sick pussy?"

"One hundred and ninety seconds? Very sick pussy!"

"What do we do?"

Voorhout looked at his watch: 21.58. "Fifteen more minutes and then..." He held up his fist and flexed his biceps.

"Action." Materne finished the sentence.

Albert looked at his watch. I'll call her at ten for the last time, he decided. And if she doesn't pick up, I'll call Jokke. He loosened his tie, got to his feet, selected a couple of leather-bound books on jurisprudence penned by counsellor de Vreux from the bookcase. On the way back to his desk, he grabbed a bottle of Johnnie Walker Black Label and a crystal whisky glass, filled it halfway and tossed back the best part of its contents. He sat down, took another gulp and looked at his watch again. Five past ten. He punched her number into his mobile and hung up after it rang twenty times. He stared into space, emptied his glass and poured a second. The alcohol invaded his mind at lightning pace. One last time, he thought. No answer. Either she was out or she was refusing to pick up. He closed his eyes, gulped at his whisky and held it in his mouth, as he always did when something was making him nervous.

The day passed through his mind like a film. The journey to Brussels. She smoked one cigarette after the other, and the smoke irritated his lungs. They got stuck in traffic outside Mechelen for forty-five minutes. A truck had spilled its contents onto the road. In the Ecailler, first Pinot Blanc with Colchester oysters. She allowed some half-pissed Englishman to chat her up. He told the guy where to get off, but she openly snarled at him in response. Called him a dreary old fart, in Flemish, fortunately, which the other clients didn't understand. Followed by a bottle of Tokay. Turbot with mousseline sauce. The most expensive item on the menu. She barely touched it. Chose a dessert and didn't touch that either. She didn't say a fucking word the entire time. One cigarette after the other. Second stab of pain in his lower belly. A long and difficult piss in the toilets. So-called "lazy flow". Back at the table. She looked right through him. Three thirty. "Still want to visit Armani, Louise?"

"Mmm…"

On foot to Waterloo Boulevard. A solid hour picking, choosing and chatting with a gay shop assistant. Endless dithering in and out of the fitting rooms. Finally an insanely expensive outfit with earrings and shoes to match. Fortunately no handbag. Bill:

a mere 117,950 francs. His monthly salary after tax, give or take. Amex gold card, confirm the amount, nonchalant signature. Back to the multi-storey parking garage on foot. Peak traffic hour. Twenty minutes to clear the Leopold II tunnel at a snail's pace. Still not a word. Serious pain near the exit for Sint-Job. Insisted on going for a ride. Saddled Yamma and headed off alone. In the bathroom mirror he looked like an eighty-year-old. Straining to pee. Igor sensed he was in pain and sat down beside him with his head on his lap. Troubling attack of self-pity. (I'm too old for her. She's fed up with me. She doesn't love me any more. But I'm still head over heels with her. When was the last time we made love? Two weeks ago. It used to be every day with her, but now she doesn't seem to be interested.)

Albert opened his eyes and gulped at his whisky. He called her number again. No answer: mobile off. For some strange reason he was reminded of *The Bold and the Beautiful*, the soap he watched without fail every evening. Just as crap as *Place Royale*, which turned Amandine mushy every Saturday. He fancied a snack. Would Maria already have gone to bed? He didn't want to bother her. Poor creature. Sixteen thousand francs per month. Pure exploitation. She had told him that she had saved enough money for two dairy cows. The pain returned. He could barely stay seated. He closed his eyes and groaned. He dialled Jokke's number.

"Hello."

"Jokke. Alberto."

"At this hour, man? What's the matter?"

"Jokke, can you recommend a good urologist?"

"Problems?"

"Pain, you know where. Peeing is a nightmare."

"Mm. You better have that checked out. Stop by the hospital early tomorrow and let me do a preliminary. Don't panic. I know a good urologist if you need one."

"What's the procedure?"

"First a rectal."

"Will it hurt?"

"Not a bit, idiot. A finger, nothing more."

"Bah!"

"The urologist, is he good?" Albert persisted.

"Among the best, if you ask me."

"Is this kind of stuff normal at my age?"

"How old are you?"

"Sixty-four."

"Nothing abnormal about it. King Boudewijn hit the jackpot at sixty."

"Hmm… Now I feel a lot better! Tell me, Jokke…"

"Mm?"

"After the operation… will I still be able to, you know, do the business?"

"Absolutely, but with one minor difference."

"A difference?"

"Yep. Retrograde ejaculation."

"What the hell's that?"

"The sperm doesn't come out."

"What?"

"You come internally."

"Ouch!" he yelped.

"Have you been drinking?"

"A touch. Internally?"

"In the bladder. But there's no problem. It's a bit late to be thinking about children. You come as before, only nothing gets wet. We call it a dry orgasm in the trade, ha ha ha."

"You wouldn't be laughing if you could feel what I feel right now."

"Nine out of ten it's a false alarm. I'll see you in the morning about ten thirty, OK?"

"Fine."

"The class structure is part of God's plan."

"You can laugh: better to say that God has monthly scores to maintain."

He hung up and immediately called her number.

No answer.

Skin against skin (she on his lap, her arm round his neck), Louise and Johan D'Hoog sat on the floor, stroking Igor's head.

Louise kissed D'Hoog's naked shoulder and her Labrador's snout in turns. She was wearing beige satin panties edged with lace, delectable against her smooth, straight thighs. Her nipples were like unripe raspberries on her small breasts. D'Hoog's hairy chest was just as brown as Louise's East Indian skin. He looked like a flamenco dancer.

Louise suddenly took hold of his neck, rested her head against his ear and whispered: "I love you more than ever, my wild gypsy thoroughbred, my Julius Caesar, my sizzling stallion."

"Crazy as ever," D'Hoog growled, gently squeezing his right middle finger into her anus (which he called *my little poop hole*).

"Mm, Johan… keep it up and you'll make me come…" Louise groaned, biting his shoulder, tugging his body hair with her teeth.

"We leave tomorrow for *Botswana*!" he shouted all at once, turning to face her and kissing her passionately.

Igor lifted his head with a jolt.

"Silly Billy, you're scaring our baby boy!"

"Come, let's stroke his head together while I work your little rosebud."

"I prefer *little poop hole*."

"Come closer so I can kiss you." He leaned forward and took hold of her buttocks. She threw back her long black hair and settled onto her belly. He pulled her panties aside and told her it was an octopus, a burst fig, a soft-boiled egg. He licked her gently and she whimpered.

"Go ahead. Do whatever you want with it. As long as you *mate* with me like a stallion."

"Your stallion's ready to go."

"Come. Doggy style. Your mare is waiting. *Mate* with me!"

"You're not going to kick me like a true thoroughbred mare when a stallion gets close?"

"Shut up and get on with it."

He lay down beside her and caressed her back, like fine silk to the touch. She opened her thighs. His penis was erect, immense and brown, its head purple and throbbing.

"Are you wet enough?"

"Drenched!"

"Whoa, horny mare."

"Come, my stallion, my stud, come!"

He groaned as he glided inside her, gently rocking to and fro.

"Deeper!"

He pushed deep inside her until he felt his penis touch her womb. She slipped her right hand under her legs and started to finger her clitoris.

"Are you ready to come?" he panted, his mouth against her ear.

"If you shoot, I'll come."

He picked up the pace.

"Ah… I'm coming!" she squealed. "*We're mating, we're mating.*"

He grunted and ejaculated while she clawed the carpet and tossed her head from side to side.

"Twelve rounds, I counted," she said as they lay gasping. She puffed and giggled.

"With you it just keeps on coming, fucking *bitch.*"

"Johan…" she said, all girly and helpless.

"Mm?"

"I can't live without you."

"What about the old man?"

"Leave it. He's out of the picture."

"He still pays his visits —"

"Yeah right, to exercise his horse and complain about his wife who won't give him a divorce, and the New Political Culture they finally managed to contain, and the never ending magistrate appointments, and how lucky he is they haven't abolished the fucking system."

"Doesn't his wife have a touch of blue blood?"

"Yes. Stinking rich, apparently. But hopeless in bed, if he's to be believed. Holier than the Pope. Last week she took a train full of sick people to Lourdes. Played the nurse."

"Pff. Why didn't she become a nun? What about him?"

"Used to be OK, but now… forget it."

"What age is he?"

"Sixty-four."

"Hmm, public prosecutor," D'Hoog pondered out loud and sat upright. He then burst out laughing and kissed her nipples each in turn.

"Come, let me clean you up," she said. She took a towel that was lying on the floor beside her and started to dry his half-erect penis and kiss it at the same time.

"Dry that pussy of yours, twit."

"Are you going to take me again?"

"Later. I'm hungry."

"Me too. There's all sorts of stuff in the fridge. Fancy some champagne?"

"Do you need an answer?"

"And there's smoked salmon, crayfish and caviar."

"Sounds like a feast."

She got to her feet and wobbled towards the kitchen, the

towel held between her thighs. "Shall we eat on the floor?" she shouted.

"If you want."

She returned with a plastic bag from which she produced three tin-foil parcels and a tin of Iranian caviar. She spread everything out on the floor and headed back to the fridge to collect the bottle of champagne Albert had opened that afternoon and recorked. She placed two crystal tulip glasses on the floor and D'Hoog filled them to the brim.

"Chin chin."

They drank. She knelt down in front of him and squirted champagne in his mouth.

He did the same and then removed the tails from the crayfish, which were already cut open, and they began to eat. He opened the tin of caviar and sniffed at it. Igor joined them and stared at the tin with interest.

"Is he allowed that sort of thing?" D'Hoog asked, his mouth full of food.

"He's crazy about caviar."

He balanced some on his thumb and Igor greedily licked it up.

"Caviar's not really my thing," he said.

"I love it," she said, "but not tonight."

"Sevruga," he said, reading the text on the lid.

"Not the best. Beluga's my favourite, but a kilo costs seventy thousand."

"Pampered, eh? Shall I give him some more?"

"Yes, but leave some in the tin in case he asks for it."

D'Hoog shrugged his shoulders, closed the lid and tossed the tin on the floor.

The computerized voice of the Travel Pilot RGS 06 announced the Oude Baan. Voorhout, who was at the wheel of the Mercedes van, stepped on the brakes. The headlights revealed a dirt track leading into a pine forest.

"What a fucking jungle," said Materne.

"Let's drive a bit further."

The track was bumpy and overgrown on either side with silver grass. They made slow progress.

"Look," said Voorhout, catching sight of a car parked ahead of them, near a house with lights burning inside. A grey Volvo hatchback. He stopped and took a photo of the car with the 3200 ASA mini digital camera, which dangled permanently around his neck. They drove past the car. Materne noted the number plate and punched it into the computer. They stopped again a little further along the track.

"Registered under Jan D'Hoog."

"The vet."

"Correct."

"It's ten-past eleven already. That pussy of hers must be in pretty bad shape."

"Shall we take a look?"

"OK. Bring Rambo."

"Rambo..." Materne muttered flatly.

The dog was lying at his feet and raised its head. They got out of the van. Materne did some stretching exercises. The dog turned in circles and finally lifted its leg against a clump of silver grass.

The shaft of light from Materne's torch flickered through the pine trees. "Looks like the lady's into privacy."

"And she has a *male* visitor."

"And she's *refusing* to answer the phone."

"Don't jump to conclusions."

They made their way towards the house.

Voorhout directed his torch towards the front of the Volvo, illuminating the vet sticker on the windscreen. "That confirms it."

"As if there was any doubt."

They stayed close to the car and looked towards the house. The blinds were down, but light was still visible inside. A bird screeched somewhere in the woods.

"An owl," said Voorhout.

A mist had formed over the paddock behind the house and a first quarter half-moon hung high in the sky. It was silent as the grave. Not a breath of wind.

Voorhout flashed his torch into the car and tried to open the passenger door. It was locked.

"D'you want me to open it?"

"No need."

They slinked towards the front door. Not a sound inside, only the whinny of a horse in the distance.

Rambo suddenly bolted and disappeared behind the house.

"Rambo! Here!" Materne shouted, smothering his voice.

Igor jumped to his feet, growled and ran out of the room.

"What's his problem?" said Louise.

"Probably heard something outside."

"Shouldn't you take a look?"

"Maybe a good idea..." D'Hoog got up and headed towards the front door.

What happened next took place at lightning speed. Barks turned to high-pitched yelps.

"Rambo!"

A halogen lamp flooded the entire area with light. The front door opened. A hirsute young man, stripped to the waist, looked around nervously, disappeared inside for a second and returned with a rifle.

"Rambo," Materne yelled, running in the direction of the yelps.

"Bastards!" the man roared, and he stormed behind him.

Materne found Rambo holding a brown-haired dog by the neck in what looked like an overexposed movie shot. He tugged at the dog's collar but the pit bull refused to let go.

"Son of a bitch!" the man yelled. He took aim. An angry rifle shot resounded through the night air. The pit bull jolted and rolled over in convulsions. The brown-haired dog, a Labrador, limped off, bleeding badly.

"Hands up, bastard!"

The man poked his rifle into Materne's chest. In the blink of an eye, Materne grabbed the barrel, yanked it out of the man's hands, tossed it aside and treated him to a karate blow to the gut. The man keeled over without a sound and lay motionless on his back.

"Let's get the fuck!..." Voorhout screamed.

"Johan!"

A young woman with long black hair, dressed in a negligee, rushed towards the vet, fell to her knees by his side, took hold of his head and held it to her cheek.

"Johan! I called emergency. They're on their way!"

The vet tried to get up. "Bastards!" he growled.

"My dog!" Materne screamed.

"Leave him! He's dead!"

"Fuckin' hell!" Materne launched himself at the vet, kneed him in the face and tossed him to the ground. Voorhout took a series of shots with his mini camera. "Move it, man! We're out of here!"

They took to their heels. When they arrived at the Mercedes van, Voorhout gasped: "We have to go back for Rambo! My address is hanging round his neck!"

"Jesus Christ, man!" Voorhout jumped into the driver's seat, turned the Mercedes round and sped towards the still-floodlit house. The woman was dabbing blood from the vet's face with a towel.

Materne jumped out of the van before it had stopped, dashed towards the pit bull, lifted him onto his shoulder and carried him with difficulty to the back of the van, which Voorhout was holding open. He tossed the dog inside. A second later, Voorhout was behind the wheel with Materne at his side, thumping the dashboard like a madman.

The Mercedes took off, its engine screeching.

8

Shortly after midnight, Baron Hervé van Reyn's daily review of the international press clippings selected by his secretary was interrupted by the buzz and whirr of the fax machine. It was a fairly long fax. When the machine stopped, he got up from his desk and collected the various pages. From Rome. In French. Sender: Joaquín Pla y Daniel. He returned to his desk and started to read. It was the transcript summary of a taped conversation between Pla and Amandine de Vreux. Extremely interesting reading, if the marginal notes he took were anything to go by.

After about fifteen minutes reading, he slipped the fax into a brand-new folder, wrote "D.S." on the front and drew a tiny cross in the upper left-hand corner. In spite of the late hour, he was still wearing a suit, a family custom he maintained with respect. He had been wearing it the entire day, but it looked as if it had just come from the dry-cleaners.

Fax (39) 66869550
Mittente: Ufficio informazione della Prelatura dell'Opus Dei in Roma
Via Sant'Agostino 5/A 00186 Roma
Indirizzo: Prélature de l'Opus Dei en Belgique. Fax (32) 2347 4916.
1999 05 25 11.56 p.m.

God and daring (Saying 401)

Querido amigo,
Please find an exact transcription of the content of the conversation I had today with the mother of D.S. I am sure it will be of interest to you in a number of respects. It should facilitate the urgent resolution of the situation at hand. Whatever the cost, resolution is essential at two different levels.

Greetings *in Christo*

Joaquín

V – When did you last go to confession?
A – Today, on your advice.
V – Do you remember anything from the evening meditation that caught your attention?
A – (She picks up a copy of *The Way* and reads the text of Saying 178) When you see a poor wooden cross, alone, uncared-for and of no value... and without its crucified, don't forget that that cross is your cross: the cross of each day, the hidden cross, without splendour or consolation... the cross which is awaiting the crucified it lacks: and that crucified must be you.
V – I would like to ask you a number of questions, which I expect you to answer truthfully, even if it shames you deeply.
A – You have my word, Father. Let sacred brazenness be my guide.
V – You appear to have misunderstood the meaning of the word. Ask your mentor to explain it.
A – *Pax*.
V – How did the relationship with your husband begin?
A – We were studying at the same university. I was studying history of art and he was at the faculty of law. He was an exceptional student. He participated in student life to the full and was president of the faculty student organization, but he

managed *summa cum laude* year after year without the slightest trouble. My father was professor of constitutional law at the time and a Supreme Court barrister…

V – Do I detect an element of pride in the way you draw attention to your father's position? Meditate on Saying 606: See how humble Jesus is: a donkey was his throne in Jerusalem!

A – *Pax.*

V – Continue.

A – Daddy took him as his assistant and invited him to the house from time to time. That's when we got to know one another.

V – What was this elite student's social and cultural background?

A – His social background was middle class. His parents owned two large delicatessens in Antwerp. They had a cottage in the country. They were hard-working shopkeepers without cultural baggage or social status.

V – Were they Catholic?

A – No, but they could hardly have been described as dyed-in-the-wool nonconformists either. They were… shopkeepers.

V – Why did they send him to a Catholic university?

A – I've no idea.

V – Are they still alive?

A – No.

V – Where did he do his secondary studies?

A – Grammar school in Berchem.

V – Didn't your father find that a little suspicious? I'm lead to believe that, as a member of the aristocracy, he is a man of deep faith.

A – With the exception of the Jesuit College, the grammar school was the best in Antwerp.

V – Where did your father study?

A – With the Jesuits.

V – Did your husband go to church with any frequency?

A – I fear not. When we were first married he came with me to mass.

V – And now?

A – Only on official occasions.

V – So he lives in a permanent state of mortal sin?

A – Yes.

V – Has your father ever been contacted by Opus Dei?

A – Yes, but he saw them as the Jesuits' main competitors and he had great respect for the Jesuits.

V – What do you mean?

A – He did not want to commit himself.

V – Were you ever approached by Opus Dei during your years at the university in Leuven?

A – You appear not to be aware that Opus Dei was completely unheard of in Leuven in 1951.

V – Your answer is correct. Don't forget to meditate on the virtue of humility. Sleep on the floor tonight.

A – *Pax.*

V – You said that your father invited him to the house?

A – Yes.

V – And?

A – We got to know one another.

V – Intimately?

A – No. Daddy found him a scholarship to study at Harvard after he finished his five years in Leuven.

V – So you didn't see much of one another.

A – Precisely.

V – My insinuating question seems to have served your purpose.

A – We married late, after a very short engagement.

V – What does late mean?

A – My husband was thirty and I was twenty-nine.

V – And the period of engagement?

A – What do you mean?

V – We ask the questions! Let me put it differently: was your engagement a chaste experience?

A – Absolutely. Daddy kept a very close eye on my social activities.

V – Did you *touch* each other?

A – We kissed when we met and said goodbye. Nothing more.

V – A *French* kiss?

A – Never! That was strictly forbidden by my confessor.

V – Who was he?

A – A Dominican.

V – Were there sins against chastity?

A – No. He tried to touch my breasts once but I managed to prevent it.

V – Did you confess the matter?

A – Yes.

V – Did you experience sinful desires when he touched you?

A – I have never been troubled by such desires.

V – Were you pure when you married?

A – Certainly. Daddy arranged a week of retreat for us in a monastery after the wedding, as advised by the pre-marital counselling book *Yes, I Do.*

V – Did you sleep in separate rooms in the monastery?

A – Of course! We were only together for the meditations and the sermons.

V – When was your first sexual contact?

A – Two months later.

V – Did you give your full consent?

A – Yes and no. My husband insisted so much I was afraid and I gave in to him. I wasn't even aware such things happened in married life.

v – Had you never received sex education?

a – People of our status did not talk about such things in those days.

v – What was the first contact like?

a – I prefer not to talk about it, Father.

v – Did you enjoy it so much?

a – Enjoy it? I never enjoyed it. I always found it unpleasant and only submitted myself because of his conjugal rights.

v – How many times did you have intercourse on the first night?

a – He was insatiable. He wouldn't stop!

v – So you never really took pleasure in it?

a – No. I considered the deed necessary for procreation and nothing more.

v – The nobility of procreation?

a – Precisely.

v – Why then did you only have two children?

a – Because he stopped insisting at a certain moment.

v – Were you happy with the situation?

a – He refused to share the nobility of procreation with me.

v – Did you ever try to change his mind?

a – No.

v – Why not?

a – Because he no longer paid any attention to me.

v – Did you ever have intercourse using a condom?

a – He asked once, but no.

v – And the pill?

a – It was no longer necessary.

v – Coitus interruptus?

a – Once. I was so outraged we never had intercourse again.

v – So your last intercourse was a mortal sin?

a – No. I didn't give my consent.

v – You clearly did!

A – I confessed everything, Father.
V – You see. Did you ever commit a sin against nature?
A – I'm not sure I understand.
V – Anal intercourse?
A – I didn't know such things existed.
V – Everything exists in the kingdom of Satan.
A – Indeed.
V – What did you do when you learned he had a mistress?
A – Nothing. What could I do?
V – Were you happy with it?
A – Of course not!
V – Do your sons know?
A – No.
V – Your father?
A – No.
V – How have you managed to keep it a secret so long?
A – Such things are not talked about in our circles.
V – How did you learn he had a mistress?
A – Someone I know had seen them together.
V – Do you and your husband sleep in the same bed?
A – Not for the last thirty years.
V – Do you ever give in to unchaste touching when you are alone?
A – Never. I wouldn't even know how.
V – So you have lived a life of abstinence for thirty years?
A – When you resolve firmly to lead a clean life, chastity will not be a burden for you: it will be a triumphal crown.
V – Saying 123. Let me respond with Saying 129: without holy purity one cannot persevere in the apostolate.
A – Impurity cleaves harder than pitch.
V – When one seeks the company of sensual gratification… what loneliness follows!
A – To defend his purity, Saint Francis of Assisi rolled in the

snow, Saint Benedict threw himself into a thorn bush, Saint Bernard plunged into an icy pond...
V – You... what have you done? blessed Josemaría asks himself in Saying 143. Let us pray together, my daughter. Before you go to sleep pray twenty Ave Marias in front of the portrait of blessed Josemaría. In the dark. And as I said, sleep on the floor. You are excused from the cilice. It is no longer necessary for women of your age. The cilice and the discipline are a male privilege.

9

On their way back to brigade headquarters in Brecht, Chief Sergeant Verhaert and Sergeant Ramael, gendarmerie on night shift, spent the entire time talking about the "shoddy affair" they had just witnessed and the handwritten report they had put together on the scene. They parked their Pontiac estate car in the garage and went inside, where they took off their uniform jackets and belts. They each poured a mug of coffee from a thermos, settled down next to a metal desk buried under piles of documents and folders and each lit a cigarette.

"Bineco, Sanitary Installations in Vilvoorde," said Verhaert, a tall, broad-shouldered character with a handsome ruddy complexion and a neat moustache, the prototypical gendarme.

"None of our business, Charley," Ramael replied. "That's one for the Public Prosecutor." Ramael was the same height as Verhaert, but wiry, pale and prematurely bald.

"I read somewhere that a pit bull never lets go, even if you thump it with a chunk of railway track."

"Possible, but the timing doesn't make any sense either."

"Miss Dubois claims she called D'Hoog, the vet, around ten thirty for a horse with colic. And a few minutes after he arrives, at ten forty-five, her Labrador is attacked by a pit bull. They note down the company's name from the side of the van, call us, we arrive fifteen minutes later, and there's the vet with a bloody nose and a ruptured lip. Doesn't waste time, does he?"

"Wasn't it a kick from a cow?"

"So he claimed."

"We should've asked the name of the farmer."

"Leave it, man."

"But everything seemed to have happened *by accident*, like some American cop movie."

"The pit bull's history. The culprits: two guys in dark-green overalls, one tall and blond, the other short and thin with a big moustache and sideburns."

"They want to press charges against persons unknown."

"And they were nervous as hell."

"Come on, how would you feel?"

"But there was something else…"

"What?"

"I heard from one of the guys at Antwerp CID that she receives regular visits from a senior Antwerp magistrate."

"Is the CID chasing magistrates these days?"

"Looks like it."

"And do I get to know the guy's name?"

"The cream of the crop."

"The Prosecutor's Office on the Waalse Kaai?"

"You didn't hear it from me."

"And there's another thing…"

"Mmm?"

"Everybody knows that D'Hoog doesn't always charge for his visits, especially if it's worth his while."

"A wise man, if you ask me. Jesus, did you get a look at the food?"

"We're small fry, my friend. Don't forget the Flemish proverb."

"What Flemish proverb?"

"It's dangerous to eat cherries with gentlemen."

"What the fuck does that mean?'

"Gentlemen pick out the ripest cherries and spit the pits in your eye, get it?"

"More or less. What do we do?"

"We type up the report, send it to the Public Prosecutor's Office and keep our mouths shut."

"You're absolutely right."

"I'd rather do something else."

"What?"

"Treat myself to a good whisky."

"Not a bad idea."

Chief Sergeant Verhaert opened a metal cabinet and produced a bottle of cheap whisky. Ramael had already found a couple of glasses.

After the gendarmes had left, Louise sat down on the sofa, lit a cigarette, her fingers still trembling, and stared wide-eyed and anxious into space. She had pulled a blanket over her shoulders. She was still wearing her negligee.

Johan D'Hoog appeared with his instrument bag and knelt down in front of Igor, who was stretched out on the floor, stock-still and clearly terrified. There were bite marks in the scruff of his neck. D'Hoog quickly filled a syringe and gave Igor an injection of local anaesthetic. He disinfected the wound, opened it, rinsed it thoroughly with antiseptic and pinched the frayed edges of the wound together with a couple of clamps.

"It's not as bad as it looks," he said.

Louise lit another cigarette and stifled a shiver.

"Are you cold?"

"No, Johan, I'm frightened," she said timidly. He wiped his throbbing nose and bleeding lip.

"I only wish I'd treated them both to a bullet in the knee," he said. "Come on my baby girl, don't let it get to you. We're both OK."

"I think *he* sent those bastards. He was jealous as hell in Brussels earlier with some English guy who was trying it on with me."

"You're not serious."

"Just to spy on us. He's in with the mafia!"

"Flemish-speaking mafia taking pictures?..."

"Why d'you think they were taking pictures?"

"No idea." He furrowed his eyebrows, trying to figure it all out.

"You have to get out of here right away. If he catches us together... Jesus, it doesn't bear thinking about..." she said.

"No, I'm staying here. You can always use Igor as an excuse."

"I just took a Seconal in the bathroom."

"But you have to call him first, just to be sure he doesn't smell a rat."

"You're a sweet, courageous man, do you know that?"

"I know, I know," he laughed and passed her the cordless phone.

She punched in Albert's number.

He made his way to the cupboard, found a bottle of whisky and poured himself a sturdy glass.

Albert woke with a start to the sound of his mobile, which he had stuffed under his pillow. He opened his eyes and looked around, still a little groggy. His nose was blocked and he had a pounding headache. His bed heaved like a ship at sea. The mobile was still ringing. He switched on his bedside lamp and looked at his watch: 2.25 a.m. He picked up his mobile and answered.

"Hello," he said, his voice hoarse and dry.

"Albert?" It was Louise.

"Mmm. Is something wrong?"

"It's Igor."

"What about Igor?" He leaned up on one elbow.

"I just got back from the vet. He was attacked by another dog, outside..."

"I don't get it. Were you with him?"

"It all happened so fast. I was reading and Igor started to bark all of a sudden. I let him out and then I heard what sounded like a dogfight. I switched on the floodlights and saw a van in front of the house. Another dog had Igor by the scruff of the neck and two guys dressed in overalls were watching. When I started to scream, they grabbed their dog by the collar and drove off."

"Did you get the licence number?"

"No, I couldn't make it out. I was too nervous."

"Did you call the police?"

"Yes. A couple of gendarmes from Brecht put together a report then I called the vet and took him over. Igor needed stitches."

"Is he all right?"

"His neck was one open wound, but he's asleep now. Everything is OK." The word OK made her giggle nervously.

"I'll be right there," he said.

"No, there's no need, really. Come early tomorrow. I've just taken a Seconal and I'm starting to feel it."

He tried to think. Didn't he have an appointment with Jokke and Saint Joseph's? "I'll let you know what time. Try to get some sleep. Are you sure you don't want me to come?"

"You sound strange. What's the matter?"

"Headache."

"Take an Optalidon."

"I'm about to do just that. Sleep well, Louise. Are you sure you —"

"Night, night. The Seconal's beginning to work."

He hung up, fell back onto the bed and stared vacantly at the ceiling for a few minutes. He slipped out from under the blankets and hobbled towards the toilet, suddenly aware of his body. The pressure around his anus had completely disappeared and, much to his relief, his urine bubbled triumphantly in the

WC. He forced the last drop from his bladder and finished his business with a leap in the air, like a soldier heading to the front, and a muffled "hurrah". "They won't be seeing me tomorrow at Saint Joseph's." His headache was suddenly a lot better.

He tottered downstairs to his office, where the bottle of Puligny-Montrachet 1975 from his father-in-law's wine cellar was still on the floor beside the chair, half full. He had opened it after several glasses of whisky, but the combination didn't work. Reason enough for his headache, he thought. A hangover and nothing more.

He half-filled a glass and savoured the burgundy's excellent nose. He then took a generous sip and pretended to rinse his mouth with it as if he were brushing his teeth, a wine-tasting tradition that made him laugh.

"Thank you, Baron de Vreux, a connoisseur if ever there was one," he said. He sat at his desk and tried to piece together what had happened to Igor.

"Well, well, well, gendarmes from Brecht," he said to himself. His eyes narrowed.

He mulled over how best to get his hands on the report. Call the local chief officer or have someone from the Public Prosecutor's Office intercept it? He was still too drunk to concentrate. He emptied his glass in one swig, but the wine didn't impress him. That whole prostate business must have been a false alarm, he thought. Jokke was right. Savelkoul was still a tough nut to crack. The best thing he could do was to grab some sleep. He had to hold on to the banister as he climbed the stairs.

She put down the cordless.

"He hasn't a clue," she said, lighting yet another cigarette. "He's coming over tomorrow."

"You see!"

"Carry me to my bed. The pill's really working."

"I'm staying here tonight."

"You're the sweetest man I know."

He lifted her off the sofa and carried her to the bedroom. She crawled, shivering, under the duvet, turned on her side and closed her eyes. He sat beside her on the bed, kissed her gently on the forehead, caressed her glorious hair and gazed at her without budging. After a few minutes her breathing became deep and regular. He got to his feet, switched out the light and made his way to the living room. He knelt down beside Igor and petted his head. He didn't react.

"Everyone's asleep," he said to himself and couldn't resist a short laugh. He rubbed his still-hurting nose, thought for a moment and decided to take a look outside to be sure everything was as it should be. The butt of the rifle had a deep scratch. He took it with him to the back door, removed the key, went outside and locked the door behind him. He switched on the lights in the stables. Soliman turned around. Yamma flattened her ears.

"Fancy a bit of a walk?" he asked, rubbing Soliman's flank.

Soliman stretched his neck, sniffed, cocked his ears and snorted.

Johan D'Hoog made his way to the saddle shed, rested the rifle against the wall, grabbed a bridle, returned to the stables, propped the bit in the horse's mouth and pulled the bridle over his head. Soliman accepted the bit, chewed at it for a moment, and allowed D'Hoog to fasten the bridle. He returned to the saddle shed and selected Albert's saddle. Before removing it from the rack, he tugged the stirrups a couple of holes shorter.

"His legs might be longer than mine," he muttered, "but that's the only thing!" Once again, he couldn't resist a laugh.

10

Wednesday 16 May 1999 promised to be yet another sunny day with temperatures around seventy-five degrees.

8.30, the start of a new working day.

The dark-blue Mercedes van was parked on the eastbound carriageway of Amerikalei, not far from where it had been parked the evening before. The morning traffic was making slow but steady progress towards the city centre, hindered by the perpetually desynchronized traffic lights. Joost Voorhout kept a close eye on house number 124A through the one-way glass. Half an hour earlier, he had faxed an observation report to Marlowe & Co.'s headquarters in Brussels. In addition to Albert's unanswered calls to Louise and the conversation between Louise and D'Hoog, reference was also made to Louise's late-night conversation with Albert. The van was in permanent radio contact with Jean Materne, who was parked a little further up the street in a Volkswagen Passat, waiting for a signal to start shadowing Albert. Materne was still enraged about the death of his pit bull, which he had dumped in the Albert Canal on the way from Sint-Job-in-'t-Goor to Antwerp. Joost Voorhout, the team leader, had submitted a false report, aware that Materne would otherwise have been dismissed on the spot. It was against his better judgement, but collegiality and his conviction that Materne was an excellent worker got the better of him. No reference was made to the pit bull. Voorhout had also run the digital camera through the computer and wiped out every trace of the compromising snapshots. Three of the photos were particularly useful: the rear of the Volvo hatchback (Johan D'Hoog's number plate), together with two suggestive shots of Louise Dubois holding D'Hoog in her arms, she wearing a see-through negligee and he stripped to the waist. There was no trace of the rifle or the dead dog. He had submitted the three relevant shots to Marlowe & Co. over the Internet.

At 8.35, chief sergeant Verhaert of the Brecht gendarmerie called his friend, sergeant Jef Vermeersch of the Antwerp CID, and told him about the events of the evening before, down to the last juicy detail. Vermeersch, who had secret, B-listed information at his disposal on the relationship between Louise Dubois and "Number 1", listened with interest and urged Verhaert to fax him the official report by way of information, a serious procedural error, but a practice that had become commonplace since the Octopus police reforms of 1998, inspired by the fact that the gendarmerie were now running the show when it came to national police policy. This was due in no small part to the former socialist Home Office Minister (a friend of the socialist corps commander) and his extraordinary support for the gendarmerie. The commander's resignation (he had "stepped aside") after Marc Dutroux's spectacular escape from the courthouse in Neufchâteau at the end of April 1998 had done nothing to curb the trend.

Vermeersch was smart enough to insist that Chief Sergeant Verhaert submit the report without delay to the procurator's office and mark it URGENT. He called this "throwing sand in someone's eyes to keep one's own hands free", an approach in which he could claim many years of experience.

At 8.42, Johan D'Hoog called Louise. He had been thinking about the contradictions in the declaration they had made to the gendarmes the night before and was in a panic. He advised Louise to pretend to be very confused if she received another visit and say that she was so upset by what had happened that her declaration might not have been entirely accurate. When Louise told him she had mentioned taking Igor to the vet for stitches when she was on the line to Albert, D'Hoog called her an idiot, insisted this was news to him, and told her he was bringing forward his plans to leave for Botswana with the UN programme "Wildlife and Cattle Interference". Louise burst into tears and wasn't even listening when he barked that one of the overalls, the tall blond bastard, had taken "*a whole fucking series of fucking pictures!*" "*And for someone else's pleasure, Jesus Christ,*" he roared and slammed down the phone.

When she had calmed down, Louise called Albert at 8.52. He was just about to leave for work. She asked him not to come over that morning because she wasn't feeling well. Albert replied curtly that he was only planning to stop by for a minute to see how she and Igor were doing and that there was no changing his mind.

At 8.55, Joost Voorhout informed Materne that the target had just left in his black Opel Omega and was probably heading for the Waalse Kaai. Address: Court of Appeal, Antwerp. Materne slipped out of the row of parked cars and was just in time to observe a black Opel Omega turn right into Graaf van Hoornestraat in the direction of the Museum of Fine Arts. He shifted into second gear and drove with screeching tyres through the red light, ignoring the double line of waiting traffic that started to move when the lights turned green. He watched the Opel slowly turn off Leopold de Waelplein into Burburestraat, heading towards the Waalse Kaai.

"I'm on his tail," he radioed his partner.

"Roger... over," Voorhout answered.

"Wait."

"Roger."

The Opel stopped no more than forty yards from the Court of Appeal building. Albert, dressed in a dark-blue suit, stepped out. The car continued and Albert walked towards the rear of building, produced a key from his pocket, opened a metal door and disappeared inside.

Materne reported what he had seen and concluded: "Mr high and mighty prefers to use the tradesman's entrance… over."

"Roger… out," Voorhout replied. It was high time for a nap, he thought. He turned the loudspeaker to maximum and lay down on the floor of the van.

At 9.11, Albert called the local chief officer of the gendarmerie, Major de Vreker, a man he had known for all of ten years and with whom he had an unusual but excellent relationship. Albert had once helped him out of a delicate situation when he was still lieutenant, something he liked to call "exaggerated diligence", another word for arbitrary and heavy-handed arrest without permission from the examining magistrate, after which the arrested individual, who turned out to be innocent, was confined to hospital for ten days.

Without offering further details, he ordered de Vreker in an official tone to copy a specific police report from the Brecht office and have it "sent to his office" by special delivery in a sealed envelope. The Major, one of the few army-trained officers still working for the gendarmerie, assured the public prosecutor that his orders would be carried out post-haste. Albert knew him well enough to be sure that the matter would be taken care of.

At 9.17, he called his friend Jokke to tell him that his prostate was in good shape and that he would make an appointment for a later date.

"I'd have my PSA measured if I were you," Jokke answered, slightly nettled.

"What's that?"

"Prostate Specific Antigen test. Can identify the presence of a tumour."

"I *don't* have cancer."

"How do you know, man?"

"There's never been cancer in the family. You're the one who's always saying it's a question of genes…"

"Dirty Jesuit!"

"Say that to my father-in-law."

"Is he still alive?"

"Barely."

"The class structure is part of God's plan."

"Bye, Doctor. You have a good day now."

"You too, Attorney General."

Albert hung up the phone with a smile, looked round and headed towards the door. A crew of workers armed with pneumatic drills were making a hellish din in the corridor, cutting a groove in the wall behind the skirting board to hide the cables for the new computer system. When they were finished, the computers were expected to work, albeit without the appropriate software. They had asked for six million francs to be included in the 2000 federal budget for a team of programmers. On the advice of a friend at the Department of Justice, Albert had requested double the required amount, because the salaries for software specialists were expected to rise dramatically in the near future. Up to that point, not a single programmer had answered the advertisement in the Antwerp newspapers. He closed the soundproof door, but it made little difference.

At 9.31, Albert called Louise on his mobile. She picked up and sounded as if she had been crying. He felt sorry for her and asked if there was anything he could get her.

"Honestly, I don't need anything," she replied, which was not her custom.

"That's right, there's still lobster and smoked salmon in the fridge from yesterday, eh?"

"I had to throw it out."

"What?"

"It had started to smell."

"And the caviar?"

"There's still a bit left."

"Did you try some?"

"Yes."

"OK, I'll stop by, but only for a quick visit. How's Igor?"

"He's lying here beside me."

"I'm on my way."

"OK. See you shortly."

"You don't sound very enthusiastic."

"Don't mind me. See you."

He hung up and muttered: "Young people these days! Everything in the bin. A couple of years on a kibbutz would have made all the difference."

He got to his feet, left the room, popped his head into the room next door and said to his secretary: "I'll be away all morning. I should be back this afternoon to run through the ethics reports with Barrister-General Bergé."

"Thank you, Public Prosecutor."

Albert headed towards the elevator, pressed the call button and the door glided open in an instant.

"Jean, he called his lady friend in the woods again," said Voorhout with a giggle. "Duration: sixty-four seconds."

"Roger... out."

A minute late Materne announced: "Target leaving the building on foot. I'm onto him."

"Roger... out."

Materne had thought that the target would head for his car, but it was nowhere to be seen. He kept him in sight as he crossed the parking lot towards the Vlaamse Kaai and turned into Pourbusstraat. He drove after him at speed and was just in time to see him disappear through the gates of a former warehouse. Lack of street parking forced Materne to position himself immediately in front of the gate, where he was able to keep an eye on Albert's movements. He hoped there was no other exit, but leaving his car behind at this juncture seemed inopportune. His wisdom was confirmed when the target left the warehouse shortly afterwards in a black BMW. As he followed the BMW towards the city bypass, he reported everything to Voorhout, including the vehicle's number plate: 9B959.

Materne's Volkswagen was fitted with a digital camera and a high-capacity zoom lens. He took a few shots of the rear of the BMW together with a close-up of the number plate. They drove at roughly forty miles per hour with just one car between them towards the E19 and the motorway approach road for Hasselt-Luik-Breda.

"I think he's heading into the bush," said Materne.

"Stick to useful information, over," Voorhout responded.

"Roger... out."

Once he had reached the city bypass, the target stepped up the pace. They ploughed along the fast lane at eighty-five miles per hour in a sixty-mile-an-hour zone. The E19 narrowed to two lanes as they passed the Sports Stadium, and overtaking trucks forced them to slow down. Just before the slip road for Sint-Job-in-'t-Goor, the BMW suddenly swerved to the right, cutting in front of a Dutch trailer-truck, much to the trucker's irritation. Materne followed the target with two cars between them. When the BMW veered right onto the slip road as expected, a wicked grin appeared on his face. A few days without shaving, together with the moustache and sideburns, made him look like a bandit, something that gave him an enormous sense of pride. They were driving to the place where his cherished pit bull had been shot dead the night before during a bungled operation that had run out of hand. His rage returned. He was determined to have his revenge, but wasn't yet sure how to go about it. When they reached Sint-Job town centre, he fell back to a safe distance from the BMW. Without being able to see the vehicle, he drove to the Oude Baan, where the tarmac road gives way to a dirt track, and saw the BMW's break lights flicker roughly two hundred yards ahead, in front of the farmhouse, which he was now seeing for the first time in daylight. He zoomed in to the maximum and waited. When the young lady came outside accompanied by the fucking Labrador, which was to blame for everything, he took an initial series of snapshots, followed by a further series of the target kissing the woman, kneeling down beside the Labrador and petting its head.

At 10.25, the telephone rang at the Prelature of Opus Dei in Brussels. The receptionist answered the call. The caller asked to speak to the director. She asked the caller's name. "Marlowe," he answered. "One moment," said the receptionist. Ten seconds later, Baron Hervé van Reyn said: "Hello…"

"Good morning, Perálta."

"Marlowe…"

"You sound surprised."

"Where did you find my number? We agreed that I would call you three times a day!" said van Reyn in a rapid staccato.

"True, but I think the information I have warrants my call."

"Where did you find my number?"

"Simple, really, but aren't you interested in what I have to say?"

"I'm listening," said van Reyn, his voice evidently restrained.

"We're seventy per cent sure of the woman in question. We have photos of her with another man."

"I asked for photos of *the man in question.*"

"You can do a great deal more with the photos that are now on their way to you. They're more… shall we say… convincing."

"So they're on their way here."

"Yes."

"I'm *not at all happy* with this procedure."

"Look here, Perálta. In less than twenty-four hours you'll have some very useable material at your disposal. If you're not satisfied —"

"No, no, it's not a question of being satisfied. I meant —"

"One moment, please, the shadow team have just reported in. Don't hang up."

Baron Hervé van Reyn held the receiver close to his ear without budging. He heart was in his throat. He sensed dampness in his armpits, something he abhorred because it was against Opus Dei rules to feel emotion. He was an officer in every sense of the word (priest and full-time servant of the army of Christ), infinitely superior to the ordinary foot soldiers, the married supernumeraries.

Marlowe kept him waiting more than ten minutes.

"Perálta?"

"Yes."

"We're now one hundred per cent certain. I have photos of the target with the lady in question. The same lady we photographed with another man yesterday evening in extraordinary circumstances. In front of the same house, no less."

"In extraordinary circumstances?"

"Yes, you'll see."

"When can I expect the photos?" croaked van Reyn.

"A second messenger is on his way."

"Can't I collect them myself?"

"Come now, Perálta. I've known your identity for a long time."

"Are you planning to continue?"

"If you say so, but if you ask me we have enough material to go on with."

"You'll send the bill?"

"The charges will be deducted from the advance. The remainder will be returned to you."

"Can you give me a figure?"

"No, our team is still on location. The operation will be cancelled in an hour or so."

"Hello?" said van Reyn, but the caller had hung up. He covered his eyes with his hands, not to pray but to stifle his regret at having been stupid and careless enough to allow the telephone number of Opus Dei to fall into the hands of a common detective agency.

At 10.45, immediately after his conversation with Marlowe & Co. – which had interrupted his customary imposed silence – Baron Hervé van Reyn telephoned the Rome headquarters of Opus Dei, introduced himself and asked in Spanish to be put through to the procurator general of the prelature. A few seconds later, Pla y Daniel's cheerful voice announced itself on the phone: "*¿Que tal, amigo?*"

"*Muy bien. ¿Y tú?*"

"*Yo tambien.*"

"Good news, Joaquín."

"Aha!"

"I have the Swiss bank account number and the balance."

"Aha!"

"And the other matter is making splendid progress. We're, shall we say, seventy per cent certain where the… eh… woman lives. Additional information is on the way."

"Allowing us to be one hundred per cent certain?"

"*Exactamente.*"

"So, my dear Hervé, what are you planning to do?"

"That's precisely what I wanted to talk to you about. It's time to give him an initial jolt before his wife gets back to Belgium."

"We can keep her here as long as you want. She's on retreat at the moment, close by, here in the house. But what do you mean by 'jolt'?"

"I plan to send someone with the news that his bank account in Switzerland has been compromised and invite him to transfer a significant portion of the balance. If he refuses, the information will be shared with the Belgian press."

"What is the balance?"

"In lire or Swiss francs?"

"Either."

"Two hundred and sixty thousand, nine hundred and twelve Swiss francs, and twenty-five centimes. Together with a substantial portfolio of shares and obligations."

"How much do you intend to ask?"

"Two hundred thousand. I like round figures."

"*Exactamente*. And who do you plan to send? Surely not an outsider?"

"Of course not! This is a strictly private matter. I had Paul Hersch in mind."

"Great minds think alike. How is he?"

"He's doing a sound job in Leuven. He had sixteen candidates on his Saint Joseph list this year. But his style is still a little, er... Flemish."

"When do you plan to make a move?"

"I'll call Hersch later this morning."

"One more thing: Baroness de Vreux is dissatisfied."

"Why?"

"She called Leuven and Paul asked her to call back around five thirty. When she did, he told her that her son was unable to speak to her because he had been *disciplined*."

"Disciplined?"

"Part of his praxis was to give a lecture yesterday evening and Paul felt that his text had misinterpreted the words of blessed Josemaría."

"Mmm. I still believe discipline is the responsibility of the local superior, in this case Paul Hersch. Time for me to get down to business. Don't put off your work until tomorrow."

"Saying 15. You'll call me if there's any progress?"

"Promise. When do you expect to visit Brussels?"

"In July. We can meet then and have dinner at l'Ecailler du Palais Royal."

"It's a date. *Ciao*, Joaquín."

"*Ciao*."

At 11:05, Baron Hervé van Reyn called Paul Hersch.

"*Bonjour*, Paul."

"Hey, Hervé."

Van Reyn smiled aloofly. He had difficulty dealing with Hersch's casual manners. His painful lack of style was sure to limit his career prospects, but he didn't take the slightest notice of the endless hints. The job van Reyn had in mind for him, however, might as well have been written for him.

"Paul, I need to talk to you about a delicate matter best not dealt with over the phone."

"Cut the ceremony, Hervé. What can I do for you?"

"Do you have time to meet?"

"When?"

"As soon as possible."

"This afternoon? Let's eat. I haven't had a decent meal in ages. The girls from the Leopoldstraat can't cook to save themselves."

"In the Cygne?"

Van Reyn regretted his suggestion immediately, but it was too late to withdraw it.

"Fine by me. Twelve thirty?"

"I'll be there, but try not to show up in that disgusting tracksuit."

"A dinner jacket any better?"

"Smart but casual is good enough."

"See you later."

Baron Hervé van Reyn returned the receiver to its cradle with a sour expression on his face. "Pity there's no one better," he muttered. "If he screws up, O Lord, God only knows what will happen."

He remembered he still had to say ten Ave Marias. He produced his rosary and started to pray out loud.

When Albert got out of his car that morning around eleven fifteen, the garage door of the farmhouse was closed. He honked his horn, but there was no response. The waste of crayfish and smoked salmon had put him in a bad mood the entire journey. How could fresh crayfish and salmon go off in one day?

"Don't you believe me?" she had snapped.

He wasn't inclined to insist. He honked a second time. Nothing. He got out and walked up to the front door. Locked.

"Shit!" he blurted, producing a key from his pocket.

Igor started to bark inside. He heard the bolt being drawn and the door opened. Louise, in black jeans and a T-shirt. She was as white as a sheet and had dark bags under her eyes. Her long hair was pulled back in a ponytail and she had a cigarette between her fingers. Jesus, she's beautiful, he thought. He wanted to kiss her, but she looked right through him and said nothing. She offered a customary cheek.

"What's the matter?" he asked, disappointed at the frosty reception.

"I feel rotten," she said in a little girl's voice. "After everything that happened..."

"Sorry…"

She nodded and puffed at her cigarette, inhaling the smoke deep into her lungs and exhaling with composure.

Igor jumped up to greet him with a yelp. He leaned over and examined the two clamps on his neck, which were bright red from the antiseptic. His stomach ached. The hangover had left him without an appetite and he had been drinking coffee all morning. He sighed and looked around, ill at ease. She lay down on the sofa, puffing at her cigarette and staring into space.

"I should take a look at the horses," he said.

"Fine."

"Come, Igor," he said, and he went outside.

He walked into the stables, with Igor running around him in circles. Soliman looked up and neighed deeply when Albert patted his flank.

"Hey, handsome," he said in a high-pitched voice, walking to the front to stroke his nose. When Soliman smacked his lips, sticking out his tongue in the process, Albert pressed his cheek against his horse's jaw and enjoyed the musky smell.

As usual, Igor playfully nipped at Soliman's legs and the horse paid little attention. The dog slept in the stables often enough, but his relationship with Yamma was a different kettle of fish. Every time Igor came close, she snorted and flattened her ears.

Soliman neighed and stretched his neck.

"No, boy, no jaunt today," said Albert. "The boss is dressed for work."

Soliman stomped in the straw with his front hoof and lowered his head.

"Come on then, I'll let you into the paddock," he said. He pulled a halter over the horse's ears, fastened it and opened the stable door. Soliman spun round with a jerk and bolted through the door as Albert pulled a halter over Yamma's ears and chased her into the paddock. Both thoroughbreds bucked and galloped wildly in the open space. Their magnificent gait filled Albert with amazement. He whistled through his fingers. Soliman pricked up his ears and trotted over to his boss with a spring in his step.

"Your mother's a jealous bitch, you know," he said, because Yamma had remained at a distance, stomping on the ground and tossing sods of grass in the air.

He made his way to the saddle shed, where there was always a bag of bread set aside. But when he caught sight of his saddle he was taken aback. It was hanging upside down. He removed it from the hook and replaced it correctly. What he saw then surprised him even more: *the stirrup straps had been shortened a couple of notches.*

He marched stony-faced back to the house, where Louise was still flat out on the sofa with her perpetual cigarette.

"What happened to my saddle?" he asked abruptly.

She looked up. "What about it?"

"It was hanging upside down and the stirrup straps had been shortened."

"I went for a ride this morning," she said with her eyes closed and a pathetic twist of pain in her face.

"With *my* saddle?"

"Wouldn't be the first time."

"Well, well... And I thought you didn't feel good..."

"I just took her out for a quick trot."

"Yamma?"

"Who else? Am I under interrogation or what?"

"Sorry. I let them both into the paddock."

"Fine."

"Do you feel any better?"

"No. I haven't had a bite to eat yet."

Talk of food reminded Albert of the crayfish and smoked salmon. He went to the back of the house and opened the garbage bin. Four crayfish tails had been tossed ostentatiously on top of a plastic bag. The shells were empty and the foil that had contained the smoked salmon was rolled up in a ball.

A heavy weight seemed to descend on his chest. His mouth became dry and he had difficulty swallowing. Emptiness filled him.

Albert slammed the door of his office with a kick, stormed over to his desk, yanked the chair so hard it crashed against the cabinet behind it, pushed it forward a little and sat down. His face was sickly pale, his eyes hollow and blank. In less than an hour, he appeared to have turned into an old man. He still hadn't recovered from his first major argument with Louise in their twenty-year relationship. For the first time in his life he had succumbed to a fit of blind rage. In response to his questions about the crayfish and smoked salmon, she had replied to his face that she didn't appreciate being interrogated in her own home as if she had committed a murder. "But you *lied*," he had screamed, "and I want the *truth*!" She had lit a cigarette, derision written all over her face.

He had started on again about the stirrup straps and she had laughed in his face.

"Typical impotent-old-man bullshit," she had said.

He was so overcome with rage at that moment that he smashed the antique Chinese horse to pieces against the wall. She attacked him like a cat and he punched her hard, causing her to fall to the floor and leaving her with a swollen cheek. She scrambled to her feet and turned towards him with bitter hatred in her eyes: "My mother always said that anyone who strikes a woman is a coward and should pay the penalty. Get out of my house this instant, and never set foot on my property again, *understood*?"

"Your funeral, bitch!" he had screamed. "I'll have Soliman collected in the morning!"

"You can stew Soliman with *onions* for all I care," she had replied, "and you can cough up the two thousand I had to pay for Igor's stitches!"

He had tossed a two-thousand-franc note in her direction and headed towards his car.

It was a miracle that he didn't have an accident on the way back to his office. He had taken some serious risks, driven through a couple of stop lights and had just managed to avoid a cyclist by a hair's breadth.

He loosened his collar and rubbed his eyes. Every muscle in his neck and shoulders throbbed with pain.

Someone knocked at the door.

"Yes," he heard himself say in the distance.

His secretary came into the room and handed him a manila envelope. "Special delivery from the gendarmerie, Public Prosecutor."

"Thank you, Miss Verdonck. Would you bring me a glass of water."

She inspected his face. "Are you feeling under the weather, Public Prosecutor?"

"I'm fine, miss."

She left the office with a look of concern on her face. Strange, he thought, finally someone who gives a damn about me. This was the first time she had dared ask such a question. He wasn't sure whether it had to do with his secretary's unsolicited concern, but reality started to seep through, drip by drip at first and then with a flood. He became aware of the irreversibility of the new situation, which had rolled over him like an avalanche.

He emptied the glass of water and stared into space for a good fifteen minutes. Without giving it much thought, he then opened the envelope from the gendarmerie, took out the police report, put on his glasses and started to read.

The document's contents had an unexpected effect on him, demanding his complete concentration. This allowed him to distance himself from the contents as if they were intended for someone else. He read the report with the same attention he would have given to a complex legal text and took notes on a notepad.

22.30 L. calls vet for a horse with colic
22.50 Vet arrives, Oude Baan.
Noise outside shortly thereafter.
In the floodl. they see I. being attacked by a pit bull. Delivery van, Bineco Ltd, Vilvoorde. Sanitary installations.
Two men in overalls pull p.b. free and drive off.
One is tall and blond, the other short with moustache and sideburns.
23.09 Gend. Brecht receive call.
23.11 Gend. arrive. Vet is already on site. Claims a kick from a cow is responsible for his bloody nose. She didn't drive Igor to his house.
Conclusion: L. made up the entire story.

Albert stared into space once again. His face suddenly changed into a contorted mask and he wrote in slow, careful capitals: THEY THEN ATE CRAYFISH AND SMOKED SALMON TOGETHER. He collapsed into his chair, rested his head against its soft leather back and closed his eyes.

It took until 12.50 before Albert was able to think straight. He stumbled, his head hung, from his desk to the solid rosewood cabinet against the wall, slid open one of the doors and selected Brussels's *Yellow Pages* from a pile of telephone books. Standing at his desk, he searched for Bineco Ltd under "Sanitary Installations", but found nothing. They probably listed it wrong, he thought. It wouldn't have been the first time.

He slammed the *Yellow Pages* shut and tossed it back into the cabinet on top of the other telephone books. It slipped to the floor and he kicked it under his desk. He had noticed his hands shaking like an old man when he was looking for Bineco Ltd. His headache had returned and he felt weak and unable to concentrate. But he was determined to get to the bottom of the fucking matter, if only to limit the loss of face he would suffer if he did nothing. He looked at his watch. Almost lunchtime. He returned to his desk, called Marc Keymeulen, the district prosecutor, and calmly directed him off the record to have a copy of the police reports from the Brecht gendarmerie sent to his office. Such requests were particularly few and far between, but given the circumstances he didn't give a toss. Prosecutor Keymeulen knew when to keep his mouth shut, he was sure of that. The man realized, of course, that a potential leak would lead back to his office, and he knew that Albert hated leaks.

"Certainly, Public Prosecutor," he had said. "I'll take care of it."

Gone were the days when he was on first-name terms with his predecessor and used to stop by his office unannounced, in spite of his lowly status as first substitute. For the first time that morning, a smile came to his lips.

He briefly considered asking Major de Vreker to collect information on Bineco Ltd, but thought it wiser to wait.

He had not eaten breakfast that morning, and in spite of the stress he felt hungry. He called home and Maria Landowska answered the phone.

"Hello, Maria..."

"Is that you, Mr Albert?"

"I'll be home for lunch."

"I've nothing ready, Mr Albert."

"Three eggs and a pot of strong coffee will be fine."

"Very good, Mr Albert."

He hung up and rubbed his painful eyes.

The prospect of having lunch in the kitchen with Maria Landowska lifted his spirits a little. It reminded him of his childhood, when he would dine in the kitchen with his mother on delicacies she had prepared especially for him.

The atmosphere at restaurant Le Cygne, where Baron Hervé van Reyn had invited Pierre Hersch for lunch, was anything but cordial. As General Vicar for Belgium, van Reyn pretended to be a teetotaller in the presence of other Opus Dei members. He ordered water and one simple fish course. Paul Hersch, on the other hand, ate with relish. He ordered an aperitif and a bottle of Rully, which he emptied while enjoying a starter (smoked eel and salmon) and main course (grilled turbot).

Hersch's table manners irritated van Reyn to the extreme, and his outfit didn't improve matters: a worn-out, ill-fitting sports jacket, a grimy shirt and a Sixties tie. He himself was dressed in an elegant pin-striped suit, a splendid light-blue shirt and an otherwise out-of-place Eton tie. The latest fashion in the tie department struck him as vulgar.

Not a word was said about the reason for their rendezvous. When van Reyn finally came to the point over coffee, Hersch listened attentively, opened the envelope he had been given and looked absent-mindedly at the photos and the Swiss bank account details. He returned the photos to the envelope and pushed it to one side.

He frowned, stretched his enormous torso, which transformed him into the incarnation of the word *Sitzriese*, and declared in no uncertain terms that van Reyn would be better off employing a professional for such a job, a private detective, for example, or a contract killer.

"Paul, *please*, it was to stay *in the family*," he pleaded with a wary grin. He pretended he'd never heard of the expression "contract killer". He spoke precious but correct Dutch, albeit with a slight Antwerp accent. He pronounced his *g*'s as if they were Scottish *ch*'s, just like the late King Boudewijn.

"No, sir."

Van Reyn pulled a face as if reacting to a twinge of pain. "My dear Paul, it's your *duty* as a numerary."

He made a snorting sound and his head quivered, as it always did when low-class individuals annoyed him, an aristocratic gesture from his extensive repertoire, implemented with precision to illustrate some or other dramatic remark.

"No, sir."

"But the plan comes from *Rome*."

Van Reyn's tone gave the impression that the word *Rome* made further discussion irrelevant.

"I don't care."

Van Reyn sipped at his coffee, ordered a jug of hot water to dilute it, breathed out, crossing his wrists in a rigid V and turning his head slightly to the left: "You know what happened to your *predecessor*..."

"Paco had a *crisis of faith*; that's another matter, Hervé."

"But now he's a curate in the Basque country, pff!"

"I hope he's happy."

"Let's pretend I didn't hear what you just said. Rome wants this. *Beyond question*."

"Who in Rome?"

Baron Hervé van Reyn's head quivered as before. "Do I have to name names?"

"Yes."

"Joaquín."

"Pla y Daniel?"

"Mm."

"I see..."

"Do you have *scruples*?"

"We're talking about blackmailing a senior magistrate, Hervé, the father of a candidate numerary." He thumped the table with his sizeable fist, making the cups and saucers tinkle and attracting the attention of one of the waiters.

"Get rid of those scruples that deprive you of peace. *Obey!*" van Reyn hissed.

"I'm quite familiar with Saying 258, Hervé."

"*Obey!* God shall vomit up the lukewarm! Fight your stupor!"

"I'm being obliged to break Belgian law..."

"If you cannot find peace in obedience, it is because you are proud. One day, it might be years from now or just a few days, you will be reduced to a pile of stinking flesh: worms, putrid bodily fluids, filthy strips of shroud... and not a soul on earth who cares about you."

Paul Hersch looked aside, angry, his eyes bulging more than ever. Jesus, he's ugly, Baron Hervé van Reyn thought to himself.

"So they've made up their mind in Rome that I'm the man..."

"Yes, Paul."

Hersch closed his eyes, folded his hands together and remained motionless for a few moments, as van Reyn sipped his cup of coffee.

He opened his eyes, looked van Reyn straight in the face and said bluntly: "*Pax.*"

Van Reyn nodded without even a hint of a smile and winked at a waiter, who hurried to their table with a burgundy-coloured artificial leather folder on a silver tray. Without looking at the bill, he slipped a ten-thousand-franc note under the folder.

He took the envelope with the photos and information and handed it over. Paul Hersch folded it in two and stuffed it into his inside pocket.

11

Around eleven thirty that night, Jean Materne drove slowly past the farmhouse on the Oude Baan, his engine purring gently. The blinds were down, but the light from inside suggested that the occupants were still awake.

Materne was at the wheel of a red Honda NSX with spoilers and four fog lamps. He had bought it the year before for four million and had put himself into serious debt with a couple of banks.

He drove four hundred yards into the middle of the woods, where he parked the car in the silver grass at the side of the road.

He looked at his watch, fished a black balaclava from a rucksack on the passenger's seat and pulled it over his head. He opened the glove compartment and took out his pistol, a 9-mm FN Browning HP, silencer attached, stuffed it into the pocket of his black tracksuit trousers and got out of the car. It was much like the night before: clear, on the chilly side, a half-moon high in the sky and streaks of mist lingering above the dirt road. He looked around and listened, opened the boot and took out a pair of magnetic number plates. He attached them front and back to the Honda and locked the doors with the remote. He removed the pistol from his pocket, checked the slide, fastened the safety catch and returned it to his pocket. He had reduced the charge of the cartridge and eased the trigger pull to dampen the noise as much as possible.

Slightly stooped, he scurried towards the farmhouse. He stopped and listened at the door. He heard the dull thuds of hard rock music playing inside. He walked past the door and looked round. He could see a couple of shadows in the paddock behind the house and realized they must have been horses.

"A stroke of luck," he muttered under his breath, suppressing a chuckle. He brushed past the side of the garage, carefully and without a sound, as he had learned in the paras, and stopped at the barbed-wire fence surrounding the paddock. The horses were about seventy yards away. They had noticed his presence and were standing side by side and motionless.

Materne crept agilely over the fence, moved towards the horses, took out his pistol and released the safety catch. When he was about fifteen yards from them, he clacked his tongue. In the moonlight, he saw one of the horses prick up its ears while the other snorted and neighed. He wasn't a horseman, but he knew enough about their behaviour to avoid taking unnecessary risks. He approached with extreme caution, raised his pistol to eye-level, arm outstretched, and aimed at the upper part of the head. All that could be heard when he pulled the trigger was the action of the slide opening and closing. The horse jolted, collapsed to the ground with a muffled groan, its rear legs convulsing, and finally stopped moving.

The other horse did not react at first, although it was only a few yards away. But then it reared up suddenly, emitted a piercing neigh that echoed deep into the woods, leaped forward on its rear legs and crashed its front legs with all its might onto the creature that had done something unusual and suspicious to its mother. The creature let out a shriek of pain and fell to the ground. The stallion's instincts instructed him to attack a second time, and he smashed his front hoofs on the wailing creature with a noise that sounded like a filled jerrycan being thumped with a rubber hammer. When the creature stopped moving, the horse lowered his head and sniffed at the body of the person who had invaded his territory and tried to intimidate him as his mother's protector. He then sniffed his mother. Her scent had changed in a matter of seconds and she no longer reacted to his signals. He snorted vigorously, stretched his neck, trotted towards the stables, stopped at the barbed-wire fence and emitted a loud, terrified, penetrating neigh that sounded more like the bellow of a cow in distress. A dog barked inside the house in response.

At 11.50, an emergency call was made from Sint-Job-in-'t-Goor to the headquarters of the gendarmerie, which was immediately redirected to the Brecht office. The same team was on duty as the previous night. Sergeant Ramael took the call – a hysterical woman rattling on about someone attacking one of her horses, probably the guys who had set a pit bull loose on her Labrador the night before, which almost bit him to death.

"Stay where you are and don't touch anything," Ramael advised. "We're on our way."

"I'm not staying here for another second. I'm going back to my mother's place," the woman screamed, clearly beside herself.

"Please, lady, try to stay calm and wait for us. We'll be there in ten minutes."

He hung up and turned to superintendent Verhaert: "Never a dull moment with that Dubois woman from the Oude Baan in Sint-Job. Now she says someone shot dead one of her horses."

"You're kidding."

The Pontiac intervention vehicle left the station shortly afterwards, its sirens wailing.

When the gendarmes arrived eight minutes later they found Louise Dubois tossing stuff into her car like a woman possessed. She was delirious and kept repeating that she was leaving "that haunted house" for good and that she was going to stay with her mother. Her cheek was swollen and she had a black eye. The Labrador followed her everywhere and seemed terrified.

The gendarmes tried to calm her by reminding her that they had to take her statement. They finally convinced her to go with them to the paddock, where she threw herself on the dead horse, sobbing and yelling, "Yamma! Yamma!"

She suddenly got to her feet, pointed to something behind her and screamed with a crack in her voice: "He's there, the murdering bastard!"

Ramael directed his torch at the body of a man in a black tracksuit and balaclava lying motionless in the grass, his knees pulled up to his chin. The two gendarmes walked towards the man, removed his balaclava and noted that he had a heavy moustache and sideburns, in agreement with the description of the owner of the pit bull. His tracksuit was soaked with blood. When Ramael shone the light in his face he started to blink and groan. In close to incomprehensible words, he managed to inform the gendarmes that his back was broken and that he could not move.

"John, call an ambulance," said Verhaert, crouching to pick up the pistol.

"What do we have here: an HP with a *silencer*, Christ almighty!"

"The same as last night and that fucking pit bull! I'm sure it is..." Louise Dubois yelled. Her desire to kick the man on the ground was stifled by her police companions.

"Call an ambulance," Verhaert repeated. "I'll cuff him."

"No, no cuffs," said the man.

"Aha, he's got a tongue, that's nice. Let's have your wrists, pig."

"No cuffs," Ramael ordered. "The man can't even walk." He turned to Louise Dubois: "Come, lady, let's go inside and take down your statement."

"Murderer!" Louise Dubois screamed.

* * *

Albert made his way to his bedroom humming blithely. He had chatted with Maria Landowska in the kitchen until midnight. She had made dinner and he had asked her to join him. She had given him a strange look and agreed immediately. She was wearing jeans and a white T-shirt. Her thick red hair was tied back in a ponytail. She had prepared entrecôte with salad and brown bread. He had asked if she fancied a glass of wine.

"*Tak* – yes," she had replied, with a snigger.

After the first bottle of Chevrey-Chambertin 1990 he uncorked a second. The wine was sublime, its round aftertaste bursting with berries.

For reasons unknown, they spent much of the conversation dwelling on childhood memories, his silk shirt open at the neck and tie discarded, and in spite of the strange language they used to communicate, there was an evident familiarity between them. This was probably due in part to her farm background and the fact that he had spent much of his youth in the countryside. When she told him she had been riding horses on her uncle's farm since she was fourteen, he launched into a lengthy description of Soliman, as if it were the most normal thing in the world.

"I knew you had a horse," she said, in a mixture of German and Dutch.

He had to smile. She had clearly enjoyed the wine, but had said nothing about its quality.

"Madame doesn't like horses," she said after a moment of silence and in the same mixture of German and Dutch.

"No, Maria, Madame doesn't like horses," he replied, repeating her words exactly. She looked at him long and hard with her penetrating blue eyes.

"I wouldn't mind a little vodka," she said unexpectedly.

He had a bottle of Wiborowa in his drinks cabinet. They threw back a couple of glasses without a blush and fell silent.

As he finished the second bottle of wine he said: "It's done me the world of good to talk about *real things* for once."

She smiled and said in German: "You needed it, Mr Albert."

"True, Maria."

Albert got up, wished her good night, jumped under a cold shower, dried himself and climbed naked into bed.

In the middle of the night he was ever so gently awakened by a warm naked body, which slipped under the blankets beside him, embraced him and started to kiss him passionately with a mouth that tasted of alcohol. His erection was irrepressible (Louise is back, he thought). He opened his eyes and gazed into those of Maria Landowska, who draped her long red hair around his neck, kissed his eyelids, took hold of his penis and rubbed her breasts against his chest. She threw one leg over his hip, let go of his penis, tossed her arms round his neck, gripping him tightly, and panted in his ear: "*Niebo!*"

"What does *niebo* mean, Maria?" he said as he slipped inside, moaning with pleasure, pressing his nose under her arm, which smelled of butter and musk.

"Heaven," she answered, "let me take you to heaven."

"Maria..."

"Mr Albert..."

"Why don't you use my first name?"

"Never. For me you will always be Mr Albert. Let me turn over. I prefer to lie on my belly."

"*Pozadku*, Maria, horse style."

She flipped onto her belly, hoisted her generous buttocks upwards and grabbed his penis once again to guide him to the right spot.

12

Albert awoke as if from a dream. A series of what seemed like electric shocks overwhelmed him with an immense joy that quickly turned to tangible reality: the warm, muscular and naked buttocks of Maria Landowska squashing his penis flat, her back, her neck, her tight curls between his lips, which he softly licked and sucked. She snored almost imperceptibly. He looked at her ears as they moved in harmony with her breath in the morning light. She smelled of soil and withered leaves. He hadn't felt so young, strong and proud in years. His prostate problems had vanished. They had made love twice, and his untarnished Polish beauty had reached orgasm, her teeth sunk into the pillow, just as he had ejaculated.

She had remained on her belly, gasping, muttering all sorts of Polish words, and then turned her head to shower him with licks and kisses. He had never experienced such pleasure with a woman before. He had never imagined it possible. Louise had vanished in a distant haze, Amandine had never been born, and all he could think of was a couple of the prostitutes from the district near the station, who would give themselves over to unbridled lovemaking on the rare occasion that the customer took their fancy.

Maria held her breath for a moment. She turned over and stared at him shamelessly: stainless-steel smile, shallow eyes, high cheekbones, auburn hair, the picture of a satisfied woman.

"Maria..." was all he could say.

"Mr Albert," she replied, stating the obvious, as the tears started to roll down her cheeks.

"Don't cry, Maria, don't cry. Please..." he said in German.

"I'm so... so *szczęśliwa*."

"What does that mean?"

"I don't know. *Radość. Błogość*... Happy?"

"I'll get the dictionary."

"No, there's no need, really. Shall I make some coffee?"

"Good idea, Maria. What time is it?

"I don't know... I don't know anything any more."

"Strong coffee and eggs."

"Beaten?"

"Yes, beaten like raindrops on the window."

He took her head in his immense hands and said with unknown tenderness: "Maria, yesterday I was a nobody. Now I'm *Jung* again!"

"I know, Mr Albert. I know everything. Just like my mother."

"How do you say witch in Polish, Maria?"

"*Czarownica*."

"You're my *czarownica*."

She placed two fingers on his lips, slipped out of the bed, leaped athletically to her feet and made her way slowly towards the door, her hips swaying like a model on a catwalk, her hands tying up her sumptuous tresses, revealing her dense underarm hair. When she reached the landing, she started to sing a well-known Russian song: '*Ochi Chyornye*', or 'Dark Eyes'.

Albert rolled onto his back, placed his hands behind his head and said aloud: "*Czarownica*, I'm *in love*."

At nine o'clock, while he was chatting with Maria after breakfast as if they had been a happy couple for several years, the telephone rang in the dining room next to the kitchen.

"Shit," said Albert, a trendy word as far as he was concerned and the first time he had used it.

"*Pan* Albert, *telefon*," said Maria needlessly. She was wearing jeans, her voluptuous breasts pert and triumphant, her hair in its usual ponytail, Albert's empty coffee mug in her hand. Barefoot and wearing nothing but a pair of boxers, Albert made his way into the dining room.

"Hello."

"Public Prosecutor." It was his secretary. She hadn't called him at home for more than a year.

"Yes, Miss Verdonck."

"Good morning, Public Prosecutor, I'm sorry to disturb you."

"No problem, Miss Verdonck."

"Public Prosecutor, you received a call from Major de Vreker, the district commander of the gendarmerie."

"Yes, and?..."

"He wants you to contact him urgently."

"At what number?"

"At the station on Boomsesteenweg, Public Prosecutor."

"Thank you, Miss Verdonck."

"And again, please excuse the disturbance, Pros—"

"It's all right, miss."

Albert slammed down the phone, sighed, swatted the air around him as if he was shooing off an irritating insect and shouted in the direction of the kitchen: "Maria, have you seen my mobile?"

"It's here, Mr Albert."

He returned to the kitchen table and gulped at his coffee. She came and stood beside him and he placed his arm around her waist. She stroked his hair and kissed the top of his head. He realized for the first time how tall she was.

He punched in the number of the gendarmerie.

An official-sounding man's voice said: "Gendarmerie District Antwerp, good morning."

They're learning, Albert thought, and answered: "Good morning, can I speak to the district commander?"

"Who can I say is calling?"

"Public Prosecutor Savelkoul," he said with a fake grin.

"I'll put you through."

Put me through, unprecedented politeness, he thought.

"De Vreker, good morning Public Prosecutor."

"Good morning, Major, good news?"

"Eh... I would prefer to discuss the matter with you in person, if you don't mind."

"Fine, Major. Shall we say in an hour at my office?"

"I'll be there, Public Prosecutor."

He hung up and was suddenly reminded that he would normally have called Louise at least twice by this time of the morning. Strange how it left him cold, he thought. What happened? He looked at Maria Landowska and asked himself if she was the one who would finally bring him the *rest* he had long been searching for.

He looked at his watch and said: "I'd better get ready. I have an appointment."

She nodded in silence.

Before she could say anything, he said: "Let's have lunch together."

"What would you like, Albert?" she said.

It was the first time she had used his first name without the Mr, and in German no less. He had to smile.

"Shall I bring some cold hors d'oeuvres?"

"Cold food is no food, we say in Poland."

"Then make a hot meal."

"*Smocze zęby*."

He looked at her questioningly.

"*Drachenzähne*."

"Dragon teeth? What's that?"

"That's what the Polish soldiers call asparagus."

"Excellent, but buy Belgian. With butter sauce and mashed hardboiled egg. I'll bring the *Tarte*." He knew how much she loved sweet things.

She started to clear the table, less hurried than in the past. Before he went upstairs to get ready, he took her in his arms and kissed her, caressing her steel teeth with the tip of his tongue. It gave her goosebumps. Her teeth had a penetrating taste he couldn't place.

She gave him a gentle dog bite on his shoulder. She noticed that he had an erection, but all she did was pass her hand swiftly over his boxers.

He climbed the stairs, humming 'Dark Eyes' to himself and thinking: if only Amandine could see us now, God alone knows how she would react. A fit of laughter seized him.

When he passed the statue of Our Lady he noticed that the usual flowers were missing. He suppressed a mocking "*Salve Regina!*" It didn't interest him, even remotely.

After taking a bath and shaving, he slipped into his room for a moment and took *The Teaching of Buddha* from the shelf. He opened it at page 440 and read:

> Of the third type there are those who are more broad-minded and do not become angry very often, who know how to control a greedy mind but are not able to avoid feelings of jealousy.

He reflected on the difference between envy and jealousy. I don't mind if Maria's *jealous*, he thought, as long as she doesn't *envy* me for my money and possessions.

He closed the book with a smile and returned it to its place between the Spanish and South African versions of the New Testament.

13

Major de Vreker waited in the antechamber with a briefcase at his side. Around ten o'clock, Albert charged along the corridor lined with portraits of his predecessors and into his office, the door of which was wide open, American style. The Major sprung to his feet. Albert waved, offered the Major a firm handshake, asked how he was, and told him he was fortunate that the workers were almost finished with the cabling job. At least they would be able to make each other out.

"Thank you, Public Prosecutor," de Vreker answered formally, slightly surprised at Albert's unexpected joviality.

He was in plain clothes: a dark-blue suit with a light-blue shirt and a red-and-black-striped tie, a colour combination that differed little from the uniform of the gendarmerie. He was a handsome man. As tall as Albert, short blond hair, slender build. He was an excellent horseman and had once had an interesting conversation with Albert about horses. They had talked about Monty Roberts, among other things, known for his training methods and his nickname "the Horse Listener".

Albert invited him to take a seat in one of the armchairs in the corner of his office, the "living room", where he preferred to receive visitors with a certain status.

"Coffee, Major, or can I offer you something else?" he enquired.

"Coffee please, Public Prosecutor."

Albert crossed to his desk, dialled an internal line and said flatly: "Two coffees, please."

He sat down opposite the Major and looked at him.

Major de Vreker advocated the no-nonsense approach. Without saying a word, he opened the briefcase, took out a folder and handed it to Albert, who opened it to reveal a few typed Pro Justitia documents. He held the first document roughly twelve inches from his face and narrowed his eyes. Wearing glasses in front of the Major was out of the question.

The Major had developed a technique for keeping an eye on things while pretending to look aside.

The further Albert read, the harder his expression became. At a certain moment, the blood drained from his face and his lips became narrow and tight. He stood up without looking at the Major, walked to his desk and dialled a number. No answer. He hung up and returned to his seat, still white as a sheet, and continued reading.

Without looking up he said: "Have you any idea which of the horses was shot, Major?"

"A mare, Public Prosecutor."

"So the other horse is alive?"

"Precisely."

Albert closed his eyes for a second, stretched his back and read further.

The secretary appeared with two cups, milk, sugar, chocolates and a nickel-plated thermos on a tray.

"Thank you," said the Major instead of Albert, who was still preoccupied with the documents.

Again without looking up he said: "Close the door behind you, Miss Verdonck." An indescribable silence filled the room.

When he was finished reading, Albert returned the documents to the folder, opened the thermos and poured a cup of coffee for himself and the Major. He sipped at his coffee in silence.

Major de Vreker waited without moving a muscle.

Albert cleared his throat and said in his usual baritone voice: "So do we have the suspect's identity and occupation?"

"No, Public Prosecutor. As you can see in the report, the man – Jean Materne – confessed that he was acting out of revenge because the vet, a certain Johannes D'Hoog, had shot his pit bull two days earlier. He had no identity card on his person. He told us his name without difficulty, but refused to give his address."

"Has all the information been checked?" asked Albert flatly.

"Johannes D'Hoog has disappeared."

Albert raised an eyebrow but made no comment. Fortunately, Louise had not been mentioned. Strange, he thought, but he said nothing about it.

"And have they issued a missing person's notice?"

"Of course, Public Prosecutor."

"Have they been able to determine why Materne was snooping around the house in the middle of the night? And what about his sidekick?"

"He's still under anaesthetic at the moment. His pelvis was fractured in two places as the result of a stamp from one of the horses."

"Did he have a car?"

"Yes, but he refused to tell us its location."

"And are they still looking for it?"

"I'm afraid so…"

The Major coughed a couple of times.

"What about Bineco?" Albert asked.

The Major appeared worried. "We've looked everywhere, Public Prosecutor, but there's no sanitary installations company in Vilvoorde answering to the name."

"Who's in charge of the rest of the investigation?"

"CID, orders from the Public Prosecutor's Office."

"Do we have any idea what we're looking at?"

"Not yet, sir."

The Major averted his gaze, lifted his cup and drank his coffee.

Albert thought for a moment and then said: "Shall we take a look at the crime scene?"

The Major had more or less expected this suggestion, but he didn't let it show. "A police vehicle is at your disposal, Public Prosecutor," said the Major, realizing immediately that his proposal was inappropriate.

"No, we'll take a private car."

Albert stood and opened the door. Major de Vreker picked up his briefcase and followed.

Something unusual happened as Albert and Major de Vreker stepped out of the car at 10.50 in front of the farmhouse on the Oude Baan. Without prior agreement, they set about what the police refer to as "divvying up the work". Everything went so smoothly and naturally that Albert was reminded at a certain moment of a French expression: *des atomes crochus* – personal chemistry. He opened the front door with a Yale key on a ring with various other keys. Major de Vreker followed him inside. Although Albert had more or less expected to see what he did, it still hit him like a kick to the stomach. He held his breath for a second, stood still and tried to breathe calmly in and out. All the decorative pieces he had once given her were gone: English hunting scenes, the horse collection, gone. Even the teddy bears, cushions and carpets were gone. Everything but the kitchen sink. The .22 rifle had been placed ostentatiously on the floor in front of the fireplace. He noticed immediately that the walnut handle had been scratched.

The definitive end of what had been a fairly happy period in his life, all things considered, he thought. She had even taken Igor, but surprisingly enough it didn't bother him. *Soliman* was still alive and that was the most important thing.

"I'm off to check on the horse, Major," he said. His voice reverberated in the hollow, empty room. He was about to say: "Why don't you take a look around the house," when the Major asked: "Do you mind if I take a look around in here, Public Prosecutor?"

Albert went outside. The sun was shining as if it was the height of summer. He looked left and right on his way to the stables to see if there was anyone around. The stables were empty. He could see Soliman in a far corner of the paddock, standing in the shade of the trees and looking at him as if he were ready to bolt.

"Soliman!" he shouted. "Come here, boy, come!"

Soliman hesitated for the briefest moment and then galloped calmly towards Albert, who felt a lump in his throat at the sight of his horse's agile canter. It hit him for the first time that Yamma was dead, the horse that Louise had ridden with such style, turned into a corpse with a single shot, rotting in the stinking hell of the abattoir. He tried to apply his psychological resistance technique, putting Yamma out of his mind, because there was nothing he could do to change things. It didn't work. He couldn't stop thinking about the fact that Louise had loved her horse so much and about the dreadful end Soliman's mother had had to face. He hoped he would never be forced to confront the killer.

Soliman stopped abruptly at the perimeter and neighed deeply, allowing Albert to rub his forehead and press his cheek against his warm jaw. I still have Soliman and Maria, he thought resignedly, I still have Soliman and Maria. He slapped the horse's flank with the palm of his hand, looked around and tried to think of a practical solution. He would have to bring Soliman to a riding stable for a while. The farmhouse was in Louise's name. He was sure she wasn't planning to change her mind and come back. He would have to call her mother to find out where she was.

"Public Prosecutor, sir," he heard the Major say behind him.

He turned as de Vreker was walking towards him, holding something between his thumb and his index finger: an empty rifle shell.

"The same calibre as the rifle?" Albert enquired with a smile.

"Precisely. In the grass." de Vreker replied in elliptic police language.

So someone used my weapon after all, thought Albert, who had only half-believed Materne's revenge story.

"Confiscate the weapon, Major," he said.

"Me, personally?"

"If you don't mind."

"Sure," the Major answered, as if it were against his better judgement.

"Didn't you say there was a missing person's out on D'Hoog?" Albert asked.

"Yes."

Albert petted Soliman pensively between the ears. "What do you think of him?" he asked without looking at the Major.

"Handsome horse. Fine hindquarters. Four perfect legs."

"Andalusian thoroughbred," said Albert, "spirited but correct."

After a short silence, Albert looked the Major in the eye and said: "Can I be frank with you?..."

The Major nodded.

"This is the pied-à-terre where I used to visit my lady friend."

"I had already guessed as much, Public Prosecutor."

"Her horse was shot by a certain Materne, whose pit bull was shot by a certain Johan D'Hoog, a vet from Brecht... With my rifle."

The Major nodded anew.

"It's essential we identify the firm Bineco..."

"Everything is being done, Public Prosecutor," the Major repeated with obvious patience.

"Who do you think is behind all this?"

"No idea, sir."

"Not even an inkling?"

"No, sir."

"*I do*. My wife."

The Major appeared hesitant but said nothing.

"And that's why I'm almost a hundred per cent sure that the Bineco delivery van is a detective agency observation vehicle."

"We'll get to the bottom of it, sir, you can rest assured."

Albert fished his mobile from his pocket and called Louise's mother. Her mother answered the call in person and hung up when she heard Albert's voice. Without blushing, he called the stable where he used to go riding on occasion and asked them to send a trailer without delay.

The reaction of Louise's mother on the phone brought Albert a degree of relief. He was reminded of Bruce Chatwin's *What Am I Doing Here?*: "Men of action have a habit of consigning past loves and indiscretions to oblivion in the hope of better things to come."

While he rubbed Soliman's lips, something the horse couldn't get enough of, Albert said earnestly: "This stays between us…"

"You have my word, Public Prosecutor," Major de Vreker answered.

While Albert and Major de Vreker waited in the Kempen for the trailer to arrive from the riding school, an old-fashioned CID investigation was underway in Brussels: clandestine, without the knowledge of the Public Prosecutor's Office – in other words, against every law and ordinance of a constitutional state. The two gendarmes from Brecht had taken the initiative and it wasn't long before they were overstepping their jurisdiction, upon the explicit request of sergeant Jeff Vermeersch of the Antwerp CID and with his assured protection. After an unforgettable night of repeated threats and verbal abuse, they had found a car key in Materne's pocket and gone in search of the car on their own initiative. They found it parked on the Oude Baan, not far from the farmhouse, opened it, recovered Materne's wallet, mobile and keys, discovered that it was fitted with false magnetic number plates and interrupted Vermeersch's sleep to bring him up to date. Vermeersch jumped into his car and arrived on the scene thirty minutes later. He noted every detail, took charge of the keys and the wallet, and found it a shame that Materne had been taken to hospital and that Louise Dubois had driven off. He gave the men orders not to tamper with the front door of the farmhouse, to type up a report, seal it and have it delivered by courier to the district chief in person. He then drove home, called Major de Vreker in spite of the late hour and gave him a detailed account. The men had an excellent relationship. They agreed not to inform the Public Prosecutor's Office as yet, and to start a parallel investigation in Brussels, Materne's home base. At nine o'clock the same morning, Sergeant Vermeersch, together with two Brussels CID officers, conducted a search of Materne's bachelor apartment on Monrosestraat in Schaarbeek without an official search warrant. They used the owner's keys, leaving no trace of a break-in. The men found an arsenal of weapons: three Kalashnikov machine pistols, two FAL NATO assault rifles with fitted infrared sights, eight Czech-made hand grenades, smoke bombs and an anti-tank missile, likewise from NATO.

The discovery was interesting, needless to say, but it took until eleven thirty before they found what they were really looking for: the address of Materne's employer (the detective agency Marlowe & Co.). The mystery of the Bineco delivery van was solved there and then, but an unexpected element came to light at one and the same time: the management of Marlowe & Co. had "special connections" with the Brussels CID. Two years earlier, the detective agency had been caught by a gendarme patrol breaking into an estate agent's in order to make copies of a number of documents. Brussels CID had struck an old-fashioned bargain. Marlowe & Co.'s licence, which would otherwise have been withdrawn on the spot, was left untouched as long as the agency agreed to pass on interesting information to the CID when required. You scratch my back, I'll scratch yours.

After the search, the CID officers informed a magistrate of the illegal procedure (the magistrate supplied them with a predated warrant – not exactly kosher but still the done thing – and told them everything was fine). They then drove to Marlowe & Co. and had a conversation with the director. When he had been informed of what had happened, he ordered Joost Voorhout, who happened to be in the office at the time, to organize a management meeting. The Dutch-born Belgian made the best of a bad bargain and tried to save his skin by confessing everything. He was fired on the spot.

The director was kindly invited to supply the name of his correspondent and the nature of the commissioned detective work. The correspondent's telephone number was typed into a special computer, which linked it with the Belgian Prelature of Opus Dei (something the director of Marlowe & Co. had known from the outset).

While the details were being noted, it became apparent that one of the CID men had more insight into the case than the others, particularly when it came to the implications of such of a surveillance assignment commissioned by an institution like Opus Dei against a senior magistrate. It could only have been blackmail, and at the highest level. But the most interesting element (the motive) still had to be found. The fact that a public prosecutor had evidently been keeping a mistress in a remote farmhouse was no more than a spicy piece of incidental information.

One of the Brussels CID men was reminded of a comment he had heard from an FBI colleague: "This is dynamite: if you push a case like this too far, the fucking shit will hit the fucking fan."

It was made crystal clear to the director of Marlowe & Co. that the matter was best kept under wraps, but he seemed to have taken the point. To his great relief, no one asked him if photos had been taken.

At around one thirty, the three arrived at the CID building on Leuvensesteenweg in Brussels. Sergeant Vermeersch called his district commander. Major de Vreker had just returned to his office after an intriguing visit to the farmhouse on the Oude Baan. He had helped to load the reluctant horse into a trailer and had driven back to Antwerp with Albert. He had barely sat down at his desk to dig in to a takeaway hamburger when the phone rang. De Vreker took note of what Vermeersch had to say, his brow furrowed. He whistled through his teeth when he heard the name *Opus Dei*, thought for a moment, and insisted that Vermeersch not blab about the affair and get himself to Antwerp as quickly as possible. Major de Vreker was a gendarme at heart, and his loyalty to the corps was his first priority. As far as he was concerned, double dealing Antwerp's Public Prosecutor's Office was all part of the picture. In addition, he was expecting to be promoted to lieutenant colonel the following October. He felt free to maintain his position, because expressions such as *Octopus Agreement* and *New Political Culture* – launched in the hysteria surrounding the Dutroux affair and aimed at the reform of Belgium's law-enforcement instances – had become something of a dead letter in the election campaign that was now in full swing. As usual, politicians based themselves on the memory of the average voter, which was a bit like a rabbit's tail, short and fluffy. Charles-Ferdinand Nothomb, a former speaker of the chamber of representatives, abundantly illustrated this reality when he said in the *Cercle Gaulois*: "The new political culture is like the Beaujolais nouveau: you drink it, you piss it."

As chair of the college of public prosecutors, Albert had always declared himself in agreement with the principles of judicial reform that had been proposed by the government (followed by inaction and waiting). Like Pontius Pilate, he washed his hands in innocence, because he knew from experience that such matters rarely progressed beyond declarations of principle. If need arose, the magistrates of the Supreme Court – who enjoyed the last word in such matters and staunchly defended the sanctity of the separation of powers – would cover him. It was fashionable among progressives to subscribe to the idea that on the eve of the twenty-first century, Belgium was being governed by a club of old men who thought they were still living in the nineteenth century.

As Major de Vreker finished his hamburger, Albert and Maria Landowska tucked into asparagus with butter sauce and chopped boiled egg, sprinkled with exquisite Meursault Charmes 1990 from the cellar of Amandine de Vreux d'Alembourg. Amandine had telephoned that morning, *nota bene*, to inform Maria that she would be returning the following Tuesday, 1 June.

"Ha haaa, then we have the place all to ourselves, Maria!" Albert cheered as Maria fed him asparagus tips like a baby bird. He was wearing jeans and a white Arrow sport shirt that set off his bronzed hairy arms. Every asparagus tip was followed by a peck on the lips.

"And if we have the place all to ourselves…" she said, her face more radiant than ever. He had never seen her wear eye make-up before, but the difference was amazing. Without her usual ponytail, she reminded him of one of Van Eyck's musical angels.

"We can do whatever we want, *kochanie.*"

"Say it again, Mr Albert."

"*Kochanie... Kochanie... Kochanie,*" he intoned. Head over heels at my age, he thought! Who would believe it?

When they had finished the asparagus, he opened a box containing a chocolate cake he had bought from the best patisserie in Antwerp.

"This calls for a Sauternes!" he proclaimed, scampering down to the cellar like a teenager.

14

At two thirty, after the director of Marlowe & Co. had more or less come to terms with the shock he had received with the help of a couple of serious whiskies and the application of a technique he called "self-brainstorming", he telephoned the Belgian Opus Dei prelature from a public callbox close to his office in a fit of paranoia, reinforced by the whisky. He was put through to Baron Hervé van Reyn, who had just returned from prayer in the chapel with the other numeraries. Fifty Ave Marias in honour of the month of Mary. Van Reyn spoke diplomatically of his appreciation for the documents and enquired once again about the invoice. The director first let van Reyn talk and then told him what had happened in elliptical police language, hiding nothing.

"I see," van Reyn mumbled sceptically. "And… er… are we facing an impasse, Mr Marlowe?" (He used the name mockingly.)

"To be honest, I would prefer to talk with you personally, Perálta —"

"Completely out of the question," van Reyn retorted. His head shuddered and his lips twisted as if he had just eaten something unpleasant, a notorious aristocratic tick he found impossible to suppress when confronted with the inane reactions of common folk.

"But I must insist, Perálta," the director persevered, "I must warn you —"

Van Reyn was immediately on his guard. "Is that right? And can you tell me why?"

"If you insist on the telephone…"

Van Reyn hesitated. He sensed that something serious was going on, but there were few things he found worse than losing face, a unmitigated betrayal of the family motto *Droit et en avant.*

"Fine, I'm listening," he said with evident reluctance.

"The bottom line is this…" the director continued, choosing his words with caution, "the documents you received from us within the framework of your assignment have been rendered unusable."

"In what way?" van Reyn interrupted in a high-pitched tone.

"Look, *monsieur*, let me tell you what the consequences would be for you should you decide to use them against my advice…"

"Mm…"

"We know, in the meantime, that the police investigators have informed the target of the incident in which a dog and a horse were shot."

"Thanks to the unbelievable gaffe of one of your, er… detectives."

"These things happen, *monsieur*," the director replied with little enthusiasm.

"So you're siding with that… that… I've no idea how to refer to such individuals."

"They were both fired on the spot."

"And so far we haven't made an inch of progress."

"May I continue?"

"Please do."

"Well, the fact that the target is the Public Prosecutor of Antwerp places him in a privileged position to dig up everything there is to be dug up about the case, if you get my drift."

"No, I don't… er… get your drift."

"We cannot use the photos under any circumstances."

"And why not?"

"Because blackmail on the basis of those photos might elicit a completely different reaction than we might have expected. The man is aware of certain information, which, should he wish to dig deeper, might point in our direction. Then we'll be left holding the baby and the authorities will turn their attention to us. There is one positive point, however: the police *are not aware* that photos were taken."

"Good, I see, but there's something else: has the relationship between... er... the target and that woman been seriously damaged by the incident?"

"The house is currently empty," the director replied in haste, a detail he had picked up from the Antwerp CID, which he shared against his better judgement, but it was the only way to calm his client down.

"The crucial element from *our* perspective is that the relationship with the woman in question remains broken..."

"I see..."

"What do you suggest we do to make sure he never meets the woman again?"

"The easiest thing would be to check his telephone calls."

"Tap them, you mean?"

"No, that would be impossible."

"Nothing is impossible."

"Believe me, Perálta. If it were possible, we would not hesitate to do it for you. Let me suggest the following: we use an electronic device to track outgoing and incoming calls, and check the corresponding addresses. Experience has taught us that interesting information will not be long in emerging."

"Agreed, but let me make another suggestion."

"Feel free."

"We're not prepared to pay for the botched operation."

"If you promise to return the photos to my office, then we have a deal."

"I presume you are insured against staff *blunders*."

"Er… Quite," was the director's cowed response.

"Then I'll have the photos returned as quickly as possible."

"Work will only recommence when we have them in our custody."

"*La confiance règne*."

"Indeed."

Baron Hervé van Reyn did not pursue the irony of the situation. Copies of the photographs had already been made and given to Paul Hersch. The originals were in his safe.

"Then I consider the matter closed," he said in a superior tone.

"*Au revoir*, Perálta."

"*Au revoir*." He was about to hang up, but continued in the nick of time: "Should I simply deposit the photos in your mail box?"

"We have a secure delivery box, similar to the one used by the banks."

"You'll have the photos this afternoon."

Hervé van Reyn returned the receiver to its cradle, placed both elbows on the desk in front of him, covered his eyes with his hands and held his breath for as long as he could. He used a breathing technique taught him by his friend Navarro Valls to organize his thoughts. He applied the technique when he was confused or when taken unawares by the occasional platonic temptation. When it slowly dawned on him that he still had an important trump card to play, namely the information on the Swiss bank account, he stretched his neck to the point that it hurt and remained in that position until he had counted to a hundred. He then stood up, stretched out his arms and started into an emotional recitation of the *Salve Regina*, Opus Dei's preferred prayer, which every numerary was expected to say at the end of every day:

Salve, Regina, Mater misericordiae,
vita, dulcedo, et spes nostra, salve.
Ad te clamamus, exsules filii Evae.
Ad te suspiramus, gementes et flentes
in hac lacrimarum valle.
Eia, ergo, advocata nostra, illos tuos
misericordes oculos ad nos converte;
et Iesum, benedictum fructum ventris tui,
nobis post hoc exilium ostende.
O clemens, O pia, O dulcis Virgo Maria.

The prayer had the desired effect. It gave him energy and a renewed awareness that he was a member of the elite guard in the army of Christ, sanctifying every second of his life by fulfilling the obligations of his state, such that his existence had become one long prayer.

He meditated further on Saying 3 of El Padre ("Let your outward conduct reflect the peace and order of your soul"), sat down and called the student house in Leuven. Without beating about the bush, he ordered Paul Hersch to postpone "the action – you know what I mean" until 1 June, after the month of Mary.

"And the photos are not to be used," he concluded.

"A very smart decision, if you ask me," Hersch responded cryptically.

After hanging up, Baron Hervé van Reyn walked over to the safe in the corner of his office, set the four-dial lock to the correct combination, opened it and removed a manila envelope. He asked himself if Mr Marlowe was naive enough to believe he would receive every existing copy of the photographs.

15

The period between Friday 28 May and Tuesday 1 June was dominated by two issues: the weather, which continued to be warm and dry with a gentle easterly wind, resulting from an anticyclone over Russia, and the apparent if temporary cessation of activities of those who, maliciously or unawares, had been spinning a web around Albert.

There was one exception: Albert's incoming and outgoing telephone calls continued to be registered by Marlowe & Co.'s Electronic Number Interceptor. Baron Hervé van Reyn called the detective bureau every evening at the stroke of six and took note of the numbers. When it appeared that Albert had not called Louise Dubois in Sint-Job-in-'t-Goor for two days in a row, van Reyn was tempted to give in to something he normally distrusted immensely: wishful thinking. He called the number himself on occasion, but there was never any answer. In order to be completely sure, he commissioned Marlowe & Co. to conduct an on-the-spot investigation. On Sunday 30 May at two o'clock in the morning, a team broke into the farmhouse using a counterfeit set of keys. In the meantime, Louise had asked her mother, with whom she was now living, to have the place emptied. This detail provided Baron Hervé van Reyn with sufficient certainty that her relationship with Albert Savelkoul had at least been compromised. He decided to wait a few more days before asking for a meeting with His Majesty's personal secretary. He had heard from Pla y Daniel that Amandine de Vreux was expected back in Belgium on 1 June. The day after, she was to be invited to appear at the office of Jozef Vromen, a lawyer in Ekeren, to arrange an important matter. Hervé van Reyn was also planning to be present.

Johan D'Hoog, Louise's vet friend, was the first protagonist to disappear suddenly from the scene. His UNESCO contract in Botswana was to begin on 1 July, but after a passionate farewell encounter with Louise in a rendezvous hotel opposite Antwerp's Museum of Fine Arts (just over half a mile from Amerikalei), he took a Sabena flight to Johannesburg on Saturday 29 May. Major de Vreker had told Albert that an international warrant for his arrest had been issued, but this was a lie. He passed through Zaventem airport unimpeded, and three hours after arriving in Johannesburg he joined a flight to Gaborone. From there he took a two-engine Cessna to Maun, where his friend David Robinson, registered guide with Okavango Wilderness Safaris, was awaiting his arrival. Robinson had taken off the entire month of June to go camping with D'Hoog in the Okavango Delta, one of the few places in Africa where the fauna still lived as it had done a thousand years ago. D'Hoog and Robinson had a particular bond. They had studied animal behaviour together in 1992 and 1993 at the University of Birmingham.

Louise was expected to fly out to Gaborone at the end of July, to stay with D'Hoog in the bungalow that UNESCO had placed at his disposal. Her first express letter, addressed to Mr J. D'Hoog, Private Bag 14, Maun, Botswana, arrived on 31 May in the box of what passed for the town's post office, a lopsided building with clay walls and a corrugated iron roof supported by pillars so riddled with termites they started to buzz when you knocked the door. The letter declared how insanely she loved him and how much she looked forward to the day they could *mate* for the first time under the sizzling African sun.

* * *

Louise lodged with her mother, who lived on her own in an enormous villa after divorcing her husband and bagging a tidy settlement. The villa was located in the leafy Maria-ter-Heide district near one of the Belgian army's artillery training grounds, where it had been as still as the grave for more than two years due to expenditure cuts at the Ministry of Defence. She spent her time smoking, walking Igor, watching TV and chatting to her mother if she wasn't in Brussels shopping or drinking coffee with one of her women's club – the exclusive "Montgomery" – girlfriends at some or other patisserie.

Conversations with her mother were conducted in a strange mixture of French and Antwerp dialect. They referred to Albert as "*le vieux schnook*", as a mark of their boundless disdain for all the stingy men in the world. Louise had told her the whole story, one hundred per cent faithful to reality for once, and she made no effort to hide the fact that she had a new lover. Her mother's only objection was to Botswana, where, like all of Africa, it was dirty, overrun with stinking Negroes and dangerous on account of the animal life. She advised her daughter to take Prozac, which she herself had done for years.

"There isn't a problem Prozac can't deal with," she claimed.

Major de Vreker thought long and hard before deciding on his tactics. He wavered between two priorities: his steadfast loyalty to the gendarmerie and his enviable relationship with Albert. The Flemish proverb "*het hemd is nader dan de broek*" – roughly equivalent to the English "charity begins at home" – finally won the toss. He hedged his bets in the first instance by putting together a carefully prepared report on the matter addressed to Colonel Spitaels, chief of the Operations Directorate at the General Staff in Brussels, and marked *Confidential*. The gendarmerie were still reeling from the voluntary resignation of corps commandant Lieutenant-General de Ridder in April

1998. The disgrace was ultimately the government's fault, which had apparently forgotten the gendarmerie's excellent record of service in the Dutroux affair for purely political reasons, namely the survival of the Deheane government at whatever cost until the crucial elections of 1999, the outcome of which de Vreker expected to be in line with the Belgian norm. The Old Political Culture (which he referred to as "that obstinate creature") had counted yet again on the manipulative capacity of disinformation in combination with the "common sense" of the average voter, who tended for the most part to make the most of it. Electoral upheaval was unlikely. In the days prior to the summer holidays, the population was more interested in practical, everyday issues, which mass marches, green protests and leftist agitation were unable to solve. The opposition conducted a short-sighted, reactionary election campaign and the gains of the Flemish National Front were considered a necessary evil (the extreme right was growing throughout Europe after all). The prime minister in question, nicknamed the cart horse, the plumber, the Texan bull and the viceroy of Absurdistan, was about to take leave of Belgian politics and be granted a well-deserved and well-paid job in one of the European institutions. The end of a chapter in Belgian history.

As a simple major, de Vreker could do no better than to secure his own position by exhibiting a degree of fair play towards Albert (keep his mouth shut in public about his girlfriend in Sint-Job-in-'t-Goor and avoid hasty conclusions about a possible connection with Opus Dei, the mysterious organization he planned to explore in the coming days out of simple curiosity). Both his identity and his future deserved priority. After all, thanks to his master's degree in law, he stood a substantial chance of being transferred to the Operations Directorate and finishing his career as a full colonel. He was surprised that Albert had not contacted him in recent days and could find no explanation for the man's silence, but he continued to keep a low profile.

Public Prosecutor Marc Keymeulen had had his suspicions about the Oude Baan affair from the outset. He was more or less familiar with "Cardinal Richelieu's" amorous relationship, but he was a humanist and he detested irrational conclusions. The matter was officially in the hands of one of his substitutes, and he allowed the man to get on with business without saying a word about the ambiguous position the Public Prosecutor's Office, which was under his leadership, now found itself in. On the one hand, it was a routine affair, which would probably result in a minor suspended sentence and the payment of damages for the loss of the horse. On the other hand, Albert had insisted on having access to the police report without making it official.

As public prosecutor, he had followed the only officially correct course of action possible: played dumb. It would have seemed a little suspicious if he had involved himself with the affair, even if only out of curiosity.

Although Marlowe & Co. had sacked Joost Voorhout, the director had lamented the loss of an excellent detective, in spite of the serious professional error related to the night of 26 May in Sint-Job-in-'t-Goor. A solution was found. Marlowe & Co. had a branch in Ghent, which was in a different judicial territory. Contact with police personnel who were familiar with the affair was virtually out of the question. He gave Voorhout a vigorous talking to, insisted this was his last chance, and then offered him a transfer to the Ghent office. Voorhout accepted and firmly resolved that he would keep his team under tight control in the future.

* * *

Jean Materne was recovering from a pelvis fracture in ward 3 on the second floor of Saint Luke's hospital in Antwerp. His condition was reasonable: forty-eight hours after the operation, the doctors had given him permission to totter around the ward on crutches for thirty minutes a day. No one, not even the surgeon, was aware of the facts of the case. CID sergeant Vermeersch, who had pretended to be a family member on a visit, had interrogated Materne on 30 May from behind a screen in relation to the illegal weapon collection in his apartment in Schaarbeek. Vermeersch, an expert in "exhorting information without intimidation", hit the jackpot in less than half an hour. He discovered a discrepancy between the first police report and the truth of the case: the police report contained nothing about the shooting of the pit bull by D'Hoog. Vermeersch was curious about the location of the weapon involved. He particularly wanted to question Louise Dubois on the matter, but if the substitute in charge of the investigation didn't order an interrogation, he could hardly ignore him and do so without permission. It remained possible that she was still in contact with Public Prosecutor Savelkoul (he had managed to tickle some of the details from an IT friend at the gendarmerie in Brussels who had also been responsible for inputting the Opus Dei information into the computer database). Unfortunately, he didn't know the substitute personally and was unable to call in any favours. His curiosity about the affair was driving him crazy.

Brecht gendarmes Verhaert and Ramael went about matters in a completely different way. Discretion was not their strong point and they hadn't so much as a notion of professional secrecy. Verhaert got drunk in a café on Brecht's market square after a provincial football match and spilled every detail, including names and places. It was the main point of conversation in the local shops the day after. The plot quickly evolved as the gossip machine invented and introduced new details. Within twenty-four hours "the tart with the horses... you know the one... hung herself from a beam in the garage because some rich bastard from Antwerp dumped her..." In some quarters, the "rich bastard" was a furniture manufacturer, in others a bigwig in the judiciary. Housewives cycling past the farmhouse on the Oude Baan stopped to peer through the windows. The empty buildings confirmed their theory that a terrible drama had taken place. Some versions were closer to the truth: D'Hoog, the vet from Brecht, regularly checked up on her horses and everybody knew he was a bit of a ladies' man who wasn't averse to settling his bills in bed. He had disappeared without a trace, and nobody believed the colleague who replaced him when he said that the man had been planning a trip to Africa for a long time. "Tell us another one..." was the usual reaction.

CID sergeant Vermeersch picked up on some of the gossip, but simply shrugged his shoulders. During a phone call with his friend Verhaert he said in his best Antwerp dialect: "Charley boy, what do women get up to when they've nothing gossip about? Ha, no idea? They look for something else to do!" At that point both men roared with laughter.

Soliman was stabled at the Black Stallion, a classy riding club in Schilde. He had a spacious box, received biologically balanced feed and fresh straw every evening, but he missed the calm of his old surroundings, Yamma his mother and the paddock where he was free to run and where every smell was familiar to him. The to-ing and fro-ing of stable boys and perfumed ladies who couldn't resist rubbing his nose made him nervous. And to top it all, he hadn't been introduced to any of the other horses! Two days after they brought him to the club in that bloody trailer, his boss had visited in the company of an unfamiliar woman, who did nice things and whispered strange words in his ear in a language his boss had never used. His boss had saddled him and they had done some dressage training in the manège, which smelled of unfamiliar sand and where a bunch of jabbering girls had taken lessons on horses that had flattened their ears when he got too close. His boss had lead him outside at that point to let him run loose in an open pen. He was able to fool around for a while before his boss dismounted to give the strange woman a ride. She had a much firmer hand than his boss and her movements were fairly abrupt, but she kept talking to him and when she had finally worked him into a gallop, he had reared up with vigour – just to free his mouth – and broken into a sprint with her, slinging his head from side to side and turning sharply, but he had not been able to shake her off. At that point, his boss did something he had never done before: clap hard with his hands. She then urged him into a comfortable trot, a gait he utterly detested, and her movements became gentler. The boss took over at the end and the woman clapped her hands as he had done.

For the first time since his ordination in 1974, in the cathedral of Toledo, where his grand-uncle had once been archbishop, Joaquín Pla y Daniel gave in to regression, something psychiatrists consider to be a natural defence mechanism against one of the most dangerous neuroses in existence, namely fixation. The focal point of his fixation had appeared thirty years earlier when he was studying philosophy at the University of Navarra, an Opus Dei institution in Pamplona: El Padre himself, the blessed Josemaría Escrivá. During a visit to the university, the extremely gifted student Pla y Daniel was introduced to Escrivá and given permission to kneel and receive his blessing, something he considered a great honour. From that moment onwards, something changed for ever in Pla y Daniel. His experience was like that of Saint Paul, who, according to Acts of the Apostles, was struck to the ground by a bolt of lightning. Pla y Daniel's youth had been marked by endless frustration at his heartless mother, which lead to his hatred of all women, and he became obsessed, with baroque Spanish fanaticism, with the figure of El Padre, pledging privately to live according to the letter of his writings and teachings. The second fixation, which appeared five years later, was a logical consequence of the first: he was appointed as mentor in the formation of a group of students who were in the preparatory phase of training to become numeraries, the highest grade of membership. His uncompromising character occasionally took him too far, and after the suicide of one of the candidates he was advised to soften his approach. His reaction was to do a nine-day retreat, fast completely, drink only water, wear the cilice throughout and endure the excruciating thigh cramps it caused, and subject himself to the discipline three times a day while reciting the *Salve Regina* at the top of his voice. After the retreat he continued his Spartan approach to formation unmitigated, as if nothing had happened. When one of the candidate numeraries flew at his throat in a bout of sudden rage, he was invited to an audience with El Padre himself, who admonished him paternally, transferred him to Rome and promoted him to procurator of the Institution, third in line to the top. His career had taken a considerably positive turn. Every door in the Vatican was now open to him, even that of John Paul II.

The regression that he was presently indulging took shape in his approach to the Belgian "girl" who was on retreat in the House. He had decided arbitrarily to "guide" her though the process, taking the Trident as his point of departure: penance; complete subjection to the mentor; strict and unremitting devotion. He intended to persevere until the goal of the Trident had been achieved: render the subject infantile, depersonalized and culpable (the condition of an innocent child bursting with feelings of guilt). Years of experience in Spain had taught him that the human spirit could be destabilized with relative ease using isolation, repetition and exhaustion. He chose the food she would eat, for example, limiting her to dry bread with a glass of Roman tap water, which tasted of chlorine. The isolation process consisted of a prohibition against conversation with others and the requirement to perform a series of duties, including the submission of a two-hourly written report to the mentor of the entire group, a Basque by the name of Pedro Ruiz Arcaute, who hailed from the same region as blessed Josemaría and was equal to Pla y Daniel in zealous piety. Lectures were given every day that paid little attention to the end of the Cold War and warned against three dangers: crypto-Marxism and Freemasonry, which destroy religion; sexuality, which turns humans into animals; and subjectivism, which leads to tolerance. According to the *amalgama* method, the said three dangers were always referred to in a single breath, as if they were one and the same.

Every day, lengthy talks and meditations were given on one's duty to be an instrument in the hands of God, according to the magisterium of the Catholic Church, which would ultimately be taken over by Opus Dei with world domination as the final goal.

If there was anything wrong in the written reports, the "girls" were collectively humiliated with one of El Padre's sayings: *Don't fly like a barnyard hen when you can soar like an eagle.* Amandine had dared to say that she did not understand the connection. She was ridiculed: a woman did not have to *understand*, she had to *function* within the role pattern ascribed to her. She needed time to discuss the matter with God in prayer, was her retort. Ruiz snapped that it was inappropriate to make reference to

God in public. When she replied with tears in her eyes that she wanted to dedicate her life to Him alone, she was advised with a snigger to dedicate herself to the "Apostolate of Not-Giving", leaving her even more confused than ever.

At a certain moment, her room was cleared of furniture and the showers were closed. Ruiz dismissed her concerns and gave her orders to write a commentary on the subject "Detachment from whatever is not of God": objects, persons, the self, one's own ideas, health, time, leisure, study, work, family, money, self-satisfaction...

Her concern about being unable to talk to her eldest son in Leuven (she had made several attempts but the line was dead) was met with an admonition to avoid the people she loved, because feelings of attachment were inclined to encourage time-wasting. In addition to this, it was forbidden to examine the origins of one's own uneasiness in this regard. An infamous Jesuit humiliation, employed on occasion by Paul Hersch, was similarly part of Ruiz's drill: the use of "spiritual *eleemosynae*", an Opus Dei expression for public humiliation by the other group members, who exposed one's shortcomings in a feigned effort to encourage a change of ways. Amandine was accused of being pretentious. She was devastated, but managed to contain herself with difficulty. She lost several nights' sleep over the remark, and even the silent recitation of the *Salve Regina* lying on the hard floor (according to the regulations, the night silence prohibited praying out loud) did not help.

At the end of three days, the lack of food had left her in a permanent state of weakness. She had also been required to hand in her credit card to cover "costs". She had left her passport in her room at the Casa Belgica on Via Omero, but someone from Opus Dei had collected it together with her luggage. Each evening, two bank transfer slips were left next to her bread and water, one for the daily "generosity" collection and one for the purchase of flowers. She refused one of her obligations without drawing attention to the fact: kissing the floor when she got up in the morning. She had been unable to overcome her obsessive hatred of dirty floors.

When the retreat finally came to an end at three in the afternoon on 31 May, Amandine felt as if she had just begun to recover from a bad flu, physically and mentally exhausted. To round off her visit, and much to her surprise, she was invited to have dinner with Pla y Daniel in one of the opulent salons of the House, the very place in which El Padre used to entertain select company in the past, what he called "the apostolate of the table".

The table was adorned with antique linen, Sèvres porcelain on gilded plates, cutlery, crystal glasses and candles in a *golden* candelabra. She was well enough informed about Opus Dei to know that it was *solid* gold.

The courses were served by female Opus Dei candidates in simple attire, who brought each plate and nodded without a saying a word. The magnificent sideboards and leather-clad walls lacked any form of religious symbolism. A glass display cabinet, containing at least a hundred porcelain, bronze, wood, terracotta, papier-mâché and metal donkeys, decorated one of the corners. El Padre insisted it was his favourite animal, and liked to tell his guests that he was "the humble donkey of Christ".

The many courses were accompanied by the most exquisite wines, at which Amandine guardedly sipped. She politely refused a serving of risotto with white truffles. Pla y Daniel ate and drank to his heart's content, summoned the waitresses with a table bell, dismissed them with a wave of the hand and launched into a series of Vatican jokes about the Pope and the curial cardinals. Puffing at a quality Havana cigar over coffee, he finally returned to the point; his expression turned cold and vacant, and he issued strict orders for 2 June, when she was to attend a meeting with a "notary of our choosing" in the company of a Belgian numerary. Pla y Daniel rounded the evening off by handing her an envelope containing a bill for the retreat, her credit card, her passport and her airline tickets.

Paul Hersch's approach to Didier Savelkoul differed considerably to the treatment the young man's mother had received in Rome. Hersch was beside himself with rage at having walked into Hervé van Reyn's trap and fallen for his intimidation technique. He was now being obliged to do something he detested – complete an assignment for which he was not trained, an assignment that would backfire on him if it were to fail. The stench of double standards was enough to make even Machiavelli proud, but he didn't give a damn.

He was tense and restless, like an imprisoned rat searching for an escape route. His paranoid mind saw only one solution: *someone else* had to pay the price. And was there anyone more appropriate for the job than Didier Savelkoul, the incarnation of moral masochism? He decided to give him his "preferential treatment", which he used on occasion to break rebellious candidates: he ignored him completely. When they crossed each other's path somewhere in the building, he would turn his head and enjoy the thought of Savelkoul's wincing face, like a terrified child looking up from a deep well. He usually invited him to visit his office once a day to discuss matters of concern and hear him out on his fellow students. He was well aware that these meetings were important to Savelkoul, providing him an opportunity to recharge the batteries of his identity. But Hersch's house line had been blocked for three days in a row. His office, where he spent up to fourteen hours a day studying new "psychological formation techniques", and where he was now taking his meals, remained unaired.

He would sit for hours ruminating and fretting, like a sitting giant with the brachycephalic head of a Saxon farmer, brooding on the best way to satisfy his lust for revenge.

He finally made his move at midnight on 29 May. With the softest of voices, he appointed Savelkoul superintendant in charge of buildings, knowing full well that his assistant hated practical matters of this kind.

His behaviour during the weekly jog was equally bizarre: he encouraged the stragglers to keep up with vulgar and foul language. All this had to do with an increasing self-hatred brought on by his inability to square up to van Reyn. The stuck-up petty aristocrat with his toffee-nosed lingo would probably have been obliged to accept his response. His usual psychological defence mechanisms had failed him one after the other. For the first time in his life he had taken sleeping pills for three nights in a row.

Baron Hervé van Reyn was in the best of form. He had spoken with notary Vroman and prospects were excellent. They had examined the notarial deed of purchase together and formulated a proposal to be presented to Amandine de Vreux. The properties were not to be *donated* to Opus Dei, for the simple reason that the Institute would thus be faced with a bill from the Belgian state for up to eighty per cent of the value of the gift (68,800,000 Belgian francs) in registration fees. Rather, Amandine de Vreux was to sell the properties to an anonymous company by the name of Rumpus, one of Opus Dei's numerous fiscal and legal fronts. Van Reyn was to hand her the sale price in cash (in an attaché case), and she was to sign for receipt in the presence of the notary. Once they had left the scene of purchase Amandine was to return the attaché case to van Reyn. The money itself came from Atlantis, a non-profit organization used by Belgium's Opus Dei to launder its undeclared income. A reduced registration fee of 12.5 per cent (8,600,000 Belgian francs) was considered a reasonable price to pay.

A notarial donation had thus been transformed by fraudulent means into an act of sale, with the sole purpose of avoiding payment of eighty per cent registration fee to the Belgian state. Baroness Amandine de Vreux was not informed that her heirs (her two sons), both partially disinherited by this fraudulent procedure, would have to face much more serious difficulties after her death. The Belgian tax authorities would then present them with a substantial bill (art. 108 of the Belgian fiscal code on inheritance rights) for the enormous revenue acquired from the property sale (of which their mother had not received a single cent). Opus Dei was completely indifferent to the fact that both Savelkoul sons would be considerably disadvantaged by their actions (Geoffroy wasn't even a member). Pla y Daniel, who had studied law in Spain, spoke with Hervé van Reyn on the telephone about the question. Wasn't Opus Dei acting in total contradiction to the principles of Belgian civil law? Monseigneur van Reyn had replied with a snigger that the boys would be ill-advised to challenge Opus Dei on the matter without the help of a very good lawyer. He was simply too euphoric to worry about it. Everything appeared to have gone according to plan. Developments in that unsavoury affair with the whore also appeared to be moving in the right direction. Strangely enough, it had become a point of honour for van Reyn that the two sons be granted an aristocratic title. After all, Belgium's Opus Dei would then be a baron richer. Before contacting the royal court, however, he had to wait for the result of Paul Hersch's operation, which was set to begin on 2 June. It was all very strange. The only person to remain completely free of guilt up to that point was the man himself, the guilty party. Van Reyn had sworn to bring him to his knees. He considered the five million francs stashed away in the Swiss bank account a mere bagatelle, which Opus Dei fully deserved.

On Monday 31 May, the date of the second fortnightly meeting of Antwerp's Rotary Club, Albert appeared an hour later than was his custom. The Rotarians were settling down to their main course and the atmosphere was the same as always, a little like a London gentlemen's club: the executive members wore ribbons of honour round their necks to signify their function, and the entire company was dressed as one would expect of such a gathering. The conversation was animated and the wine abundant. Albert's chair, between Walter de Ceuleneer and Georges Weyler, was empty. He took his place, emptied a glass of water in one gulp and asked for a refill.

"Alberto, how are you?..." enquired Weyler with a roguish wink.

"Jokke, prostate is all in the mind," Albert answered with a hoarse voice and pointed to his forehead.

"You look the worse for wear, if you don't mind me saying," Weyler continued.

Walter de Ceuleneer took over: "You look like a dog after a night's scavenging, man," he said and burst out laughing.

Albert did not react. His main course was served – traditional guinea fowl with peas and mashed potatoes. He started to eat with little enthusiasm and said nothing. He sipped at the wine. Mediocre. Baroness Amandine was expected home the next day. No more hours of contentment in the company of Maria Landowska, who would have to appear once again in her prim black dress, white collar and starched cuffs and say "yes ma'am, no ma'am". The most important thing was that he keep their sexual relationship a secret. Amandine had a special nose for such things. Hypocrite that she was, she would keep it to herself and then strike at an unexpected moment, like a spider attacking a fly caught in its web. He knew precisely how it would happen. He would arrive home one fine day to find that Maria Landowska had been summoned urgently to Poland for the funeral of a family member. The Canon of Antwerp's cathedral chapter would take care of a replacement. The piss-smelling old bugger had a set up a profitable business with some or other Polish bishop providing irreproachable young Polish servant girls for irreproachable Catholic Belgian families. The very thought of it sickened him. After no more than fifteen minutes he was bored to death. When dessert appeared on the table, he looked at his watch and said: "Sorry, gents, time for me to go."

"Aha, Alberto has a date," said Georges Weyler.

"Of course I have a date," he replied calmly. "Why else would I have to leave?"

"By the way, man," said de Ceuleneer, placing a confidential arm around Albert's shoulder. "We're off stalking in Scotland again next week," he said, unashamed of his Antwerp brogue. "Stag. Fancy joining us? Bring young Louise along. The horses are standing by and Patricia's looking forward to a visit from her Scottish Sister, hahaha."

"Sounds good," said Albert expressionlessly. "Give me a buzz when you know the exact dates?"

"Righto. Enjoy yourself, eh?"

Albert stood, waved to his fellow diners and they waved back.

After he had left, de Ceuleneer asked Weyler if something was wrong. "He looks *terrible*."

"Problems downstairs."

"And him with a young filly to entertain… That's a problem all right."

"We're all in the same boat, Walter. It's just a matter of time."

Walter de Ceuleneer, who hadn't really understood what Weyler had said, peered at him wryly and tossed back the remainder of his wine.

Albert turned the front-door key, pushed it open and was embraced there and then by a pair of muscular arms.

"Oh Maria, *moja kochanie*," he whispered in the warmth of her ear. Lips met lips, teeth, a warm tongue... Two hands deftly loosened his tie and she threw her legs in the air like a dancer, gripping his waist with her knees. They staggered up the stairs of the vestibule and he grabbed her ponytail, pulling it until she groaned.

"Mr Albert, oh Mr Albert, I'm soooo *bosko*," she said in a mixture of Polish, Flemish and German, her vivid boyish voice turning suddenly hoarse. She rested her head on his shoulder and started to cry.

"Maria, don't cry," he said. He put her down on the marble floor, kicked open the door with its ground-glass windows and embraced her. His hand disappeared under her skirt, pulling her panties aside and penetrating her warm, damp and slippery pussy with his middle finger.

She buckled in his arms and held her breath. He kissed her naked arms and gave her goosebumps. Her skin was covered in fine blond hair and there was a vague scent of perfume. He bored his nose into her armpit and bit at the fur. He recognized Davidoff, his own deodorant. When his finger found its way to her clitoris, her lips tightened and she pushed back her buttocks until he had slipped out. She took his head in both hands and said: "I've made dinner."

"First champagne?" he asked, eye to eye, his nose rubbing gently back and forth against hers.

"I'd rather have *wódka*."

"*Wódka* it is."

He chuckled, happy, reckless, young, anticipating what they would do together in the hours that followed, without a thought for the next day, when the arrival of the lady of the house would plunge him into the same bloody grind he would have to endure until the end of his days. He could barely stomach the idea.

The table in the kitchen was set for a feast, with a white embroidered tablecloth, porcelain, crystal, silverware, candles and napkins.

She gazed at him wide-eyed, pressed herself against him and asked if he was *zadowolony*.

"What does that mean?"

"Content."

"*Absolutnie*."

"Aren't you going to change?"

"You're right. Let's go upstairs."

They climbed the stairs. When they passed the statue of Our Lady on the first landing he noticed fresh lilies.

"Fuck," he snorted.

She quickly blessed herself.

"Why do you do that?" he asked bluntly.

"It's not right to curse in front of Our Holy Mother."

"Fuck."

"Mr Albert, it's not up to me. *Madame* insists on flowers. And tomorrow…"

"Stuff tomorrow," he hissed.

"Stuff tomorrow?"

What he wanted to say was: "They can kiss my arse", but he contained himself: "I couldn't care less," he translated.

She nodded, still not quite sure what he was talking about. "Madame also uses a word I don't understand," she said, looking him in the eye.

"What word?"

"En-cyc-lical," she spelled.

He exploded with laughter and she stared at him in surprise.

"That's from her father. If something annoyed him he would always say '*Encyclique*', in French. Then he would tell his household *what* had annoyed him. It was usually something to do with leaving lights on, using too much toilet paper or forgetting to lock the door."

"Was he a poor man?"

"No, Maria. The richer the tighter! Do you know what an 'encyclical' is?"

"No."

"It's a letter from the Pope to the Catholics of the world containing his infallible teaching."

"Infallible?"

"Without the possibility of error."

"Oh, I see," she said, pursing her lips.

"Don't you like the Pope? Isn't he Polish?"

"No," she replied, her eyes pinched.

He looked at her with a smile. You're so cute, he thought.

"Priest, bishop, the Pope, they're all *gówno*."

"Mmm?"

"Shit?" she translated.

"And I thought you were such a good Catholic!"

"I know all about that sort. My mum was screwed by the local parish priest and when she got pregnant he dumped her."

"And then?"

"Abortion," she said, gesturing with her hand in front of her belly as if she were chasing a fly. "But she put a curse on him. *Rak*. Cancer. Dead."

"Oh Maria..." He took her face in his hands and kissed her gently on the lips.

"Mr Albert, *ich liebe dich*," she announced. "I don't want to leave you." She pressed herself against him with all her might.

Albert had to control his emotions. "You're a good woman, Maria," he said. "You're type three according to Buddha."

She closed her eyes and did not ask what he meant. She unbuttoned his shirt, ripped it open and kissed him again and again on his hair-covered chest. She then checked between his legs. Nothing.

"Tonight," she said resignedly, and she tapped his nose with her index finger.

God preserve me, thought Albert. They had pushed out the boat the last three days and he needed a miracle to get him through the last night. If only he had met her twenty years ago, he thought, running his hand over her back.

She stood on the tips of her toes and held her breath, lifted her skirt, slipped her panties to one side and stretched her labia apart with two fingers to reveal her clitoris. He kneeled and started to talk to her pussy at first, telling it not to be naughty, that it was his "rascal", his "honey pie", his "ball of quicksilver", his "sweet little party animal". When he started to lick it, she stretched her back and squeezed her thighs together until they were hard as ivory. And she came quickly, violently, howling like a wolf.

She loosened her ponytail, knelt beside him and covered his neck and face with an abundance of fragrant hair.

"When I rode Soliman, I had the same… The same happened," she said, and she started to laugh.

"You ride like a she-devil."

"Soliman is a man-devil. Good horse… very good horse."

"He'll throw you off one of these days if you keep pulling at his mouth like that."

"Pff…"

"How many times have you fallen from a horse?"

"Hundreds of times."

They burst into a fit of laughter.

Out of the blue she said: "Come with me to Poland, Mr Albert. There's so much countryside in Poland. You're a farmer at heart..."

"That's true. I was raised on a farm."

"Poland has plenty of wild boar to shoot with your rifle."

They walked arm in arm to the bedroom, where he put on a pair of jeans and a black T-shirt.

As they made their way downstairs, he asked her where she had learned to ride a horse.

"My uncle had horses. I learned bareback."

"Really?"

She formed a saddle with her hands.

"Did you get the same... er... in those days?" he said, pointing to her lower belly.

"Sometimes," she replied in perfect Antwerp dialect, her eyelids fluttering coquettishly.

He stopped in his tracks. "Feel this," he said proudly.

She pressed her hand against the front of his jeans. "Hurrah!"

They rushed downstairs together.

She stood to attention next to the kitchen table like a soldier. "En-cyc-lical," she said dramatically and saluted.

Albert looked on as she set the table. He had never felt so young, so delightfully indifferent to the consequences of his deeds.

"Maria, the fork with the teeth downwards! White wine glass right. Red wine glass left. Water glass to the rear! Oh, but what have you done, this is simply *ghastly*!" he said in French, imitating his wife's high-pitched voice. "Don't forget, Maria, Madame is a *baroness*..."

She looked at him enquiringly.

"People like her always call this sort of... crap *ghastly*. Serious matters are usually *unpleasant* or *bothersome*." He gave a perfect imitation of the aristocratic gesture of the hand with which "people who don't belong in our circles" tended to be dismissed.

"In Poland, the Russians shot every one of them," she said. "Bang, bang, bang!"

"That'll never happen here in Belgium," he replied absently.

"Bah!" she yelled all of a sudden, lifting her dress and exposing her buttocks.

He gave them a sound slap.

She jumped forward in the direction of the fridge and took out a bottle of vodka.

"Dreenk?"

"Why not. Let's get plastered."

She returned to the fridge, took a five-ounce tin of caviar from the door, fetched a knife and opened the lid.

"Spoons!" he exclaimed, opening the sideboard drawer.

She poured two stiff vodkas. They drank and spooned caviar from the tin.

"Mr Albert..."

"Maria..."

"What are we going to do when Madame is here?"

"Encyclical," he announced solemnly, throwing back his head and pouting his lips.

She was clearly taken aback.

"I'll come... to your room. *Schluss!*"

"D'you mean it?"

He held his fingers to his mouth in a v-sign and licked.

They ate caviar and drank vodka.

"Mr Albert..."

"Yes, Maria..."

"Why am I type three?"

"Later, Maria. Later..."

16

Tuesday 1 June, 10.35 am. Dressed in a beige two-piece with milky nylons, black patent shoes, glasses hanging from a chain around her neck and the perfect Queen Paola hairdo, Baroness Amandine de Vreux emerged from exit two of the national airport, pushing a baggage trolley with a grey suitcase and a Louis Vuitton travel bag. Albert's chauffeur caught sight of her and rushed to her assistance.

"Good morning, Madame," he said stiffly, taking over the trolley. She glanced at him and nodded.

"The car is close by," said the chauffeur.

She nodded again and looked in the opposite direction.

The chauffeur took the suitcase and travel bag and carried them towards the exit. It was chilly outside and rain had settled in the day before.

Baroness de Vreux looked at the sky as if it was to blame for everything. The chauffeur held open the passenger door of the black Opel and she stepped inside.

He loaded the baggage, hissed "arsehole", settled down at the wheel and drove off.

The telephone rang at the Public Prosecutor's Office at 11.05. A gentle, polite male voice asked to speak to the Public Prosecutor in person. The switchboard put him through to his secretary, who enquired as to the reason for his call.

"I would prefer to discuss the matter with the Public Prosecutor himself," the man answered calmly.

"I'll put you through, sir."

She transferred the call to Albert's office, where he was listening attentively to Barrister-General Bergé's weekly briefing, a duty he found relatively interesting, all things considered.

"Yes," he answered.

"I have someone on the line who wishes to talk to you in person, Public Prosecutor."

"On the phone?"

"Yes."

Albert had a hangover from the vodka and wine he had guzzled the evening before, but was nevertheless in the best of spirits. He had managed – *in extremis* – to satisfy Maria *completely*, and this had given him the energy to deal with the less pleasant prospects of the day ahead.

"Put him through," he said, lifting the receiver. "Hello?"

"Is this Public Prosecutor Savelkoul?" a soft male voice enquired in standard Dutch with a hint of a French accent.

"Speaking."

Barrister-General Bergé stood according to custom and enquired with a gesture if he should leave the room, but Albert waved him back to his seat.

"Would it be possible to meet?" the man asked.

"What about?"

"I would prefer to tell you in person."

"But… with whom do I have the honour?"

"Jean Maraudy de Moretus."

Not another aristocrat, Albert thought, but his curiosity had been aroused.

"Fine. When would you be free?" Albert enquired, pen and paper at the ready.

"This evening."

"Where?"

"In front of the church in Kortenberg."

"Kortenberg? That's miles away!"

"Would you prefer to meet somewhere else?"

"No," Albert snapped. "What time?"

"Would nine o'clock suit?"

"Nine is good for me. How will I recognize you?"

"I'll be standing in front of the church door in Brouwerstraat. I'm small-built and a little chubby. I'll be wearing glasses… and a hat."

"Good. See you in Kortenberg at nine."

Albert hung up and invited Barrister-General Bergé to continue his briefing with a nod.

Bergé was short, bald and corpulent, sixty-two going on seventy. His blue lips betrayed a heart problem. In addition to holding his own top-level position at the Public Prosecutor's Office, he was also designated "the inquisitor". His job was to deal with disciplinary matters relating to CID officers, the metropolitan police, the gendarmerie, court bailiffs, lawyers, notaries public and lower-ranking sitting magistrates. He did his job with painstaking accuracy, which basically meant he was absolutely unrelenting, especially when it came to the conduct and good name of the legal system. Bergé examined every anonymous letter in minute detail, and he worked hard and late whenever necessary to get to the bottom of the accusations they contained. His own conduct was unimpeachable. He had been a widower for six years and belonged to one of Antwerp's most conservative Catholic families. In legal circles, however, he wasn't the brightest. It was thanks primarily to the support of the right wing of the Christian People's Party that he had been able to climb to the upper echelons and establish himself at the same time as a staunch defender of the Old Political Culture. He mocked Belgium's New Political Culture as "an insecticide" and "interference". He was an expert in the typically Belgian procedure of mixing unrelated conflicts in such a way that they neutralized one another. He thus gave the impression that he favoured change, but his real goal was to maintain the status quo, the only plausible stance an intelligent conservative could take, he insisted. Albert hated him with a vengeance but never let it show. He was a dirty old man, with liver spots on his scalp and a disgusting body odour. Bergé's only positive side was that he kept Albert up to date with the gossip that was doing the rounds, most of which contained more than a grain of truth. In addition, the man reminded Albert Savelkoul of the fact that he was two years older, yet still had the look of a playboy. He gave him every due respect, following the adage of ex-president Lyndon B. Johnson about Edgar Hoover: it's better to have him inside the tent pissing out than outside the tent pissing in. Bergé's attitude to bourgeois society was nineteenth-century. He considered it a sort of insurance policy for the hereafter.

What fascinated Albert most about the man was his face: Barrister-General Bergé's face was an amalgamation of expressions that appeared to be divided into unconnected units, leaving him, at least so it seemed, completely faceless. He was incredibly meticulous and methodical, puzzlingly ambiguous, nitpicking and one-dimensional, making him particularly useful for certain tasks, such as prying into other people's sex lives. Albert himself could not abide such business and only took pleasure in it during mundane meetings or get-togethers at his club.

But he was finding it difficult to stay focused. Thoughts of the wonderful night with Maria and the imminent return of Amandine soured his mood, although he planned to make an adventure of the situation: the stupid nun, that sanctimonious bitch, was not going to prevent him from continuing a bloody satisfying relationship under the roof of the house she had received from her daddy to celebrate the tenth anniversary of her failed marriage. The opportunity was not to be missed.

By 11.25 he had had enough. He looked at his watch and said he had to go. Out of politeness, he asked Bergé how far he was with the inaugural speech he was writing on Albert's behalf, which was to be delivered at the opening of the judicial year in September. The presentation rejoiced in the title: 'The Administration of Justice and Territorial Jurisdiction'.

"It'll be ready on time, Public Prosecutor," Bergé answered with a contented grin, which made his chubby lips curl.

Condescending little bastard, thought Albert, knowing full well he would have to adapt the style of everything but the footnote references, which, as ever, would be perfectly correct.

When Bergé was gone he thought once again to himself: what a wreck! He had once scribbled an excellent description of "Old People" in a luxury desk diary he had received from the General Bank, which he used for the sole purpose of noting his thoughts and musings. He fished the diary from the drawer, surreptitiously slipped on his reading glasses and found the text almost immediately: "One should be on one's guard when old people appear helpless. When they can no longer rely on their powers of persuasion, they're reduced to bragging about their authority. Experience can help in this regard, but most of the time they've forgotten it. They talk incessantly, because they're afraid of losing track of their thoughts. They resort to tyranny because they sense that others no longer respect them. They're impatient because they know their life is coming to its end. They're distrustful, because they can no longer check up on things, and irritable, because they know people are laughing at them behind their back."

Albert closed the diary pensively and was overwhelmed by a surge of melancholy. Am I irritable, he asked himself? Do I lose the thread sometimes in conversation? Am I authoritarian? Perhaps the latter was true, he conceded, recalling his enthusiasm for one of Napoleon's adages: "Obedience is only for officers beneath the rank of general".

He looked at his watch and cursed. The nun was about to

arrive at her ancestral abode and recite the first of many *Salve Reginas* in front of that infernal statue, he thought. Shit!

At 11.30, the precise moment that Baroness Amandine de Vreux crossed the threshold of her town house on Amerikalei in Antwerp, the door having been opened by Maria Landowska dressed in a black below-the-knee dress with a white collar and cuffs, nylon stockings and cheap black moccasins, Paul Hersch telephoned Baron Hervé van Reyn and immediately came to the point: everything was "in the bag" for that evening at nine o'clock in front of the church in Kortenberg.

"You're kidding," van Reyn responded with a nervous giggle. "Was it as easy as it sounds?"

"You'll see. I'll call you again tomorrow. Cheers," said Hersch and he hung up.

He was still furious with himself for falling into van Reyn's trap. The very idea that he had also given his word on the matter in a moment of rash haste simply infuriated him even more.

After looking her servant girl up and down a couple of times, Baroness de Vreux's first word was: "*Encyclique.*"

Maria Landowska looked at her. Maria had bags under her eyes and appeared to have touched up her eyelashes.

"In my house, the servants do not wear make-up," Baroness Amandine snapped. She pointed to her suitcase and travel bag and slowly ascended the vestibule's marble stairs. Maria Landowska followed with the baggage. She was reminded of the way Mr Albert had carried her up the same stairs the evening before and hissed: "Shit!"

At the stroke of twelve, Baron Hervé van Reyn telephoned the detective agency Marlowe & Co. and was immediately put through to the director.

"Perálta," he said.

"I'm listening," said the director.

"Can you send one of your men to the church in Kortenberg this evening at nine sharp?"

"What would he be expected to do?"

"Shadow the same… er… target as in Antwerp. Someone is expecting him at the church door. Only the target is to be shadowed."

"Should we take photos?"

"No! No unnecessary risks."

"We never take unnecessary risks, Perálta," was the director's uppish response.

"I should hope so. I'll call back tomorrow at nine."

"Ten would be better."

"Shadow the man, Mr Marlowe, nothing else."

"Bye bye, Perálta."

Hervé van Reyn returned the receiver to the cradle, looked at his watch and realized he was fifteen minutes late for the Angelus in the chapel. He pulled the same face as that of his great-grandfather, whose portrait still graced the walls of "Beukenloo", the family castle in 's-Gravenwezel, picked up the wooden figureless cross that enjoyed a permanent place on his desk next to his right hand, kissed it, held it tight and thought of Josemaría Escrivá's Saying 82: "First prayer; then, atonement; in the third place – very much in the third place – action."

"*Salve Regina, Mater misericordiae,*" he prayed, his eyes closed, cross in hand.

After five *Salve Reginas*, he meditated for a time on penance and atonement. He would wear the cilice after lunch. After thirty minutes the pain would be unbearable. He preferred not to think about "action" for the time being.

At two thirty, Baroness Amandine de Vreux was opening her mail, her glasses perched on the end of her nose. She arranged the letters into two piles: *reply* and *file*. The second pile consisted of worthless junk mail and advertising material, which she collected, nevertheless, in a sturdy cardboard folder held shut with an elastic band. It was an obsession she had inherited from her mother: never throw anything away. A row of cupboards in the house was filled to bursting with things she had been keeping for years. Her grandmother's evening dresses, military uniforms of family members who had fought during the war, toys belonging to her parents, her sons and herself, school books, piles of newspapers and magazines tied together with string, boxes, wrapping paper, bed linen, etc., everything neatly arranged and folded, each cupboard with a list of contents on the inside of the door. Every now and then she would walk through the rooms, open one of the cupboards, gaze at its contents and savour the enormous satisfaction it brought her.

After dealing with her correspondence, she studied the list of telephone messages Maria had scribbled in her crooked handwriting. There was only one worth answering immediately, from Thérèse de Montignac, old French aristocracy and married, like herself, to a commoner. Thérèse loved gossip. Amandine returned the call.

"*Ma chère* Amandine..."

"*Quelles nouvelles, ma chère* Thérèse?"

"You were away last week."

"Yes, I was in England looking at gardens."

"Where did you stay, if it's not indiscreet of me to ask?"

"With Edith and Noël Beiresford-Peirse."

"Mmm... Do they still have that *sublime* estate?"

"Yes, it's truly *incredible*. And the weather was *magnifique*."

"Just like here. *Insanely* beautiful, all last week, until yesterday in fact."

"You called when I was away?"

"Mmm..."

"Do I get to know why?" Amandine tested the water with a nervous chuckle.

"But of course, *ma chère*; but it's... eh... a little *delicate*... if you get my drift. Are you alone?"

"I'm alone."

"*Eh bien, ma chère*, I'm duty bound to keep you informed... let me see... on Saturday 29 May around seven in the evening, I was at the Zwarte Hengst in Schilde, you know, where I keep my horse..."

"Mmm..."

"And I saw your husband there."

"..."

"Hello?"

"I'm listening."

"*Eh bien*, he was horse-riding in the company of another woman."

"Nothing new."

"Perhaps, but they were in jeans and T-shirts with those vulgar training shoes, you know the sort. And the woman was like a savage on horseback..."

"Well, well. And what did she look like?"

"Sturdy. Well endowed. A red ponytail... a real floozy. And they were so sweet to one another. I was struck by one particular detail: when I passed them in the bar, I noticed she had a row of metal teeth... a *ghastly* sight..."

Baroness Amandine de Vreux turned pale, closed her eyes and was unable to speak. "*Un grand merci*, Thérèse," she squeaked. "I'll call you back later, *au revoir*."

She slowly returned the receiver to its cradle, removed her glasses and rubbed her eyes. She dragged herself to her feet, shuffled step by step to the corner of the room, where a tiny statue of Our Lady was perched on a plinth against the wall, folded her hands and started to pray.

17

Albert parked his car on Brouwerstraat, which opened out onto the Church of Our Lady in Kortenberg. He got out, closed the door and looked around. Little traffic, empty streets. Typically Belgian, he thought, everyone's glued to the box. He made his way towards the church, its ridiculous tower peeking out above the rooftops. The man was standing next to a larger-than-life statue of the Sacred Heart carved in stone. He was wearing a dark raincoat and hat, and was, as expected, short and rotund.

Albert approached the man with confidence, stopping about fifteen yards from where he was standing. He was sure the man had seen him, but without some sign of recognition he couldn't be certain.

Albert marched over to him and said unabashedly: "Didn't we have an appointment?"

"Indeed."

He had the same voice as the man on the phone, but he didn't look the least bit aristocratic. Albert had consulted a list of aristocratic families, the Gotha Almanac, at home and the name Maraudy de Moretus was not mentioned.

"What should we do?" Albert asked curtly.

"Shall we go to my car?"

"Do we have to?"

"Don't you trust me?"

"Depends on you."

Albert had a canister of CS spray in his Burberry raincoat pocket and was determined to use it if he had to. He broke into a sweat.

"It's parked close by," the man said.

"On condition that you don't put the key in the ignition."

The man smiled briefly. His broad, flat face had something Tartar about it.

"Don't be nervous, Mr Savelkoul, I'm not planning to kidnap you."

When he heard the man say his name, he suddenly regretted having agreed to the meeting in the first place. His mood had deteriorated in the course of the afternoon, after reading a message from Amandine, in which she informed him of her agenda for the next two days. The following evening, there was a charity function organized by the Neckerspoel de Dickpus family to collect money for gifted yet needy children. The proceeds would allow their parents to send them to an exclusive school in Lima. He wasn't sure it was a worthy cause. He remembered a similar function organized by the same family to collect money for a school, the Villa Madero in Buenos Aires, to which the crown prince himself was later invited for the opening ceremony. It later turned out to be an Opus Dei institution. Scandalized readers sent letters to the press but the case fizzled out. He would have to come up with "something urgent" to get out of it. It made no difference to him that she insisted on being chauffeured to the event in his official car.

"Let's get a move on then, I don't have much time," he said bluntly.

The man smiled yet again. "This won't take long, Mr Savelkoul."

Albert noted that the man's French inflection had disappeared and detected a hint of a Flemish accent, perhaps Mechelen.

They entered a side street. The fact that he was head and shoulders taller than the other gave Albert a degree of self-confidence.

The man stopped a hundred yards or so into the street next to a wine-red Ford Scorpio. Albert took a mental note of the registration number: 7RS 225.

The man unlocked the car with the remote. Albert opened the car door and got into the passenger seat, still holding tight to the CS spray in his raincoat pocket.

The man glanced at Albert, drew in his chin, produced an envelope from his inside pocket and handed it over. It was open.

The envelope contained a letter. He started to read its contents with his heart in his throat. He closed his eyes and gritted his teeth. When he opened his eyes again, the street outside seemed blurred, as if seen through an out-of-focus camera. He had difficulty breathing and his mouth was dry as a bone.

The man stared ahead in silence.

When Albert had recovered from his initial shock, he croaked: "What do you plan to do with this?" He was finding it hard to maintain his composure.

"What do you think?"

Albert stifled an outburst of rage. "*I* asked *you* a question," he growled, barely able to control his voice.

The man made a sort of hissing noise and started to stroke the steering wheel. "Look, Mr Savelkoul," he began, as if he was about to make some kind of reasonable proposal. "I would like the sum… in the er… bank account… to be transferred… er… to *my* bank account."

Albert took a deep breath, doing all he could to refrain from emptying the CS spray in the ugly little bastard's face. "And if I refuse?"

They faced one another.

"Then the press will hear about it."

Albert closed his eyes again and thought about the situation. As ever in such critical situations, his mind was working at full tilt. The procedure was too obvious. He knew from years of studying blackmail cases that this sort of unprofessionalism rarely achieved the desired goal. He was relieved, in a sense. He was more or less convinced that the man was bluffing, but he still found it difficult to understand how he had managed to get hold of his secret bank account number and details of his account. He decided to put him to the test.

"Did you say *transfer*?" he enquired with caution.

"No, no... I meant cash."

"I see. And what makes you think I can lay my hands on that kind of cash at short notice?"

"How much time do you need?"

"Where can I reach you?"

The man snorted with laughter. Albert noticed his bad breath.

"Mr Savelkoul, do you honestly think I'm *that* crazy?"

"Mr Maraudy de Moretus, call me tomorrow morning at ten o'clock sharp," said Albert in an authoritarian tone. He noticed that the man shuffled uncomfortably, probably realizing how stupid he had been to use an aristocratic family name that didn't exist.

Albert's plan was taking shape in the meantime. His heart was beating normally, but his forehead was still clammy with sweat.

"So you agree..." the man said, as if surprised that it had all been so easy.

"Do I have a choice?"

"You'll hear from me tomorrow at ten. Same number?"

"Of course," Albert snapped. He opened the passenger door, stepped out and slammed the door behind him. He made his way towards his own car, his head held high, without looking back.

He cursed and cursed under his breath in an effort to calm himself. He walked as quickly as he could, which helped him to think and give shape to his plan. He knew from experience that repetitive action was the only way to get the better of his nerves. Once back in his car, he scribbled the registration number 7RS 226 in his pocket diary, grabbed his mobile and called a number.

"Hello!" a deep baritone barked.

"Walter? Albert here..."

"Ah, how are you, my friend?" Walter de Ceuleneer enquired in his inimitable West Flanders accent.

"Good. Do you have a moment?"

"You're in luck, man. This is the only evening in the week I'm at home. Come on over. I'll see if there's a bottle or two of Le Pin in the cellar. Good choice?"

"Excellent. I'll be there in about an hour."

Albert switched off his mobile, started the car and drove slowly out of Brouwerstraat and onto Leuvensesteenweg. He turned right at the lights towards Brussels's ring road and stepped on the gas. Determination was written all over his face and he was able to think clearly without the slightest effort. He was hypersensitive to the world around him, which enabled him to trust fully in his sixth sense (survival whatever the cost).

He put his foot down as he took the on-ramp for Brussels. The powerful six-cylinder motor purred with ease. An unfamiliar feeling took him by surprise – the conviction that revenge was his only remedy.

He had not noticed the car that had followed him from the church in Kortenberg. The driver of the VW Passat had employed the "hare" technique, driving one car behind the target for a while and maintaining full eye contact.

Albert didn't need to get out of his car to ring the bell. The ten-foot-high gate made of high-grade steel glided open as he stopped in front of 'Evergreen House' on Baillet-Latroulei, one of the most exclusive residential enclaves of Antwerp's leafy Brasschaat. He knew that the concrete pillars supporting the gate had scanner cameras attached, which registered the presence of vehicles stopping at the drive and sent video images to the house.

Albert drove through the gate and found himself at the beginning of a drive lined with mature beech trees, which wound its way through a broad-leaved wooded area. The BMW's headlights illuminated a couple of full-grown rhododendrons as a pair of startled rabbits scuttled into the shrubbery, their white bobtails in the air. Roughly a hundred yards into the woods, he reached the edge of a lawn the size of a golf course, surrounding a residence that looked like a Moorish palace built for a Hollywood film set. A postmodern glass porch in the form of a truncated cone gave the place a Dallas-like finish.

The drive continued across the lawn, bordered on each side with halogen spots, and came to an end close to the porch, where a man appeared, dressed in a white bathrobe, glass of wine in hand, accompanied by a large, dark-brown dog. The man waved.

Albert got out of his car to a warm and friendly welcome from Walter de Ceuleneer, who embraced his friend and walked with him into the house, his arm over his shoulder. He was a good six inches shorter than Albert, and his bathrobe was pulled tight over his corpulent and unashamedly protruding belly. With the exception of a thin line of dark-blond hair, his expansive scalp was completely bald, and his head rested neckless on his massive shoulders. His movements were surprisingly swift and agile, a characteristic feature of many chubby-yet-healthy individuals. The magnificent Rottweiler sniffed Albert's hand and disappeared.

They walked through an immense hallway with stairwells on either side leading to a pillared balcony and a circular stained-glass window, a miniature version of the famous rose window in Chartres cathedral. The marble floor was carpeted with a sixteenth-century map of the city of Roeselare, the owner's birthplace.

"A glass of wine first!" exclaimed de Ceuleneer on his way to the salon. "Can I take your jacket?" His voice blared like a trumpet.

Albert took off his jacket and loosened his tie and collar.

The impressive hallway and enormous salon differed considerably in terms of style. The salon was the creation of a French interior designer, who had worked for the *président de la république*, among others. Straight lines, discreet colour combinations, modern fitted furniture, refinement itself if one didn't include the paintings, most of which had been produced by artists from West Flanders in exchange for some favour or other. A life-sized replica of the Venus de Milo on a white pedestal graced the centre of the salon. One of the walls was completely taken up by Picasso's famous dove, with the added features of a jet airplane and the word PALOMA on its tail, the name of Walter de Ceuleneer's personal Lear Jet.

They sat back on a leather sofa in front of an open fire with a Cape buffalo above the broad mantelpiece. De Ceuleneer half-filled a crystal red wineglass with an unusual "crackle" stem.

"New glasses?" Albert enquired as he tasted the wine.

"From Alain Chapel in Mionnay," de Ceuleneer replied, in his opinion the best three-star restaurant in France, "eight points a piece…" (He had the habit of referring to a thousand Francs as *one point.*)

Albert couldn't help smiling. He was used to de Ceuleneer's comments, and this sort of camaraderie put him at ease for some unknown reason. He took a second sip and muttered approvingly.

"Annie's not here," said de Ceuleneer good-humouredly. "She's trying to lose a few pounds at a fat farm in California."

At that he slapped his belly hard and roared with laughter, far enough from Albert's right ear not to do any damage.

"Sam!" he bellowed. The Rottweiler sidled towards him and rested at his feet, his head on his front paws.

"Most women are content if their men are a little more attractive than a chimpanzee," said Albert. He stretched and stared in silence at the tips of his fingers. He was having trouble coming to the point, especially about the amount of information he would divulge. He was confident nevertheless that Walter de Ceuleneer could keep his mouth shut, in spite of his extravagant manners, particularly when it was a matter of trust between friends.

"I'm being blackmailed," he blurted, turning to face his friend.

De Ceuleneer raised his eyebrows, put down his glass and leaned back in his armchair.

Albert related the entire story with meticulous clarity, as if he was explaining a complicated legal case. He kept nothing back, except the break with Louise, something he considered completely unrelated to the blackmail question.

When he had finished his story, de Ceuleneer filled their glasses and stared pensively into space. "What are you going to do?" he enquired.

"Not cave in!"

"So you think he's bluffing?"

"Yes. I've a fair amount of experience with this kind of thing. He's an amateur. He made some major mistakes, the use of a non-existent aristocratic family name for one. And he used his own car without any attempt to disguise the plates. He also seemed to be unaware that a Swiss bank account can never be directly associated with a name and that their commitment to secrecy can only be challenged when drugs or murder are at stake, and even then it takes for ever and costs a fortune."

"Any thoughts about the source of the account number?"

"I suppose we could force it out of him, but I'm not in the mood."

"What then?"

Albert took a sip of wine, waited for a moment and said: "Show him who he's playing with…"

"And how do you plan to do that?"

"Put him in hospital for a couple of days."

"Just like that!"

Albert hesitated for a moment, took another sip of wine and said decidedly: "We let one of your Albanian friend's sidekicks have a go at him."

De Ceuleneer didn't react. He furrowed his brow and whistled gently through his teeth.

Albert thought: West Flanders! Typical commonsense wariness.

"Mmm… I see," de Ceuleneer muttered. "Mmm…"

"Then he'll give up," said Albert, "guaranteed!"

"Are you sure?"

"Of course I'm sure. He doesn't have a leg to stand on."

"Only a number and a code name," de Ceuleneer pondered. "And you're certain that there's no paper trail leading the codename to Albert Savelkoul?"

"Come on, Walter, haven't you got an account in Switzerland? Only two people know about it: the manager of the bank and a lawyer."

De Ceuleneer pretended not to have heard the last part of what Albert had said.

"The only possible connections between me and Geneva are telephone calls, but that's circumstantial evidence."

De Ceuleneer nodded understandingly. "What phone did you use?"

"My mobile."

"Certain?"

"Yes."

"Then the chances of them tracing you are close to none."

"That's what I figured," said Albert.

De Ceuleneer thought for a second, nodded and said: "OK, I'll give our friend Shehu a call, if that's what you want."

Albert thought: it's just like having an everyday business conversation.

"Please," said Albert and he sipped at his wine.

De Ceuleneer produced an ultra-thin mobile from his bathrobe and called a number without having to look it up.

"Ramiz, my dear brother, Walter here. How are you?" he said in a painful Flemish accent.

He gazed at the ceiling as Ramiz Shehu responded and when he had finished he held the phone close to his mouth and whispered so quietly that Albert had difficulty making him out: "It would be better to see each other personally, OK?"

He listened and looked at his watch.

"I'll be there within an hour. At your place?"

De Ceuleneer ended the call and carefully slipped his mobile back into his bathrobe pocket.

"At his place…"

"I heard," said Albert. "I'm grateful, Walter."

De Ceuleneer nodded. He liked his friend's no-nonsense approach.

"So… and how's our Louise getting on?" he enquired.

Albert sensed that the question was an innocent one. "Fine. She's spending a couple of days with her mother."

"Aha! Then you're on holiday," said de Ceuleneer, thundering with laughter.

"Exactly," Albert replied expressionlessly.

"Pretty little thing, that Louise of yours, very pretty," said de Ceuleneer, meaning every word. "Lucky bastard…"

"So you'll be seeing Ramiz later today?"

"He's not a man to waste time."

"Does he have… er… *muscle*?"

"Muscle and respect. He only has to snap his fingers and it's done," said de Ceuleneer, and he snapped his own fingers, making a noise that sounded like someone uncorking a bottle. "I'd better get a move on if I want to be there on time. I also think I should go alone…"

"I wasn't planning on joining you…"

"What the eye doesn't see…"

Precisely, Albert thought. He was about to ask if there was any need to mention his name, but he stopped just in time.

"Nothing beats Le Pin," he said to fill the void.

"I ordered ten boxes of the 1990 last week. Forty-five points a bottle. Wine for connoisseurs…"

"Didn't you say something about a hunting trip to Scotland during the Rotary dinner?"

"That's right… Completely slipped my mind. Second weekend in June. Paloma's ready and waiting."

"Where is it?"

"Dalchruin, fifteen miles from the castle."

Albert nodded absently, his thoughts elsewhere.

"Only six-point racks and none of that hanging around stuff. Stalking's the game… But there's something I'd like to know first…"

"I'm listening…"

"Where exactly do you want it to happen, and can you provide a detailed description of the bugger?"

"No problem."

"Wait. Let me get a scrap of paper and something to write with."

Albert relaxed, arched his back and closed his eyes as de Ceuleneer left the room. The Rottweiler lumbered over and lay down at his feet. He petted the creature between the ears and couldn't help thinking of Igor… and for the briefest of moments Louise.

Albert leaned up in bed, held his breath and listened. Thirty years getting used to the house's creaks and groans meant he could identify every sound. The house dated back to 1891 and was built on an allotment of land on the south side of Antwerp once used for the 1885 World Expo. In the very place where he now lay listening, they had built a Congolese village housing "real Negroes". Renowned for their tact, the people of Antwerp had tossed bananas and monkey nuts at them. He was convinced that Congolese spirits – twelve had died on the spot of TB – occasionally filled the house on Amerikalei 124A with evil forces. Sometimes he heard noises in the middle of the night, shuffling and panting he couldn't place. He liked to believe that the place had a ghost that wandered silently through the corridors, listening at doors and then disappearing. He secretly hoped it would suddenly manifest itself in Amandine's room, which was locked from the inside at ten o'clock sharp every night, after Maria Landowska had brought up Madame's lime blossom tea, her last duty of the day. Madame got up every day at six and attended mass at seven thirty in a side chapel of Saint Michael's church, seventy yards from the house on the opposite side of the street, where an Opus Dei priest from the Oosterweel student residence said mass in Latin every day for a number of supernumeraries and associates, unmarried men and women who live alone and follow the rules of Opus Dei.

He had once confessed to Jokke Weyler about his wife's bedroom and its sturdy lock. The man immediately explained that her custom was classic, the projection of a primal need, an irresistible desire to be brutally raped. "You should try to break in one night," said Weyler in his unmistakable Antwerp dialect.

"You'll soon see that I'm right." They had enjoyed a good laugh about it. Jokke thought he was right to take a mistress given the circumstances. He had only seen her in a photograph, but had whistled approvingly.

Albert slipped out of bed, made his way barefoot to his wife's door and settled an ear against one of the panels. Not the slightest sign of life. Baroness Amandine de Vreux was a paragon of good manners, even when she was asleep. Aristocracy did not snore! Albert, on the other hand, apparently did, at least that's what Maria had told him. She didn't mind in the least. All animals snore, she explained, it was common sense. He had told her about prehistoric cave dwellers who clubbed snorers to death because they betrayed the group's position to the enemy at night. She hadn't believed him. "Idiot," she had said.

Without a sound, he crept upstairs in the darkness to the third floor, stopping at her bedroom door and peering through the keyhole. Her light was on. He suppressed a spasm of laughter. He was about to do something the aristocracy and bourgeoisie had been doing for centuries with their servant girls: wheedling clandestine sexual favours without the knowledge of the lady of the house. A wave of youthful recklessness washed over him. He was without a care in the world. He had made up his mind to settle scores with the blackmailer before the week was out. The little fucker would be hearing from him soon. Finally a little action, he thought to himself, exhilarated by the idea.

"Hmm..." he groaned, his mouth close to the keyhole.

"Hmmmm," she responded.

He opened the door. She was tucked into a single bed, her auburn tresses fanned out proudly over the pillow, the sheets pulled chastely up to her chin.

Before he knew it he was cradling her head in his hands and kissing her passionately, the tip of his tongue exploring the inside of her upper lip.

"Oh, Mr Albert, come to me, come to me," she whispered in his ear, pulling the sheets from her body in a single movement. He crept into bed beside her and pressed himself from head to toe against her warm body.

"*Moj kotek*, my little kitten," he said, and he kissed her nose on both sides, knowing the effect it would have on her. She groaned and grabbed him by the hair. An erection was inevitable.

"Spend the night with me," she panted in German.

"Yes, Maria, my kitten. Every night from now on. But let's lock the door first, to keep out the ghost."

"Ghost?"

"The phantom!"

"Is there a ghost in the house?"

"Yes. How do you say ghost in Polish?"

"*Duch*. But is there really a ghost?" she insisted.

"Yes there is, and he visits people who snore and bashes their brains in."

"Idiot," she replied, as before. She ran her fingers through his hair, kissed his eyes and pointed at something above the door. He looked up to see a string of garlic hanging on a nail.

"*Czosnek*," she said, "from my mother. Ghosts are scared of it."

She slipped her hand under the sheets.

"Ahaaaa!" she said and started to giggle.

"Give me your hand," she said, grabbing it tightly and pulling it under the sheets.

His middle finger slipped inside her, probing and searching.

"Squeeze," he commanded, skilfully stroking what he called "her little tangerine" with the tip of his finger.

Baroness Amandine de Vreux woke up in the middle of the night, in spite of the sleeping pill she had taken before going to bed. She switched on the light. It was twelve thirty. The telephone conversation she had had with Thérèse de Montignac earlier in the day suddenly filled her mind. The horror of those words still haunted her. Without knowing why, she pulled the quilt to her chin and stared at the ceiling, clenching her teeth until it hurt. She forced herself to listen. Nothing, except the occasional passing car on the street outside.

But then it dawned on her: *he's not snoring* (and he always snores!). She listened hard. Nothing. Perspiration formed on her brow. She got out of bed, put on her dressing gown and pompon slippers and tightened her hairnet. She stood at the door, unsure, wavering. In spite of her good intentions, this was the first time in her life that she was about to lower herself to something as *unheard of* as eavesdropping.

She opened the door and stepped out onto the corridor. He always snores, she thought once again. She stood still and listened for some time, but there was nothing. She climbed the stairs, slowly and with the greatest of caution, and stopped on the landing. She stopped again at the last couple of narrow, uncarpeted stairs leading to the servants' quarters as if she had run out of breath. When she finally reached the third floor, she could see light burning in the maid's room. Light! At twelve thirty!

And then she heard it. She refused to believe it at first, but then she heard it again. *Voices! A man and a woman.* She held her breath in an effort to suppress the dizziness that was inching over her body like a second skin. Paralysed, Baroness Amandine de Vreux d'Alembourg underwent a second initiation: the most profound humiliation a person can imagine. The first was thirty-six years earlier, when *he* had raped her and robbed her for ever of her precious innocence. Now she was facing something her family considered so appalling it was never spoken about. If one talked about such matters, it meant they were real!

When she sat on the edge of her bed (minutes or hours later?), her hand covering her face, she tried her best to picture how she had managed to return to her room without falling over the banister on the stairwell, which had turned into a heaving ship, and disappearing into the murky depths. She tried to pray, but even prayer was beyond her.

18

Wednesday, 2 June 1999. Breakfast in the dining room. Albert in shirt and tie. Amandine in beige twinset and brown pleated skirt. In complete silence, as they had done for years. Amandine ate yogurt, with measured spoonfuls. Albert guzzled down a plate of scrambled eggs. They drank tea. Maria Landowska waited table. She wore a black dress with white collar and cuffs. Amandine was pale as the grave. The wrinkles extending from her nose to her chin were clearly defined.

Albert's hatred for *the fucking family nun*, as he called her, was eating him alive. He had already grown accustomed to the pleasant atmosphere in the kitchen, watching Maria in her jeans and T-shirt, his sturdy, supple, sweet, scrumptious, sexy Polish poppet. A second earlier she had looked him in the eye and licked her lips. He had smiled back unobserved.

After dabbing her lips affectedly with her napkin, Amandine produced a folded piece of paper from her sleeve, where she also kept a handkerchief, and placed it next to his plate in silence. He unfolded it and read: I NEED THE DRIVER AT 10. He narrowed his eyes, took the pen that had evidently been placed for the purpose next to his coffee cup and wrote: AFFIRMATIVE. She read his response and stood up without the least reaction, crossing herself in the process. He looked at his watch. Eight fifteen. His official car would be at the door in a quarter of an hour. At eight forty-five, he was to phone Walter de Ceuleneer as agreed, and at ten o'clock he was to expect that all-important call.

He heard Amandine slowly climb the stairs. Stiff joints, he thought, unable to curb his immeasurable contempt: her sagging belly, her double chin, her pug-nose, her swollen hands, the saliva on her lips, the underarm perspiration stains on her blouse, the handkerchief in the sleeve, the Our Lady of Fatima pendant around her neck, the Queen Fabiola hairspray, the wedding ring, the signet ring with the family crest and device. Albert thought: where creatures like Marie-Amandine de Vreux d'Alembourg make their appearance, the rancid oil of tedium begins to drip from the walls.

Just as he was about to let loose a series of muttered curses, Maria came into the dining room. She was beside him in an instant, her head on his shoulder.

"Mr Albert," she whispered.

"*Kochanie...*"

"Will I see you again tonight?" she said in German.

"Yes, Maria. Every night... every night."

He took hold of her wrist and looked at her hand as if he had never seen it before. It was a strong hand, yet slender and smooth. He held it to his nose and sniffed.

"*Pozadku*," she said contentedly, sounding as if she had expected nothing less.

She kissed the top of his head, hurriedly squeezed his shoulder and set about clearing the table with single-minded determination, as if she were cutting grass with a scythe.

Albert closed his office's padded door and took his place at his desk, where a file awaited him. He took out his mobile phone and called Walter de Ceuleneer.

"Hello!" The familiar de Ceuleneer blare.

"Everything OK?" Albert enquired.

"Are you alone?"

"Yes."

"Safe?"

"Yes."

"Good news," said de Ceuleneer.

"Oh..."

"He agreed."

"What do you mean?"

"That he's going to send someone who can do what you're asking."

"Oh..."

"You don't sound very pleased."

"No, I am, honestly."

"But there's a condition."

"What condition?"

"He wants to rehearse the whole thing, on location."

"Does he have to?"

"These guys are professionals. Ramiz says you can trust him. Hundred and ten per cent!"

"An Albanian?"

"What did you expect? And there's another thing I was thinking about..."

"What?"

"That blackmailer of yours has a contact at the bank. If you ask for a rendezvous to hand over the money, he'll probably call the bank first to make sure you've withdrawn the money. Himself or some go-between or other."

Albert thought about it. De Ceuleneer was probably right.

"OK," he said. "I'm expecting his call in an hour. I'll arrange to meet him near the courts in Antwerp, not in Kortenberg."

"Why not?"

"Because I'll have more control over the situation should something go wrong."

"*Go wrong?*"

"What did you think? This is a risky business, all things considered."

"Have you thought about a location?"

"Yes, but I haven't made up my mind yet. How can I get in touch with you?"

"My mobile number."

"OK. Thanks, Walter."

"Call me as soon as you've spoken to the bastard?"

"OK."

"Cheers."

De Ceuleneer hung up.

Albert leaned back in his chair, deep in thought. A trip to Geneva in the BMW seemed the best option, although it would take an entire day. The day after next he had to be in Brussels to chair a meeting of the college of public prosecutors. It would have to be tomorrow. He looked at his watch. Almost nine. He opened his correspondence folder, put on his glasses, and started to read the first letter without paying much attention. He automatically removed the fountain pen from his inside pocket and unscrewed the top.

At 9.55, Albert's secretary informed him that he had a call.

"Please put it through."

"Aha... Good morning Mr Savelkoul." Polite, apprehensive, curious.

Albert clenched his teeth, his heart in his throat.

"Yes..."

He was furious.

The man revelled audibly in his victory.

"Is there news?"

"News? What do you mean?" asked Albert, trying to maintain his calm.

"About the... eh... the handover. The date... The place..."

"You can count Kortenberg out for a start. Not safe enough."

"As you wish. Your preferences will be accommodated, where possible of course."

Albert had an image of the peasant bastard's mocking grin.

"I'll know more the day after tomorrow," he said.

"When should I call back?"

"The day after tomorrow. Same time."

"Friday 4 June at ten."

"Yes…"

Albert carefully returned the receiver to its cradle and took a couple of deep breaths to stave off a looming headache. Knowing he could rely on Ramiz Shehu's help put his mind at rest, and there was no point in fretting about potential consequences. His usual defence mechanism (not thinking about a problem until it ceased to exist) didn't work this time. He clenched his fists and pictured his hands around the little fucker's neck, bashing his fat head against a wall until the blood squirted out of his nose…

The headache refused to subside. He called his secretary and asked her to bring a cup of strong black coffee. The word coffee made him think of Major de Vreker. He'd heard nothing from him about the strange goings on in Sint-Job-in-'t-Goor. Louise, Yamma, Soliman flashed through his mind. He would have to take his horse out for a ride one of these days. Without Maria.

He slammed his desk with his fist. She was alone at home, dressed in that infantile maid's outfit while Madame was on her way to her appointment in his official car. He would ask the chauffeur later where they had been.

Much to his own surprise, he asked after his secretary's health when she arrived with the coffee.

"Good, Public Prosecutor, thank you," she replied, a rosy blush invading her cheeks.

"And your mother?"

"She'll have to go into a care home, Public Prosecutor."

"And have you found one?"

"No, not yet. It's not easy..."

"I know, I know. I'd be happy to do what I can if you have no success."

"Oh... thank you... Public Prosecutor," she said with difficulty, her face now bright red.

She asked permission to return to her desk.

He responded positively with a friendly wave of the hand.

As he enjoyed his coffee, he yielded to a second urge: he called home on his mobile.

Maria Landowska picked up the phone.

"Hello, *kochanie*."

"Oh, Mr Albert..."

"Hello."

"What's the matter?"

"Nothing, Maria. I just wanted to hear your voice."

She started to sob gently. "You make me so happy..."

"See you this evening, Maria..."

She blew her nose. He hung up and slowly savoured his coffee, a strange smile on his face. He suddenly felt tired and old. The bloody pain had returned that morning, but hadn't lasted long. Perhaps I should give Jokke a call one of these days, he thought.

He heard a cough at the door. His secretary came in with a fax. He waited until she had left the room and started to read: licence number 7RS 225 was registered to Avis Rent-a-Car in Leuven. Pity, he thought, no reference to driver. He folded the fax and stuffed it into his wallet.

At ten thirty on Wednesday 2 June, the sale of properties belonging to Baroness Marie-Amandine de Vreux d'Alembourg, presently residing at Amerikalei 124A, 2000 Antwerp, to

Rumpus Ltd, domiciled in 1180 Brussels, proceeded in a most extraordinary manner.

Jozef Vromen (seventy-four), notary public resident in Ekeren, received her together with Baron Hervé van Reyn, General Vicar of Opus Dei in Belgium, in his run-down castle, surrounded by trees in the middle of a neglected park. The notary was a small man, gaunt and bald, and he wore a loose-fitting grey suit with stains on the lapels. He was slowly recovering from a stroke, which had left him with partial paralysis on his left side and speech problems. A confirmed bachelor, he lived alone with an elderly maid in the castle his grandfather had purchased in 1891, when he took over a colleague's legal practice. With the exception of a coal-fired central heating system, the interior had been left unaltered since its purchase. Jozef Vromen occupied a couple of rooms above the offices and lived like a hermit. He started his working day in the house chapel with the recitation of a series of Ave Marias and ended it in exactly the same way. He had been an Opus Dei supernumerary for twenty years and served the institution as titular notary for the province of Antwerp. He did so on the sole condition that he would never be asked to accept a fee for his services. He was prepared to do whatever was permitted – or thereabouts – by law to promote the interests of his respected client. Even Baroness de Vreux was taken aback by the bizarre conditions in which the transaction took place. The three first made their way to the chapel, Vromen in front with his walking stick, dragging his left leg. Hervé van Reyn then recited a series of twenty Ave Marias at the top of his voice, so loud it echoed around the room. Van Reyn held Baroness Amandine's hand as he prayed, evidently eliciting a sort of hypnotic trance and the dulled awareness generally associated with brainwashing as she accompanied the two gentlemen to the office.

Jozef Vromen then read the most important paragraphs of the deed of sale in a monotonous voice akin to the chant-like rhythm of the prayers they had just recited. Every ten seconds he moistened his lips with a reptilian lick of the tongue.

The property included a penthouse apartment located on the sea dyke at Knocke-het Zoute valued at forty million Belgian francs, a villa in Wijnegem with garden, swimming pool and caretaker's residence valued at twenty-two million francs, and forty acres of woodland near Neupont-sur-Lesse valued at 6.8 million. The total value of the sale amounted to 68.8 million Belgian francs.

During the reading of the deed of sale, Hervé van Reyn kept his hand on that of Baroness de Vreux, an elated grin on his face. She seemed vacant, like an old woman with Alzheimer's. Dressed in a blue blazer, grey trousers, striped shirt and military tie, van Reyn was the personification of *la noblesse belge*, a caste that had created privileges in centuries gone by, which they still enjoyed to the present day.

Van Reyn signed the deed of sale in the name of the purchaser, Rumpus Ltd. He underlined his flamboyant signature and concluded it with a full stop, a graphological characteristic of a dominant personality.

Amandine placed her signature mechanically to the right of his.

Baron van Reyn then handed her a dog-eared brown leather attaché case, and opened it himself. It was stuffed to the brim with ten-thousand-franc notes.

"Should I count it for you?" he said with a grin.

She shook her head and signed a receipt for the sum of sixty-eight million Belgian francs. She handed the receipt to van Reyn, who popped it in the blink of an eye into his inside breast pocket. Vromen spent the entire time apparently distracted by the contents of another dossier.

Van Reyn coughed. Vromen looked up, shook their hands and muttered: "Congratulations."

The three made their way to the front door and took their leave of one another. Before they had left the castle, Vromen tore up the receipt for his standard fee of 131,941 francs, as a sign that he wished to donate the sum to the non-profit organization Atlantis, used by Belgium's Opus Dei to launder its undeclared income.

Baron Hervé van Reyn gallantly carried the attaché case outside. When they arrived at the park's open gate, he bowed and took his leave, the attaché case firmly under his arm.

"Haven't we forgotten something?" he enquired with his trademark grin.

Noticeably taken aback, Baroness de Vreux pursed her lips, opened her handbag and handed him a bulging envelope without saying a word.

Inspired by the Opus Dei precept of Sacred Brazenness, Hervé van Reyn turned abruptly, without the usual courtesies, and walked towards his car, which was parked nearby. The envelope contained around ten million francs in shares and obligations, which Pla y Daniel had requested of her in Rome.

She made her way slowly and with difficulty towards the black Opel Omega, which was parked half a mile along the road near Saint Lambert's church, with Albert's chauffeur at the wheel.

Albert called Walter de Ceuleneer at ten thirty sharp and made an arrangement to meet the Albanian the following Thursday at nine in front of the church in Overbroek, a sleepy village between Brecht and Sint-Job-in-'t-Goor, which he knew like the back of his hand. He also informed de Ceuleneer that he planned to drive to Geneva that same day in a private car. De Ceuleneer cracked one of his classic jokes: prominent Belgians *always had their chauffeur do the driving* when they visited Luxembourg to deposit undeclared earnings. Albert did not miss his friend's allusion to the so-called "KB-Lux" affair. He replied that the affair was destined to be swept under the carpet because Belgium's elite had compromised itself yet again. You could compare it with the Nijvel robberies, he added, but without the twenty-eight deaths. De Ceuleneer was the only person with whom he dared to share such allusions. He asked if the stalking trip to Scotland was still on for 12 June. "Of course," de Ceuleneer thundered.

After the call, he was seized by a fit of gloom. What in God's name was he doing? He was the Public Prosecutor of Antwerp! He was in one of the most precarious situations you could imagine, for the simple reason that he had no authority to start a judicial inquiry. But once the mist had cleared, he was determined to conduct a discreet investigation into the whys and wherefores of the affair. Was there any connection with the attacks on Igor and Yamma? How had they managed to get hold of information on his account in Geneva? Who might benefit from driving him into a corner? Who had rented the car from Avis in Leuven? Was Amandine the spider at the centre of the web?

The thought of Amandine's involvement particularly disturbed him. Powerlessness was like a vacuum he found impossible to square with his position of power as a magistrate, and his narcissism of course, which had helped him come to terms with events so quickly, even the sudden break-up with Louise.

A quip from François Mitterand's French biographer seemed to fit the moment: "Power is anarchy at its worst", although he had never spoken about it with anyone else before. He considered such statements his "private property".

He was reminded of a discussion he had had a few years earlier with a senior officer on the Dutch police. The man had argued that Belgium was not a democracy because it was ruled from the wings by aristocratic, French-language, armchair politics.

Pure Dutch chauvinism, of course, but being forced to admit that it wasn't far from the truth and having been unable to offer an intelligent counter-argument at the time still bothered him and seemed to contribute to his present state of melancholy. To cap it all, the fucking pain in his anal region refused to go away. He was even finding it difficult to urinate, but had decided not to call Jokke unless it was a genuine emergency.

Albert glanced at his watch before getting out of the car. Forty-five minutes past midnight. He had parked the BMW in a side street adjacent to Overbroek's main thoroughfare. The side street lead to a solitary neighbourhood dotted with pine trees and farmhouses, and gave out into an artillery training ground known as the Polygon. He had decided to make his way to the church on foot. An icy south-wester drove the clouds across the night sky, intermittently exposing a full moon. He was wearing a khaki raincoat he used for hunting.

He made his way towards the town square at his own pace. It was five minutes to one when he reached the church. There wasn't a soul in sight. The village slumbered in the sodium-lit darkness.

He looked around and walked towards the partially lit square in front of the church. A man suddenly appeared from nowhere dressed in bike leathers. Albert was taken aback.

"Yo," said the man.

Albert nodded.

"Not much time," said the man. "What I do?" he asked with a broken Antwerp accent.

He appeared nervous, very unprofessional.

"I plan to bring someone," said Albert hesitatingly.

"When?"

"I'll let Mister... Mister Shebu know in due course."

"Yo."

Albert could clearly make out the man's face in spite of the poor light. Short black hair and a moustache. Small, robust. Dark eyes staring at him unrelentingly.

"What I do?" the man repeated.

Albert hesitated once again. What in God's name should he tell the man?

"Say it in English," said the man. "I understand better."

"A good beating," said Albert. It seemed easier to say the words in a foreign language.

"OK."

"But no broken bones. Only a stiff beating."

The man started to laugh noiselessly, his shoulders shuddering up and down. In the blink of an eye, he conjured something metallic from his pocket and violently swiped the air around him muttering: "Yo… Yo."

Albert was shocked. The man had a telescopic truncheon, one of the most efficient combat weapons on the market.

"I said no broken bones," he repeated.

"Yes, sir. Aga Ramiz gave me orders…"

Albert was pleased to hear it, and his use of Shehu's first name came as an agreeable surprise.

He wanted to ask where the man was parked but held his tongue just in time.

"When do?" asked the man.

"I'll contact Mr Shehu about that," said Albert.

"OK."

The man telescoped the truncheon against his chest, slipped it into his pocket, turned, and disappeared without a word.

Albert returned to his car. Not a single vehicle had passed while they were talking. The only sound was that of a dog barking somewhere on a nearby farm. He needed to urinate badly. It took a long time, with long interruptions. Although his bladder still seemed half-full, the flow had stopped for the time being.

He looked at his watch. Twenty past one. He decided to set off for Geneva. Amandine had grown used to his occasional unannounced absences. Maria Landowska, on the other hand, knew all about it. She had kissed him and said she would miss him. "Not another night without you, Mr Albert," she had said.

Just as he was getting into the car, a heavy motorcycle raced through the centre of Overbroek at high speed.

19

On Thursday morning around six thirty, Albert wolfed down coffee and brioche at a Restoroute near Bourg-en-Bresse and continued on the last leg of his journey, maintaining the local speed limit of eighty miles per hour. He arrived in Geneva at eight forty-five, just in time for the beginning of the working day. He knew that the Crédit Suisse was somewhere in the city centre, close to the lake. He asked a policeman to direct him to Place Bel-Air. The man looked at his number plates, shared nothing of his thoughts on the matter, and then explained in peculiar French how to get to his destination. Shortly after nine o'clock, he drove into the bank's underground car park. When he got out of the car, he was immediately struck by the cleanliness of the polished, billiard-green concrete floor, which had caused his tyres to squeak like someone removing a pair of rubber gloves. The ceiling was dotted with cameras that moved almost imperceptibly back and forth. He took the elevator to the hall: lofty, impressive, Carrara marble from floor to ceiling. He informed the blond, chubby, friendly girl with flushed cheeks at the reception that he had an appointment with Monsieur Rossy. She checked her appointments list, nodded enthusiastically and called an inside line.

"They'll be delighted to welcome you on the first floor," she said cryptically, revealing her petite yet level teeth. "Present yourself at the reception, *s'il vous plaît.*"

Albert took the elevator, which opened on the first floor into a stately corridor lined on either side with paintings of important bankers, the floor bedecked with oriental carpets. The air was discreetly scented.

A grey gentleman in dress suit manned the reception, his hands folded, his gaze penetrating. "Beaver?" he asked. Albert nodded, slightly taken aback.

The gentleman scribbled something on a scrap of paper, stood, and accompanied Albert to his appointment as if he were a royal courtier. He opened a door and ushered Albert into a small windowless room with only a table, four chairs, a computer and a cube-shaped object he had never seen before. A metal tube, similar to a gas pipe, protruded from the ceiling.

The man closed the door behind him. It felt as if he had been locked up in a radio studio.

The door suddenly flew open and a short, portly fifty-year-old man in a three-piece grey suit and a dark-blue tie burst into the room. He bowed discreetly and introduced himself: "Jean Rossy, *responsable du compte.*" He had lank blond hair and shiny skin. He smiled cheerfully, invited Albert to take a seat, folded his hands and looked at him with an honest, upright expression.

"I am Beaver," said Albert for the lack of something better. His first impression of the man was not good. "I would like to withdraw two hundred thousand Swiss francs from my account."

Mr Rossy raised his eyebrows and nodded. "Monsieur, the new regulations oblige us to ask for evidence of your identity," he said, with evident reluctance.

Unruffled, Albert took out his passport and placed it on the table.

Rossy opened it, glanced at the photo and the name, excused himself with a beaming smile and returned the passport. He started to type nervously at the computer, keeping his eye on the screen, and pressed a button attached to the table that looked like a bell. The sound of compressed air hissed from the pipe above their heads followed by a dull thud. Rossy opened a clip and removed a cylindrical plastic container, which he proceeded to open. He hurriedly placed a bundle of banknotes into the unfamiliar cube, which Albert now realized was a money counter. In the space of a few seconds it whirred through the 1,000 Swiss franc notes. A total of two hundred thousand.

"Would you like to check it for yourself?" he asked.

"That won't be necessary," Albert replied, overwhelmed by the speed of the service, which was even faster than the average Singapore Bureau de Change.

He signed a receipt. Rossy quickly compared it with the model signature of the Beneficial Owner – *Wirtschaftlich Berechtigter* on the computer screen – and slipped the money into an unmarked envelope.

Albert stuffed the envelope in his pocket and thanked Jean Rossy, who finally offered his client a friendly handshake.

They walked together to the elevator, passing the grey gentleman on the way. Rossy bowed with military formality, turned on his heels and disappeared.

"Dirty kraut," Albert mumbled, in spite of the fact that they had spoken nothing but French.

He took the elevator to the underground car park and headed towards his car. But he changed his mind halfway. He was hungry. He made his way to the exit, found himself on the busy Place Bel-Air and looked around for a place to eat. He crossed the square and sat down at a table in a café-restaurant where he ordered an omelette with bacon and a large espresso.

He called home while he was waiting. Amandine answered with her affected "*Oui!*" He hung up immediately and blurted: "Stupid bitch!" The words lightened his humour to a degree. After spending the entire night behind the wheel, reality around him had evolved into a Magritte painting, a vacuum divided into compartments with surreal objects floating in the air.

By the time the delicious-smelling omelette had arrived, presented in a copper frying pan with what looked like genuine home-made bread, Albert was verging on the euphoric.

The first thing Jean Rossy did after taking leave of Albert was carry out the orders given him by Ernst Jacobi, who had been warned the day before by Hervé van Reyn to keep an eye on Albert's account. Rossy called Jacobi's inside line without going through the switchboard. Jacobi grumbled approvingly when he heard the news. Uncharacteristically, he showered the *responsable du compte* of one of the bank's most important affiliates with praise, so much so that the man could hardly believe his ears.

The conversation had lasted twenty-four seconds. The international call Jacobi then made to Hervé van Reyn lasted a little longer. Van Reyn was delighted at the good news and during the small talk that followed he promised he would pay a visit to Zurich a week later on his way to Rome, where he had an appointment with procurator Pla y Daniel and his good friend Navarro Valls.

Jacobi insisted he join him for dinner at restaurant Kunststuben in Küsnacht, where they served the best *foie gras de canard aux queues de bœuf* he had ever eaten. Hervé van Reyn, who was something of a connoisseur in matters of gastronomy, found the combination a little strange (he had his doubts about Swiss cuisine), but he crooned an elongated *Mmmm* nevertheless, a typical quirk of Belgian aristocratic style when conversing about good food.

When Jacobi concluded their otherwise mundane conversation with a formal "*Pax*", Hervé van Reyn raised his eyebrows and slowly returned the receiver to its cradle. Although he prided himself in his knowledge of the Swiss character, this unusual form of forced politeness surprised him time after time. He put it down to the peasant origins of the entire Swiss population.

He was so optimistic about the way things were going, he decided to dispense with the services of Marlowe & Co. The fact that the target had visited a friend after the encounter in Kortenberg seemed irrelevant to the situation and its investigation a waste of money.

He called Paul Hersch and told him the news. He insisted that Hersch arrange a rendezvous with the target as soon as possible.

20

On Friday 4 June, beginning at ten past eleven, Albert chaired a meeting of the college of public prosecutors, which took place in a room on the second floor of the Ministry of Justice, decorated with imitation Louis XV furniture. The respected college, which had been established the year before to introduce a degree of uniformity into Belgian penal policy, had evolved in practice into a sort of committee of arbitrators, charged with coordinating the tug of war between the five Belgian Public Prosecutor's Offices, each with its political bias towards Flanders, Wallonia or Brussels. Their job, in fact, was to limit hostilities where possible. The installation of a federal prosecutor's office in 1999, with a sixth public prosecutor at its helm responsible for serious crime and its international expansion, had done nothing to settle Belgian communitarian rivalries.

Albert adjourned the meeting at one thirty, realizing that they were still dealing with point one on the agenda: a precise description of the concept "criminal organization". The actual discussion had turned around the amount of power to be given to the federal police chief, which would have to work closely with the new federal public prosecutor in the reformed structure. As often happened, the meeting had degenerated into a futile hair-splitting session, the representatives of Flanders, Wallonia and Brussels each refusing to give an inch on the matter.

The meeting's actual agenda had been interrupted to such a degree that the assembled college decided to vote on whether to continue after lunch or to schedule another meeting at a later date. The vote favoured another meeting.

In line with tradition, lunch was taken in Chez Duparc, a restaurant still considered by many Belgians to be among the best in Western Europe, probably because the menu, which had remained unchanged for years, was determined by certain prescriptions of classical nineteenth-century gastronomy and, with equal probability, because the place was so expensive only an elite few could afford to set foot inside.

By the time dessert arrived (crêpes suzette with ice cream and a sauce of Pernod and pepper, one of the house's secret and more daring combinations) together with a glass of Château d'Yquem 1964, the eight invitees at table were in a particularly jovial mood (the minister of justice's private secretary, a French-speaking aristocrat who had attended the last half-hour of the meeting, had joined the college for lunch). The problems raised during the meeting had been set aside (it was the weekend after all), and should similar teething trouble be encountered in the future, a typically Belgian compromise was sure to be reached after joint consultation, with a view to the maintenance of existing power structures, which the upcoming elections – the following week – were likely to leave untouched, thanks to an atrociously expensive disinformation campaign organized by the ruling party and the population's short memory. Only those with half a brain remained convinced that the elections would lead to an unashamed and unsubtle restoration of the *ancien régime*.

The bill (46,768 francs, including service and VAT) was paid by Albert with a special credit card he reserved for the purpose.

The Opel Omega slowed to a halt in the weekend rush hour as it entered the Leopold II tunnel, only to find that the tunnel's ventilators were out of order yet again and the exhaust fumes were percolating into the car. Albert started to agonize over the only real problem on his mind: his appointment with the unknown man on Monday 7 June in front of the church in Overbroek, the man who was intent on blackmailing him for five million francs. He had made the appointment when the man phoned him at ten o'clock sharp that morning. He had detected a degree of enthusiasm in his voice. Something new, he thought. He had toyed with the idea of installing a tracking device for incoming calls, but he feared it might raise suspicions among his own staff and was not convinced such gadgets would work with a mobile phone.

He called Walter de Ceuleneer, who was on his way to his villa in Knokke in the back of his Rolls Royce. He was also stuck in traffic between Drongen and Nevele due to an accident.

Albert informed him of the day, place and time of the appointment. "We'll take care of it," he replied. "If there's a hitch I'll be in touch. By the way, will Louise be joining us in Scotland?"

"I think so," Albert replied.

"The horsies are ready and waiting!"

"I'll have a word with her," said Albert and he hung up.

"Bloody traffic's a pain in the arse," he said to his chauffeur.

"It's the same every Friday, Public Prosecutor."

"I suppose so," Albert answered, bereft of inspiration.

The pain in his lower belly had stopped and he had been able to urinate normally, but he had other worries. How long before Amandine smells a rat, he fretted. The very idea of a weekend in her clawing presence, with Maria hovering in the background radiant with desire for him, made him question his *savoir-vivre*, the *virtù* of the Renaissance man, a much cherished narcissism in which he had believed unconditionally until that moment.

21

After a couple of days of "Belgian weather", the first weekend in June 1999 turned out to be warm and sunny, with temperatures reaching into the eighties. A stiff east wind blustered along the coast. Surprisingly enough, the ever optimistic nit-pickers at the meteorological office hadn't declared it a "catering industry weekend", as they were often inclined to do, which meant that the exodus of apartment dwellers – with surrogate outdoor lives – to the traditional coastal resorts got off to a slow start. But it wasn't long before the motorway police were obliged to introduce traffic controls, although their efforts were not enough to prevent a pile-up between Nevele and Aalter, which created a twenty-five-mile tailback. As a result, many day trippers only reached the coast in the early afternoon, with the cheerful task of finding a parking space waiting to greet them on arrival.

The Belgian, Italian and Swiss protagonists involved in the affair surrounding Public Prosecutor Savelkoul were, for the most part, unaware of one another's existence. As such, their behaviour during this unexpectedly pleasant weekend was what one might be inclined to call normal, that is, they continued to be convinced that what they were doing or planning to do was in complete harmony with Christian ethics.

As was his custom in the summer, Walter de Ceuleneer spent every weekend in his "cottage by the sea", as he liked to call it, in leafy Knokke-het Zoute. It was in fact a pretentious replica of a Victorian country house with an ivy-covered façade, rejoicing in the equally pretentious name "Manderley". His wife's continued absence, trying to lose a pound or two at her favourite Californian fat farm, allowed him to invite a lady friend for the weekend. Mouche was a forty-something divorcee who lived close to his home in Brasschaat. He referred to her as "my regular". While he played golf in the company of the cheats and swindlers surrounding the local mayor, she relaxed in the sun by the pool drinking gin and tonics, to which she had developed a remarkable immunity over the years. She was blond, slender and, thanks to a couple of costly facelifts in Davos, Switzerland, more or less wrinkle-free. She lived for her body, and enjoyed flaunting it in the company of "our Walter", whose excessive generosity towards her could not be said of every man. His slightly ridiculous obsession with parading her in public – in spite of his age and excess weight – was the result of certain symptoms of the penopause, for which he tried to compensate with an exaggerated passion for her husky bedroom voice and regular use of the American wonder drug Viagra.

"I can still manage a second round," he would bluff in male company, "and with live ammunition!"

His wife was aware of his relationship with Mouche, but she preferred to make the most of a less-than-ideal situation, primarily because of her determination to protect her status as well-to-do married woman whatever the cost, and turning a blind eye was a tried and tested face-saving technique.

That Saturday evening, de Ceuleneer was planning to take Mouche to a restaurant in Sluis specializing in mussels. After dinner they would have a drink at home – she in her negligee, he in his bathrobe – until the moment arrived when he would trumpet: "Time for me to give you a good seeing to!"

Notary Vromen had maintained the same Friday evening ritual for more than fifty years: mass at St Lambert's followed by a glass of port with the parish priest – Karel Jacobs – a former classmate at the junior seminary in Hoogstraten. They would talk about the good old days when they were children, an innocent form of regression they both enjoyed immensely. At seven o'clock sharp, the notary said goodnight and made his way to his "castle" a couple of hundred yards along the street, taking his time on account of his stroke. Elza, the seventy-year-old maid, would serve him buttermilk porridge with brown sugar in a gloomy dining room full of nineteenth-century furniture illuminated by a single forty-watt bulb. She would place his medication in a plastic pot next to the plate and leave the room without saying a word. She refused to wear a hearing aid, in spite of her chronic deafness, and her bad back made it difficult to get out of bed in the morning, but she continued in service nonetheless. She saw herself as one of the Vromen family heirlooms, an important part of her psychological identity that would be irretrievably lost if she were to be dismissed for reasons of old age or sickness. Notary Vromen seldom spoke to her, partly because he was taciturn by nature and partly because she rarely understood a word he said. She had carte blanche when it came to the housekeeping, although he checked every bill and invoice to the last franc, and left them unpaid for at least a month (cash in a used envelope). She also had the key to the wine cellar, where hundreds of bottles from the Twenties and Thirties awaited consumption, something the notary was unlikely to achieve in his lifetime.

He emptied his plate, dribbling right and left on both the tablecloth and his napkin, and then turned with suspicion to the plastic pot and his medication: Zestril for high blood pressure, Hydergine to prevent narrowing of the cerebral arteries, and Rytmonorm for cardiac arrhythmia. He finally gulped down the lot with a glass of tap water.

He drew the faded velvet curtains around nine o'clock, transforming the dining room into a dimly lit cave in which he felt completely at home and safe from the wicked world outside, a characteristic symptom of geriatric paranoia. He then collapsed into an armchair, the springs of which had long given up the ghost, closed his eyes and withdrew into the womb of the past, his face resembling a death mask. He tried to recall fragments of scenes from his unhappy youth, in which his dominant mother was intent on seeing him elevated to the priesthood one day. Her plans came to nothing when he was expelled from the seminary for reasons that were not made public. He decided to study for his notary examinations instead. Brooding on his failed vocation was the only form of self-torment he had left, a poor surrogate for his weekly visits to the friendly prostitute with the beery laugh in Antwerp's red-light district. She would tickle his neck with her toes while he ground his teeth and tried to jerk his penis into an erection. Failure was inevitable.

After half an hour of melancholic musing, he would grope his way up the unlit stairs to his bedroom and put on his musty flannel pyjamas. He would hoist himself into the same elevated bed in which his mother had died, roll over onto his back and set about praying a series of ten Ave Marias, out loud and in Latin, for the forgiveness of his own sins and the sins of the world. He rarely got beyond the fifth. He would drift into sleep, snoring gently, his exhalations sounding on occasion like a death rattle. The room slowly filled with an unpleasant odour, as if someone had sprinkled vinegar on the bed.

Joaquín Pla y Daniel was in the habit of reserving one weekend per month for an "excursion", as he liked to call it, and he allowed little if anything to disturb this routine. This was due in part to his obsessive behaviour (the only way to survive in an organization such as Opus Dei), but it also allowed him to vent some of the stress his obsessive behaviour tended to create in staggering proportions. In reality, he only had himself to blame.

His fanatical implementation of Opus Dei's strict discipline – he was after all one of its senior members – resulted in an unusual form of schizophrenia. To the outside world he was the personification of the elite Basque numerary, and he did not intend to fall short in this regard. But at the same time, he was a highly intelligent man and he realized that the rules of the organization had narrowed his mind and left him with such tunnel vision that he had come to consider every form of openness to the world as sinful. His all-consuming curiosity clearly did not square with his role as the Opus Dei functionary he had become.

To facilitate the mental openness he needed to fulfil his administrative duties, and for this reason only, he permitted himself one single weekend per month of "recreation", a word he had borrowed from the Jesuits, with whom he had a love-hate relationship. He considered their intellectual flexibility objectionable, but he knew well enough that without Ignatius of Loyola there would never have been a Josemaría Escrivá. He also had to admit that it was the Jesuitical casuistry of men such as the infamous Doctor Eximinus, Francisco de Suárez, that allowed him to rationalize his monthly escapades.

No one in the Opus Dei headquarters on Viale Bruno Buozzi had the slightest idea where he spent his notorious weekends, and none dared allude to them in public. The truth, in fact, was unremarkable. Pla had secretly rented an apartment in a seventeenth-century palazzo on Via delle Botteghe Oscure, close to Isola Tiberina, an upmarket quarter that was built to house the city's pharmacists and was now populated by diplomats and senior Civil Servants. Much to his delight, the district was more or less abandoned at weekends. He called the flat his "captain's castle", taking inspiration from the English author, whose name he had forgotten, who had secretly furnished a room as a ship's cabin, and used it to lie low for a couple of days every month.

Pla's weekend was riddled with rituals, each with a hint of infantile paranoia, all of which made him think he was in some sort of spy film. This satisfied him enormously because it differed completely from the universal, divine paranoia that gave foundation to the miracle of providence embodied in blessed Josemaría Escrivá, a providence he was convinced would one day govern the Catholic Church. The miracle filled him with intense pride and at the same time with a perverse delight in the fate of all the damned outside Opus Dei, a typically Basque characteristic that had twice the vigour in Pla because it had been passed on to him literally at his mother's breast. His hatred for women had its origins half a century earlier when he refused the breast for no apparent reason as an infant and was forced to take a beating from his mother for his trouble. For this reason, his veneration for El Padre was greater than his veneration of the Most Holy Virgin, whom he invoked 150 times a day with Escrivá's glassy stare peering over his shoulder.

The first ritual for the month of June 1999 was the celebration of Holy Mass for the female numeraries resident in the house. He distributed Communion – always received on the tongue – with abrupt indifference. He then took a cold shower, selected an unobtrusive beige linen civilian suit, a brown shirt and a black tie, got dressed and skipped breakfast. At quarter to eight, he slipped out of the building via a rarely used exit that gave out into the park behind the house. The high stone wall concealed a moss-covered door, for which he had a key.

He locked the door behind him without looking around, waded cheerfully into the ocean of the world, and strutted towards Viale Bruno Buozzi, his head held high and a grin of triumph on his face, where he stopped a taxi.

"*Piazza del popolo, per cortesia,*" he said to the driver. This was part of the ritual: the use of polite formulas that had long gone out of fashion.

The traffic in Rome was exceptionally calm at that hour. The city was probably preparing itself for a heatwave after three days of heavy rain and serious flooding, which had resulted in the evacuation of the streets along the Tiber and an ensuing traffic chaos. Pla enjoyed the short drive in the yellowish sunlight for which Rome was so famous. He got out of the taxi at Piazza del Popolo, one of the finest squares, he thought, after Salamanca's Plaza Real. He gave the driver a ten per cent tip. He produced a pair of dark sunglasses from his jacket pocket and put them on. He looked round as if searching for someone he expected to find, someone with whom he had made an appointment, but nothing could have been further from the truth.

He glared suspiciously at the terrace of the renowned Caffè Rosati from a distance of about fifty yards, where a few people were already enjoying breakfast. He found a table under the awning, took a seat and waited until an elderly waiter in a white waist apron appeared with a silver platter under his arm. He ordered breakfast, a large espresso and "*pasteles*", in Spanish, in spite of his fluent Italian. The waiter handed him the silver platter and disappeared. Pla y Daniel sauntered inside to peruse the ample assortment of breakfast pastries with raisins, almonds, icing and whipped cream, arranged in glass display cabinets. He selected four items using a pair of pastry tongs, returned to his table and did not wait for his coffee. He gobbled one of the pastries, wiped his fingers on his napkin, and quickly lit a cigarette. He inhaled with evident pleasure, held the smoke in his lungs and leaned back in his chair. His recreation had started. He waited to see what would happen next.

Caffè Rosati was known by every gay Roman of standing as a meeting place. Pla y Daniel hated gays almost as much as he hated women. His hatred had started almost fifteen years earlier in the Opus Dei house in Pamplona, where he had been responsible for training young candidate numeraries. Manolo, a twenty-four-year-old Madrileño of exceptional beauty, had been taunted by him to such a degree about his looks that the boy threw himself to the floor in tears one day, grabbed his ankles and started to kiss them. At that point, his hand shot upwards with lightning speed and he started to stroke Pla's penis, groaning with desire. Pla was so taken aback he was unable to move for a few seconds, but when he came to his senses he began to kick and beat Manolo, and shower the boy with curses, *hijo de puta* and *mala leche* being among the least offensive.

At the moment his espresso arrived and the pastries had been devoured, the reason for the Caffè Rosati's reputation became clear. An elderly gentleman dressed in a black, raw-silk suit with purple stripes, a purple shirt and a heavy gold chain set with dark-blue precious stones instead of a tie, had been sitting at a nearby table for some time. A white Jaguar pulled up abruptly in front of the café and a tall, skeletal, yet strikingly elegant young man, wearing an enormous black hat, stepped out. He was dressed in a white silk suit with a black-and-white-striped breast-pocket handkerchief, a black shirt with white polka dots, black shoes with white tips, and wore a red-stoned ring on top of black gloves. He moved with feline agility towards the elderly gentleman's table and offered him his hand. He kissed the ring. The young man sat down, produced a round hand mirror with a golden handle, and commenced a careful examination of his face. The elderly gentlemen beckoned the waiter and started to talk to him with rounded gestures.

Pla y Daniel stubbed out his cigarette, nervously finished his coffee and summoned the waiter. The irritating spectacle had elicited an allergic reaction, which he quickly suppressed by spraying Rhinocort in his nose. He knew exactly how much he would have to pay because he did the same thing every month. He gave the waiter a ten per cent tip and got to his feet.

The walk to the "captain's castle" via the Corso and the Vittorio Emmanuele – and past the Gesù, which did not warrant a glance – took roughly half an hour. The shops were still closed and the terraces more or less empty.

The magnificent palazzo on Via delle Botteghe Oscure had a dreary grey-stone façade and a large, half-open entrance. It was impossible to imagine from the exterior that the building had been divided into luxurious apartments with an enormous variety of occupants, from drug dealers, successful artists and diplomats to the kept women of those who could afford it. The doorman was napping in his cubbyhole in the side wall of the overgrown courtyard, with fountains and pedestalled Roman busts sticking out of the shrubbery. He raised his hand and continued his nap. Pla climbed the wide marble staircase to the third floor – the building had no elevator – and turned, puffing and panting, into a lofty, dimly-lit corridor. He took out his key.

The spacious room was reminiscent of a monastic cell. Plain white walls, antique Castilian furniture, but not a single Catholic symbol in sight.

He lowered the white venetian blinds until the shadows faded, considerably increasing his sense of security. He removed his jacket, draped it over the back of a chair, yawned and stretched, lit a cigarette and started to pace around the room to the imaginary measure of a military march, humming to himself in the process. He stopped after a couple of rounds and knelt down in front of a TV with an enormous screen. He selected a video from a sturdy wooden box with iron mountings, which had once served to store food in a Basque farmhouse. He dragged an impressive, elaborately carved, high-backed chair to its regular place, where he would settle down for hours on end to watch the same videos of celebrated bullfights with toreadors from the classical school such as Paco Camino and El Caracol. He would intersperse his viewing with two films: Saura's *Blood Wedding* and

Mario Camus's *The House of Bernarda Alba*. Every now and then he would give in to another element of his obsessive behaviour, the repeated recitation of 'Romance Sonambulo', which he believed to be García Lorca's most beautiful poem:

Green, how I crave you green.
Green wind. Green branches.
The ship out at sea
And the horse on the mountain.

During the scene in which Bernarda Alba's youngest daughter Adela masturbates, he would mutter an uninterrupted series of misogynistic expletives, which, according to ancient Spanish tradition, usually had something to do with animal organs, vegetables and fruit.

As ever, he would dine in a dark corner of the same unsavoury restaurant in the Trastevere district two nights in a row, where they served decent square meals at reasonable prices and allowed the customers to smoke at table. He would then wander aimlessly through the dark streets of the Jewish quarter and submit himself to a storm of historical associations full of pogroms and mass executions, after which he would return to the palazzo, stub out his last cigarette and climb into bed a satisfied man. Without prayer, without meditation, without even a quick sign of the cross, he would fall asleep like a child, undisturbed by his usual allergies.

At seven o'clock on Saturday morning, Ernst Jacobi awoke to the melancholic opening strains of Anton Bruckner's Seventh Symphony, reverberating from a powerful pair of Bang & Olufsen speakers attached to the radio-alarm next to his bed. Jacobi did not move a muscle. At two minutes past seven, his paddle-like hand slowly emerged from beneath the Swiss crochet-work bedspread and started to pet the head of an Alsatian dog, which lay asleep on an artistically carved bed from Graubünden next to his. The twelve-year-old Alsatian bitch was named after Hitler's dog Blondi. Jacobi took enormous pleasure in using the name Blondi in public. He blamed the lack of reaction to a deficiency in the Swiss teaching of history.

He listened to the music, a recording made by the Berlin Philharmonic conducted by Otto Klemperer, which he considered the best performance available. His adoration of Anton Bruckner had nothing to do with his love for music and everything to do with the fact that he was the Austrian composer's double. A large photograph of Bruckner graced the hall of his house, and when visitors caught sight of the bald and double-chinned Swabian peasant face, read the name underneath and expressed their amazement, Jacobi would glow with pride.

At ten past seven he got out of bed with a groan, popped in the false teeth he kept in a glass by the bed, leaned forward and buried his nose in Blondi's shaggy coat, without paying the least attention to the smell, which was due to his elderly companion's poorly functioning kidneys. Blondi did not stir.

Jacobi put on a shabby dressing gown and a pair of equally shabby leather slippers and shuffled towards the bathroom, where he urinated with extraordinary vigour. The prostate operation he had undergone two years earlier had done its work. He shaved with a cheap Philips razor without washing.

In the musty dining room, with its pinewood walls and ceiling, heavy furniture and enormous table, he peered in passing through one of the tiny double windows at the geraniums on the balcony that surrounded the entire house.

The main feature of the room was a massive tiled stove, which ran like a pillar through each floor of the house, from the cellar to the attic. It was fired with pinewood logs and kept each of the rooms comfortably warm throughout the winter.

A red-and-white chequered tablecloth covered one half of the table. He sat down and blessed himself. His hand quivered as he poured milk on a shallow bowl of muesli, sprinkled it with sugar, stirred it and started to eat, slurping from his spoon and carefully chewing every mouthful.

At five minutes to eight, a shiny black 1975 Mercedes climbed the steep drive towards the house in first gear. Jacobi appeared on the veranda at eight o'clock sharp, and descended the wooden stairs with obvious difficulty. The chauffeur opened the rear passenger door.

"*Grüezi, Herr Doktor,*" he said.

"*Grüezi*, Heinrich, how are you?" Jacobi responded good-naturedly.

"Excellent, *Herr Doktor*, thank you."

The chauffeur followed a country road, past meadows and crops of pinewood forest, onto the Zürich bypass and into the city. Before reaching the city centre, he drove into the car park of a Spar supermarket and Jacobi got out while the chauffeur remained behind the wheel. Half an hour later, Jacobi appeared with a trolley containing three plastic bags, which the chauffeur helped unload into a wooden wine case in the boot.

The Mercedes then continued to the headquarters of the Credit Suisse on Paradeplatz, the pompous façade of which was constructed from greyish-white sandstone from Ostermundingen and decorated with statues of heroes, warriors and robust women, symbols of the unshakeable traditions of the Swiss mentality, still known today as traditions without the least tolerance towards any form of critique considered "disruptive of our cultural affiliations".

Jacobi stepped out of the car and disappeared behind the enormous wrought-iron gate, which was slightly ajar. The chauffeur drove off, aware that he had to return to collect him at five o'clock sharp.

Jacobi took the elevator to his office on the fourth floor of the empty building, where he hoped to spend the entire day working uninterrupted on a number of difficult accounts. This was his idea of the ideal Saturday. He never worked on Sundays. "Otherwise I'd grow horns," he would laugh when friends teased him for his idleness. His grandfather, a wealthy farmer from the canton of Aargau, always said the same.

On Saturday morning at half past ten, Paul Hersch was so fed up with Leuven that he gave in to an urge for which he was renowned in Arenberg. He left his office dressed as he was (jogging outfit and trainers), told no one, jumped into his car and drove like a madman to the Hoge Venen, a fenland park near the border with Germany. His reasons were simple and, to a degree, understandable: he was angry with the entire world. For the first time in his life he had received an instruction from Hervé van Reyn that was little short of a reprimand: give Didier Savelkoul (or *junior* as he liked to call him) some space. It was obvious that the wimp had gone whining to his superior in Brussels. His suspicion that "the financial matter" had been settled had been confirmed: junior had been promoted. Van Reyn's characteristic silence on the matter barely surprised him.

When junior had asked permission the day before to spend the weekend at home, he had written a "*nihil obstat*" until ten o'clock on Sunday evening without saying a word. This was the first reason for his agitated state. The second was his dwindling interest in picking up a stack of cash from Savelkoul senior in the middle of the night in some miserable country village east of Antwerp. He had said nothing to van Reyn about his Monday appointment, in spite of Opus Dei rules to the contrary.

An hour and a half later he arrived in Eupen (a motorway camera had caught him speeding between Liège and Herve, but he couldn't have cared less). He then drove from Eupen to Ternell, a forest keeper's station in the Herzogenwald on the road to Monschau. When he got out of the car he breathed in the country air, angry with himself for not enjoying it as others would, put on a pair of rubber boots and started walking. Half a mile further on, he left the woodcutter's path and jumped down towards a waterfall, where he sat on a tree trunk that had been cut down, ready for transport. He rested his chin on his clenched fists and set about what he called "autohypnosis", a special technique he had developed to help him reach practical conclusions on problems he considered worth the effort. He cut himself off from the world around him, stared like a snake at an invisible point in space and emptied his mind.

After roughly half an hour, he got to his feet and started to throw pebbles at a tree fifteen yards or so from where he stood. He had done the same for hours on end as a boy, and under normal circumstances he considered it a transparent form of childhood nostalgia. When he turned out to be just as good as he used to be – a disappointment since he was already sick to the teeth of it – he took out his mobile and called Hervé van Reyn. The female numerary who answered the phone at weekends on Avenue de la Floride informed him that the Regional Vicar was absent.

"*Merci,*" Hersch grunted.

He called chateau "Beukenloo" in 's-Gravenwezel and van Reyn finally answered. "*Allô, oui,*" he said with a high-pitched voice.

Hersch was determined to stick to his guns. "I'll keep it short, Hervé. I just wanted to say that I'm willing to do that you-know-what business, but only under one condition: someone drives me there and back. Not in my own car and not in an Avis hire drive."

"*Ooh la la!*" was all van Reyn could manage in response.

"Clear?" Hersch retorted, irritated by the stupid reaction.

"And do I get to know the time and place?" van Reyn asked.

"Yes."

"Yes, what?"

"Monday morning at three a.m. in a village called Overbroek east of Antwerp. In front of the church..." (He wanted to say "the local priest is also involved", but swallowed his words.)

"How long have you had this information?" van Reyn enquired.

"Not long!"

"Hm... and will he have the money?"

"That's the idea."

"I'll call you back."

"Why?"

"To tell you who will be picking you up."

"Aha! That's good to hear."

"OK. I'll call you back later."

"Fine by me."

"Where are you, by the way? The connection's fading in and out."

"A forest in the heart of the Ardennes," said Hersch in an explosion of gravelly laughter.

"Are you pissing me around?"

"Not at all. If you want I can let you hear the birdsong."

"*Bon*," van Reyn concluded. "I'll call you."

"That's the third time."

The connection went dead. Hersch closed his eyes and rubbed his forehead. He sat still for a couple of minutes and tried once again to empty his mind. But something unexpected happened, something he feared, especially when he was alone with nature's intimacy: he got an erection. He jumped to his feet and raced up the hill towards his car. He reached Ternell out of breath and sweating like a horse. Strings of ejaculatory prayers buzzed incessantly through his head. The combination of running and praying had done the trick: the temptation of the flesh had released him.

He parked his car in Eupen not far from Sankt-Nikolaus-Pfarrkirche and stopped at a butcher's shop, where he purchased a couple of *Eupener Würste*. He ordered a glass of Funckbier at a café, whipped out his pocket knife, and started to cut one of the sausages into slices, which he popped unashamedly into his mouth without paying the least attention to the café owner, who watched him with suspicion from behind the bar.

The telephone call from Paul Hersch had interrupted something van Reyn had done every weekend for years, something he considered a Duty to the Future of the Country (its youth), an "apostolate of friendship", which Saying 973 interpreted in part as "discreet indiscretion… whispered in the ear… with which you open up unexpected horizons". Baron van Reyn gave his own personal twist to the Saying, treating the "apostolate of friendship" as a sort of upper-class scouting activity.

On the grounds of his ancestral castle, which was set in five hundred acres of forestry and pasture, leased out to local farmers, he had had a log cabin constructed in which twelve carefully selected boys between the ages of twelve and seventeen (the twelve apostles) were permitted to camp at weekends and during the holidays. He selected the boys himself according to four criteria: they had to come from conservative Catholic families, be excellent students, fit and healthy, and free from physical impairment. In other words, perfect candidates for Opus Dei's future "fishermen" in Leuven. Three of the twelve had an aristocratic background and spoke better French than Flemish, and two were what might be called "pretty boys". Hervé van Reyn, who wandered around in a scout's uniform with khaki shorts and an authentic Royal Canadian Mounted

Police hat, sublimated this fact by silently comparing them with the apostle John, the beloved of Jesus. Their uniform tie was light blue (for Mary) and they wore a wooden cross on the left pocket of their khaki safari shirt. The weekend camp started according to custom at two o'clock on Saturday afternoon with a game of football and a natural-history quiz. The latter was organized by Gustje the gamekeeper, who confronted the boys with unusual aspects of the forest's animal life: the shooting, trapping, skinning and butchering of birds and mammals. "Mister Hervé" considered it essential for the boys to learn such things. It prepared them for the future – there was little doubt that a knowledge of hunting in all its dimensions would be of benefit later in life and further their careers – and at the same time, should Armageddon arrive, such prehistoric techniques, as he called them, would help them survive.

Around six in the evening, the apostles took a cold shower, dressed in suit and tie, and attended mass celebrated by van Reyn in the chapel. They were then served a lavish evening meal with one glass of wine per person. After dinner a debate was organized in the salon on some question of contemporary politics, philosophy or a spiritual topic. At ten o'clock they would make their way to the log cabin, where they slept on the floor in lightweight sleeping bags. Van Reyn also slept in the cabin, but he had the habit of arranging a confidential conversation in "discreet indiscretion" with each of the boys in turn before he retired, gently holding their hand in his. He called this an "exercise in divine love" and credited himself for never allowing any further form of "corporality". Heroic deeds of self-control were unnecessary, of course, since he had never suffered a moment's trouble from his libido in his entire life. Rumour had it that he was gay but unaware of the fact, which for some explained his somewhat effeminate appearance and high-pitched voice. But Baron van Reyn was an exception in every respect, including sexuality. He differed completely from his noble forefathers, who had often taken the family motto – "*Droit et en avant*" ("upright and forward") – quite literally by siring a respectable number of descendants with the servant girls and the daughters of the local farmers. He was also the first priest in the family since his great uncle, a canon of the cathedral, drowned under suspicious circumstances in the castle lake in 1902. Rumours abounded in those days that he had been "messing around with young boys", but there was no hard evidence to confirm them.

The weekends of sport and intellectual activity Hervé van Reyn enjoyed with his twelve apostles were considerably more upright and deserving than the work he did as Regional Vicar of Opus Dei for Belgium, a position that often called for unrelenting rigidity and, of course, Sacred Brazenness. None of this bothered him in the least, however, since he could always find a Saying in *The Way* to justify his behaviour. He liked to use the Jesuit expression *pia fraus* or white lie. His whole existence was a tissue of preciously formulated white lies, even during the whispered conversations with that day's *préferé*, who, he would inform repeatedly, belonged to the elite of his people, in training for the rigid doctrine of Opus Dei, which considered Catholic non-members as ordinary foot soldiers and sinners as vessels of stinking garbage. The only corporality that bothered him during these indiscreet discreet conversations was a build-up of saliva in his mouth, which forced him to swallow every five seconds and transformed his Flemish gutturals into a throaty Arabic rattle.

At half past twelve that same Saturday, Albert and Maria were sitting in the kitchen drinking vodka and cokes. She was wearing her usual black dress. "Madame" had called a taxi half an hour earlier and had driven off without saying a word.

"Madame's gone to visit her father with Master Didier," said Albert.

She smiled.

"I thought as much," she said, taking his hand and running the tip of her finger over his knuckles.

He ran his fingers through her loosely brushed hair, a pleasure he enjoyed intensely.

"And how is my old man getting along?" she asked.

Albert pointed tellingly at his forehead.

"Too old, if you ask me," she said and nipped at her vodka and coke. "Like my *babka* Maria…"

"Really?"

"What's your star sign?"

"Star sign?"

"What month were you born?"

"October… tenth."

"I'd never have guessed. Libra."

She raised her eyebrows.

"A good sign for a woman."

"And you?"

"Twelfth of April. A good month for men."

"What do you call it?"

"Aries. An animal with horns this size," he said, illustrating with his hands.

She sipped her drink and said nothing.

"Why does Madame always take a taxi or the official car?" she blurted.

"Because she never learned to drive and now it's too late."

"Huh?"

"Can you drive?"

"I took lessons in the Polish army."

Albert laughed in disbelief. "You never told me."

"You never asked."

"How long were you in the army?"

"Three years. I can also drive trucks and tanks, and I'm pretty handy with a Kalashnikov."

Albert was bent double with laughter.

He kissed the tip of her nose, and she grabbed his hair with both hands and kissed him firmly on the lips.

She stood beside him. He caressed the back of her thighs, but when his hand ventured upwards she sat down and took his hand in hers.

"Not now. It's not a good time..."

"*Pozadku...*"

"Midsummer is on a Monday," she said out of the blue.

"True," he said, slightly taken aback.

"On Midsummer's day I want to cook you a Polish meal. And burn lots of candles."

"I can't wait, Maria. How do you say 'candle' in Polish?"

"*Świeczka.*"

Albert nodded. It sounded pretty.

"Where can we celebrate Midsummer?" she persisted.

"I know a good place."

"*Pozadku...*" She smiled.

They sipped their drinks every now and then and enjoyed the moments of silence.

"So what is it like to be a lawyer in Amsterdam?" Baron Pierre Philippe de Vreux asked his grandson Didier, who had been invited to lunch with his mother every first Saturday of the month for as long as he could remember. Opus Dei always gave permission. According to custom, French was spoken at table.

The question caught Didier unawares and he returned his desert spoon to its place. He had barely managed to taste the vanilla custard.

"Didier is a lawyer in *Leuven*, Papa," Baroness Amandine patiently corrected her father, gently caressing his small emaciated hand, like the hand of a corpse. He was in a wheelchair.

They were taking lunch in the dining room of the family's town house on Marie-Josélaan in Berchem, which looked more like a museum for Delft porcelain. The characteristic white and blue vases, jugs, pots and decorative platters filled every corner, and even the lunch was eaten from Delftware plates. Coffee had just been served.

One of the walls was graced with an almost life-size statue of the Sacred Heart with a red lamp burning in front of it, making the place appear like a chapel. Two portraits decorated the opposite wall, one of them depicting Baron Pierre-Philippe in his red ermine-collared robes, with an excess of decorations pinned to his chest. The fragile old man in the wheelchair, with the ridiculous napkin tied like a baby's bib around his neck, had little in common with the proud Supreme Court justice in the painting beyond his white combed-back hair and his austere gaze.

His hand quivered and he was barely able to control the spoon, but he refused help from whatever quarter. The other portrait depicted Baroness Louise-Marie de Vreux, née de Wasseige, a generously proportioned lady with a double chin and a tiny mouth, wearing a diamond tiara and a silk evening dress. A four-stringed pearl necklace adorned her ample bosom.

"My dear Didier, a lawyer should never forget article sixty-nine of the Belgian constitution," said Baron de Vreux, his index finger wagging admonishingly. "The King ratifies the laws of the land and promulgates them."

"Yes, *bon-papa*," Didier replied. He glanced furtively at his red fingertips and ate another spoonful of custard. He was wearing a greenish sports jacket and a tartan tie. He had bags under his eyes, which accentuated the paleness of his skin.

Baroness Amandine nodded cheerfully and said: "Didier's practice is doing very well, Papa..."

"I suppose it would... there's a lot of criminality in Amsterdam, but that's because they don't respect the constitution. It's different here in Belgium. We still have article sixty-nine. Fortunately..."

"True, Papa," Amandine concurred. She stood up, spooned a lump of custard from the corner of her father's mouth and quickly licked the spoon. She caressed his hand once again and sat down.

"Madeleine!" the Baron roared with his incredibly sonorous bass voice. He groped for the brass bell shaped like a Dutch farmer's wife with a clapper under her skirts, but couldn't find it. The door opened and a chubby woman dressed in black with a white cap on her head entered the room.

"You called?"

"*De la soupe*, in the name of God!" he thundered, thumping the table with his fist. "Will there be soup? Yes or no?"

The maid appeared to be at her wit's end and turned to Baroness Amandine, who smiled and shook her head.

"Have you forgotten, Madeleine, that my daughter and son-in-law are joining us for lunch today?" the Baron snapped with a strong Antwerp accent. "Is the soup ready? Yes or no?"

Baroness Amandine got to her feet a second time and kissed her father on the head. The Baron suddenly took hold of the arms of the chair and yelled: "*Je dois faire pipi!*"

The maid rushed over to him, grabbed the back of the wheelchair and pushed him out the door. The Baron ripped off his napkin on the way and tossed it to the floor.

"I suppose we should leave," said Amandine with a sigh. She folded her napkin and looked at her watch. "It's not even one o'clock..."

She blessed herself and got to her feet.

"I'm taking an earlier train," said Didier. "I still have a lot of work…"

"Whatever you think best, my dear."

She reached out to caress his hand, but he pulled it away as if she had given him an electric shock.

"Does Daddy still think I'm a lawyer?" he asked without looking at her.

"You're still a member of the bar, aren't you?"

"Yes, but I don't have an office…"

"Pff… He hasn't a clue. When did he ever show any interest in his children?"

A look of disgust covered her face. She quickly turned away and sniffed.

"There's a train at seventeen minutes to two," said Didier. He blessed himself and got to his feet. He hesitated.

"What's the matter?"

"Shouldn't we say goodbye to Grandpa? He usually has a cheque for me…"

"Let me take care of that. Let's go. Madeleine will be busy for a good half-hour" (changing his soiled Pampers, she thought).

They left the dining room and passed through a salon full of dark furniture, carpets and nineteenth-century paintings. She stopped briefly in the corridor, opened her handbag, to which she had attached a Hermès scarf, donned the glasses hanging on a chain around her neck, removed a cheque from the bag and handed it to her son.

He glanced coldly at the amount, handed it back to her and said: "Add Grandpa's money and something extra for the flowers you forgot to pay for in May."

"But then I'll have to write another cheque."

"Whatever…"

He glared reproachfully at his mother, and pursed his lips as his grandmother had done in the portrait.

She returned to the salon, sat down at a bridge table, tore up the cheque and produced another.

"Forty thousand," he commanded.

His abruptness surprised her. "But Didier —"

"Forty thousand."

She stifled a groan and scribbled the amount. He took it from her without saying a word, slipped it in his wallet and looked at his watch.

"Here," he said, breaking the silence, and he handed her an envelope.

Amandine looked at him.

"The dentist's bill."

She nodded and stuffed the envelope into her handbag, aware that candidate numeraries were expected to submit themselves to a thorough dental examination.

"I'll order a taxi," she said.

He nodded stiffly.

There was a telephone on the bridge table and she called a taxi.

"Come, it's time we got moving..."

She looked back into the salon for a moment, as if she had forgotten something, and sighed.

They walked down the marble stairs in the vestibule. Didier opened the door, stepped outside, stood at the edge of the pavement, looked at his watch and started to chew the nail on his little finger, or what was left of it.

On Saturday 5 June at three thirty in the afternoon, an impressive Honda CBR sports bike stopped in front of Sacco's junk shop on Antwerp's Falconplein. The man in black leathers astride the fiery red machine took off his helmet, dismounted, looked around and made his way into the shop, his legs stiff, his back arched. He was small and wiry with pitch-black hair, a moustache and a handsome brown pockmarked face. A portly man with a heavy moustache was leaning on his elbows at the counter. He recognized the motorbike rider, gave him the thumbs up and pointed to the floor above. The man left his helmet on the floor, opened a door and headed upstairs.

When he returned to the shop roughly an hour later, he took a seat at a table in the corner. Moments later, the portly shopkeeper appeared with a kebab sandwich and a glass of tea on a tray. They exchanged a few words and the man started to eat.

His name was Mehmet Alia and he was thirty-four years old. He was a distant cousin on his mother's side of Ramiz Shehu and worked for his uncle on a full-time basis as a messenger and money launderer. He flew every week to Sofia with a case full of dollar bills, which he transferred into the account of an international criminal organization using an import-export firm as a front for trading in expensive stolen cars. He had managed to save enough in three years to buy a house in the old city, which he was renovating with a couple of family members. The Honda was worth at least half a million francs.

Before coming to Belgium, he had done his apprenticeship as a "hit man" in Istanbul. This had nothing to do with contract killing. He had an ordinary day job with a private collection agency, visiting debtors and using violence where necessary to make them pay up. The incredible inertia of the Turkish courts tended to encourage this method as the only way to ensure payment. Mehmet Alia was known as a hard man. He had fled to Belgium in great haste after crippling someone for life with an iron bar.

He was prepared to do anything Shehu asked of him. He called his uncle *aga*, an old-fashioned form of respect borrowed from the Turkish occupiers of Albania, which had fallen out of use and been replaced by the simple *baba* or father.

They had just discussed the "hit" he was to carry out the following Monday at three in the morning in a village called Overbroek roughly twenty miles from Antwerp. He had already made an exploratory visit.

22

Monday, 7 June. Paul Hersch and the detective from Marlowe & Co. waited side by side in the same Volkswagen Passat used by Materne the week before to shadow Albert on his way to Sint-Job-in-'t-Goor. The man at the wheel was an old hand, fifty-five years of age, plenty of experience, and able to remain calm in difficult circumstances.

Hersch, on the other hand, had barely slept the night before and was as nervous as a kitten. He was dressed in a dark suit and wore the same hat as he had done in Kortenberg. He hadn't said a single word during the journey and his shirt was soaked with sweat. They drove into Overbroek's sodium-lit high street. The village was sound asleep. He looked at his watch: 2.55.

Albert waited in the shadows at the side of the church, where he had an excellent view of the square. He could see a urinal against the wall of a café. He had parked the BMW on a country lane roughly five hundred yards from where he stood. He was wearing a denim jacket, jeans and trainers. The CS gas spray was tucked away in his trouser pocket. He was holding a package made to look as if it contained 1,000-Swiss-franc banknotes. In reality, it was stuffed with pages from a marketing magazine folded to size. The package had been taped shut using what appeared to be an entire roll of tape. Albert was nervous and angry. He looked at his watch: 2.55. A car appeared from nowhere and stopped on the other side of the street. He presumed the driver had let it roll for fifty yards or so with the engine off. The car reversed into a side street, its headlamps dimmed. A man stepped out.

Mehmed Alia had pushed his Honda CBR Blackbird to its maximum 120 mph on the motorway between Merksem and Brecht, slowing down moments later to what he called his cruising speed of 100 mph. He was aware of the risks – make a mistake at 120 mph and it's over – but he couldn't resist. The rush of adrenaline left him shaking. When he rode the bike he felt like an *ülkücü*, a Turkish samurai, a warrior with the courage of a lion. He had learned the *ülkücü* doctrine from his Turkish-born uncle Gunca Us, who was known for his heroism in the struggle against the Serbian oppressors and for his leadership role in the Black Malissors. His uncle had disappeared without a trace one day and had never been seen since.

He took the exit for Brecht, tilting his machine to the limit in the sharp bend, and ripped through Sternhoven crossroads at 110 mph, slowing down abruptly when he reached Overbroek high street. The four cylinder 1,100 cc engine purred gently in second gear and was barely audible.

Alia got off his bike at the same discreet spot, roughly one hundred yards from the church, from which he had observed the Belgian gentleman's last meeting. He glanced at the Honda's digital clock: 2.55 precisely. He took off his gloves, placed his helmet on the saddle, opened a metal box at the rear of the bike, and removed what looked like a length of gas pipe, but was in fact a telescopic truncheon with a leaded tip, a weapon he knew how to use. He crept silently towards the church.

The bell of Saint Willibrord's church sounded three. At that moment, Paul Hersch wandered onto the square. Albert immediately recognized the heavy-set man with the short legs and the dark hat. He came out from the shadows at the side of the church, walked towards him, handed him the package and told him in a muffled voice that he should count it (the sign agreed with the Albanian). Paul Hersch started to remove the tape with difficulty. Albert looked around and was thinking that the Albanian had failed to deliver on his promise, when a figure in black suddenly appeared and hit the man with the hat on the head with a short baton. He fell to the ground and the Albanian set about his task.

The man tried to avoid the blows and started to shout for help at the top of his voice. The sound echoed through the entire village.

A light went on in the café next to the church and a man opened a ground-floor window that looked out onto the square. "What the fuckin' hell is goin' on?" he yelled. The man with the black hat had grabbed the man in black by the ankle with both hands. The beating continued but he refused to let go. His cries for help sounded like the squeals of a pig in an abattoir.

The man at the window turned around and shouted: "Bruno! Attack!"

A dark-brown Doberman leaped through the window with amazing agility and attacked the man in black, who stopped beating the man on the ground and took his turn at screaming for help. The Doberman had dug its teeth into his arm and was refusing to let go.

The animal's owner had dialled 101 in the meantime, the number of the local gendarmerie. His name was Jan Vissenberg and he was owner of a café, The Pigeon Fancier.

The detective, who had timed the whole incident (it had lasted exactly seventy-two seconds), drew the appropriate conclusions. His client had apparently dug himself into a hole without telling the firm the truth about the nature of the assignment. He was also fairly certain the police would be on their way.

Marlowe & Co. regulations prescribed immediate departure from the scene in such circumstances. He did not hesitate for a single moment. He drove out of the side street with his headlights dimmed – once he was on the main street he switched to full beam and hit the floor.

The Brecht gendarmerie appeared at 3.14. Chief sergeant Verhaert was accompanied this time by his apprentice, twenty-year-old sergeant Peeters, who had been awarded his first stripe a month earlier. The crime scene they encountered on arrival included Jan Vissenberg with a shotgun poking the chest of a man on the ground. The Doberman sat close by, its ears pricked up, determined not the let the man out of its sight. A second man was lying unconscious on his back, his arms spread out like Jesus on the cross. He had lost his hat and his bald head gleamed like ivory in the neon light.

"Hey, Jan. What's been goin' on?" said Verhaert, who had known Vissenberg for years.

"Let me think: I couldn't sleep, and had just put out a cig when I heard someone outside squealing like a pig. So I open the window and what do I see? This dirty Moroccan bastard laying into a bald guy with a one of those special truncheons. I've got it here…" Vissenberg handed Verhaert the telescopic truncheon.

"Where's the Moroccan?" said Alia in a thick Antwerp accent. "I'm Albanian!"

"OK, the dirty Albanian bastard laying into the bald guy with one of those truncheons," Vissenberg repeated. "I set Bruno on them and he put a stop to it in no time, eh boy!"

The Doberman wagged its short tail a couple of times.

"And the other gent?" enquired Verhaert, who had the habit of referring to everyone not in the force as a "gent". He checked to see if Hersch was still breathing and examined the telescopic truncheon, but said nothing.

"He's been well taken care of, if you ask me," said Vissenberg. "One of his legs is broken. That brown fucker was like a madman."

"Nothing else?" asked Verhaert.

"Wait a minute. Yes! There was a car parked in the street next to the girls' school. He drove off without lights when the bald guy started to squeal. I'm pretty sure it was a Volkswagen."

"And you? Where's your bike?" Verhaert asked Alia, pointing to his leathers.

"Back there, not far," Alia answered, pointing in the direction of Sternhoven.

"Cuff 'im, Jos," Verhaert ordered, "and see if you can find his bike."

"Right away, boss," Peeters answered, skilfully cuffing Alia and disappearing towards Sternhoven.

"Let's get the whole shebang on paper," said Verhaert, "and maybe we should call an ambulance for the bald gent."

"Fancy a pint?" Vissenberg enquired.

"Never been known to say no..." said Verhaert.

He made his way over to the police van, switched off the blue rotating lights, grabbed a pile of official statement forms and brought them to the café, where Vissenberg had switched on the lights.

Verhaert sat down at one of the tables, removed his cap and placed it next to the pile of papers.

Vissenberg arrived with a couple of pints. They clinked glasses and Verhaert said: "Can I see your ID card? Just a formality..."

"No problem," said Vissenberg, and he disappeared behind the bar.

"Shit! That bloody ambulance," said Verhaert. "Let's see if the bugger's come to..."

He made his way outside. The Albanian was on the ground with his hands behind his back; the bald gent hadn't budged an inch.

"These cuffs are too tight," Alia complained.

"Shut it, Mustafa!"

Verhaert returned to the police van and called St Joseph's hospital in Westmalle.

Vissenberg reappeared in the café with a blanket under his arm.

"Shouldn't we get the bald guy inside?" he asked. "I brought a blanket."

"Not a bad idea," said Verhaert, emptying his glass in one go.

As they were carrying the wounded man into the café, Vissenberg noticed something on the ground: a brown paper package, sealed with sticky tape. He pointed it out to Verhaert.

"We'll take it along for evidence," he replied formally.

The man regained consciousness when they laid him on the blanket. He started to groan and grabbed at his right arm, which appeared out of joint.

23

On Wednesday 9 June around quarter past eleven, Baron Hervé van Reyn readied himself for an unusual event: a tête-à-tête with His Majesty's private secretary, Baron Pierre van Peers de Grâce, known to those who did not appreciate him as "the viceroy of Belgium". He was a man of tradition in every respect, and his family had enjoyed political and economic influence since the time of Leopold II. Several members had been associated with the Société Générale de Belgique since the birth of the Belgian state and many of them held senior military and diplomatic ranks. The van Peers had a long-established reputation for tremendous piety, extreme conservativeness and, unusually among the aristocracy, acute intelligence.

Pierre's wife, Baroness Charlotte Drieu de la Rochelle, had been responsible for the civil list for a considerable number of years in the Royal Household of King Boudewijn. None of his family had ever married a "commoner", as the nobility disdainfully described it. He had no direct connections with Opus Dei, although he taught Forestry Law at the Université Catholique de Louvain, Belgium's Opus Dei stronghold, and the Institut Catholique des Hautes Études Commerciales in Brussels. Although he was supportive of Opus Dei, Baron Pierre belonged to a sect established in Belgium by Cardinal Suenens – The Catholic Charismatic Movement – which preached a strict interpretation of the Gospel, with an emphasis on the power of the Holy Spirit. In terms of ethics and religiosity, he was more or less on the same wavelength as King Boudewijn. Queen

Fabiola also appeared to have been over the moon with the appointment of such a devout personal secretary. Her husband the King lived in fear of the Lord, was a furious opponent of abortion, and was not afraid to declare paedophilia, prostitution and woman-trafficking to be sins crying out for revenge. Baron Pierre still joined Fabiola, Albert, Paola, Lorenz, Astrid and Filip every week for prayer and praise in the palace chapel at Laken. He was also Crown Prince Filip's "spiritual director". There was little doubt that he had personally inspired King Boudewijn to refuse to ratify the law on abortion.

Baron Pierre, who was a secret admirer of Machiavelli and Baltasar Gracián, must have taken great pleasure in his influence on the King. Infiltration and intrigue were in his blood. He openly idolized Baldassarre Castiglione and his book *Il libro del cortegiano*, and had learned lengthy passages off by heart: "The perfect courtier must use his accomplishments to win the heart and appreciation of the prince in such a way that he is able and determined to tell him the truth in everything he should know without fear of displeasing him; and if he is aware that the prince is of a mind to do something wrong, he should have the courage to contradict him and make use of the favour won by his accomplishments to rid his mind of every false intention and keep him on the path of virtue."

He had only three arch-enemies: freemasons, Marxism and the supporters of liberalizing abortion. He had two nicknames. The humanists called him *Saint-Pierre* and the leftist fanatics *Rasputin*. He never gave the slightest hint of his rancour towards everything related to free-thinking or secularism. The smile of the perfect courtier was a permanent feature, no matter what the circumstances. He also possessed an aristocratic talent for correctly gauging the amount of affability one should display. He was considered a "*Grand Commis de l'Etat*", a nobleman who exercised power behind the scenes, someone with a blind devotion to his origins, an obsession taken to be a proper respect for the past. Such individuals find life difficult to grasp and tend to take refuge in formalism instead.

A black court Mercedes, registration number 31, pulled up in front of the restaurant Comme Chez Soi at twelve o'clock sharp. The chauffeur, in dark-grey uniform and cap, opened the rear passenger door, and a balding man in a dark-grey suit stepped out. He was short and thickset, with a heavy ball-shaped head and a stubby neck. He was wearing glasses with thick lenses and looked for all the world like a church verger or a complaisant Civil Servant. He looked anxiously left and right until he caught sight of Hervé van Reyn hurrying towards him. He smiled and held out his hand as they exchanged the customary high-pitched "*Mon cher Pierre, mon cher Hervé*". Van Reyn had sent Baron Pierre the de Vreux file in an envelope marked "Strictly Personal", and the Baron had managed to review it in a short couple of days, something van Reyn considered "ominous, in the third sense of the term", in other words: promising.

The King's private secretary was known to enjoy veiling himself in a cloud of mystery. Van Reyn, on the other hand, was barely able to control his curiosity. They descended the stairs into the restaurant, where they were warmly greeted in French by a female manager wearing a multicoloured silk outfit decked with jewellery. She led them into the "salon royal", which was reserved for the royal family and a few select non-royals. While they relaxed in one of the salon's comfortable armchairs, a waiter appeared with two glasses of orange juice on a silver tray. When the waiter, whom they completely ignored, had left the room, they sipped their juice and stared at each other with wide innocent eyes, as if they had met for the first time.

"*Et comment va Brigitte?*" van Reyn enquired.

"She's in Tuscany with a friend who cultivates the most exclusive roses in the world. *La contessa della Gherardesca…*"

"Aha, I met her once with Prince Aquaviva."

The King's private secretary did not only speak with a high-pitched voice, he was also exceedingly nervous, a characteristic he put down to his high IQ. He was a member of an international club of extremely gifted individuals, many of whom were inclined to babble at a rate of knots without listening.

"Mm… Tuscany is one of the most magnificent places I know, especially in the spring. In July and August… pff," scoffed van Reyn, who never took his vacation in the tourist season.

Van Peers agreed wholeheartedly, gestured stereotypically with his limp wrist, his head to the left, his nose in the air. He wore his wedding ring and nothing more. The idea of a signet ring with the family coat of arms was pure ostentation. After all, everyone knew well and good who he was.

"You and yours?" he enquired, with a noncommittal allusion to Opus Dei.

"Procurator Pla y Daniel is particularly pleased with the Belgian prelature."

"Did I ever tell you, *mon cher* Hervé, that I once received a blessing from his great uncle, the primate of all Spain, on the Feast of the Ascension 1963."

"In Toledo?"

"No, in Avila. He was inaugurating a statue of some local saint or other."

"Is it true that he was the last to insist that people kiss his red slippers?"

"I wasn't aware of it."

Van Peers sipped at his glass and smiled charmingly in van Reyn's direction. He had a knack for being able to transform his smile from run of the mill to broad in a second, a bit like switching an electric radiator on and off. He had indeed kissed the slippers of a senile old man in red who weighed more than four hundred pounds, but he preferred to keep it to himself.

"Shall we?" said van Peers, glancing at his watch and abruptly standing up.

"We still have a few minutes, I hope..."

"I have an appointment at two, but the menu was agreed on the phone."

Van Reyn nodded and followed the private secretary into the small dining room next to the salon royal, where an oval table with a large candelabra had been set for two. He noticed that van Peers had no documents with him and this made him uneasy.

They had barely taken their place at table when two waiters appeared with the first course – mixed salad with chunks of lobster. Spa mineral water was served in crystal glasses. The private secretary liked to give the impression that he was a teetotaller, although in private he was a keen drinker of wine and champagne.

They looked at one another, made a synchronized sign of the cross, closed their eyes and prayed in silence. After a second sign of the cross they began to eat.

"Mm..." both men droned after tasting their first forkful.

"Nothing can beat Comme Chez Soi," said van Reyn, who preferred De Karmeliet in Bruges, but knew that van Peers did not share his opinion.

They ate in silence, tearing portions from an elegant bread roll, dabbing their lips after every sip of the glass, knife held like a paintbrush between thumb and middle finger, little finger stiff and upright.

"So, how is our friend Paul Hersch getting on these days?" van Peers enquired without looking at van Reyn. He ate quickly without savouring his food, as if he wasn't interested in fine cuisine.

Van Reyn was taken aback. Had van Peers smelled a rat? After being informed by Marlowe & Co. on the telephone about what had happened that Monday night, he had reacted exactly as the Jesuits had done for centuries: he pretended there was nothing going on. Opus Dei's Belgian prelature was thus prepared to leave its senior numerary in the lurch and would deny any involvement in blackmail. Van Reyn had made enquiries at Saint Joseph's Hospital in Westmalle via a doctor – an Opus Dei cooperator – who informed him that Paul Hersch was in a bad way. He had spent twelve hours in intensive care with a double cranial fracture, a herniated neck disc, a broken arm and a host of bruises and contusions over his entire body. The doctors only realized at the last minute that one of his kidneys had been punctured and they had to operate to remove it. The surgeon had smiled and told him to look on the bright side: he could still live a normal life with one kidney. Fortunately, Hersch had been wise enough to offer no further details about his address, which was taken to be an ordinary apartment on Leuven's Tervuursevest. According to van Reyn, the Marlowe & Co. detective had reacted adequately, ensuring the avoidance of any direct association between the crime and Opus Dei. If it were necessary (he had already consulted Pla y Daniel on the matter), they were even prepared to deny ever having known Paul Hersch. A barrister at the Public Prosecutor's Office in Brussels and an Opus Dei supernumerary had already been informed of the affair. He had promised to keep a close eye on developments at the Public Prosecutor's Office in Antwerp with the help of a cooperator who worked there. Appropriate measures would be taken in due course and he was prepared to intervene if necessary, although convention disapproved.

"Paul Hersch is on holiday," van Reyn answered indifferently. "He needed it."

"Mm... A relative of mine at the university has rooms in Arenberg Residence," said van Peers, implying that he knew more.

"Paul Hersch is a very capable director..."

The waiters cleared the plates, although they were not yet empty, replaced them with soup plates, and served a particularly refined *mouclade* made with Breton mussels.

Both men started to eat, slurping inaudibly from the side of the spoon, following the example of the British aristocracy.

They left half of the soup in the plate, nibbled some bread, sipped some water, wiped their mouths... and finally van Peers de Grâce came to the point.

"I think we've reached a reasonable compromise in the de Vreux affair," he said stiffly.

"Aha," said van Reyn, "I'm pleased to hear it." His mouth went dry.

"*Eh bien*... As far as we are concerned, and as a matter of principle, the father's name should not be related in any way to an aristocratic title."

"Understandable," van Reyn concurred. He tried to contain his nerves. He knew from experience that van Peers was not to be trusted completely. He was a master of the oblique.

"The name de Vreux enjoys an impeccable reputation and the family has served its country and its Royal House for centuries. After talking the matter over yesterday with His Majesty, we think the following solution to be opportune."

"Mm," van Reyn mumbled, his nerves quivering.

"Bearing in mind that the family de Vreux has been part of the country's nobility for several generations, I suggested to His Majesty that it might be better to make an abstraction of the name Savelkoul and adjoin the title baron to the name de Vreux, clearly warranted by Didier's status as a numerary and by the Department of Foreign Affairs's glowing report on Geoffroy's diplomatic career."

Van Peers had said what he had to say in a single, well-formed and syntactically correct sentence.

"Did you say *baron*?"

"That's what I said."

Van Reyn closed his eyes for a moment and breathed deeply in and out to alleviate the tightness in his chest. He could barely contain the urge to fidget with excitement, his usual reaction to good news.

"An excellent compromise indeed, *mon cher* Pierre," he rasped.

"We had to avoid putting them on the annual honours list at all costs, of course, otherwise His Majesty would have been obliged to include the *father* when he dishes out the titles on 21 July (Belgian Independence Day), which would have been inopportune for a variety of reasons. We simply extended an existing and long-standing title. A brief visit to the Heraldry Office and Foreign Affairs and there won't even be any need to publish it officially or let the press get wind of it. *Voilà!*"

"And what if Public Prosecutor Savelkoul refuses to accept the procedure?"

Baron van Peers de Grâce stopped smiling. It was impossible to tell if he was annoyed at van Reyn's naivety or simply at the very suggestion that such a thing could happen.

He narrowed his lips and said: "Then we'll just have to appeal to his common sense. We certainly cannot accuse Savelkoul of being short of ideas." His voice seemed much deeper than before.

"Baron Didier's inheritance has also been taken care of," said van Reyn, without going into detail.

"I know, *mon cher Hervé*, but the internal affairs of your organization are really none of my business. I'll pretend you said nothing about it. Just be grateful that the Belgian prelature has another nobleman in its ranks. I'm sure Foreign Affairs will feel the same, although Geoffroy is a tad more… er, more *liberal* than his brother."

"Please accept my gratitude for this service in the name of Opus Dei."

"We do what we must, *mon cher* Hervé."

Van Reyn nodded elatedly. "Shall I inform Baroness de Vreux?" he asked. Probably a tactical mistake, he thought, but nothing could have been further from the truth.

"As you please," van Peers answered with a smile.

He gestured towards the door and the two waiters responded immediately.

The soup plates were cleared and, much to van Reyn's surprise, the maître d'hôtel brought the bill. He was familiar with the private secretary's lifestyle, but he had at least expected a main course and a cup of coffee. This is a superb example of Sacred Brazenness, he thought with some degree of admiration. Few of *us* could do better. He took it as a matter of course that the bill would not be settled in the restaurant. The Royal Household would take care of it in due course, within the year if they were lucky.

The manager reappeared and thanked them for their custom. Baron van Peers took the opportunity to praise the quality of the food.

The chauffeur opened the rear passenger door of the Mercedes. Van Reyn thanked the private secretary once again and took his leave.

He waited until the court limousine had disappeared and asked the restaurant's parking attendant to call him a taxi.

Baron van Reyn fidgeted with nervous excitement in the back seat of the taxi as it made its way to Ukkel. Beyond every expectation, the operation against Public Prosecutor Savelkoul had been a singular success. Opus Dei had acquired almost seventy million Belgian francs worth of property, shares and obligations, Baroness de Vreux's two sons had bagged an aristocratic title thanks to the ingenuity of the King's private secretary and Savelkoul's whore had disappeared from the scene. Paul Hersch lay alone and abandoned by his Opus Dei confrères in Saint Joseph's Hospital, but van Reyn didn't give him a second thought.

He gave in immediately to a sudden urge, something he considered sinful and usually did everything in his power to suppress.

He flipped through his address book in search of Baroness de Vreux's telephone number and grabbed his mobile.

He was greeted by a guttural yet evidently female voice: "Huloo."

"With whom do I have the pleasure?" he enquired.

"The Public Prosecutor's housekeeper."

"Is the lady of the house at home?" van Reyn asked, with an air of superiority.

"I'll connect..."

"*Allô, oui,*" a high-pitched female voice interrupted.

"Madame de Vreux?"

"*Oui.*"

"Hervé van Reyn speaking."

"*Ah, mon cher* Hervé..." she answered with little enthusiasm.

"I have news..."

"Mm..."

"*Good* news."

"Mm."

"I just had a meeting with His Majesty's private secretary."

"Mm, and is he well?"

"Very well. He spoke recently with His Majesty about Didier and Geoffroy, and the matter has been settled."

"What do you mean, 'settled'?"

"They will soon be granted the title of baron, but on one condition."

"And that is?"

"That they change their name from Savelkoul to de Vreux."

"Oh, good news indeed. Have you informed Didier?"

"Not yet."

"May I call him?"

"I would prefer not. Blessed Josemaría's Saying 639 says: 'Remain silent, and you will never regret it, but speak, and you often will'."

"*Pax.*"

Hervé van Reyn was surprised at this unexpected reaction. "Let me continue," he said abruptly. "We offer our felicitations on the distinction acquired by your sons and we hope that you, as supernumerary and mother of a numerary, will remember us each month..."

"*Pax.*"

Van Reyn hung up and rolled his mobile back and forth in his hand. He then did something he hadn't done for years: he enjoyed the hustle and bustle of Brussels as he started to devise a brand new plan to relieve the Public Prosecutor of his five million francs. The stupidity of others had lead to the failure of the previous endeavour, in spite of Opus Dei's considerable investment in terms of time and money. The pleasure he derived from this "spiritual exercise" was equal to the thrill and excitement of the city streets, and he took this to be a good sign.

Baroness Amandine locked the door of her boudoir and prostrated herself on the floor in front of a porcelain statue of the Virgin Mary. She spread out her arms as she had done the week before in the crypt of Opus Dei's mother house in Rome in front of the tomb of blessed Josemaría. She said three Ave

Marias slowly, paying close attention to every word, struggled to her feet, organized her clothes and returned to the table with the telephone, where she had just received incredible news from Baron van Reyn. She put on her glasses and started to flick through the telephone book, smiling from ear to ear.

She noted the number of a travel agency and dialled it.

"I would like some information, please," she said in reasonably correct Dutch.

"How can I be of assistance, madam?"

"Is it possible to book an international *billet de train* with your agency? No, one way… Yes, second class. I'll call you back later with the name and destination. Merci."

Without wasting any time, she called Canon Zwaegermans of Antwerp Cathedral.

"Ah, Reverend Canon," she said, once again in reasonable Dutch. "I would like to ask you a favour."

An elderly male voice answered: "*Madame la Baronne*, how could we ever refuse you?" A parrot-like giggle followed.

When Baron van Reyn arrived at Avenue de la Floride in the best of moods around two o'clock that afternoon, a piece of paper was waiting on his desk asking him to call a certain number urgently. He knew the number by heart: the office of Barrister-General Deweerdt at the Palais de Justice in Brussels, an Opus Dei cooperator. Good news, Deweerdt informed him. He had finally managed to get hold of the Hersch dossier via a friend at Antwerp's Court of First Instance. But there was a problem: he was morally bound by his position not to pass on the documents he had at his disposal, but he was prepared to read a few excerpts, which he believed might shed some light on the matter.

Van Reyn raised an eyebrow, grabbed a notepad with a contemptuous sneer, and started to write down Deweerdt's dictation, telegraph style:

Mehmet Alia. Albanian national. Refused to say a word up to now about the incident. Remanded in custody in Antwerp. Appeared before the examining magistrate on Monday 7/6. Grievous bodily harm. Art. 398,399,400 of the Criminal Code. Telescopic truncheon (???) A brown paper package 12x8x2 containing folded newspaper, sealed with tape. Partly opened. Albanian drove to the scene on a powerful Honda motorcycle. Address: Zirkstraat 56, Antwerp. Lives alone. Occupation: mechanic. Unemployed, on the dole (!!!). Immobilized by a dog until the gendarmes arrived on the scene (???) Paul Hersch: room 242, Saint Joseph's Hospital, Westmalle. Questioned by Antwerp CID after kidney operation. White-collar: Rumpus Ltd, Tervuursevest 123, Leuven. Serious skull fracture. Broken arm. Bruises. Doesn't know how he got there or why he was there. Probably drugged in advance. No vehicle found.

"*Voilà*," Barrister-General Deweerdt concluded, "that's all we have available for the moment. Is that enough, *cher ami*?"

"*Un grand merci*," van Reyn answered mechanically, dissatisfied with the inadequate information, which wasn't of much use to him.

"You're welcome, *au revoir, cher ami*."

Hervé van Reyn folded his hands and stared vacantly into space. His cheerful mood slowly subsided. He was the type of person who needed to have everything go according to his wishes, otherwise he could make life a misery for those around him. His poetry teacher, a priest at a boys-only school for the wealthy in Loppem, once said: "Hervé, you are a genuine absolutist." He was still proud of the fact, convinced it was in his blood, as it were. His family had cultivated a considerable nostalgia for the historical absolutism of the French Bourbons.

He reflected on the situation. The package full of newspapers intrigued him most. Didn't this prove that Savelkoul was planning to con Paul Hersch? The whole affair was riddled with inconsistencies. Had Savelkoul even shown up in the first place? The only person who could answer this question was Paul Hersch, but he preferred to uphold Opus Dei rules on the matter and stay out of his way for the time being. And what the hell was the *Albanian* doing there? Was he trying to bag the cash? How did he find out about the meeting? And the dog? Wasn't it all a little over the top?

Frustration was beginning to rattle Hervé van Reyn's nerves. The entire affair had escaped his control. He couldn't find a plausible explanation for the facts and there seemed to be no logical connection between them. His right leg bounced nervously, a quirk he had picked up when he was at school, but then the cause had been quite different. In those days he used it to suppress a sudden urge to urinate. It was strictly forbidden to go to the bathroom alone during classes. The real reason for this rule was never made public (the temptation to sin against purity was twice as intense in an abandoned WC). He had once wet himself in class, and the laughter of his teacher and classmates still resounded in his ears from time to time during what he called his school nightmares.

What should he do to take his mind off things? Prayer wasn't likely to help in the present circumstances, he was aware of that. He looked at his watch. Quarter past two. His stomach rumbled. Lunch at Comme Chez Soi had been far from sufficient. Although Opus Dei rules advised against it, he decided to wine and dine himself. He faked a smile, tugged at his double chin, grabbed the phone and reserved a table at La Villa Lorraine, where they served an excellent Pulligny Montrachet, his favourite wine. He needed something to boost his spirits.

He got to his feet and glanced automatically at his watch again. He had to find out without delay what had happened in Overbroek in order to present Joaquín Pla y Daniel with a plausible report during their meeting the following week in Rome. Perhaps it would be best to abandon the blackmail given the circumstances. He would emphasize the enormous success of the inheritance question while in Rome, and draw attention to the seventy million notary Vromen's cunning manoeuvre had managed to bag for the Institution's coffers. There was one thing he had to avoid at all costs: the suggestion that Opus Dei might be connected in any way with the police investigation surrounding the Overbroek affair and the possibility that the press might get hold of such information. Opus Dei had made the news more than once in Flanders in 1997. This was simply unthinkable prior to 1975, when El Padre was still alive. Paul Hersch could be dropped like a hot brick if need be. He already had an alternative candidate in mind to take the helm at Arenberg Residence.

At quarter past two, Albert was in his office studying a "politically tainted" file from the Court of First Instance in Turnhout. A company specializing in refuse disposal had dumped 24,000 tons of poisonous waste without a licence on a plot of agricultural land near a meadow full of grazing cows. The creatures had all died. Tests (insisted upon by the Greens) revealed the ground and the animals' blood to contain *sixty times* the European norm for heavy metals, nitrates, cyanides and pesticides. The Greens had found out that the Christian Democrat Minister for the Environment and Environmental Planning had bent over backwards to issue an antedated licence, making it almost impossible to bring the company to court. Albert knew the owner of the refuse-disposal company from his Rotary Club dinners in Turnhout. The man was a sickeningly wealthy Christian

Democrat with plenty of influence and all sorts of friends and connections in the conflict-of-interest-ridden Belgian politico-economic network. He avoided publicity like the plague, principally because many of his commercial activities tended to teeter on the edge of illegality and corruption. Albert, who had developed a serious aversion to "people with connections", was aware that the man's in-laws were related in one way or another to the family of the minister in question.

He was of a mind to grit his teeth and keep at it, but finally decided to let the file simmer for a while, at least until he was one hundred per cent sure of his personal situation. It was nothing short of a miracle that he had managed to avoid involvement in the incident at Overbroek. He was determined not to interfere in the inquiry, and had even avoided casual mention of the affair to be sure no one got suspicious. He also avoided de Vreker, since he could never be quite sure whether he would connect the "horse affair" in Brecht with the incident in Overbroek, a village nearby. He had still heard nothing from Walter de Ceuleneer, but the man travelled a lot and he considered a telephone call inopportune under the circumstances. In spite of everything, he found the slightly paranoid atmosphere stimulating. He had a gut feeling that everything would turn out fine.

The telephone rang and his secretary informed him a moment later that Mr de Ceuleneer was on the line. Jesus, he thought, talk of the Devil...

De Ceuleneer's blaring voice bored into his eardrum. He held the receiver six inches from his ear. Just when de Ceuleneer was about to launch into the "you-know-what" affair, Albert interrupted him:

"Let me call you on your carphone. Where are you?"

"On my way to Paris."

"In the Rolls?"

"No, the Ferrari."

Albert called the Ferarri's carphone number, which he knew by heart. "I'm listening," he said.

De Ceuleneer always came straight to the point.

"Ramiz is pissed off," he said. "You know what happened, don't you?"

"I think so."

"Look, my friend, I don't usually get involved in other people's business, but this time you're going to have to help him out…"

"What d'you mean?"

"Do I need to spell it out?"

"Enough said."

"Make sure the man Ramiz sent gets off."

"Impossible," said Albert categorically.

"No way! What do I tell the man?"

"That it's impossible. There are limits…"

"But you've managed to fix similar situations…"

"Maybe, but intervening now would raise questions."

"You've lost me."

"It would mean I'd have to call up the file from the Court of First Instance. The whole business is such a… such a mess. Somebody's guaranteed to smell a rat."

"Mm… and?"

A silence fell between them, interrupted only by the background rumble of the Ferrari.

"Hello," said Albert.

"So, you're trying to tell me it won't be easy…"

"It will be impossible!"

"Ramiz said, 'Make sure *he* doesn't leave me in the lurch…'"

"Is that a threat?"

"No, take it easy. All he said was that *he* shouldn't leave me in the lurch…"

Albert said nothing.

"Wouldn't it be better to have a word with Ramiz in person?"

"Impossible," Albert answered in an official tone.

"Look, Albert. I'll tell him what you've told me, but the lackey who helped you is related to Ramiz and he's now in the shit. Family comes first for Albanians, you know that. It's like…"

Yeah, like the National Front, he thought to himself, but held his tongue. He thumped his desk hard with his fist.

"What was that?" asked de Ceuleneer.

"Nothing, I'm trying to think."

"D'you want me to call back later?"

"No, Walter, it won't be necessary."

"OK, cheers…"

"By the way, is the hunt still on for Saturday and Sunday?"

"Of course, my friend, two different questions altogether. Paloma is ready and waiting on the runway at Deurne."

"What time?"

"Friday at seven. Gets us in on time to do a bit of stalking on Saturday morning at four."

"Stalking?"

"It's good for the middle-age spread. Will sweet Louise be joining us?"

"Not this time, I'm afraid."

"Shame! Never mind… Bye."

"Bye, Walter."

Albert hung up and collapsed into his chair. The blood throbbed in his head. He stretched his lips, exposing his teeth, and stared at the photos on the wall opposite, pictures of himself in illustrious company.

"*Fuck!*" he yelled, thumping the desk so hard his fist hurt. He looked around in a rage, opened and closed his fist a couple of times and finally punched in his home number.

"Hallooh."

Maria Landowska's boyish voice. His mood improved with leaps and bounds.

"Maria…" he whispered. His heart quivered.

"Oh, Mr Albert, what's the matter?"

"When does Madame get home?"

"This evening late, Mr Albert. That woman with the red car came to get her," said Maria in her usual mixture of Dutch and German.

If Nadine Tahon, the wife of a wealthy Brussels notary, had taken her to her villa in Knokke, there was no doubt she would be home late.

"Good, I'll be right there," he said, "get the glasses ready."

"Oh oh… which glasses?"

"You choose."

"*Pozadku.*" She blew a kiss into the receiver.

He hung up, stretched and remained seated, indecisive.

He then ripped a sheet of paper from the memo pad on his desk and wrote in block capitals: "FRIDAY EVENING 11 JUNE I LEAVE FOR SCOTLAND FOR THE ENTIRE WEEKEND."

He growled as he got to his feet: "They can all go to hell, every last fucking one of them!"

Something else still bothered him. His chauffeur had told him he had driven "*Madame*" to *Ekeren* the previous Wednesday, but he had been unable to say exactly where in Ekeren.

Albert and Maria Landowska clinked glasses and toasted one another. It was pure vodka. He sat beside her on the attic floor in front of the enormous wardrobes he had just opened. He had picked out a sky-blue taffeta evening dress trimmed with pearls and sequins that had once belonged to one of Baroness Amandine's grandmothers and tossed it on the floor as if it were a worthless rag. The attic reeked of mothballs.

Dressed in her usual black outfit with white collar, Maria took another gulp of vodka and gave him a kiss.

"Look at me," Albert shouted after taking another gulp of

vodka. "I'm a little bird, and I'm *thirsty*! Look, guess what kind of bird…"

"*Orzeł!*" she shouted.

"What's an *orzeł*?"

"An eagle."

He jumped to his feet and started to circle round the attic with his arms outstretched. A half-empty bottle of *Wiborowa* stood between them on the floor.

She fell on her back and laughed. "Tell me about the *Third Woman*. You promised!"

"First the *proper* outfit," he said, picking up the evening dress.

She threw off her maid's uniform and stood in front of him in her bra and panties. He fell to his knees and pulled her panties to the floor.

"No pussy," she said with a perfect Antwerp accent, "not until I'm *properly* dressed."

Barefoot and in jeans and a sports shirt, Albert pulled the evening dress over her head. It was much too big.

"Aristocratic bitches with their fat tits and sagging bums. Tea and biscuits and cucumber sandwiches my fucking arse! Fuck the lot of them!"

"It's beautiful," she said, returning to her preferred German. "Fasten the buttons! I want to keep it on."

"It's your funeral, Maria Landowska."

"Mr Albert, do what I say!"

"The Third Woman would never speak like that, Maria Landowska."

"I love it when you use both my names. It makes me horny. Here, feel…"

"Is pussy getting wet?"

"Feel for yourself!"

"No, first let me tell you what a Third Woman isn't, then you'll know exactly what I'm talking about."

He started to button the bone-ribbed, reinforced bodice. He held her shoulders, turned her to face him, bowed to her and kissed her hand. She accepted with Polish good manners.

He filled the glasses.

"Perfect," he said. "Just perfect."

She did indeed look like a picture. He sat cross-legged on the floor.

"Let down your hair, Maria Landowska."

A shock of red hair tumbled over her shoulders.

"Von Eichendorff's angel. Third Woman. Lusty and wet down below!" She exploded with laughter and pirouetted in front of him.

"Tell me… now," she insisted and sat down beside him.

"Women who are scared of spiders mice cats dogs dust on cupboards smudges on floors that there isn't enough to eat in the fridge that they don't have enough money and will die in poverty who never throw anything out and moan and groan about everything are never satisfied with a man's efforts who think they're better than everyone else who can be sweet as pie to your face and run you down behind your back who exaggerate little details that make most people laugh and turn them into affairs of state who are never content who are quick-tempered who are permanently lying in wait to belittle you who say do this do that from morning till night and why didn't you do this or that who can't drive shoot or ride a horse who never let go tell a dirty joke get pissed as a fart who are always dressed to the nines in twinset pearls and a handbag and wear milky nylons and refuse to wear suspenders or sexy underwear to make a man horny who never wear jeans and a T-shirt who recite *Salve Reginas* in front of fucking statues of a woman who had a kid without getting screwed who place a towel under their arse before they do the deed who stare at the ceiling and never come and so forth and so forth… Not like you Maria Landowska, my *Dritte Frau von Herrn*

Buddha who would be happy to fight a guerrilla war with me and reload my Kalashnikov every time it's been fired..."

Albert took a gulp of vodka and looked at her with a grin.

"Mr Albert, I'd do anything for you, anything, anything..."

"OK, then from now on you're my Third Woman."

They emptied their glasses in one go. Maria tossed her glass in an arc above her head. It shattered to pieces on the floor behind her.

"*Nitsjevoo!*" she yelled in Russian and spread her arms.

He filled his glass and gave it to her. She emptied it and gave it back.

She stood directly in front of him and said: "Feel..."

He placed the glass on the floor and slipped his hand under the stiff silk dress.

Just as he was about to slip her panties to one side, she jumped backwards and quickly undid the dress.

"*Madame* is back," she gasped.

"Don't be silly," he said. "I didn't hear a sound."

"I heard her come in, I mean it. I'm off to my room."

She rushed downstairs in her bra and panties, her black maid's uniform draped over her arm.

Albert, who was too drunk to give a damn, shrugged his shoulders, grabbed the bottle and ambled down the stairs at his leisure. Third floor, second floor, first floor.

And there she stood, Baroness Marie-Amandine de Vreux d'Alembourg, in front of the etched-glass vestibule door. Rigid as a statue. She watched as a bulky, dark-haired man, with a square jaw and a classic Greek nose, barefoot, in jeans and a sports shirt, with a bottle of vodka in one hand and a glass in the other, appeared on the first-floor landing. He stood there and started to laugh, waving a piece of paper in his hand, which he tossed at her with a derisive bow.

The look she gave him was devastating, a look of contempt that was verging on the cosmic.

24

On Thursday 10 June, Albert arrived home a little earlier than usual, jumping up the vestibule stairs at ten to five as he contentedly hummed 'Dark Eyes'. He couldn't help thinking of the day Maria jumped on top of him as he walked in the door, crossing her legs behind his back and refusing to let go. Crazy, he thought. He found it strange that there was no one in the kitchen. He wasn't sure whether Amandine was at home. As he was hanging up his raincoat, he heard Amandine talking with Maria upstairs. He crept up to his office without being heard, closed the door behind him, made his way over to his gun cabinet, took out his favourite stalking rifle and placed it carefully on his desk. It was a magnificent Mannlicher SSG.308, with a rotating magazine, a dark-brown grained and polished butt with cheek rest, made to measure by Steyr AG in Austria and fitted with a Kahles Helia 3x telescopic sight. The combination of the weapon industry's finest products had produced the perfect rifle, accurate enough to shoot a cigarette from someone's mouth at two hundred yards.

Albert was an excellent marksman, but two things brought him just as much pleasure as the perfect shot: talking about weapons with people who understood them and readying a weapon for the hunt.

He took a white linen cloth, an aerosol can and a box of cleaning materials from a drawer beneath the gun cabinet. I've been looking forward to this all day, he thought.

He sat down at his desk, quickly unbolted the chamber, sprayed some white foam into the magazine, and left the whole thing to dry. The pungent smell of Ballistol filled his nostrils, cheering him immensely. True to the hunting tradition, he maintained the rituals to the letter, convinced that the outcome of the hunt depended on following the correct sequence.

He screwed together the three-part cleaning rod, attached a felt cleaning patch, sprayed a second shot of Ballistol into the magazine, pulled the cleaning patch through the barrel, took a look inside and admired the fluted, white manganese spirals in its interior. He deftly slipped the bolt back into the slide and polished the outside of the weapon, removed the rubber caps from the telescopic sight and checked to see if the cross-wire contrasted sufficiently with the lenses. He replaced the caps, slipped the rifle into a worn leather sheath tucked away in the cupboard and leaned it upright against the wall.

He pressed his ear to the door and listened. Silence. He crept back to his office, took a Japanese lacquered box from the drawer of his desk, removed a deck of cards and stared thoughtlessly at the inane figure of Johnnie Walker.

"What shall we play for today?" he asked aloud. "Two things," he answered. "First: whether I should call Prosecutor Keymeulen and ask him to send me the file detailing the assault and battery case in Overbroek on 7 July ASAP?; second: whether I'll shoot a first-rate six-point stag in Scotland as a surprise for Maria Landowska?"

He shuffled the cards and identified Maria with the Queen of Hearts. He, of course, was the King of Spades.

The first game lasted less than two minutes, ending without him drawing a single ace. He was relieved. He probably wouldn't have called the procurator anyway. The third card in a row of seven was the Queen of Hearts. "Come on, King of Spades, let's see you!" he pleaded. The row of seven was left with an empty space. At the last minute, he drew the card and slapped it onto the empty space. He turned the card he had landed on: *Queen of Diamonds*!

"Bah!" he grunted, collecting the cards and stuffing them back into the box.

He leaned backwards and stared at the stag trophies on the wall above the wild boar tusks. He heard someone coming down the stairs. He didn't move. The last thing he wanted to do was bump into Amandine. And if it was Maria, he would be unable to stop himself from embracing her. She had only winked when he had told her the day before that he was spending the weekend hunting in Scotland. She had said something in Polish he didn't understand, but he had not asked for an explanation. He had also mentioned that he had an appointment the following morning with Jokke for a complete check-up. Although he felt better, the usual fucking pain had been bothering him the last couple of days. The vodka from the evening before hadn't done much to help. They had enjoyed a quiet night together for the first time in their relationship.

He had left her asleep when he had slipped back to his bedroom at five the following morning after his alarm had gone off.

He had asked her what she had done after "*Madame*" had returned so unexpectedly. With an incredibly cool head, she had changed back into her maid's outfit, quickly cleared away the broken vodka glass, returned the evening dress to its proper place and closed the cupboard. She had then made her way downstairs as if nothing had happened.

"I would go to war for you," he had said, a colourful phrase he had borrowed from his grandfather for addressing people you can trust, whatever the circumstances. "My grandfather used to say: 'You're the best horse in the stable'," she had replied.

She had also been quite taken aback at Madame's uncharacteristic kindness towards her, the first time in all the years she'd worked for her. It had reassured her. They had managed to escape a major disaster in the nick of time. He hadn't seen Amandine for the rest of the evening. She had even taken breakfast in her boudoir after the seven-thirty mass and Maria had told him she was still being conspicuously pleasant towards her.

He stood up, walked over to the gun cabinet, stretched, and removed one of the stag trophies from the wall. He gently rubbed the antler's shiny ivory-coloured points with the tip of his index finder and then the dark-brown warts on the shaft. He could still remember every detail of beautiful Balnacoil in the Scottish Highlands and how the stag had warily emerged from a cluster of juniper bushes and proudly jaunted into a valley, shrouded in a light mist.

He returned the trophy to its hook, opened the door and checked the landing. There was a strange silence in the house, as if it had been empty for months.

His mobile suddenly started to beep. He closed the door, returned to his desk and picked up the mobile from the floor.

"Hello..."

"Albert?" Walter de Ceuleneer's trumpeting voice was immediately recognizable.

"What's the matter, Walter?"

"Am I free to talk?"

"Yes, no problem."

"I just had a call from Ramiz..."

"And?"

"He's adamant..."

"And what does that mean?"

"He wants to know if you've forgotten about previous services rendered... you know..."

Albert said nothing.

"He said this was the last time he'd call..."

"Is that a threat?"

"Not sure, but I didn't like the sound of his voice."

"Tell him I can't do anything for his nephew. It's impossible."

"He also said something about finding it hard to respect those in power when they leave their friends in the lurch."

"I just cleaned my Mannlicher," said Albert.

"So you can do absolutely nothing for him?"

"Nothing, and that's the end of it."

"I'll pass it on. He wanted to know if he could have an audience at your office."

Albert burst into a gravelly laugh. "Tell him I'll be at my office tomorrow morning from nine o'clock. It's a public place, open to Belgians and Albanians. Only the Pope gives audiences."

"You seem to think it's a laughing matter..."

"Far from it, I've never been so serious in my life."

"Can I quote you?"

"With my compliments."

"See you tomorrow then, seven o'clock at the airport?"

"I'll be there, dear Walter. *Weidmannsheil!* Good hunting!"

"*Weidmannsheil!*"

Albert returned his mobile to its place beneath his desk, walked to the door, opened it and stuck his head outside. He could still hear Amandine talking to Maria upstairs. Were they rummaging through old clothes together? Amandine was prone to such whims, then everyone else had to drop what they were doing. If she were to kick the bucket before him, he knew exactly what he would do. On the day of the funeral he would empty those fucking wardrobes, pile those fucking outfits in the garden, douse them with a jerrycan of petrol and whoof!

Ramiz Shehu took a deep breath, swelling his torso to make himself look even more than the massive three hundred pounds plus he actually weighed (his scales stopped at three hundred).

He lit a cigarette and inhaled, held the smoke in his lungs for some time then gently exhaled. His pig-eyes gave him a cold, empty, shark-like look. A large moustache dyed with henna accentuated his baldness. A scar ran all the way from his right eye to his neck. He was relaxing in a leather armchair in the unventilated living room above his shop "Sacco", on Antwerp's Falconplein. He shuddered with what people in the desolate mountains of Eastern Albania call *Malisor Madness*: an unshakeable determination to settle scores for a deeply wounded sense of honour, a sacred duty to be fulfilled by every man of principle, which took second place to one thing only: *gjakmarrjé* – blood feud.

He grabbed the telephone with his broad hairy talon and slowly punched in a number.

"Nazim?"

He had a deep, throaty voice. Something resembling a smile appeared on his lips.

When the remarkably agile Albert caught sight of a couple of stag and half a dozen hinds sauntering over the mountain ridge about two hundred yards from where he stood, his evident sense of harmony with his surroundings (heather, juniper bushes and the occasional crooked spruce) prompted a series of associations and mental leaps, which cheered him immensely. Neolithic *joie de vivre*, he thought. The creation of humankind on the sixth day was one big mistake. He held his breath and turned to his guide, John Cummings, who was lying flat on his belly beside him, binoculars pressed to his eyes. The ghillie concentrated his gaze, completely absorbed in one thing only, a privilege normally reserved exclusively for animals. Albert peered through his binoculars and observed the stags grazing undisturbed, the hinds following their example, but more skittish, looking up from time to time, stationary, nose to the wind, ears open and alert, tails wiggling. The wind was blowing towards him, ideal conditions. One of the stags had magnificent antlers and an ash-brown coat, darker than the other, which was clearly younger. Suddenly, one of the hinds leaped playfully away from the others, pretending to take flight. Then it sauntered back and propped its nose under the larger stag's tail. The stag turned its head, stretched its neck and emitted a short barking sound.

Cummings looked up and whispered: "They'll probably mate tomorrow..."

Albert nodded. "Is the dark one good enough?" he whispered back.

"I'm not sure," said Cummings laconically, returning to his binoculars.

Cummings was short and thickset, with red curly hair and a heavy beard, in which only his nose and eyes were visible. His blond-haired hands grasping his binoculars were covered with scars. His clothes were dog-eared and worn, and his green wellingtons covered with patches.

Albert removed the rubber caps from his Mannlicher rifle's sight and checked to see if the lenses were misted. They were clear. He replaced the rubber caps and grabbed his binoculars. It was cold and wet. The sun had just risen and the dew was beginning to glisten here and there on the heather. Lying on his belly in the wet grass next to Cummings, Albert bowed his head to relieve the pain in his neck. He wriggled his toes in his brand-new wellingtons. He could feel the sweat building up under his sleeveless body warmer. The dreaded pain was absent. Jokke had done an internal examination the previous morning, but his prostate had turned out to be normal. He felt reassured, at his best here in the wild loneliness and silence of the Highlands, in his element.

Cummings spat tobacco juice into the grass by his shoulder, looked to one side and whispered: "We wait. They'll hang around. Probably."

The wind picked up and the mountain ridge disappeared in a bank of dark-grey clouds. Albert knew from experience that the weather could be unpredictable in this part of the world. According to Cummings, unexpected showers of heavy rain were called "rain-buffs". Cummings said little and only spoke when he had to. From time to time he would volunteer information about the wilderness around them – tracks, smells, the landscape, the behaviour of the fauna – but even then it sounded as if he was talking to himself.

Albert liked Cummings and preferred to have him as his stalking partner. He also preferred stalking to coursing with dogs.

"The big one looks fairly good," Cummings whispered without removing his binoculars. "Six points…"

Albert knew that the man was prone to understatement. His heart started to race and his mouth became dry, as it always did immediately before a shot. Maria was going to be delighted with her surprise trophy, he thought. He pushed back his Gore-Tex cap and took in the unparalleled open landscape. It must have been the same in Roman times, he thought, when they built the wall to keep out the Picts. All he could hear was the gentle rush of the wind. It started to drizzle, but Cummings pretended not to notice. He snorted and spat tobacco juice into the grass for the umpteenth time, a tic he repeated at ten-minute intervals. He could pick out a target at six feet and more. Albert couldn't resist a smile.

Cummings was one of those people he could tolerate for ever. He reminded him of some of the farmers he had known as a boy. Walter called him "the Shadow", because he never wandered further than a couple of yards from Albert's side during a hunt. Walter was stalking in a nearby valley with Will Mackenzie. They had made the usual bet: a bottle of malt for the biggest deer. The bottle was given to the ghillie, but usually emptied by the entire group.

"Sir," Cummings whispered.

"Yes..."

"He's a good one. Get him."

Albert cleared his throat, removed the caps from his sight, rested the butt against his cheek, unfastened the safety catch and waited until the herd came into view. He slowly lined up the cross-wire with the chest of the larger stag – the place hunters refer to as "the spot" – held his breath and pulled the trigger.

Bang!

A second shot followed, then something unexpected happened, something so unexpected it set his heart thumping: *the herd had vanished from the face of the earth.* He checked his sights and glanced at Cummings: *Cummings had also vanished.*

A wave of panic ran through his body. He jumped to his feet and shouted "*John!*"

Albert woke with a jolt, startling the warm body pressed against him.

"Mr Albert, what's the matter?" a woman's voice asked.

Albert was shaking from top to toe. His back was soaked with sweat.

"It was a dream..." he spluttered. "I was hunting..."

She switched on her bedside lamp.

"It's five o'clock. You should get up."

He turned on his back, closed his eyes, rested his hand on her belly and started to fiddle with her pubic hair.

"How about *your* belly?" she asked.

"So so," he said. "I'm seeing a doctor friend later, at ten."

"Mm... I know..."

"Maria..."

"I'm going to miss you in Scotland."

"Me too, Mr Albert."

He remained on his back, panting for breath like an old man, and said nothing.

"When do you get back?" she asked.

"Sunday evening..."

"Will you come to my bed? To our bed?"

"Yes, Maria, yes..."

She fell silent. He looked at her and saw the tears in her eyes.

"*Kochanie...*"

She threw her arms around him and rested her warm head against his cheek. He buried his nose in her thick auburn hair, which drove him wild. He wanted to say: "I'll bring back something for you", but he checked himself. He wanted to surprise her.

"You should get up," she said for a second time and sniffed away her tears. Albert had to laugh. Just like Cummings in my dream, he thought. For one reason or another he longed to go hunting. At the same time the following day he would probably be wandering around the Highlands with "the Shadow".

Maria freed herself from his arms, jumped out of bed stark naked, ran to the door, got up on the tips of her toes and plucked a bulb of garlic from the string her mother had given her to ward off evil powers, witches and ghosts.

She sat beside him on the bed and gave him the garlic. He gently caressed her smooth, warm, muscular back.

"Take it with you," she said.

He kissed her and got to his feet. He knew she didn't like long farewells.

"See you Sunday."

"Keep the *czosnek* with you all the time," she said.

"Will do, *kochanie.*"

"Say something else."

"You're my Third Woman according to Buddha."

She whimpered and shook her head back and forth.

He turned quickly, opened the door, peered outside and listened. Nothing but the sound of traffic on Amerikalei. He looked back, but she was already in bed with the sheets pulled over her head.

He crept silently downstairs. As he passed Amandine's bedroom, he thought: even if she were to catch me in bed with Maria she would pretend nothing had happened.

He sat on his bed and sniffed at the bulb of garlic. It was so dry it had lost its smell.

25

Albert adjusted his alarm clock to six forty-five, lay back, pulled the duvet up to his neck and fell asleep immediately.

Maria Landowska got up around five thirty, washed herself with cold water at the sink in her room, pulled her black maid's outfit over her bra and panties, and made her way downstairs to the kitchen, where she clattered around as she did every day, preparing breakfast for Mr Albert and Madame, who usually ate in the dining room. She poured herself a cup of coffee and warmed the teapot with the idiotic cosy with hot water.

Baroness de Vreux got up at six o'clock sharp, took out her curlers, brushed her hair, sprayed it with lacquer, splashed some water under her arms and put on pantyhose, a skirt, a blouse and a three-quarter-length jacket. She appeared in the kitchen ten minutes earlier than usual and invited Maria with a smile to accompany her to the chapel to help her carry a large box of candles. It wasn't the first time. Maria reluctantly slipped on a nylon anorak and sandals. At twenty past six, the women left the house and crossed Amerikalei. Maria Landowska was head and shoulders taller than the woman at her side. She was carrying a heavy package under her arm as if it weighed nothing. She had to slow down her pace to allow the woman to keep up. They entered Saint Michael's church via a side door that lead to the library. A door at the end of a corridor opened into the shadowy chapel, where a dozen or so elderly men and women were on their knees at prayer. Candles were burning next to the altar in front of a statue of Our Lady with a crown on her head and a sceptre in her hand. A child with the features of a wizened old man rested in the curve of her left arm.

"Stay with me until mass is finished," Baroness de Vreux whispered. She pointed to a chair at the end of the row. The Opus Dei priest, a thin forty-year-old with a pallid complexion, hurried into the chapel accompanied by an altar boy, and started to recite the prayers of the mass according to the Latin rite in a loud voice, his back to the assembled congregation. The men and women, who had nodded to one another when they arrived, all held sets of rosary beads. They prayed with their eyes closed. A vague odour of candle wax, incense and damp cellar filled the chapel. They got to their knees during the consecration, and everyone – with the exception of Maria – went forward to Communion, which they received on the tongue, returned to their places and knelt in prayer, their hands covering their faces. Baroness Amandine pretended not to notice that Maria had not gone to Communion. When the mass was over, those present exchanged a "kiss of peace", placing their hands on each other's shoulders and touching cheeks.

Baroness Amandine gestured that Maria could leave the candles where they were. When they stepped out of the chapel into the busy morning traffic, Baroness Amandine suddenly stopped in her tracks, looked at Maria with a strange grin, removed an envelope from her handbag and said: "This is a ticket for the train to Warsaw. The train leaves at ten thirty from central station with a connection in Brussels South for Cologne and Berlin. I've included twenty thousand francs as a reward for loyal service."

"But… what about my clothes?" Maria spluttered, her face ash-grey, gasping for breath. She stared at Baroness Amandine with her eyes wide open.

"They'll be sent on later by mail. And now I would like you to get out of my sight for ever," Baroness Amandine concluded. Her final words were uttered with complete indifference.

She raised her head, fleetingly covered her mouth with a limp right wrist, turned and carefully crossed Amerikalei with a look of satisfaction on her face.

Maria Landowska was stunned rigid. She staggered backwards, sat down on the bluestone steps of the church and stared vacantly at the envelope, which she held in her hand as if she had no idea what to do with it.

At seven thirty, Albert was preoccupied with his daily ritual in front of the bathroom mirror. The pain in his groin was gone and he had filled the WC with a healthy waterfall. These old muscles of mine are still made of iron and steel, he thought, pulling in his belly, inspecting his hirsute athletic torso, admiring his profile and humming his favourite 'Dark Eyes'.

He brushed his teeth, rinsed his mouth with water, checked to see if there was any blood in it (there wasn't) and returned to his bedroom in good cheer, where he dressed at his leisure in a beige shirt and a lightweight Prince de Galles jacket and trousers, which suited him to perfection. He selected a black tie with flecks of gold. Maria knew exactly what he was planning to wear that day. Gone with the Grand Cross emblem! Today was to witness the return of the Renaissance man in all his glory: a flash of the eye here and there at the office, just like Cardinal Richelieu always did as he wandered the corridors of the Trianon, his head held high, before going hunting in the forests of Fontainebleau.

He made his way downstairs two at a time and found Baroness Amandine in the dining room affectedly spooning yogurt into her mouth, her hands chubby and white, the traditional teapot-with-cosy in front of her nose.

He took his place beside her and waited for Maria to appear with a plate of scrambled eggs as she did every morning. Baroness Amandine unexpectedly returned her spoon to the table. "By the way, *la Polonaise* is no longer with us," she announced as if it were a piece of trivia.

Albert was taken aback. "No kidding..."

"You're not an American. You know what Daddy thinks about such *barbarie*. All I said was that *la Polonaise* is no longer with us."

Albert felt as if someone had grabbed him by the throat. He was speechless.

"Besides, you went a little too far, *mon ami*," Amandine continued, her voice trembling. "There's one thing I will not tolerate: being humiliated *under my own roof*!"

"Where is Maria?" Albert whispered through gritted teeth.

"Ha ha, on the train to Warsaw. I took care of the ticket and arranged for another maid. *Le chanoine* Zwaegermans already has someone in mind. "And another thing," she continued in a triumphant tone, "Didier has recently become a full member of Opus Dei and I have arranged through connections with *Sa Majesté* for both him and Geoffroy to be granted the title of baron, *linked only to the name de Vreux*."

Albert was dumbfounded and slowly began to realize that his muscles were refusing to work. His stomach contracted and a twinge of pain shot from his groin to his kidneys. His heart skipped several beats. He took a deep breath, stared at her with eyes full of venom and said in a low voice: "Didier's well suited to that sect. He's always been too stupid to be a lawyer. Hardly surprising, since he inherited the brains of his mother and Granny de Wasseige, the result of years of intermarriage."

"I'll never forgive you for those words," she snapped. "God will punish you. You have dishonoured the name of my eldest son and that of my family!" Her eyes glistened with hatred.

She's never looked so real in her life, Albert thought. "I don't give a damn about the title and that Opus Dei nonsense," he said, mimicking her aristocratic flick of the wrist, "but one thing is sure: no one has the right to change a family name to that of the mother without mutual consent. And God can go to hell!"

She pretended not to hear his final words and started to sneer.

"*Sa Majesté* has the right. Pierre van Peers *confirmed* it."

"Oh, that..."

"They'll never give you a title. A man who cheats on his wife with the maid... Bah!"

"People of your sort have been cheating on their wives with the maid for centuries and I wouldn't give them the light of day. But none of that's important. I demand to know where *Maria* is!"

"On her way to *la Pologne*."

"Do you know what you remind me of?"

"Pff."

"A fat ugly spider in its web, waiting to suck the blood of the next defenceless fly."

She brushed off his remark with her customary flick of the wrist.

Slowly but surely he started to feel better. Now he was certain and there was no stopping him. "Do you think for one minute you can get the better of me?" he sneered. He balled his fists and recovered control of his muscles.

She stared at him, beady-eyed.

He leaned over and said with his face inches from hers: "I'm bringing Maria back, and she's staying with *me*, goddamnit!" prodding his chest with his finger.

"Not in this house!"

"What did you think? That I would let her play the slave for the pittance you gave her? People like you think the *ancien régime* is still in business. But those days are gone for ever, *madame la baronne.*"

"The whore," she sneered. Saliva appeared at the corner of her lips. She was bright red. She quickly produced a handkerchief and blew her nose.

He threw back his chair, grabbed her by the wrist and yanked her to her feet. She squealed and tried to break free. He had never realized how limp her muscles were. He pushed her hard and she fell to the floor. Her legs flew into the air, exposing her pale pantyhose and white slip. He stared at her stubby white thighs and could barely stop himself from laughing as he marched out of the room, ignoring her whimpers. He slammed the door so hard it sounded like a rifle going off and raced upstairs. He opened a drawer in the art deco table in his office, removed an envelope containing 200,000 Swiss francs and tried unsuccessfully to stuff it into his inside breast pocket. He grabbed an attaché case from under his desk, opened it, popped the envelope inside, adjusted the numerical code, snatched the leather gun case leaning against the wall by the gun cabinet and hung it over his shoulder, glanced around the room, took the framed photo of the little boy on the Shetland pony and stuffed it in his pocket.

He stopped and thought for a moment. He looked at his watch, grabbed his mobile and called the number of his official car. It was ten past eight.

"Chauffeur?"

"Public Prosecutor?"

"Can you bring the car…"

"I'm on my way, Public Prosecutor."

He hung up, but his telephone started to beep.

"Hello?"

"Mr Albert!" a woman's voice squealed.

"*Kochanie!*"

The gun case slipped to the floor and he sat down.

"Oh Mr Albert, I'm so happy to hear your voice..." She started to sob.

"I know everything, Maria, everything. Where are you?"

"Central station in Antwerp."

"*Pozadku.* Wait there. In the buffet upstairs. I'm coming to get you. You're staying with me!"

"Do you mean it, Albert?"

"*Kochanie.* I can't live without you for another day. Come with me to Scotland. Let's go *hunting.* Stay with me *for ever.*"

"Albert, *ich liebe dich* so..."

"I'm on my way, *kochanie.*"

He hung up, draped the strap of the leather gun case over his shoulder, grabbed the attaché case and ran downstairs.

There was silence in the dining room. He made his way to the vestibule, opened the door, stood outside on the pavement and looked up and down the street. Traffic whizzed by. The clear liquid of morning, in which passers-by swim like goldfish in a bowl, enveloped him. He clenched his teeth and stretched his back. I am the Public Prosecutor of Antwerp, he thought, they can't touch me. I've finally made a decision that's going to make life worth living. I have Soliman and I have Maria. I'm taking her with me to Scotland. In a private Lear Jet. Walter will understand my situation. This time tomorrow, we'll be wandering across the Scottish moors in the company of John Cummings, my shadow.

Albert gazed at the busy traffic on Amerikalei. He enjoyed it. His chauffeur was on his way. He was reminded once again of John Edgar Hoover, who had terrorized his chauffeur in the most refined manner. He promised himself to be nice to everyone from then on. He wanted to live life to the full for years to come. I'm one of the five most important men in the country, he thought. I have power. I have my health. And I have a *woman.*

The black Opel Omega stopped in front of his neighbour's garage. The chauffeur got out and leered at the gun case.

"Good morning, Public Prosecutor."

"Good morning, how are you?" Albert enquired with a broad smile.

The chauffeur almost collapsed with surprise. "Eh... v...very well, thank you," he babbled.

"The Kaai, as usual," said Albert after settling into the back seat. He took pleasure in the luxury of such a short journey. He thought about Jokke, who would have considered it absurd to take the car. He would call him later and cancel the appointment. *Prostate is all in the mind!*

He gazed at the traffic, which was bumper to bumper at that hour.

The chauffeur stopped in the car park of the Court of Appeal. Albert let himself out. "Would you mind waiting for me?" he asked.

"Of course not, Public Prosecutor," the chauffeur replied, and he drove to the main entrance of the building. Albert made his way to Cockerill Kaai, humming 'Dark Eyes' and paying little attention to what was going on around him. He fished the key from his pocket, stopped in front of the rusty metal door, opened it and stepped inside.

What happened next was compressed into a couple of crystal-clear seconds, unrelated to biological time, which faltered and stood still.

A tall, athletic, dark-haired man, smelling of aftershave, with a neatly trimmed Balkan moustache, gleaming white teeth surrounded by a cinnamon-coloured face, gloved and dressed in a dark tracksuit, appeared from nowhere, grabbed Albert's shoulder, forced him to turn around on the spot, pushed him down the concrete corridor, produced a heavy pistol with silencer attachment in the blink of an eye, pushed the barrel to his chest and pulled the trigger. There was a sort of hissing sound, like air being released from a tyre. Albert opened his eyes wide and shouted what sounded like "*Wahoo!*" but the man fired again, this time lower. Albert fell forward, his lungs rattling, grabbed his throat, but was unable to speak. The man grabbed him by the hair, yanked him to his knees, pressed the barrel against his right eye and fired. Blood spattered everywhere. He then did exactly the same with the other eye.

He let Albert fall to the floor. A pool of blood formed and quickly spread across the concrete.

The man, whose name was Nazim Tahir, tossed the nickel-plated Colt .45 with rubber grip on the ground next to Albert, turned, and carefully closed the metal door. Without looking back, he swaggered like a cowboy towards a bicycle leaning against a house on the corner of Cockerill Kaai. He opened the lock, took off his gloves, put them in his pocket, threw one leg over the saddle and cycled at his leisure towards the old town.

Baarle aan de Leie, 5 July 1998.

BACK TO THE COAST

Saskia Noort

Maria is a young singer with money problems, two children from failed relationships and a depressive ex-boyfriend. Faced with another pregnancy, she decides not to keep the baby, but after the abortion, threatening letters start to arrive. She flees from Amsterdam to her sister's house by the coast, a place redolent with memories of a childhood she does not want to revisit. But when the death threats follow her to her hiding place, Maria begins to fear not only for her life, but also for her sanity.

Saskia Noort is a bestselling author of literary thrillers. She has sold over a million copies of her first three novels.

PRAISE FOR SASKIA NOORT AND *THE DINNER CLUB*

"A mystery writer of the heart as much as of the mind, a balance that marks her work with a flesh-and-blood humanity."
Andrew Pyper, author of *The Wildfire Season*

"Affairs, deceit, manipulation, tax dodges and murder – there's nothing Noort shies away from stirring into the mix, nicely showing off the sinister side of the suburbs." *Time Out*

"While there are echoes of Desperate Housewives here, this is closer to Mary Higgins Clark and is a good bet for her fans."
Library Journal Review

£8.99/$14.95/C$16.50
CRIME PAPERBACK ORIGINAL
ISBN 978-1-904738-37-4
www.bitterlemonpress.com

THE VAMPIRE OF ROPRAZ

Jacques Chessex

Jacques Chessex, winner of the prestigious Prix Goncourt, takes this true story and weaves it into a lyrical tale of fear and cruelty.

1903, Ropraz, a small village in the Jura Mountains of Switzerland. On a howling December day, a lone walker discovers a recently opened tomb, the body of a young woman violated, her left hand cut off, genitals mutilated and heart carved out. There is horror in the nearby villages: the return of atavistic superstitions and mutual suspicions. Then two more bodies are violated. A suspect must be found. Favez, a stable-boy with blood-shot eyes, is arrested, convicted, placed into psychiatric care. In 1915, he vanishes.

PRAISE FOR JACQUES CHESSEX AND *THE VAMPIRE OF ROPRAZ*

"A superb novel, hard as a winter in these landscapes of dark forests, where an atmosphere of prejudice and violence envelops the reader" *L'Express*

"An admirable story-teller, Chessex surprises again with this terrifying portrait of a region, of an era and of a man with an extraordinary destiny." *Livres Hebdo*

"Stark, wintry prose... disconcerting novella that alternately seduces and appals." *The List*

"Packs visceral punch and unlikely to be quickly forgotten." *Crime Time*

£6.99/$12.95/C$14.50
CRIME PAPERBACK ORIGINAL
ISBN 978-1-904738-33-6
www.bitterlemonpress.com

A NOT SO PERFECT CRIME

Teresa Solana

MURDER AND MAYHEM IN BARCELONA

Another day in Barcelona, another politician's wife is suspected of infidelity. A portrait of his wife in an exhibition leads Lluís Font to conclude he is being cuckolded by the artist. Concerned only about the potential political fallout, he hires twins Eduard and Borja, private detectives with a knack for helping the wealthy with their "dirty laundry". Their office is adorned with false doors leading to non-existent private rooms and a mysterious secretary who is always away. The case turns ugly when Font's wife is found poisoned by a marron glacé from a box of sweets delivered anonymously.

PRAISE FOR *A NOT SO PERFECT CRIME*

"The Catalan novelist Teresa Solana has come up with a delightful mystery set in Barcelona... Clever, funny and utterly unpretentious." *Sunday Times*

"Teresa Solana's book may be full of murder and mayhem, but it's also packed full of humour, acute observation, a complicated plot and downright ridiculousness... I cannot recommend it highly enough." *Oxford Times*

"Scathing satire of Spanish society, hilarious dialogue, all beautifully dressed up as a crime novel." *Krimi-Couch*

This deftly plotted, bitingly funny mystery novel and satire of Catalan politics won the 2007 Brigada 21 Prize.

£8.99/$14.95/C$16.50
CRIME PAPERBACK ORIGINAL
ISBN 978-1-904738-34-3
www.bitterlemonpress.com

DOG EATS DOG

Iain Levison

Philip Dixon is down on his luck. A hair-raising escape from a lucrative but botched bank robbery lands him gushing blood and on the verge of collapse in a quaint college town in New Hampshire. How can he find a place to hide out in this innocent setting? Peering into the window of the nearest house, he sees a glimmer of hope: a man in his mid-thirties, obviously some kind of academic, is rolling around on the living-room floor with an attractive high-school student... And so Professor Elias White is blackmailed into harbouring a dangerous fugitive, as Dixon – with a cool quarter-million in his bag and dreams of Canada in his head – gets ready for the last phase of his escape.

But the last phase is always the hardest... FBI agent Denise Lupo is on his trail, and she's better at her job than her superiors think. As for Elias White, his surprising transition from respected academic to willing accomplice poses a ruthless threat that Dixon would be foolish to underestimate...

PRAISE FOR IAIN LEVISON
author of *A Working Stiff's Manifesto* and *Since the Layoffs*

"The real deal... bracing, hilarious and dead on."
New York Times Book Review

"Witty, deft, well-conceived writing that combines sharp satire with real suspense." *Kirkus Reviews*

"There is naked, pitiless power in his work" *USA Today*

£8.99/$14.95/C$18.00
CRIME PAPERBACK ORIGINAL
ISBN 978-1-904738-31-2
www.bitterlemonpress.com